Also by Jonathan Wylie

SERVANTS OF ARK
Book One: THE FIRST NAMED
Book Two: THE CENTRE OF THE CIRCLE
Book Three: THE MAGE-BORN CHILD

THE UNBALANCED EARTH
Book One: DREAMS OF STONE
Book Two: THE LIGHTLESS KINGDOM
Book Three: THE AGE OF CHAOS

DREAM-WEAVER

and published by Corgi Books

SHADOW-MAZE

Jonathan Wylie

CORGI BOOKS

SHADOW-MAZE
A CORGI BOOK 0 552 13929 7

First publication in Great Britain

PRINTING HISTORY
Corgi edition published 1992

This book was set in 10/11pt Times by
County Typesetters, Margate, Kent.

Corgi Books are published by Transworld Publishers Ltd,
61–63 Uxbridge Road, Ealing, London W5 5SA, in Australia
by Transworld Publishers (Australia) Pty Ltd, 15–23 Helles
Avenue, Moorebank, NSW 2170, and in New Zealand by
Transworld Publishers (NZ) Ltd, 3 William Pickering Drive,
Albany, Auckland.

Made and printed in Great Britain by
Cox & Wyman Ltd, Reading, Berks.

For Sue,
with much love.

'Thinking of you, little one.'

INSIDE THE SHADOW-MAZE . . .

There had always been a garden here. Even before mankind came to the land, the endless cycles of growth and decay had cast their spell. Flowers bloomed and died, leaves unfurled and withered, fruit ripened and fell, seeds were sown and sprouted, beginning the process anew.

Halana was the last of the Guardians who still respected the old ways. She had tended the garden for more years than anyone could remember, and she herself had now become a part of the ceaseless patterns. But men and women have their seasons too. Halana was old now, and frail, and could no longer move among the trees and plants as she once had. Yet her vigilance did not cease. Some of the more perceptive Lords had recognized her worth, and had given her one last task.

For a full year, Halana merely watched, marking the myriad lives of the garden day by day. Nothing escaped her notice, whether it was the subtlest change or the grandest transformation. The seasons passed within her memory as well as in the world.

And then she began. Old hands moved with a delicate, spider-like motion and the portrait, almost imperceptibly, took form. The task took many years, the seasons overlapping in her images, but Halana's hands never faltered. Even when her eyes grew weak and her vision darkened, she did not hesitate, seeing now with her nose and tongue and ears. The scents, tastes and sounds of the garden were more vivid to her than the sights of a sunlit day in a child's eyes.

At last her work was almost done, but she did not slow her pace. Her time had come and she was content. In a way, the tapestry was the story of her life; in another, it *was* her life.

As the last stitch fitted into place, Halana gratefully drew her last breath, and bid farewell to the garden and this world.

PROLOGUE

The attack began at dawn. By the time the sun rose, the only people left in the village were dead. They were the lucky ones.

*   *   *

Four days earlier, two boys had left their homes. They were returning as men. Emerging separately from the forest on to the track which would lead them back to the welcome of their families and friends – and to the celebration of their success – they grinned at each other in sudden comradeship as they met. Although they were still two hours' walk from home, their time of trial was over.

Each carried a trophy of their manhood ritual. Varo, the elder by a year, carried a pack from which the wickedly curving tusks of a wild boar protruded. Brostek stared open-mouthed at this trophy, and whistled in admiration. Like everyone who made their living in the deep forests and upland ranges, he knew that an adult boar was the most ferocious of all the predators of that wild region.

Varo's grin widened, and laughter sparked in the warmth of his deep brown eyes.

'Want to see it?' he asked.

As Brostek nodded eagerly, Varo shrugged off the leather straps and dumped the boar's head unceremoniously on to the damp ground. Small red eyes glared accusingly up at them from either side of the bristle-covered snout. The yellowing tusks curled on both sides of the monster's open mouth, from which the broken end of Varo's spear protruded. Blood caked the creature's teeth and lips.

Brostek shuddered. He had never before seen such a hideous creature – and hoped fervently that he would never meet its like alive.

'It's *big*,' he breathed, unable to think of anything better to say.

'I know.' Varo's smile grew a little smug. He was secure in the knowledge that no boy had matched this kill in living memory, and he could afford to be generous. 'That's a beauty too,' he remarked, indicating the head and pelt of the grey she-wolf draped over Brostek's shoulders.

For a moment, the smaller boy hesitated, but then he responded as confidently as he could.

'Not bad,' he said. 'She put up quite a fight.' Until now, Brostek had been feeling more than a little pleased with his own kill, but suddenly, all he could remember was the icy terror as he had stalked his oddly tentative prey, and the panic-stricken fury of the wolf's final desperate defiance. The boy's victory had been hard-won and messy, as the rips in his clothes, vicious-looking scratches on his arms and the matted blood stains on the animal's thick fur attested. He glanced at the still-snarling jaws and the death-glazed eyes, and his achievement suddenly seemed less notable.

'Wolves are the worst,' Varo commented. 'How did you separate her from the pack?'

'I didn't have to,' Brostek admitted. 'They'd gone on without her.' When the other made no comment at this surprising information, he added awkwardly, 'I was just lucky, I suppose.'

'The hunter makes his own luck,' Varo replied, quoting an old proverb. 'Let's get home. I need a proper meal!'

'Me too!' Brostek grinned. The thought of returning to their village warmed him more than the weak sun of early autumn, and he was eager to get back. At fourteen years of age, he had volunteered for the trial out of bravado, and it had only been his stubborn pride which had convinced the village elders to let him go. Varo, older, stronger and already taller than many full-grown men, had met with no such doubts.

The test of manhood was a generations-old tradition, dating back to the first settlement of the upland wilderness, and in essence was a simple enough test. All the aspiring hunters had to do was survive alone for four days in the still wild forest, using only their skills and instincts, and armed only with a single, hand-held weapon of their choice and a hunting knife. No kill was necessary, but over the years the boys themselves had made it a matter of honour to bring home a trophy, and now few returned with nothing to show for their first solo expedition.

The trials took place either in mid-spring or autumn, avoiding both the harshness of winter and the relative ease of summer warmth at night, but each boy was free to choose his own time, subject to the approval of the village elders. Varo and Brostek had been the only youths to volunteer this year, and it seemed appropriate that they should return together, even though they had never been particularly close. Varo was the son of one of the settlement's best hunters, a man noted for his cunning and intelligence as well as his physical prowess, and the young man had inherited these abilities in addition to his own self-assurance and ever-present sense of humour. Brostek on the other hand was an orphan, abandoned as an infant by travelling folk. He had been adopted by an elderly couple, whom he loved with a fierce, protective loyalty, but who could never make him forget his earlier abandonment, however hard they tried. Even now, the gap between the two young men was not fully bridged, but the shared camaraderie of the trial made them friends – at least for the day.

As Varo pushed the boar's head back into his pack, there was a rustling in the undergrowth next to the track. The youths turned as a small grey wolf-cub emerged and

11

stared at them with unnerving intensity. For a few moments, neither of them moved, then Brostek drew his sword, brandishing it wildly.

'Go away!' he yelled. 'Go!'

The wolf-cub watched him warily but did not move, even when the young man took a threatening step forward.

'Looks like you got more than you bargained for,' Varo remarked, unable to keep the laughter from his voice.

'There aren't supposed to be any cubs at this time of year,' Brostek complained bitterly. 'Go away!' he yelled again, but still the cub took no notice.

'That's obviously why the mother was separated from the pack,' Varo said.

'I wouldn't have killed her if I'd known,' Brostek defended himself awkwardly. The hunter's tradition which forbade the killing of mothers of young extended in his mind even to wolves.

'It's a wolf!' Varo responded incredulously. 'The less of them the better. Kill him now and get it over with.'

'It's a her.'

'What?'

'The cub's female,' Brostek muttered quietly.

'You got close enough to tell?' Varo asked, laughing.

'She was hurt,' the other replied defensively. 'I cleaned out the cut, that's all.'

'You did what!'

His face burning red, Brostek did not reply. *Go away!* he implored the tiny creature silently. He knew he could not bring himself to kill her. Yet to hand the task over to Varo would be the ultimate humiliation.

The wolf-cub yawned suddenly, displaying a mouthful of tiny, needle-sharp fangs. Then she yelped questioningly. Varo laughed again.

'She's rather fetching,' he commented drily.

'It's a wolf!' Brostek retorted angrily. 'And I want to get rid of it, but it keeps following me.'

'It's picking up the scent of the mother's pelt,' the older boy said.

'I know that,' the other snapped irritably, cursing himself for not having realized this obvious truth before.

They stared at the watchful bundle of fur, both knowing her endearing appearance to be misleading.

'It won't be so friendly when it's a bit bigger,' Varo said. 'You'd better decide what you're going to do with it.'

Brostek made one last attempt to scare the cub away. The animal tensed, but did not move, and he gave up in the face of such unreasonable persistence.

'Come on,' he said. 'Let's go. We can easily outpace her in the open, and anyway, she'll never follow us into the village.'

Varo refrained from comment, and fell into step beside his companion as he strode silently along the track. Neither looked back.

'How did you manage to get the boar?' Brostek asked eventually, hoping to return to their earlier sense of joint satisfaction.

'I made it so angry that it killed itself,' the young hunter replied, then launched into an animated account of how he had trailed the boar, driven it to fury by pelting it with stones and clods of earth, and of how he had then allowed it to charge at him – but only at those places where he could escape by pulling himself quickly into the branches of a tree. This course of action sounded like insanity to Brostek, but Varo had repeated the process several times until the enraged boar – a creature whose eyesight was never good at the best of times – had charged for the last time. The boy had stood his ground, his heavy spear held unnoticed, braced firmly against the trunk of a tree. Varo had steadied the point so that the maddened animal impaled itself, and died in a squealing fountain of blood.

'Skewered itself from head to tail,' Varo concluded happily. 'I could have roasted him there and then.'

Brostek was both sickened by the tale, and lost in admiration. He knew that he would never have had the nerve to attempt a kill with such audacity. Failure would have meant certain death.

'Took me a while to hack the head off with just my knife,' Varo added contentedly. 'I could have done with your sword then.'

Brostek looked for the hidden barb in his companion's words but could find none.

'That's amazing,' he said truthfully. 'Your father'll be proud of you.'

'And yours of you,' the older boy replied promptly. 'A wolf is no mean prize.'

They walked on in silence for a while, each thinking about their reception at the village and the boasting they could indulge in when the younger boys gathered to greet them. The morning grew warmer, and their spirits rose even higher. They kept up a fast pace as the excitement grew inside them, and laughed immoderately at each other's meagre store of jokes.

While they were still some distance from the village, their mood changed abruptly, though in later years neither would be able to recall how they had known that something was wrong. Perhaps it was a deeper silence beneath the constant rustle of the forest; perhaps their nostrils caught a faint tang of acrid smoke; or perhaps it was just an indefinable distortion in the atmosphere of a place they knew so well. Whatever the cause, the two hurried on, their small triumphs forgotten. Almost running now, they came into the clearing which surrounded the village and knew immediately that their worst fears were justified. They stood quite still, shocked into disbelieving silence by the horror of what they saw.

At this time of day, the village would ordinarily have been a hive of activity; gardens being tended, buildings repaired, children shouting and playing, men and women going about the many routine tasks of daily life. Yet now the place was deserted, deathly still. Nothing

14

moved, not even a bird. Some of the wooden houses had been reduced to mere piles of ash, and a few grey wisps of smoke rose in the sluggish air. But many homes remained untouched, as though their owners had just slipped out for a mid-morning stroll. Varo and Brostek knew differently, but were still struggling to come to terms with the appalling disaster that had befallen their home.

'No,' Varo breathed. 'Not here. Not *here*!' There was a note of pleading in his anguished, useless denial.

Brostek was the first to recover the use of his legs. Flinging down his pack and discarding the wolf's pelt, he ran towards his parents' hut in the centre of the settlement. The sturdy wooden door had been torn from its hinges and cast aside.

'Mam?' he screamed. 'Da?'

The boy plunged inside, and shuddered to a halt. In the sudden half-light, he could not see properly at first – but then his eyes adjusted, and his gorge rose. He turned and lurched outside, gasping for breath, as though all the air had been sucked from his lungs. He doubled over and was violently sick.

Gradually, his convulsions subsided, leaving him aching and empty, and he forced himself to look inside once more. A single glance was enough to confirm what he had seen. All the uplanders had heard the stories, of course. But this was the first time he had ever come face to face with the true terror of the Knifemen of Bari.

His parents lay side by side across their own table, barely recognizable as human beings now. Their skin and sinew were stretched tight over frail skeletons. Eyes stared sightlessly in wide horror; teeth were bared in grotesque snarls between thin, chalk-white lips. There were several needle-thin cuts in their necks and arms, but there were no stains about the dead couple. Every drop of blood had left their bodies.

Brostek's nerve snapped.

'No!' he screamed. '*No!*'

15

Drawing his sword, he swung violently at the door-post, burying the blade in the time-hardened wood, then wrenching it free. He hacked again, swearing and shouting, as if venting his fury on the now-departed enemy. Tears of rage and sorrow fell from his maddened green eyes as he worked the insanity of grief from himself in oaths and uncontrolled violence. He ranted and raved, howling incoherently, his vitriolic stream of words ending only when he ran out of breath. His strength failed him, and casting his blade aside, he fell to his knees and wept.

Some time later, slow measured footsteps sounded behind him, and he forced himself to turn and face his companion. The expression on Varo's handsome face told its own story.

'You've seen?' Brostek asked, his voice cracked by horror.

Varo nodded, his face expressionless. Nothing showed in his eyes, no hint of emotion, no trace of feeling. It was as though he had withdrawn into himself, leaving his body a cold, frigid shell. It was almost a surprise when he spoke.

'All those that are left are the same,' he said flatly.

'Your . . . your parents?'

'My mother's gone,' Varo reported, his voice a calm monotone. 'So are my sisters. My father's dead. He died fighting, at least. There was blood on his wounds.'

The knife in Brostek's gut twisted again.

'And *his* parents?' he whispered. 'Are they dead too?'

Varo's grandparents had been among the most respected of the village elders.

'Yes.'

'Like that?' He gestured towards his own home.

'Yes.'

Brostek swore under his breath, and hung his head. It wasn't supposed to be like this! Today should have been a day of celebration and joy. Instead . . .

16

Only one thing had not changed. Now he had no choice but to become a man.

'Come on,' Varo said. 'We have to burn the bodies.'

Comprehension slowly dawned on Brostek, and he forced himself to his feet. He knew that if the victims of the Knifemen were not cremated soon, they would putrefy and become a source of plague.

The youths laboured throughout the rest of that day, building a vast funeral pyre from wood hewn from those houses that had been left standing. The dead – the hideous corpses of the Knifemen's victims, and the bodies of the men who had died trying to defend their homes – were laid in huddled rows on top of the pile. At dusk, in a tacitly agreed gesture, Varo and Brostek added their trophies to the pile. The grim heads of the boar and the snarling wolf added a final macabre touch to the scene as the fire was lit and the two young men stood back to watch their last links with the past dissolve into smoke. They spent a sleepless, seemingly endless night watching the flames and sparks shoot up into the sky, sickened by the stench of burning flesh, and brooding helplessly about the fate of those who, unlike the dead, had vanished without trace. The Knifemen only took the young and able-bodied, and none of their captives – man, woman or child – had ever been seen again.

*   *   *

The next morning, they gathered together a few belongings – mementoes of their former lives – and their travelling gear, and prepared to leave. But before they set off, Varo led his companion to the largest hut still standing, and pointed to marks that had apparently been branded into the wood of the door-post. Inside a large circle were seven symbols, none of which meant anything to Brostek. One of the seven, the central symbol in the circular pattern, was repeated below. It was an inverted triangle, that seemed to point towards the ground.

'Remember those signs,' Varo instructed his companion.

As they stared at the curious symbols, flecks of an unnatural green-blue light twisted within the marks, like dying sparks in sorcerous embers. Brostek shivered, knowing that he would indeed remember these signs for the rest of his life. They were the only real evidence he and Varo would have in their search for revenge.

Without another word, the two young men turned away, leaving the village and heading west, away from the mountains and towards the heart of Levindre. Neither of them looked back.

A few dozen paces behind them, limping slightly, a wolf-cub followed, like a small grey shadow.

PART ONE

TREVINE

CHAPTER ONE

Shadow looked up from the gently rocking floorboards, where she lay with her head between her forepaws. She always felt a little unsure of herself in this strange house – and even more so around its even stranger inhabitant. The wolf rarely understood exactly what humans were doing – her world was a much simpler place – but the woman who lived here was a complete mystery. At least Shadow recognized her peculiar combination of scents now – the tang which marked her as female, the must of books, and the scent of invisible flowers. This last confused the wolf, but humans appeared to like it.

And the woman always seemed to be talking. Even Shadow's master was quiet by comparison.

'Haven't you done enough?' Magara asked, her voice tinged with exasperation. She was cutting Varo's hair, snipping carefully, trying to bring some sort of order to the white-blond chaos.

'All we've done so far is rid the world of a few human maggots who were allied to the Knifemen,' Brostek replied. He was sprawled sideways in a chair, eating fruit pie with evident relish. 'They'll always be able to find replacements. We want the seven themselves.'

'But you've been trying for four years . . .' she began.

'Nearly five,' Brostek mumbled, sounding almost glum for a moment.

'With no success, and no thanks from anyone,' Magara persisted. 'Even the villagers you've saved have short memories. You've earned a rest.'

'No.' The single word of flat denial was Varo's first contribution to the lengthy and fruitless discussion, and his interjection startled Magara.

'Don't talk while I'm doing this, unless you want to lose an ear,' she remonstrated. Then she smiled, aware of the irony of her commanding Varo. Even sitting down, his head was only just below the level of her own; standing he towered over her, yet he took no offence at her command.

If only he wasn't always so polite, she thought. *If only he got angry or happy or sad once in a while – anything! I'd understand him better then.*

Magara was justifiably proud of her insight into people. Many came to the heron lady for advice, or just to talk. But Varo remained a closed book to her. Only his surface – the perfectly proportioned, stunningly handsome surface – was clear. It was all he ever showed to anyone.

Now Brostek, on the other hand . . .

She glanced towards Varo's constant companion, and smiled. He was still spooning food into his mouth, making shameless slurping noises, as though he had not eaten for days.

'Go on like that and you'll get as fat as me,' she chided.

Brostek grinned and swallowed. They had had this conversation before. 'You're not fat,' he replied.

'I can't get into half my clothes any more,' she countered.

'They must be shrinking in the damp,' he remarked.

'And you're just trying to cheer me up.'

'You are small,' the traveller answered solemnly, 'but perfectly proportioned.'

'Small, yes.' Even Brostek, who was of only average height for a young man, stood more than a handspan taller than her.

'And you make the best fruit pie in the crater,' he went on.

'My problem exactly,' Magara sighed.

'What's more,' Brostek continued, not to be put off, 'your hair is the colour of summer corn, your eyes are as blue as the sky . . .' Magara burst out laughing, and had to stop her work with the scissors, but he went on unabashed. 'You've read more books than any scholar, and you know more about everything than I'll ever have time to forget. Small children and animals love you. You are an excellent barber, seamstress and cook.'

'Stop babbling,' she ordered, smiling.

'No. There's more. You are also the perfect drinking companion because – through some grossly unfair aspect of the inner workings of your body, denied to us mere mortals – you never get a hangover, and are thus able to tell us all what happened the night before!' He paused for breath. 'You are, in short, perfect.'

A few moments passed in silence.

'Oh, have you finished?' Magara asked eventually, disappointment evident in her tone and downcast face.

'I have laid my heart bare,' he replied promptly, spreading his arms wide. 'What more can I do?'

'You are a joy,' she said. 'No one else ever tries to make me feel good.'

Brostek put down his dish, then left his chair in a fluid tumble, ending on one knee with his hands clasped over his heart. His expression contrived to be both affronted and solemn, and there was a sparkle in his green eyes.

'May Talisman run me through with his beak if I spoke one word of a lie,' he declaimed.

'I could fall in love with you,' Magara told him fondly. 'If only you weren't so ugly.'

'Ah, cruel fate!' he exclaimed. 'To have my infirmity cursed by the lips of beauty. I shall retreat behind a mask, never more shall the world see my face!' He slumped back into his seat, an ungainly tangle of limbs, then grinned at his hostess. 'Any more pie?' he asked hopefully.

'No,' she replied, smiling back. 'Go and fetch me some water, so I can shave this big lump of a friend of yours.'

Throughout this exchange, Varo had sat stoically, silent and unmoving. Brostek went to do as he was bid. Shadow immediately looked up, and watched until he returned with the bowl. Magara watched him too.

He's not really ugly, she thought, *but . . .*

In isolation, Brostek's features were fine, but somehow their combination produced an odd effect. His face was not misshapen, but it was certainly plain, and disconcerting. It was as though he were a statue cast in sections by a master craftsman, and then assembled by a clumsy, talentless apprentice. Much as Magara liked him, she could not deny that she found him physically unattractive.

Taking the bowl of water from him, she pushed such thoughts aside and went to get some of the foaming crystals which her friend, Iro the alchemist, had made by mistake. Then she began to rub the mixture into Varo's thin, pale beard. Dark brown eyes, which should have been friendly and warm – and which looked unusual with his blond hair – stared back at her, ice-calm, somehow reminding her of cold metal – and somehow seeming almost colourless. Varo's expression rarely changed from a steely watchfulness. He spoke little, and never idly.

How do such an ill-matched pair make such a good team? she wondered, not for the first time.

And yet the two men were inseparable, held together by a bond deeper than any words, which dated from the time, nearly six years ago, when they had lost their families, their homes, and the innocence of childhood in a single day. Magara had known them both for close to three years now; her home had become the refuge to which they returned after their travels. Their ceaseless, bloody and seemingly futile vendetta was all too familiar to her now.

With a last sweep of the razor, Magara finished shaving her subject, revealing the strong jaw in the perfect face. Broad shoulders, a tapering torso – bare now, to keep the hair cuttings from his clothes – and well-muscled limbs completed the picture.

If any man could be called beautiful, she thought, *then it's Varo*. Yet she knew that she was not the only one to be unnerved by the unswerving gaze of those cold eyes and his unfailingly calm demeanour.

'You're done,' she announced, and tossed a small towel at Varo's face. He caught it, dried himself and stood up, not bothering to brush away the clippings from his shoulders. 'Now you,' Magara said, turning to Brostek. 'Get that cream off your face!'

Brostek uncoiled obediently and lay down on the floor. 'Come on, girl.'

Shadow immediately trotted over and began to lick the cream from her master's whiskers. It was a comical sight, but Magara could never suppress a shudder at the sight of the wolf's frightening teeth so close to her friend's vulnerable neck. She knew that Shadow was devoted to Brostek and was normally mild-mannered, just like a well-trained and well-loved dog. The wolf even wore a collar that her master had put on her as a concession to civilization, but the wilderness still showed in her eyes sometimes – and then it was as though she were only a moment away from running with the pack, howling her fierce message over the snow-covered mountain wasteland. In spite of the fact that she was supposedly 'tame', Shadow still made many people nervous.

The wolf finished her impromptu meal, and Brostek rose, stripped off his shirt and took Varo's place on the stool. As the two men moved, the house rocked gently.

'Thank you,' Varo said evenly.

'You are welcome, kind sir,' she replied, curtseying in the vain hope of inducing a smile.

But the tall man only gave her a polite nod, before turning and striding out of the open door. Outside he halted, leaning on the railing of the walkway. The summer sun bronzed his impressive frame.

Magara began Brostek's toilet by trying to comb his tangled black hair with her fingers.

'Ow! Be careful,' he protested. 'There's valuable livestock in there.'

'Perhaps I should try to smoke them out,' she said thoughtfully. 'Setting fire to this thatch would be a lot easier than cutting it.'

'I think I'll go for a swim,' he said quickly, trying to get up.

'The scars would heal soon enough,' she told him as she pushed him back down. 'Quiet now, or you really *will* lose an ear.'

She began to cut, hanks of dark hair falling to the floor. Outside, Varo was still and silent.

'Is he ever going to stop?' Magara whispered, half to herself.

'No,' Brostek answered quietly, serious for once. 'And neither am I.'

CHAPTER TWO

The Knifemen's attacks had begun over a decade ago. At first, their victims had been lone travellers or isolated shepherds, and many of the corpses had been discovered only when they had become pestilent, rotting husks, hardly recognizable as human. Later, the raiders grew bolder, attacking remote farmsteads and hunters' cabins, and then whole villages. At each site, with an arrogance reflecting their growing audacity, they left their signature branded into the fabric of the violated homes – sometimes even upon the skin of their victims.

Fear grew in the upland communities. While many people left for the safety of the western plains, most remained, clinging to the only life they knew. It was assumed that the bloodthirsty raiders were from the neighbouring country of Bari, although there was no proof of this. Reliable eye-witness accounts of the Knifemen's attacks were few; those who were not captured or killed outright often succumbed to the ensuing plague that made the village sites uninhabitable for months afterwards. This scarcity of information meant that some villagers actually believed the Knifemen to be creatures of myth, stories to frighten children with. They thought that something like that could never happen to them. Until too late.

There had been little regular communication between Levindre and Bari. The two countries were separated by a huge mountain range, one of several that ran like spokes down from the unimaginably vast, ice-bound wilderness which formed the hub of their continent. The gigantic peaks at the centre of this frigid desolation were forever hidden behind swathes of cloud; even the border range proved a formidable barrier, discouraging all but the most daring – or foolish – travellers. Today, no one attempted to cross the high passes. Fear and rumour had put paid to that. Some said that the seven Knifemen, known only by their symbols inscribed within the fateful brand, were evil wizards who had rediscovered the old powers; others believed them to be vampires, who drank the blood of their victims. A few claimed that they were the leaders of a warrior cult and that they worshipped vile nameless gods. Yet more suppositions were held about the people who had been taken during the attacks. They were used by the Knifemen as slaves or sacrifices, or in arcane experiments. But nothing was ever known for certain – because not a single captive had ever returned to tell his tale.

Very few claimed to have seen the Knifemen at work, and what reports there were proved unreliable. Their ghastly experience had been enough to drive the onlookers half-insane, and their reports were vague and contradictory. Despite all this, some firm beliefs about the Knifemen had emerged over the years. It was assumed that each of the Seven worked alone, identifying themselves by branding their own symbol below the encircled group, but that each was accompanied by a sizeable troop of warriors. Whether these men were volunteers, lured by the rumoured promises of eternal life, or other more mundane riches, or whether they were forced to aid the Knifemen by sorcerous means, was the subject of further speculation.

Varo and Brostek had gathered together a small band of dedicated followers, made up of rare survivors like themselves, adventurers and assorted human misfits. They had accounted for many of the enemy assailants, who had seemed like ordinary men in all but one aspect. None ever surrendered, preferring to fight to the death. If any one of them was ever forced into submission, then his heart would simply stop beating. Varo had surmised that they had a deadly poison secreted upon their bodies, but others attributed these mysterious deaths to sorcery. Whatever the reason, the fact that no prisoners were ever taken was immensely frustrating.

Yet this frustration paled into insignificance beside another. In spite of their small successes, neither Varo nor Brostek had ever seen any of the Seven, let alone come near to capturing or killing one of their mortal foes. How the Knifemen travelled, or why they occasionally chose to abandon their followers were questions no one could answer.

However, in the process of chasing their elusive enemies, the self-appointed guardians of the uplands had stemmed the evil tide a little, and had saved some villages – at least temporarily – from annihilation. Once an attempt was foiled, the Knifemen would not return to that area for months, sometimes even years. However, the area under threat was vast, and with the meagre force at his disposal, Varo could not hope to defend it all. He and Brostek had to rely upon a not always reliable network of messengers and look-outs. More often, they could trust only their own hunters' instincts.

Some years earlier, when their band had been newly formed, and was beginning to realize the immensity of its self-imposed task, they had tried to enlist the help of the landowners, powerful men whose organization, known as the Cartel, effectively ran Levindre. But they had been unable to convince these men of the danger, and the Cartel had seen no profit in financing expeditions to unimportant, sparsely populated areas on the strength of what they regarded as exaggerated rumours. They did not believe that these upland 'skirmishes' would ever lead to war with Bari – the only consequence that might have led them to action – because the logistics of taking any army across the mountains would prove well-nigh impossible.

Although Brostek and Varo had to concede that the

landowners were right about this point, they knew that war was not the only way in which their land might be invaded. The enemy they faced was far more vile and insidious. Although Varo had accepted the Cartel's decision calmly, Brostek had been furious at the complacency of those who spent their lives in safe prosperity. His companion had had to force him away before his angry reaction led him into trouble.

Only the people of the uplands and the other remote communities were grateful to Varo and his men and, as Magara had pointed out, their gratitude was usually short-lived, soon supplanted by the harsh necessities of everyday life.

*   *   *

The Cartel had not always ruled Levindre. For centuries after the continent was first settled, its people had been guided by the Linking Lords – known to the general populace as wizards. These 'lords' were not noblemen in the accepted sense – the pioneers had rejected such notions – but were men of special talents, spiritual leaders of their people who had harnessed the innate magic of the land and used it for the benefit of all. Their powers had reputedly been prodigious – but were now reserved only for storybooks.

The first landowners, like the rest of the population, had revered the Linking Lords, and had ensured that all their material needs were supplied, leaving them free to concentrate on arcane matters. Gradually, though, the wizards had become less intrinsic to Levindre's way of life. Over a long period of peace and increasing prosperity, their guidance was heeded less and less, and the landowners and their money became correspondingly more dominant.

The wizards themselves had grown accustomed to ease and plenty. As their powers declined, so the peoples' faith in their judgement and confidence in their leadership wavered. Their downfall had become inevitable, and for many decades now, the so-called Linking Lords had been enfeebled, disregarded by all but a superstitious few. The handful who remained were mostly wanderers, little more than vagabonds, performing fairground tricks for those still amused by such. Others had retreated from the world, living in hermitages in those few locations where magic still existed – once sites of reverence and awe, now shunned or ignored.

The Cartel, once the second tier of government in the land, was now its undisputed ruler. They had little interest in the problems of the unprofitable, far reaches of their country.

* * *

'There's another wave coming,' Varo stated. 'I can feel it.'

The three friends were sitting on the walkway outside Magara's house, their feet dangling over the side into the cool water of the lake.

'But it's been quiet now for months,' she protested.

'That's always been the pattern,' Brostek answered, running a hand through his now trim hair. 'There'll be a lull, followed by a spate of attacks. All we have to do is anticipate where and when!' Like Varo, he had recently experienced a sense of foreboding. Both men had learned to take note of such feelings.

'But you're exhausted! You've spent the last six hands travelling almost constantly,' Magara persisted. 'How can you hope to cover even a fraction of the border country in your present state?'

'We can't,' Brostek replied simply. 'But we have to try.'

'We need help,' Varo said flatly.

'Is it worth another trip to Mathry?' his long-time companion asked, after a moment's pause.

Mathry was the castle home of Bullen, one of the most

31

influential of the land-barons, and one who often hosted Cartel meetings.

Varo stared out over the lake, and did not respond. Brostek glanced at Magara.

'No!' she said quickly. 'I can't.'

Brostek laughed. 'I sometimes wonder why I have a tongue in my head. You know my thoughts better than I do.'

'That's because you're so obvious,' she retorted, grinning. *Unlike Varo*, she added to herself.

'Why won't you help us?' he asked. 'Don't you think it's at least worth a try?'

'It won't do any good.'

'You don't *know* that.'

'Yes I do! I've been gone too long. My father wouldn't take any notice of me now.'

Brostek shrugged. 'At least you still *have* a father,' he muttered.

'That's not fair!' Magara shot back. There was a flash of anger in her eyes, but also hurt, and for a moment she was close to tears.

'Sorry,' Brostek said quietly.

The ensuing silence was broken by the sound of strong, slow wingbeats. Magara's adopted heron, Talisman – so named because he had been the first creature to greet her on her arrival at the crater – flew towards them over the water, landing clumsily on the walkway a few paces away. Shadow, who lay just behind her master, raised her head slightly and inspected the new arrival. Wolf and bird eyed each other disdainfully for a moment, then studiously ignored the other's presence. Talisman settled himself on one long leg and appeared to fall asleep, while Shadow's muzzle rested once more on the wooden boards.

'We'll be needed in the mountains,' Varo stated, as if he had just come to this decision. 'We'll leave in a day or two.' He had evidently dismissed any thought of a journey to Mathry.

Magara began to object, then decided to accept his words quietly. Arguing with Varo did as much good as arguing with a tree.

The sun had gone down below the edge of the crater, casting the town into premature shade as always, though the eastern walls were still brightly lit. This was normally a time Magara loved for its colours and its peace, but today she felt restless and uneasy.

'I feel like making the most of our time here first.' Brostek grinned, obviously not sharing her mood. 'Starting tonight. I hope Newberry is ready for us.'

'Always,' Magara reassured him, brightening a little.

'Tonight, the stars will shine from our eyes,' he declaimed, laughing. It was a phrase he often used but no one, not even Brostek himself, knew exactly what it meant. However, it was safe to assume that his evening would involve a great deal of laughter, music and drink, and that it would ensnare many others in its joyous web before the night was over.

The crater-rimmed town of Trevine was uniquely suited to such an enterprise.

CHAPTER THREE

Local legend had it that the town of Trevine was named after the first man to climb down into the crater. In fact, this may have been a historical inaccuracy, because among the things he found at the bottom were bones – both animal and human. What was certain, however, is that Trevine was the first man ever to climb *out* again.

His long-ago journey must have been immensely perilous – as were all the other expeditions to his discovery before the wallmen turned the art of crater-climbing into a science. The cliffs which formed the internal walls of the crater were almost vertical; even at their lowest point they towered fully one hundred paces above the rock below. No one knew what had prompted Trevine to make that foolhardy descent, but the results of his exploration began a chain of events that eventually produced the now-thriving community which bore his name. Most of the town's inhabitants reckoned that he would have approved of the place, had he lived to see it, and the founder's health was drunk with some regularity. The citizens of Trevine were proud to think of themselves as different; outsiders and renegades, cut off from the mundane world by the massive cliffs which encircled them – and they considered that early explorer to have been made of the same special stuff.

The first thing remarked upon by visitors to the crater was the colour of the cliffs – a soft, dusty orange-red that reminded many of rusting iron. Indeed, the rock contained many minerals, and the quarrymen of Trevine would occasionally shear away a section of the surface to smelt for the ores within. In doing so, they would expose the true colour of the strata beneath, which varied from midnight blue to coal black. The newly bare surface would make a striking contrast with its surrounds for a few days, but the effects of air and moisture would gradually change its colour back to rust, and within four or five hands, the new section would once more be indistinguishable from the rest of the cliff.

The vast majority of the area within the circular crater was filled with a huge lake, and land was consequently very precious. For four-fifths of its circumference, the cliffs plunged from the crater's rim straight into the calm water. Only on the western side did the descent lead to solid ground. At the base of the cliff there was a line of unstable scree, and below that the thin strip of land on which Trevine was partially built. Here the surface was made up of a mixture of stone and a little fertile soil. By careful husbandry over the decades, this arable land had been well utilized, and provided the town with its few truly fresh crops. Because of the valuable nature of this soil most of the early building in the crater had been on the boulder-strewn shore of the lake, but solid-ground construction had stopped decades before Magara's arrival. Most of the homes and some public buildings were built on specially treated wooden stilts over the water's edge and, even further out, many more actually floated upon the lake. These rafts were connected by walkways, complete with steps and handrails. Magara's small dwelling was one of the most recently constructed, and stood at the end of a long walkway that stretched out into the lake at the southern end of the town. When she had first arrived in Trevine, she had lain awake for several nights until she became accustomed to the feeling of the house as it moved gently under her. Her new neighbours had informed her that the dark water beneath her floor was probably ten to twenty paces deep – a fact that did little to dispel her initial unease, but which she now took for granted.

The lake itself was enormously deep in the middle but had never been measured accurately. The level of the water never changed, seemingly unaffected by either tides or rainfall. The only waves ever seen were those caused by the mercurial winds which swirled round the crater. These never amounted to much, and indeed on some days there was no wind at all, leaving the lake as smooth as glass. The townsfolk called such occasions 'mirror days' and, by long-held tradition, no boats or swimmers disturbed the magic of those times, when the depths of the lake presented perfect replicas of the cliffs and the sky above. Gazing at such a surface for too long was enough to induce vertigo and confusion in the minds of all but the strongest-willed.

Yet for all its stillness, the water in the lake was not stagnant; it was always clear and pure. On sunlit days, its deep bed was visible in some places. Some unidentifiable currents had been detected by the divers, and theories put forward that there may be underground rivers flowing in and out of the lake, their inlets hidden in the inaccessible depths. Others claimed that the strange geology of the crater contained some sort of purifying element, ensuring that the water never became polluted. A further theory stated that the fish within the lake – varying from common species to strange, rarely glimpsed creatures in the deeps – were responsible for keeping the water clean. As yet, no one had come up with a theory that explained how the fish had got there in the first place. However, their existence was undeniable, and they were a valuable source of food, the size of each year's catch being strictly controlled.

In spite of the controversy over the source of the water's purity, the people of Trevine respected its vital importance to their way of life, and ensured that all refuse which could not be recycled was buried in the specially hewn pits and caves at the furthest point from the lake. The task of maintaining these pits was a community project, and although it was an unpleasant task, each citizen was happy to take their turn. It was a small price to pay for life in this unique town.

Most necessities, such as timber and the majority of foodstuffs, had to be imported into the crater. In the past, various traders had tried to take advantage of this situation, but the citizens of Trevine soon made it clear that they would not stand for profiteering. They paid a good price for all they received, but expected to be treated fairly in return, and ensured that the cliffs which separated them from the 'outside world' were not used as an excuse for shoddy goods or poor value. Enterprising merchants had soon realized the potential of trade with Trevine, and the honest men among them had prospered with the town. Indeed, extensive settlements had been established on the rim above the crater precisely for this purpose.

At various times during the town's history, ambitious visionaries both above and below the cliffs had devised various grandiose schemes to make access to the crater easier. These had all come to naught, much to the relief of most of the inhabitants. The plans had been of varying degrees of insanity, ranging from the boring of a gently sloping tunnel starting half a league from the crater, to a gigantic spiral road which was to have been cut around the entire circle of the cliffs. Neither of these ideas – or any of the other extravagant proposals – had progressed beyond their theoretical beginnings, and thus Trevine was left to rely on more mundane but eminently practical methods.

There were several routes up the cliff face, but most traffic moved along the easiest and well-established paths. A complex system of ropes, pulleys, staging platforms hewn from the rock, and a variety of foot- and hand-holds made vertical movement possible. The people whose lives were devoted to the care and constant renewal of these systems were known as wallmen; they were understandably regarded as important members of crater society. There were no horses or other large animals within the crater, but it was the wallmen's proud boast that anything else that Trevine wanted, Trevine got.

Most newcomers found their first descent a terrifying experience, despite the numerous safety measures and professional manner of their guides, but even old hands on the journey found the sight of the wallmen scurrying spider-like over the precipitous routes most unnerving. Accidents and even fatalities were not unknown, but given the number of people and the volume of goods which traversed the cliffs each day, these sad events were considered remarkably rare.

The wallmen themselves were a phlegmatic breed, revelling in their dangerous calling and the awe it inspired in less experienced climbers. They worked hard, but when they were away from the cliff face, they played hard too. Within the lore of the town's history, the wallmen had their own legends. They claimed Trevine himself as one of their number, but there were many other colourful figures in the tales they told, most commemorated by the naming of the routes that they had pioneered – names like Diamond Crag, Craven's Trellis, and Rakespill's Folly. And yet their bragging was regarded with good humour by the rest of the community; the fact that any sort of commerce with the outside world was possible was quite remarkable given the effort involved. On the face of it, it seemed strange that any sort of community should have survived – let alone thrived – in such a place. That it had done so was due to a number of factors, but key among them was an unsolved mystery, buried in the darkness of the distant past.

That the crater had been formed many centuries before man came to Levindre was accepted by everyone, but there were two schools of thought about how the massive formation had come into being. The majority of people believed that it had once been a giant volcano, its enormous ramparts formed by the molten outpourings of the earth itself. However, a few eccentrics put forward the argument that the crater had been hollowed out by a devastating explosion, caused by the impact of a huge boulder that had fallen from the sky. Both sides claimed to see clear evidence for their conclusions in the shape of the land and the formation of the rock, but whichever theory was correct, the forces that had striven to produce such a natural marvel were long since dormant. The crater and its lake were tranquil enough now – despite the intrusion of man – and yet the legacy of whichever ancient cataclysm had formed it was present still.

Elements and exotic alloys were present in the crater's rocks which existed nowhere else on the continent, and it was this freak of geology that had ensured Trevine's early prosperity. The most famous of its hidden treasures was a metal that became known as blue gold, greatly prized for its incredibly delicate beauty as well as for its rarity. It was found, not as an ore as most metals were, but as pure nodules that varied from the size of a pea to giant nuggets as big as a man's fist. There were other metals rarer still; the orange-yellow firedrake, the pale grey wearstone, which was harder than steel, and many others, as well as rich deposits of more ordinary elements. And yet even this was not all. For some, the most exciting prospect was the unearthing of any of the crater's many varieties of gemstone. These were rarely found, but greatly sought after. Diamonds and the enigmatic pink lake-stones from Trevine had found their way to almost all the richest households of Levindre, and their brilliance was said to be a jeweller's dream.

Although the first pioneers could not have known just how extensive the crater's treasure trove was, they recognized a good thing when they saw one. When they realized that each trek up and down the cliff face was an undertaking of considerable effort and danger, a camp was established on the narrow strip of land beside the lake. As the years passed, this camp expanded and became permanent; amenities were added, and it gradually became transformed into a genuine community, whose reputation spread far and wide.

However, the early settlers were faced with a major problem. The reserves of valuable metal, ores and stones that were easily accessible had been exhausted within a few years. All of the crater's other riches lay beneath the lake. Human resourcefulness and the lure of wealth had then devised an entirely new occupation, that of underwater mining. In the years that followed, the techniques and equipment of this enterprise had been greatly refined, but the process still relied upon a remarkable group of men and women. These were the divers whose extraordinary skill, bravery and endurance were already part of the living folklore of the crater.

The divers were literally a special breed, who had – over many, many years – developed physical differences from their fellow human beings. Enlarged lungs and an uncanny ability to slow their heartbeats even when working underwater were added to an immunity to the bone-chilling cold of the depths. All these traits had been enhanced down the generations, and the present-day divers were the most highly regarded citizens of Trevine. Several of their number sat on the council that decided matters of general interest, and were the adjudicators in any dispute.

Divers of both sexes worked side by side. Although the women were generally more agile, and had a greater tolerance for the extremes of cold, dark and pressure, the men could harness their greater strength to bring the heavier loads to the surface. The divers were the people from whom all the wealth of Trevine originated, and were even more proud and self-confident than the wallmen. They were the driving force behind the entire community, and their intense practicality, combined with their determination to live life to the full – in all its aspects – made many demands upon those about them. And yet they could also be generous patrons and the best of friends to those they respected.

Over the years, many different types of people had

been drawn to the crater by the almost magical lure of its treasure. Smiths, alchemists and self-styled scientists came to work with and study the unique metals. Jewellers then turned them into art forms. Merchants and craftsmen arrived to serve the needs of the expanding town, while others specialized in trade with the outside world. Eventually, lack of space necessitated the restriction of the number of settlers, and the council invoked a simple yet strictly held rule.

Any prospective newcomer could only stay if they demonstrated that they would genuinely contribute to the general good. Those with special practical skills relevant to the needs of the town were always welcome, but others had a harder time convincing their judges.

Part of Trevine's attraction was its sense of being 'apart', its independence and peculiar pioneering spirit that was retained long after the crater had been tamed. It developed a reputation for attracting renegades and dreamers, the rebels and misfits of the outside world. Among these were many artists, musicians, writers and other visionaries, who had been regarded beyond the rim as mere entertainers, of little worth – indeed on a level with the lowest of household drudges. Within the red walls of the crater, however, those of true talent were welcomed. This steady influx of creative energies had turned Trevine into a melting pot of many cultures and ideas, and had enriched the lives of its inhabitants beyond measure. It was a volatile brew, but a potent one, and it was said that the citizens of Trevine experienced more of the world by staying at home than they could hope to do in a lifetime of travel. The town attracted many visitors, who came to sample the special talents contained within the town for the few days spared from the toil of everyday life.

Conventional skills – whether practical or artistic – were not the only means of acceptance. Magara was proof of that. Young as she was, she had put herself forward as a teacher, as a storyteller, and as a talented

41

seamstress, and yet it was her keen intellect and almost supernatural insight into the thoughts of others that had impressed the council. She had been welcomed and was now regarded as a healer of sorts.

Magara was not alone in utilizing an unusual skill in order to gain admittance. Two years ago, a large man had made the perilous journey down from the rim, presenting himself to the council as an artist. When asked to describe his particular talent, the newcomer replied that he was a cook. After the council members had laughingly informed him that they had cooks enough, he replied eloquently, and with an almost total lack of modesty, that he was no ordinary cook, but was a master of his art. The council agreed to put him to the test, and instructed him to prepare a meal that would convince divers, wallmen and musicians alike that he was indeed what he claimed to be. If he succeeded, then he would be allowed to stay.

The following evening, eight men and women sat down to his meal, surrounded by a group of curious onlookers. Several courses were presented, each sufficient in itself, but complementing those that had gone before, and at the same time preparing the diners' palates for what was to come. The expressions of amazement and delight as culinary wonder followed wonder told their own story. At the end of the meal, the cook stood confidently before them, his arms folded across his ample chest.

'Now tell me I am not an artist!' he had dared them, smiling.

The big man's name was Newberry, and he now ran the most popular tavern in Trevine. It was there that Brostek, Varo and Magara were headed to begin their night of revelry.

CHAPTER FOUR

Newberry's tavern, straddling the water's edge, was one of the largest buildings in Trevine. The main hall was lamplit in the evenings, and was filled with delectable smells from the adjoining kitchen and the murmur of conversation from the customers seated at the functional, wooden tables. The only decoration was provided by the racks of wine bottles and barrels which lined one long wall. Newberry rarely gave his customers a choice of food, reckoning that his creations were good enough for anyone. He made no allowances for personal taste – other than his own – but his patron's plates were almost always wiped clean. However, he was not so dictatorial about their choice of drink, and each customer was free to choose from the tavern's wide range of ale, wine and other beverages. Newberry did not hold with the theory that certain drinks were more suitable for certain dishes. He believed in drinking just what you liked – so long as you ate what he gave you.

The tavern's clientele was as varied as the town's population. On any night you could be sure of finding councillors, divers, wallmen and musicians, as well as a varied assortment of all the other professions and inhabitants of the crater. Here they were all equals, drawn by their host's superlative food, and submitting gladly to his authority. Once his duties in the kitchen were complete, Newberry, red-faced and beaming, would join his satisfied customers and enjoy with them whatever entertainments the evening presented.

Tonight's main meal was almost over, and the big man was already moving among the tables, accepting the shouted praise as his due, while his staff cleared away the empty plates. Soon there would be music, and it was one of Newberry's rules that good music, like good food, should be appreciated at its best. No one was allowed to eat and listen at the same time.

The musicians were at a side table, drinking the dry white wine which was stored in metal racks beneath the lake to keep it cool. There were four of them, all men and all young. Their dress was unkempt and careless. Like many others in the room, they glanced occasionally at two newcomers, who had come in a little while ago, and who were now seated at one of the small tables in a corner. The older of the two looked perfectly normal. He was dressed plainly, with dark hair and fierce eyes set in an angular face. A lute was propped against his chair. He had finished eating, but his younger companion was still struggling with his food. Much of it was smeared round his mouth and some had fallen on to the table and the floor. He looked for all the world as though he were imitating the eating habits of a young child, but neither he nor his companion seemed to find anything unusual in such behaviour. The boy's eyes seemed permanently out of focus, and he took no notice of anything going on around him. The older man merely sat still, avoiding the curious glances directed their way.

Although there had been some whispered speculation about the newcomers and the nature of the simpleton's affliction, no one had approached them directly. Now one of the musicians rose to his feet. Hewitt was respected for his talent, and nobody cared that his clothes were deliberately ragged or that his dark, wavy hair fell below his shoulders.

'Can you play that thing?' he asked casually, indicating the lute.

'No. My cousin is the musician,' the man replied.

Hewitt's thin lips curled in a disbelieving smile.

'He can hardly get his spoon into his mouth,' he began. 'How . . . ?'

The boy looked up from his plate, his pale eyes wide.

'Be careful what you say,' the dark-haired man said in a quiet voice that cut like steel. He glared at Hewitt, who raised his hands defensively.

'No offence,' he insisted quickly.

'He don't look like he has the wits to pick his nose!' someone called out. 'Let alone pick out a tune.'

The exchange was being watched with interest by many of Newberry's customers, and a few laughed at this comment. The older of the strangers looked round angrily.

'Let him play something,' another voice suggested in a milder tone.

The fierce eyes of the newcomer swept the room as if in challenge

'"Cradle Time",' someone suggested, naming a lullaby which had the simplest of tunes. This prompted more laughter, and drew the boy's companion to his feet.

'Ignorance is no excuse for bad manners,' he said angrily. 'Don't insult what you cannot understand.'

'He doesn't seem insulted,' Hewitt replied mildly, nodding at the boy. The young man wiped ineffectually at his mouth and looked up at the musician with a curiously blank expression.

'What do you say, lutist?' Hewitt asked.

'What do you say, lutist?' the boy replied, mimicking the musician's tone and inflection perfectly. Yet his face remained neutral, and there was neither humour nor understanding in his gaze.

Hewitt frowned, and glanced at the other man.

'He's not made like you or I,' the stranger explained sullenly.

'We can see that!' a voice called out, provoking more laughter, albeit uneasy.

Still standing, the stranger took a couple of paces forward, glaring about him as if trying to find the heckler.

'We came here . . .' he half-shouted, his face colouring, then paused. It was as though his words were choking him. 'Here, of all places, we thought to escape such prejudice. My cousin is the equal of any of you.' He looked around at the people gathered there, but no one held his gaze. Silence settled over the room in the face of his fury. 'There are some simple tasks, which you take for granted, that are beyond him,' he went on, quieter now but still impassioned. 'But he has talents beyond your understanding – and any man who calls him an idiot will answer to me!' His eyes still swept the company as though looking for challengers, but none was forth-coming. Clearing his throat, he seemed about to say something more, but evidently thought better of it. It was as though he had decided that he had already said too much.

'Musical talents?' Hewitt asked appeasingly.

'Yes.' The stranger's face showed a measure of relief.

Hewitt turned to the boy again.

'What will you play for us?' he asked slowly.

'Play for us?' the young man repeated, in the same deliberate tone. He had been making minute adjust-ments to the way in which his cutlery was laid upon his empty plate, and he now returned to this pointless task.

'He can play anything,' his companion stated angrily.

'*Anything?*'

'Yes. All he has to do is hear it once,' came the stranger's answer.

This outrageous claim was greeted with a low murmur, but any hostile comment was forestalled as Newberry chose this moment to intervene. He drew close, eyeing the mess on the table, and faced the newcomer.

'You are willing to put this to the test?' he enquired.

'Why not?' the man snapped, still angry and defiant. 'Anything!'

Newberry's imposing build and calm manner had helped him deal with many awkward situations at the tavern. It was his proud claim that no violence had ever marred proceedings on his premises, and he had no intention of allowing that record to be broken now. The cook was an expert at sizing up a situation and restoring good humour. He judged the boy to be aged about sixteen or so, but obviously with the mind of an infant. His older cousin was probably making his absurd claims in a futile attempt to defend him from ridicule. Newberry had hoped that the newcomer would back down without exposing the boy to such cruelty – but that was clearly not going to happen. The cook had no choice now but to press ahead. He felt sorry for the lad, but knew that some of his customers did not share his sensitivity.

He and the stranger faced each other, neither willing to back down – and both knowing that they were treading on dangerous ground.

'You think me a liar?' There was a quiet menace in the words, but the speaker's hands were trembling.

'I do not,' Newberry replied. 'But what of your cousin? Does he *wish* to play?'

'Always . . .'

'Can he not answer for himself?' the cook interrupted. After facing the other's sullen silence for a few moments, he knelt in front of the boy, so that their faces were level. Close to, the young man's eyes were stranger still, unfocused yet intense, the irises a pale mauve. 'Will you play your lute for us?'

The boy appeared to concentrate, thinking hard before answering. He stared at Newberry, then glanced down at the lute and back up again.

'Play. Yes,' he murmured. His slight nod was more of a wobble, as if his neck were unstable, not quite under control.

Nothing for it now, Newberry thought ruefully. He straightened up, and looked first at the silent stranger, then at Hewitt.

'What shall it be, then? One of the old songs?'

'No – a new piece,' someone cried out. 'If he only needs one hearing.' Others voiced their agreement.

'What about *your* song, Hewitt?' one of the other musicians put in. 'The one you've been working on for months and won't let us try.'

'But . . .' Hewitt hesitated, glancing at Newberry and wishing that he had never started the conversation. 'It's not meant for the lute.'

'It doesn't matter,' the stranger said eagerly. 'He can transpose it.'

'But . . .'

'Play it, Hewitt. It's about time you gave us something new.' The speaker was one of the divers, and his tone brooked no argument.

Reluctantly, the musician went to fetch his viol and the background noise in the room faded away as he checked the tuning. The boy was attentive now, his eyes fixed upon the instrument.

Hewitt began to play; slow, drawn-out notes flowed forth as his bow slid smoothly over the strings. It was a melancholy melody, evoking images of mist-enshrouded hills. His audience was quickly entranced.

Magara and her two escorts arrived just at that moment, but waited quietly in the doorway, not wishing to disturb the music.

Hewitt began to sing, adding his mellifluous voice to the harmony of his viol. His words told of lovers parted by ill-fortune and deceived by a cruel father, and of a young hero who, believing his love to be dead, left his home, intending to sail away to foreign lands. The music depicted the foggy uplands, becoming faster and more lively as the journey reached the sunlit plains. The listeners heard the galloping hooves and the wind rushing past the traveller's tear-stained face.

Then the tempo became even more dramatic as the girl – who was not dead – learned of her father's betrayal and of her lover's departure. The song told of how she fled after him, of how recklessly she rode, always gaining – but never quite enough.

Hewitt stumbled over a particularly difficult piece of fingering, and stopped briefly.

'Damn,' he muttered under his breath, then replayed the passage, getting it exactly right this time.

The story ended tragically as the girl reached the port just as her lover's ship drew out of the harbour. The young man was not aware of her presence as she fell from her horse and died from a broken neck – or a broken heart.

As Hewitt finished, a little awkwardly, he was greeted with great applause, his audience recognizing a superb composition, but the musician was clearly unhappy, and took his bows reluctantly.

'It needs a coda,' he muttered, playing a few notes from the original theme.

Then the tavern grew quiet again as the boy picked up his lute and settled it in his lap. In the spell cast by the new song, everyone had forgotten its purpose. Several people glanced at the older newcomer, who merely smiled, saying nothing. Newberry looked on miserably and half considered stopping the travesty. But he knew that he could not.

The boy began to play, and discomfort turned instantly to wonder. The first notes echoed the sad stately tune perfectly, the notes drawn out in seeming defiance of the nature of the instrument. This time, the audience was transported to the grey, misty hills, and many felt their skin turn cold and wet. They exchanged disbelieving looks.

No one expected the boy to sing, but he did, precisely on cue. His voice was higher than Hewitt's, but perfectly pitched, ringing clear and true in contrast to his earlier muttered monosyllables. The music quickened; crystal notes hung in the air while others flickered like sunlight on a dragonfly's wings – and all the time the bass strings thundered out the rhythm of the flying hooves. Hands which had seemed so clumsy when wielding a spoon now skipped nimbly over the frets.

He reached the point where Hewitt had made a mistake, played exactly the same sequence of incorrect notes, and stopped.

'Damn,' he mumbled quietly, then began again,

playing perfectly once more. Many of his enraptured audience smiled, a little bewildered, but no one made a sound.

The story reached its fateful end, but instead of stopping as Hewitt had done, the boy returned to a version of the initial melody, improvising a delicate, slow epilogue. No words accompanied the music, but everyone there with any imagination saw the hero's ship sail away into the grey sea-mist, while unknown to him, his lover's heart grew still.

As the last echoes died away, the mesmerized audience sat still and silent. Then, to a man, they rose to their feet, and the room was filled with a tumult of cheering and applause. Many were crying openly, tears running unnoticed down their cheeks, moved not only by the sadness of the song but by the paradox that such beauty and wonder had been produced by such a pitiful human being.

Hewitt, who had led the applause, stepped forward, his eyes shining. The boy stood to face him, grinning shyly. He seemed to take pleasure in the acclaim, yet was obviously still uncertain. He took Hewitt's proffered hand gingerly, his head tilted towards the floor.

'Thank you,' the musician said, his voice thick with emotion. 'It is your song now. No one else will ever play it.'

'Forgive us,' someone else said.

The boy nodded again. Though his eyes were still downcast, pride was clear in his satisfied expression.

Now everyone wanted to talk to the two newcomers, to buy them drinks. Requests for more music filled the air, but one voice rang out above all the rest.

'Slaton, is that really you?' Magara's voice was choked and her cheeks wet as she pushed her way through the throng, Brostek and Varo in her wake.

The older stranger turned to her and smiled in delighted recognition.

'So, all the black sheep are here,' he said.

CHAPTER FIVE

Magara and Slaton embraced warmly. He was all smiles now.

'It's good to see you,' he told her quietly.

'And you,' she replied, then introduced her companions as they all sat down at the table. 'Slaton is another ungrateful offspring of the landowning classes,' she explained. 'Just like me. Our homes were only five leagues apart, and we've known each other since we were small.' She paused, then glanced at Brostek who merely grinned at her. 'Don't say a word!' she warned, returning his smile.

'Even *I* am occasionally capable of gentlemanly behaviour,' he replied haughtily, then turned to the newcomer. 'Welcome, Slaton. What brings you to Trevine?'

'Him.' They all looked across at the boy, who was now seated with the other musicians, exchanging phrases, and apparently unaware of the admiring audience that surrounded him. There was a rapt expression on his face.

'Who is he?' Magara whispered.

'He's Aunt Celia's son. His name's Lisle.'

'I didn't know Celia was married.' Magara remembered a soft-voiced, timid woman, who was always singing.

'She isn't,' Slaton replied. 'They kept it quiet for a long time, but secrets like that are impossible to hide. Celia wouldn't ever say who the father was, but rumour had it that he was a travelling musician. And I for one find that easy to believe.'

'Lisle certainly has a remarkable talent,' Brostek commented.

'Both a blessing and a curse,' Slaton replied.

'Why a curse?' Varo asked.

'You see what he's like. Everyone has always thought of him as an idiot, to be pitied and then forgotten. Celia was left to raise him as best she could. Only a few tried to help her, but she didn't care. She loved the boy, nurtured him, and sang to him all the time in that bird-like voice of hers. No one expected that he'd survive more than a few years, but Celia knew differently. Lisle became an unnoticed fixture around the place – rather like one of Father's dogs – but then people got to know about his musical talent, and everything changed.' Slaton paused to drink, swallowing hard. 'Some of us had known for a long time, but we'd kept it to ourselves. I still don't know how Father found out, but when he did, Lisle became an exhibit, a freak to be paraded before guests. They laughed at him and stared while he amazed them. And Lisle loved it! He was always pleased when someone listened to him play, but it broke the bond between him and Celia. I got sick of them patronizing him, the cruel insults that he could never understand.' Slaton's earlier anger made a brief return. 'In the end, I had to get him away,' he ended abruptly, the pain in his voice obvious to them all.

'Why here?' Magara asked gently.

'I could ask you the same question,' he replied, forcing a smile, and obviously glad of an opportunity to change the subject.

'I feel at home here,' she answered. 'There's nowhere else quite like it.'

'You're not exactly living in the lap of luxury in a place like this, though,' he said. 'Don't you miss the comforts of Arenguard?'

Magara had not heard the name of her former home spoken aloud for years. It felt strange.

'The only thing she claims to miss,' Brostek put in, laughing, 'is the library. Yet she's got dozens of books here!'

'There were *thousands* there,' she retorted.

'What use were they?' Varo asked calmly.

It was an old argument, and Magara was not to be drawn.

'I'm not going to waste my breath explaining such things to a musclebound behemoth like you,' she said haughtily. 'I am in civilized company now.'

Brostek and Varo exchanged long-suffering glances. Slaton, watching, grinned uncertainly, recognizing their camaraderie but unsure of his own position.

'Have you been to Arenguard recently?' Magara asked.

'Not for some time. We've been travelling for over fourteen months now. Almost a full year.'

'Why has it taken you so long to get here?' Brostek asked.

'All Levindre's outcasts end up here sooner or later,' Magara explained to the puzzled Slaton. Then she and her childhood friend went on to exchange news of their respective families, of their own travels and present way of life, while Brostek and Varo organized some food and drink. Once his more immediate appetites had been satisfied, Brostek's curiosity brought him back into the conversation.

'Tell us more about Lisle,' he suggested.

Slaton appeared reluctant, and glanced at his cousin. The boy was still playing, and seemed quite happy. Apparently reassured, Slaton turned back to his new friends.

'He was always a weak and sickly child, and after a while, it became obvious that he wasn't . . . normal. He didn't begin to walk until he was four, and he still only speaks a few words – though he can repeat exactly anything that's said to him. His eyes are weak, and he can barely manage to dress himself. Most people think he's just a simpleton, but to me he's someone special. It's as though his real mind is trapped somewhere, and can only get out through his music.'

'But in that he's a genius,' Brostek put in.

'You've only seen a glimpse tonight,' Slaton went on. 'He knows hundreds of songs, tunes, even complicated pieces for several instruments. And he never forgets a single note.'

'It's uncanny,' Magara breathed.

'I still find it hard to believe, and I've been witnessing it for years now.' Slaton was angry again. 'He was taken advantage of. They treated him as an amusing plaything, a performing monkey, not as a person. Sometimes I hated my father . . .' He paused, avoiding their eyes. 'After a while Celia couldn't face the cruelty either, especially when—' He stopped again, but nobody broke the awkward silence. Then Slaton spoke again, the pain clear in his voice. 'She ran away, abandoned him. She left me a note saying that she'd gone to the mage-garden at Nevern. We never saw her again.'

'I didn't think anyone went there any more,' Magara said quietly.

'They don't.'

'What is this place?' Varo asked.

'It's a tiny valley, like a bowl,' she answered. 'It's one of the old wizards' special places, and was supposed to be a great centre of power, healing and magic.'

'So why don't people go there any more?' Brostek wanted to know.

'We tried,' Slaton said. 'It doesn't exist.'

'What do you mean?'

'Just that. The garden, or whatever it was, isn't there any more. The valley is permanently full of mist. It's cold and grey, and when you walk in, all you can feel underfoot is bare rock. Nothing could grow there. I tried to cross the valley, but it's like being blind, and I lost all sense of direction. After a while, I found myself coming out again near the point where I'd entered. Most people don't try a second time.'

'But you did?' Magara asked.

'Several times,' Slaton replied. 'With the same result.

If Celia's in there, she's lost for ever. And the place scared Lisle, so I gave up.'

'It certainly sounds frightening enough,' Brostek remarked. Varo made no comment.

'You don't look like men who scare easily,' Slaton said, with half a smile.

'All men of sense become frightened,' Varo stated. 'It is a necessary mechanism of the body. But some things are so important that they allow you to overcome fear.'

Slaton regarded him speculatively.

'You sound to me like a man with a mission,' he said.

'I am,' Varo replied seriously. Then he and Brostek went on to explain their work. It was one of the few times that Magara had ever seen Varo become so animated. Slaton had heard of the border raids, but had never before met anyone with first-hand knowledge of them. He was horrified by the scale of the problem, having believed until now that it was confined to rare, isolated incidents, and was saddened by the tale of misery and death. He felt an affinity with their forlorn attempts to stem the tide, but was not surprised by the Cartel's lack of action.

'That's typical of their self-satisfied, self-serving arrogance!' he exclaimed. 'How *can* they be so short-sighted?'

'Do you think you could help us persuade them?' Brostek asked hopefully.

'I doubt it. I'm not exactly popular at home just now, and anyway, my father's only a minor landowner. But if we had a strong enough case . . .' He leaned forward across the table. 'Tell me more about the most recent raids, those nearest the lowlands.'

Magara was already familiar with the gruesome details of these attacks and wanted, for a time at least, to forget about them. Her earlier conversation with Slaton led her now to memories of her earlier life. Although her own reasons for leaving home had been quite different, she still felt sympathy for her childhood friend.

Neither of us can go back now, she thought ruefully.

Magara was the youngest of four daughters. Her father was a landowner of considerable wealth and power, and when his wife failed to bear him a son, he had decided to continue his dynasty through the carefully arranged marriages of his girls. Magara had watched uneasily as her elder sisters all meekly accepted his will. Agreements were reached with families of similar standing, and the resulting matches greatly expanded her father's sphere of influence.

It had been assumed that Magara would follow in her sisters' footsteps, but the young girl had other ideas. Always an independent spirit, she had long felt stifled in the role assigned to her, and took every opportunity to learn of faraway places, of the wonders of history and legend. She lived in a world of books and dreams, occasionally enlivened by the visit of a genuine traveller. Two of her sisters and their husbands lived at Arenguard, the rambling complex of stone, brick and wood that was the family home, and so she was able to see the effects of marriage at first hand. That there were pleasures as well as difficulties was obvious, but Magara knew it was not for her. Not yet.

When eligible suitors began to call, her dreams took shape and her resolve hardened. It was time for her to make a stand. Her father, for all his greed and singlemindedness, loved his youngest daughter dearly, and was confused and hurt by her defiance. After many arguments, accompanied by her tears and his rage, he finally agreed to her request that she be allowed to travel, 'to see what life really is'. In that time of upheaval, Magara became an adult in her own eyes as well as those of others. She learnt that her sisters were envious as well as shocked, and her resolve grew firmer still. At last, her wish was granted.

'One year,' her father had decided. 'No more, no less.'

Grateful for the reprieve but almost convulsed with

nervousness, she made her preparations, and left. That had been three and a half years ago.

Long before her year was over, Magara had freed herself from the travelling companions her father had insisted upon, and had arrived in Trevine, knowing that she could never conform to her family's expectations. As the year drew to a close, she sent a message to Arenguard to that effect. The initial replies were a mixture of threats and sadness, pleading and disbelief, but the young woman stood her ground, and as time went by, contact with her home had lessened to almost nothing. No attempt was ever made to force her to return. It was never actually stated that she had been disowned, but her father made it plain that if she no longer wished to be an active member of the family, then she would have to accept the consequences of her decision.

Now, as she sat in Newberry's tavern, she wondered whether they would take her in if she returned, or whether they had cut her off completely. She had no intention of trying to find out. She had no regrets.

But I do miss my books! she reminded herself, smiling.

As she thought of the old library, she was reminded of another aspect of her former life that she missed. Her grandfather had been a keen beekeeper in his later years, and had passed its secrets on to his favourite granddaughter. Magara had been frightened at first, but soon came to love the swarms, with their noise and industry. Before she left Arenguard, she had made her farewells to the hives, speaking aloud as the old man had taught her. 'They may not hear your words,' he had said, 'but they understand well enough.'

It had been a tradition that the bees were informed whenever a death occurred in that extended household, and that had been Magara's duty when her grandfather died. She had spoken solemnly, with tears in her eyes, and she believed that the drone of the bees had deepened in mourning. Magara had decided that happier

57

events should also be relayed to the swarm; it seemed only fair, and so she had started a new tradition.

Magara closed her eyes now, shutting out the scene in the tavern, and recalled one particular morning in vivid detail. She saw herself leaning out of a second floor window in the old house, shouting to the hives the news that her eldest sister had just given birth to a baby boy. The jubilant tone in her voice, or perhaps the news itself, had roused the swarm, and they flew in a huge circle as if in celebration. Magara had been delighted by their reaction, and could hear them again now, just as if she were a ten-year-old girl once more.

She opened her eyes, smiling at the memory, and returned to the present. But the buzzing of the bees still sounded in her ears.

Lisle was staring at her. His lips were parted, but his teeth were held together as he made a noise that perfectly imitated the rise and fall of the swarm's buzzing. As he became aware that she was looking back at him, a strange glow lit up his eyes.

For a moment, Magara was too stunned to react. Then she turned to Slaton, who was watching her and the boy.

'You're not telling me everything, are you?' she said.

CHAPTER SIX

'Most people don't see it so soon,' Slaton replied. He was smiling, though he sounded dreadfully tired.

'You can't hide anything from Magara,' Brostek told him. 'She reads minds.'

'I do not!' Although her annoyance was muted by Brostek's grin, she had glimpsed the momentary shock and fear in Slaton's eyes. 'Does *he*?' she asked quietly.

'Sometimes I think so,' he replied, lowering his voice.

'So music is not Lisle's only talent,' Varo said, fascinated by this latest incident.

Slaton shook his head.

'Unfortunately not,' he agreed, clearly reluctant to say more.

'Let's go. You can come back to my place,' Magara suggested, divining the reason for her friend's reticence. Although Lisle had now resumed his musical exchanges, several onlookers had obviously been intrigued by the interruption.

Their departure was a lengthy process. The musicians did not want to let Lisle go, and the boy himself seemed willing to play all night. Once started upon a tune, he would finish it no matter what, and it was a while before his audience could be persuaded to make no further requests. Eventually, Magara and her group managed to leave, thanking Newberry as they went.

It was quiet outside the tavern, and the lake's water was a black void, its glassy surface studded with the reflected light of remote stars. Magara guided the group confidently along the walkways, explaining for Varo and Brostek's benefit about her memories of the bees and Lisle's uncanny reaction. Slaton listened in silence.

As they neared her home, Magara suddenly changed the subject.

'You will stay with me, won't you?' she said, then added awkwardly, 'Though there won't be much space.'

'Don't worry. We can find somewhere else easily enough,' Brostek put in quickly, and Varo nodded in agreement.

Do they think we want to be alone together? Magara wondered. She and Slaton had been friends for as long as she could remember, but there had never been any hint of a romantic attachment between them. Indeed, the pang of loss she felt at the thought of not having Varo and Brostek under her roof was surprisingly strong. Neither of them had ever been her lover, and yet they were more than friends.

'You're sure?' Slaton asked uncertainly.

'Yes,' Varo answered promptly. 'You are new to Trevine. And old friends are dear.'

'Thank you,' Slaton said quietly.

'Thank you,' Lisle echoed, exactly copying his companion's tone of relieved gratitude.

Magara turned to the young man and smiled warmly.

'You are welcome here, Lisle.' His extraordinary eyes seemed to reflect more than the dim starlight, and she wondered what secrets lay behind his gaze. 'Come inside.'

Shadow greeted them at the doorway, a ghostly shape of starlit grey. She growled deep in her throat, disturbed by the presence of strangers.

'Friends, Shadow!' Brostek called. 'Come greet.' To Slaton he added, 'She's tame.'

Slaton flinched a little as Shadow nuzzled his hand, learning his scent, but Lisle immediately sat down on the floor so that his face was level with the wolf's. He showed no sign of fear as he reached out to ruffle the soft fur below her ears. The two clearly felt an immediate rapport, while the others just stared in surprise.

'Music is *not* his only talent,' Brostek remarked.

60

Magara led the way inside, eager to hear more of her visitors' story. She lit lamps and ushered the men into chairs.

'We ended your evening prematurely,' Slaton said. 'I'm sorry.'

'If I'm any judge,' Brostek answered, 'your tale will be worth more than anything Newberry's tavern could have offered us. Besides, I took the precaution . . .' He grinned and produced two wine bottles from the voluminous recesses of his jacket. 'You can't talk with a dry mouth!'

Slaton glanced uncertainly at Magara.

'You don't have to tell us anything you don't want to,' she assured him. 'But you can trust these two.'

The ensuing silence was broken only by the pop of a cork and the sound of wine being poured out.

'I'm sorry,' Slaton said eventually. 'I'm not hesitating because of you. It's just that until now it's been easier to try and hide the truth. Most people don't like ideas that upset their view of the world. They're frightened by them.'

'Most people are frightened by what they don't understand,' Varo said evenly.

'Are you?' Slaton asked.

'A little. That's why I try to learn.'

The newcomer nodded, his face serious. 'I'd better begin at the beginning,' he said. He sipped his wine, and glanced at Lisle, who was still seated on the boards by the door, Shadow beside him. 'Will he be all right out there?'

'Shadow won't let anything happen to him,' Brostek replied.

'He's not used to water . . .' Slaton was still anxious.

'There are railings on the walkway,' Magara said, 'and Shadow won't let him wander. Stop worrying, and tell us what this is all about.'

Brostek smiled to hear the impatience in her voice.

'Celia told me,' Slaton began, 'that Lisle knew what

she was thinking, even when he was a baby. He couldn't do much then, of course, and at the time, I didn't think much of it. After all, Celia had often had some very strange ideas! But later, I saw the truth of it for myself. I'd think of a toy or a book, and turn to find he'd already got it in his hand, ready to pass it to me. Then he'd look at me with those eyes of his . . .' He paused and drank again. 'And there were times when I was on the point of knocking at the nursery door, only to have him open it for me first.'

'Could it be that he had heard your footsteps?' Varo asked.

'I thought it might be that at first, so I tested him. I'd approach in bare feet, and I'd swear I never made a sound, yet there he was. And it wasn't just *my* approach that he reacted to. He used to hide whenever Father came near – not that he often did,' he added resentfully.

'Did you *feel* anything?' Magara asked.

'In my head, you mean?'

She nodded.

'Not a thing. I wish I could. Perhaps I'd understand him better then.'

'Did *you*, tonight?' Brostek asked, looking at Magara.

'No. I don't think so. I wasn't expecting . . .' She shrugged, leaving the thought unfinished, and Slaton took up his tale again.

'Then we began to notice other things. He would know exactly when the sun was going to rise, and would take us to watch. He'd know when a flower was going to bloom, or an apple fall from a tree. There was no way he could predict such things from other people's minds. No one saw this but Celia and me. Idiots are not supposed to have talents, after all.' His voice was bitter again. 'Even when his musical ability was discovered and he became a public figure, no one noticed much – all they saw was his entertainment value. But when the eclipses started, everything changed.'

'Eclipses?' Magara looked puzzled.

'Yes. They began about a year and a half ago.'

'What eclipses?'

'You *must* have seen them,' he replied, surprised and puzzled by her reaction.

Magara shook her head.

'There haven't been any here,' she insisted. She remembered the only eclipse she had ever seen, many years ago. Her grandfather had shown her how to watch it safely through smoked glass. Although she had been a little afraid, she had gazed in fascination as the moon slid over the sun, mesmerized by the sinuous geometry of the planet's curves. Now, however, she became aware that all three men were looking at her oddly.

'There haven't!' she insisted again, glancing between them.

'There have been more than a dozen since we left home,' Slaton responded. 'You must have seen some of them, even hidden away down here. There was one only yesterday.'

Brostek and Varo, who had been nodding their agreement, suddenly frowned.

'Yesterday?' Varo queried sharply.

'Yes.'

'When?'

'Around noon.' Slaton seemed confused now as puzzled looks were exchanged.

'We didn't see it,' Varo stated evenly.

'You must have. We were only about ten leagues from the crater – and it almost went dark!'

'Nothing happened here,' Magara said. 'I'm sure of it.'

'We've seen several eclipses,' Brostek put in, 'but we certainly didn't see that one.'

'You never told me about them,' Magara said accusingly.

'It didn't seem important,' he replied.

'I don't understand,' Slaton began. 'How . . . ?'

'Never mind that now,' Magara interrupted. 'What has this got to do with Lisle?'

Slaton shook his head as if to clear it, then glanced suspiciously at his wine.

'Have some more,' Brostek suggested. 'I usually find it helps.'

'Be quiet,' Magara told him, then turned back to Slaton. 'Well?' she prompted.

'Lisle could sense them coming,' he said. 'I'll never forget the first time it happened. Father had guests, and as usual, Lisle was ordered to play for them in the Great Hall. It was mid-winter and cold, but the sky was clear, and sunlight was streaming in through the high windows – you remember?' Magara nodded, and Slaton went on. 'All was going well. Lisle was playing, not hearing the cruel remarks, and most people were even listening to him. Then, all of a sudden, he stopped and screamed, pointing upwards. Father was furious, but when the light faded a few moments later, he became as frightened as anyone. Lisle was not the only one yelling when it went dark. The whole place was in an uproar, but I managed to fight my way outside to see what was going on. I couldn't make out much, but the air felt crackly, as though a storm was brewing, and it was hard to breathe. After a few moments the sun reappeared, but the damage was done by then. The hall was in a complete shambles, and Lisle was crying and lashing out at anyone who came near him. He was shaking like a leaf. Some people were looking at him as though he was a sorcerer – as if he'd *made* it happen, rather than just reacted to it. I heard them whispering, saw the signs . . . It made me feel sick.' Slaton swallowed hard, his face a picture of disgust, then went on. 'Celia calmed him down eventually, and managed to protect him from my father, who wanted to whip him for disrupting his feast. The old man was never so eager for his musical talents after that.'

'I'm not surprised,' Brostek remarked drily.

'It was a small mercy,' Slaton said. 'But after that first eclipse, Celia became increasingly desperate. Each time there was another one, Lisle would know it was coming –

64

and earlier and earlier too. He would try to hide, shivering and crying, obviously terrified. And then he started reacting several days before it happened.'

'What harm could an eclipse do him?' Brostek asked.

'I don't know, but they began to frighten me too. It just wasn't natural for there to be so many, so regularly. And for Lisle it was obviously becoming unbearable. Celia was at her wit's end, until finally she gave up and ran away. I can't blame her. Father still bore a grudge, and treated them both harshly. After she'd gone, I knew I had to get Lisle away.'

'And while you were travelling?' Magara asked.

'He still knows when they're coming, but it doesn't seem to affect him so badly. I've learnt to recognize the signs, but his reaction is not nearly so violent. Maybe he's getting used to it. This last one was the easiest of all.'

'But it never reached the crater,' Brostek murmured.

'None of them have!' Magara added.

'Perhaps you and Lisle should stay here then,' Brostek suggested. 'He wouldn't be bothered by them here.'

'Why not?' Magara said eagerly. 'The council would certainly accept Lisle. His music alone . . .' Her voice died away.

Slaton smiled ruefully.

'Unfortunately, all *I* am good for is looking after him,' he said gently.

'No . . .' she began.

'I'm a typical landowner's son,' he cut in. 'Very good at getting other people to work for me. It's Lisle who's earnt our passage, not me.' He raised his hands to forestall her protest. 'It's no good, Magara. We're still looking for answers. Someone somewhere must understand and be able to help him. So unless you think anyone here has those answers, we have to move on.'

Varo had not spoken for some time and had hardly touched his wine.

'Join us,' he offered simply.

Slaton blinked in surprise. 'We . . . we'd only be a hindrance,' he replied eventually. Even Brostek was puzzled by his companion's offer.

'I don't think so,' Varo stated coolly. 'Besides, this way you can keep searching for Lisle's answers, and in the meantime we may be able to get that evidence you'd need to help us convince the Cartel.'

'But . . .' Magara began. Varo glanced at her, his perfectly matched eyebrows raised, and she subsided.

'I appreciate the offer,' Slaton responded slowly.

'Sleep on it,' Varo suggested. 'You can decide tomorrow.'

'I'm no swordsman.'

'You can learn to be,' Brostek put in, warming to the idea.

'And Lisle . . .'

'It would be an honour to ride with both of you,' Varo stated.

'I don't know what to say,' Slaton said, clearly bewildered by this turn of events.

'Well, I do!' Magara exclaimed angrily. 'This is madness!'

The three men regarded her calmly, waiting for her to voice her objections.

'If you can't see—' She stopped, and sighed with exasperation. 'Men!' she breathed.

'Nothing's decided yet, Mags,' Slaton said, his expression concerned.

Magara was disconcerted by his use of her childhood nickname, but ignored it.

'Oh, isn't it?' she demanded. 'You don't know these two. Logic stands no chance against them.'

Varo frowned, but Brostek only laughed.

'And of course you would be the first to champion logic over intuition,' he teased her.

Magara glared at him, then could not help smiling.

'Perhaps not *female* intuition,' she countered.

Brostek leaned closer to Slaton, and said in a loud

whisper, 'Be very careful what you say now, or you might find your bed floating in the middle of the lake come sunrise.'

'If you're not careful, I'll throw you in now,' she threatened.

'What we're doing is important,' Varo put in. He was the only one whose expression had remained serious throughout the exchange.

'I've never denied that,' Magara said resignedly. 'But let them stay a while first. Please.'

Varo only shrugged in answer, and nodded towards Slaton, implying that the decision was his.

'Speaking of which,' Brostek announced, 'the wine's all gone, and we need to find lodgings for the night.' He stood up, a little unsteadily, and the others followed suit, Slaton going to the door to check on his cousin. Lisle was fast asleep on the boards, with Shadow lying next to him. The wolf's eyes were alert, as if she were on guard, and she gave a tiny yelp as Slaton picked up the sleeping boy. At Magara's direction, he carried him to the makeshift bed that Varo had been using.

Brostek and Varo collected their belongings and prepared to leave.

'Good night, Slaton,' Brostek called softly. 'Good night . . . Mags.'

Magara seized an empty bottle and threatened to throw it at him.

'Call me that again,' she said fiercely, 'and I'll have the divers take you to the deeps and leave you there!'

'Yes, mistress,' he answered, cowering ridiculously.

'Get out of here,' she commanded, laughing.

He and Varo obeyed, Shadow padding silently behind them on the walkway.

'Do you really think they can be of use?' Brostek asked his partner.

'Perhaps. Being able to see the future like that could be useful.'

'I don't see how it helps *us*.'

'Think back,' Varo said carefully. 'Am I imagining it, or has each spate of attacks by the Knifemen been preceded by an eclipse just a few days earlier?'

They walked on in silence, Brostek remembering some of their times in the hills.

'Gods!' he breathed eventually. 'You're right!' As the significance of the discovery sank in, he whistled softly. 'So if Lisle can predict the eclipses . . .'

'Think on,' Varo said.

'What?'

'Slaton told us there was an eclipse yesterday,' Varo replied. 'So how many days does that give us?'

CHAPTER SEVEN

'So your mind's made up?' Magara asked.

'Yes. I'd like to stay for a while, but . . .' Slaton shrugged.

'No second thoughts?'

'None,' he replied promptly. 'It was obvious last night that no one in this place has ever seen someone like Lisle before. You said yourself that you couldn't think of anyone who might help. Going with Varo and Brostek just feels right – at least now our travels will have a purpose. The more I think about it, the more certain I am that we should go.'

'That doesn't say much for my powers of persuasion,' she commented, smiling.

'No one could have been more eloquent,' he replied, grinning back, 'and your concern is appreciated. But I . . . let's just say that I *know* we have to do this.'

The two old friends had talked long into the night, only to be roused soon after dawn by Varo and Brostek with the news that they were to leave that morning. Both men had seemed pleased by Slaton's bleary-eyed confirmation that he would be going with them, and had then left to complete their own arrangements.

'I don't see why they should be in such a hurry all of a sudden,' Magara complained.

'They must have their reasons.' Slaton finished slicing an apple, and passed the plate over to Lisle, who was quietly absorbed in arranging crumbs on the table. The young man looked up briefly and smiled before beginning to eat.

'They'll come back here eventually,' Magara suggested

hopefully. 'Why don't you go with them next time instead?'

'And what would I do until then?' Slaton asked. 'They might be gone – and I quote – "for months on end". We'll take our chance while we can.'

'It'll be hard on Lisle.'

'No harder than what he's already had to cope with.'

They had been through this countless times during the night, having discussed the mystery of Lisle's gifts and disabilities, the raids and eclipses, as well as the strangeness of Varo and Brostek's way of life.

'Perhaps you will be able to help them,' Magara conceded. 'But I'll miss you. It was so lovely to see you – and now you're leaving so soon.'

There had been such a lot to talk about that the two old friends had had no time for much reminiscence or family news. Magara felt a twinge of homesickness for the first time ever as she and Slaton got to their feet. They embraced warmly.

'We'll be back, I promise,' he said softly.

Behind him, Lisle's chair scraped on the boards as he too stood up. Magara held out her arms to the boy, who came to her slowly, blushing and blinking furiously. She gave him a gentle hug.

'We'll be back,' Lisle echoed quietly.

Magara met Slaton's eyes over the boy's shoulder.

I hope so, she responded silently.

* * *

Many of the first-time visitors to the crater who plucked up enough courage to make the descent were persuaded to go down by a route known as The Swing. The wallmen guides described this – truthfully – as the quickest way to and from Trevine; it held the record times for trips in both directions. Most people equated speed with ease, and wanted to get their ordeal over with as quickly as possible. However, a traveller's first trip by this route was usually their last, because of what they were *not* told – that two-thirds of their descent was made in one huge drop. Passengers were suspended, either in harness or net, from the counterweighted pulley system on the Rim, then swung out into thin air from the overhanging rock and manoeuvred to a tiny platform atop Diamond Crag, seventy paces below. The route's name suddenly seemed much more sinister while they were swaying gently in mid-flight, and the sensation had been known to cause a range of disturbing effects in the passengers, varying from terrified paralysis to hysteria bordering on temporary madness. Ironically, this stage of the journey was perfectly safe – the wallmen knew their business too well for it to be anything else – but that did not lessen its impact on crater novices.

The wallmen themselves used The Swing frequently, delighting in its speed and, for them, lack of effort. Old hands walked down over the Rim backwards before launching themselves into space, but the younger and more foolhardy among them would sometimes don a harness and then leap into the void. This usually occurred when impressionable young ladies were present. The pulley systems allowed them to break their fall gently enough and, provided they did not jump too far out – and thus risk swinging back into the unforgiving cliff face – it was quite safe. However, their actions did little to reassure prospective travellers.

As if The Swing itself was not enough, the terrors of the descent were not over once the temporary haven of the small ledge had been reached. The journey continued, assuming the traveller's legs were still operative, down the zig-zag path that gave the Crag its name. Although the way was marked with iron pinions and carved hand- and foot-holds, there were no confining safety ropes – and the crater floor was still some thirty paces below. The last half of this distance was covered either on free-hanging ropes or on a man-powered pulley. When the first-timers finally reached the bottom of the cliff, most of them were so relieved that they were unable to walk for quite some time. Remarks from the wallmen, such as 'You were lucky the wind dropped when it did', or 'It's amazing how those birds manage to keep their nests from falling off those tiny ledges, isn't it', rarely helped their condition. However, anyone who had braved The Swing and was still in a fit state to patronize any of Trevine's taverns the same night could be sure of having his or her first drink – and possibly several more – bought by one of their guides.

The nature of The Swing meant that no heavy goods and few regular travellers went that way. There were two other main routes, and it was these that Varo and his companions would use to leave the crater. Both began at Home Platform, a natural wide ledge of flat rock, just above the scree, which had been improved by the wallmen and which was reached by either of two rough-hewn stairways or by a gently sloping chute. This chute had been painstakingly smoothed over the years, and was used to roll or push goods too heavy to carry comfortably.

From Home Platform, a large, counterweighted pulley system lifted goods and people to Yellowwine Ledge, just over half way up the cliff face. Properly handled, this system could take two loads – one up, one down – of up to six people or the equivalent weight, either in nets or harnesses. The only difficult part of this journey was crossing The Point, a jagged spit of rock overhanging Home Platform, about thirty paces up. This took time, patience and the assistance of wallmen using Craven's Trellis, a network of iron studs hammered into the rock. This had been first designed and put into place decades earlier by the inappropriately named Craven, and enabled the wallmen to manoeuvre bulk and assist passengers from all angles. The work required agility, strength and supreme confidence, and the sight of the cliff workers scurrying about like human spiders unnerved many travellers. Once past The Point, the route was once again straightforward as far as Yellowwine Ledge, named for an infamous incident when a barrel had fallen from the Rim, hitting the ridge with explosive force and staining the area orange. The ledge had been levelled and broadened by the wallmen, who had also enlarged the natural caves to provide either storage space for goods in transit, or somewhere for waiting passengers to be left in relative safety.

From Yellowwine, there were then two routes to the top. The most direct was on a second pulley system rising directly to Rimgap One, via a wide but jagged funnel known as The Serpent's Jaws. In this part, quite close to the top of the cliff, especially bulky loads needed guidance between the sides, but everything else passed freely enough. The wallmen tried to encourage passengers to use the other route, thus leaving the pulley free to haul goods, but some people still preferred to use it, for reasons of size, disability or nervous disposition.

The second route began at the southern end of the ledge, and followed Rakespill's Folly, a narrow but well-defined path which was now roped off for safety. When this traverse had been pioneered, it had been little more than an extended crack in the cliff face, and every finger- and toe-hold had had to be sought out carefully. Now all that was needed was a combination of careful movement and steady nerves.

Rakespill's Folly led to a much smaller, level resting place, known simply as Crag. From there, the journey continued with an almost vertical climb up The Cake Walk – a series of metal rungs, hoops and rails – to an even smaller ledge, named, with an unusual lack of originality, Little Crag. Here, the traveller was once again faced with a choice; either another short roped walk and then ropes and a harness which allowed him to climb or be pulled to the top, or a series of three rope ladders, each about seven or eight paces high, which ran up crevices in the upper level of the cliff. Both routes emerged at the way-station known as Rimgap Two.

Safety devices were available on each section, enabling travellers to attach themselves to ropes or pinions whenever they felt insecure. However, this process of coupling and uncoupling inevitably slowed progress, and seasoned climbers gained status by refusing them. Brostek and Varo almost always chose the Rimgap Two option, preferring to rely on their own fitness and agility as much as possible. However, the wallmen always had the final say about a traveller's chosen route. When, the day before, Slaton had requested a passage down, they had taken one look at Lisle and directed the two men to Rimgap One. The cousins had descended the entire distance in a rope cage, first swallowed by the Serpent's Jaws, then transferring to the second pulley at Yellowwine. They had both been terrified, but Slaton had also been greatly impressed. Now they would be leaving by the same route.

Varo and his group all began their ascent from Home Platform. Having paid the necessary toll, they were loaded into the wooden-floored rope cage, and held on tightly as the pulley lurched into action. Brostek and Varo, old hands now, helped the passage over The Point, exchanging greetings with the wallmen on duty there.

'Leaving so soon?' one of them called.

'This little crater is so boring!' Brostek shouted back. 'We need some excitement in our lives.'

'We have work to do,' Varo added more soberly.

'Work? You two? You don't know the meaning of the word!' a second wallman cried.

'Come with us and see,' Brostek challenged.

'No thanks. Bring the lutist back soon. He *is* worth listening to.'

News of Lisle's astonishing performance had spread quickly.

The group split up at the mid-point of the journey. Varo and Brostek finished the climb under their own power, emerging from the rope-ladders in time to walk along to Rimgap One and watch their companions and Shadow being pulled up from the Serpent's Jaws. The wolf curled placidly at Lisle's feet, an old hand herself now at this unnatural journey. Ordinarily she would have completed the trip alone – few travellers were eager for her company – but the boy seemed to accept her presence as normal, and even Slaton was beginning to feel more at ease with the creature. Compared to their precarious mode of transport, having a wolf as a fellow-passenger did not worry him.

'Gods! I'm glad that's over,' Slaton remarked when he was helped out on to firm ground. He glanced back down into the crater. Lisle also looked over the edge and pointed shakily. Far below, now only a tiny speck of humanity amid the scree, Magara stood looking up at them. As they watched, she waved in farewell. The four men waved back, then watched her turn around and make her way towards the distant town.

As the travellers followed her progress, three of them – in their own ways and in varying degrees – felt the sadness of loss in their hearts.

PART TWO

BROTHERS IN BLOOD

CHAPTER EIGHT

'Do you have your own horses?' Varo asked as they walked towards Melton, the larger and more southerly of the two Rim settlements.

'Horse,' Slaton corrected him. 'She carries us both easily enough.'

'Is that practical?' Brostek wondered. 'We travel fast – and we've spare horses if you need one.'

'If we can't keep up, then leave us behind,' Slaton replied firmly. 'The last thing I want is to slow you down.' Seeing the uncertainty on the faces of his new friends, he added, 'Lisle has never ridden alone. And we've covered many leagues since we left home, sometimes at a gallop.'

'Doesn't it get uncomfortable?'

'No. I had a special saddle made for the two of us, and as a last resort, Lisle can be strapped to my back. We've done it before when we had to.'

'That sounds fair enough,' Brostek decided.

'Where *is* your horse?' Varo asked.

'In the stables at the far end of town,' Slaton replied, pointing.

'Go and fetch her then, and meet us at Manhire's. It's that big place on the main street.'

Slaton nodded.

'We'll introduce you to some of our men there,' Brostek said. 'And your horse can meet Shadow.' He grinned. 'For some reason, she seems to have a bit of an adverse effect on horses – at first, anyway.'

Slaton glanced back at the wolf, who chose that moment to yawn expansively, displaying rows of ferocious-looking teeth.

'Can't think why,' he remarked, grinning.

They went their separate ways.

'Still think having them along is a good idea?' Brostek asked, watching Lisle's ungainly progress.

'Time will tell,' Varo replied evenly. 'Let's find Langel.'

The two men strode into the town. As always, the most immediate contrast with Trevine was provided by the dirt that seemed to inundate everything. In the crater, the purity of the lake was paramount, but here the streets carried the usual mixture of horse dung, rubbish and the dust of summer. Their nostrils were assailed by a pungent variety of smells; the stench of manure and rotting garbage, the odours of food, drink and wood-smoke, as well as the unidentifiable mixture produced by a dozen trades and a thousand people.

The buildings in Melton ranged from solid stone houses to flimsy shacks – and their inhabitants were as varied as the dwelling places. Prosperous merchants, some with guild insignia embroidered on their fine clothes, rode well-groomed horses, while beggars and ragged children competed with street buskers and a wall-eyed juggler for the coins of well-to-do passers-by. Between the two extremes, the Rim settlements boasted many tradesmen and women, the citizens whose industry – or lack of it – determined much of the town's character. Blacksmiths, bakers, carpenters, innkeepers, fortune-tellers, farmers and butchers – all claimed their share of the general commerce, and others, jewellers and crafts-men, took advantage of the link with Trevine and the crater's treasure.

The morning's business was already well under way, and the streets were full of people, horses and carts. Vendors loudly proclaimed their wares, dogs barked and cats prowled in the alleyways, defending their territory with hisses and yowls. First-time visitors were easy to spot by their bemused expressions, and were usually descended upon by the enterprising inhabitants, who hoped to take advantage of their inexperience.

However, few locals gave Varo and Brostek more than a passing glance. Even Shadow caused little comment. The Rim was used to many peculiar travellers.

Manhire's was a large wooden building, built around three sides of a square courtyard. Two sections of the U-shape were stables; the third was a basic boarding house that consisted of a large communal room where food and drink could be purchased, with dormitories to either side. The notice outside proclaimed: 'MANHIRE'S. The best stabling and the softest beds on the Rim.' The latter claim owed more to the owner's sense of business than to the truth, but his stables were indeed well-maintained and supplied. When so much depended on their horses, Brostek and Varo felt it was worth paying the extra charged by Manhire to be sure that their mounts received wholesome grain and clean water, as well as secure housing.

Entering the main room of the hostel, they came upon two men playing Dragons, a battle game of strategy and cunning fought out upon a board of alternate black and white squares. A third man – the one they were seeking – sat nearby in a deep, padded chair, studying lists and muttering to himself. All three glanced up at the newcomers.

'You're back early.' There was a slight note of panic in Langel's voice.

'We have to leave,' Varo stated flatly. 'Today.'

'Today?' Langel rose to his feet, waving his pieces of paper. His rotund frame radiated indignation, as though he took Varo's decision as a personal affront. 'Our supplies are nowhere near complete!'

'Are the horses fit?' Varo demanded, ignoring the other's outrage.

'Yes, but—'

'Then we go with what we have,' Varo said with finality.

Langel glanced at Brostek, who grinned.

'You'll cope, Langel,' he remarked. 'You always do.'

81

The other man opened his mouth to remonstrate, then thought better of it and shrugged his acceptance.

Varo turned to the younger of the two players. He was barely twenty-years-old, but was tall, with sandy hair and a muscular frame.

'Ross, go round up the others,' Varo instructed. 'Get your brother to help if he's here.'

'I don't know *where* he is,' the young man replied. 'He never tells me anything. Or anyone else for that matter. I sometimes think—'

'Well, you know where to find Keredin,' Varo cut in. 'Get *him* to help.'

'What's the rush?' Ross protested. 'I was going to win this time.'

Varo studied the board for a few moments.

'You would have lost in four moves,' he stated categorically. 'Now get going.'

After a puzzled look at the board, Ross glanced at his opponent, who was smiling smugly, then left quietly – for once leaving someone else with the last word. The other player, an older man with close-cropped greying hair and beard, looked up at Brostek expectantly. He folded scarred arms across his iron-studded leather tunic.

'Come on, Bair,' Brostek said. 'Let's try and rouse some of Manhire's stable lads.'

'Keep a look out for Slaton!' Varo called as the two men left the room.

'Slaton?' Langel queried.

'We've two new recruits.'

'Horses?' Langel asked quickly, practical as ever.

'Their own,' Varo answered. 'They ride together.'

The older man raised his eyebrows.

'No time to explain now,' his leader said. 'Show me what you've got.'

*   *   *

Slaton and Lisle arrived a short time later. Brostek was relieved to see that their mount was indeed a large animal, built for both speed and stamina. He had already explained a little about the newcomers to Bair; the old soldier was curious about them, and also a little bemused. Brostek was concerned by his reaction – the veteran hated the Cartel, for reasons he had never explained, and Slaton was the son of a Cartel member. Although Varo and Brostek were the unquestioned leaders of the group, Bair was the oldest, and his voice carried weight with the others. They could not afford any serious divisions within their ranks.

Bair watched the new arrivals as they dismounted, noting the well-practised manoeuvre and their plain travelling clothes with approval. Slaton and Bair clasped hands as Brostek introduced them, each taking the measure of the other, their expressions serious. Lisle nodded in his own odd way when he was named, but ignored the veteran's outstretched hand. Bair stood awkwardly for a moment, then withdrew. Slaton began to try and explain, but the older man stopped him.

'If half of what young Brostek here tells me is true,' he said gruffly, 'then you've no need to say anything. Lisle is welcome here.'

Behind him, Brostek smiled with relief, and returned to the task of readying the horses.

*   *   *

Langel and Varo had just completed their inventory.

'It's not much for the mountains,' the quartermaster said doubtfully.

'We've managed on less,' Varo countered. 'And we can travel faster this way.'

A sandy-haired man entered the room.

'What are you doing back so soon?' Langel demanded.

'That's Rogan, not Ross,' Varo told him.

The brothers were identical physically, but were complete opposites in temperament. Ross could talk a dragon to sleep, as the saying went, whereas Rogan was habitually silent, making even Varo seem voluble by comparison. One was always laughing, while the other seldom even smiled. Only when they fought were they entirely alike, working together as a formidable team – their gracefully precise movements allied to an almost berserker violence. Like Varo and Brostek, the twins had also been orphaned by the raids, and that fact had moulded their characters in markedly different ways, yet their dedication and loyalty to Varo's group and to each other were equally unswerving.

'Well met, Rogan,' Varo said. 'Your brother is out gathering the group. Go and help. He'll have gone for Keredin first, so if you know where any of the others are . . .'

Rogan nodded and left without a word.

'I should have known,' Langel remarked. 'There's no way Ross could have kept quiet for that long. Though how you can tell them apart by looks alone I'll never know.'

*   *   *

It was a testament to the twins' skill at rooting out their comrades, and to Langel's organization, that the entire group rode out of town only an hour after midday. Varo set a steady but not hectic pace, and the horse carrying Slaton and Lisle kept up easily, much to everyone's relief.

There were sixteen men in all. Slaton's thought, which he kept to himself, was that it did not seem many to pit against a force as powerful as the Knifemen. He had been introduced to them all before they left, but the speed of the introductions and of their subsequent departure meant that he could not yet put names to more than a few of them. Their reactions to him had varied

84

from the cordial to the cool, and Lisle had received many questioning looks. But whatever their private thoughts, none of the men had queried Varo's decision to include the two newcomers. Once on the road there was little opportunity to talk, and Slaton longed for the evening, when he would get a chance to begin to get to know his companions, and perhaps win their trust.

One member of the group whom he *did* remember was Keredin. This was partly due to the man's striking looks – a crooked, beak-like nose and a mane of jet-black hair – and to the fact, relayed by Brostek, that he was an ex-wizard. Slaton had met a few wizards at his former home, but they had been mostly pitiful creatures, objects of derision, and little better than beggars. But he had never met an *ex*-wizard before, and certainly not one who carried a sword, rode a fine stallion, and whose dark brown eyes seemed alternately ablaze and faraway. Riding alongside Slaton now, he appeared almost to be in a trance.

Looking about him, Slaton knew one thing for certain. He had never been in stranger company. This point was emphasized by an incident, one hour into the journey, when the seventeenth member of the group joined their ranks.

CHAPTER NINE

Varo led the party along a broad trail circling a hill that was topped by an outcrop of grey, weathered rock. To their left, the ground fell away in a gentle, grassy slope to a plain where copses and heathland were interspersed with cattle pasture. To the right, the tor rose high above them. The small cliff was sheer at one point, with a dangerous looking overhang ten paces over their heads, and it was here that Varo halted, leaning close to the rock face. He carefully touched some mud plastered on to the surface in the shape of an X, then examined his begrimed fingers.

'He's here,' Varo stated, and glanced at Bair. The old soldier raised his fingers to his lips and let out a piercing, drawn-out whistle. The sound was answered by an outlandish wail from above, a cry like nothing they had ever heard before.

Expressions of surprise and alarm registered on the group's faces – then *something* leapt from the top of the cliff. Horses and men scattered in confusion as the monster plummeted towards them, the ravening howl ringing out once more.

The creature landed on the dusty grass with a shuddering thump and lay brokenly, its tusks askew and legs sprawled at unnatural angles. Although its glassy eyes and bloody maw were evidence that the boar had been dead before its plunge from the cliff-top, Varo still stared at it in horror. His face was chalk-white, as though he had seen a ghost – and only Brostek knew why.

The others were now looking upwards expectantly, trying to hide the fright the dead animal had given them. Slaton, himself thoroughly unnerved, whispered words of comfort to the trembling Lisle. Below them, Shadow crouched rigidly, her eyes fixed on the boar and a low growl rumbling in her throat.

'Get down here, Ryker, you maniac!' someone called.

As a figure appeared on the cliff-top, his outline dark against the summer sky, Brostek filled the air with obscene invective – and only managed to control his anger because several of his companions were laughing now.

'At least you could have *looked* before throwing that thing down,' he ended lamely.

'I thought you'd appreciate my hunting!' Ryker shouted back, his voice full of glee. 'It was a fine kill,' he added enthusiastically.

'Get down here,' Brostek ordered. 'We have to ride.'

'On my way.'

Ryker dived head-first over the drop. Once more, horses scattered in panic and shouts of alarm filled the air. But when the falling body was no more than two paces above the unforgiving ground, a rope attached to Ryker's ankle pulled him up just short of impact. The self-styled acrobat swung to and fro upside down, laughing at the effectiveness of his latest piece of theatrics. Then he reached up, untied the knot, and flipped himself down to the ground.

However, he was confronted by Varo almost before his feet hit the floor. Although the group leader's face was expressionless, he lashed out with an open-handed blow to the side of Ryker's head. The small, wiry man staggered from the unexpected force of the hit and fell, then looked up in aggrieved surprise. In the sudden silence, Varo's voice sounded impossibly calm – yet the menace conveyed by his words was unmistakable.

'If you *ever* risk any of us with another show like that,' he said evenly, 'I will kill you myself.' His face was a mask, betraying no emotion.

'Death is our trade, Varo,' Ryker snarled. 'Certainly mine. Why should you be so afraid of a dead pig?'

Varo turned away wordlessly and remounted. No one else moved or spoke until Ryker got slowly to his feet.

'The boar could have crushed either man or horse,' Brostek said, breaking the silence. 'Use your talent on those who deserve to die.'

Ryker stared sullenly at the ground.

'Where's your horse?' Langel asked.

'Round the next outcrop,' was the muttered answer.

'Then let's go,' Brostek urged.

'Do you want the meat?' Langel asked, nodding at the carcass.

'Leave it,' Varo commanded, and spurred his horse on. Shadow approached the boar cautiously and sniffed, but then left at her master's command. Varo led the way silently for the rest of the afternoon, keeping up a good pace. The new arrival rode at the rear, and soon regained his good humour, laughing and joking with his companions. Slaton and Lisle rode in the middle of the band, with Keredin alongside.

'Is he always like that?' Slaton enquired cautiously.

'Ryker? He's a creature of the wild,' the ex-wizard answered. 'He doesn't like towns.'

'So you meet him out here?'

'Yes. I wouldn't want to be responsible for him in a civilized place.'

'Why?'

'He likes to kill things,' Keredin replied. 'Preferably people, but if that's not possible, animals will do – and the fiercer the better. He's good at it too,' he added casually.

Varo called a halt at dusk, and they set their camp in a wooded glade above a small stream. Shadow and the horses drank eagerly, while the riders busied themselves with a variety of tasks. Slaton watched, not knowing what to do.

'Bring the boy and join me,' Keredin suggested. He was sitting cross-legged on the ground, building a fireplace with a ring of stones around dry leaves and wood. Slaton obeyed gratefully, ushering Lisle before him.

'Just how do you become an *ex*-wizard?' he asked, after watching the other's preparations for a few moments.

Keredin smiled.

'By the fact that your colleagues no longer deem you fit to be counted among their esteemed number,' he replied.

'Why not?'

'Oh – for a number of reasons.'

'Such as?' Slaton prompted.

'So you want the juicy details of my fall from grace, eh?' Keredin remarked, sounding rather amused.

'I'm sorry,' Slaton responded, realizing that he was prying. 'You don't have to tell me if you don't want to.'

'Oh, I don't mind,' the fire-builder said casually. Slaton waited, content to let Keredin take his time. Lisle seemed perfectly happy, oblivious to everything around him.

'My crimes were threefold,' the ex-wizard began. 'The first was that I failed to pay sufficient respect to the elder wizards, or to our masters, the Cartel. No matter that they were doddering old cretins and grasping tyrants respectively. It seems that my idea that wizardry should still carry some responsibility towards the people of Levindre, rather than concentrating solely on our own comfort and wealth, was wrong-headed – to say the least.'

'Wizards have never struck me as being particularly wealthy,' Slaton commented.

'Most of them aren't,' Keredin replied, laughing. 'They're too stupid.'

'But a few?'

'A few who know how to milk the system,' the ex-wizard said, nodding. 'Keeping their miserable secrets to themselves and rotting in luxury while their dupes did all the work.'

'It sounds familiar,' Slaton said ruefully. 'My family

made living off other people into an art form.'

'Cartel?'

'Yes.'

Keredin nodded again.

'You have my sympathy,' he added quietly.

'Your second crime?' Slaton prompted after a moment.

'My second mistake was to want to learn about *real* magic,' Keredin said. 'The old magic. And that is frowned upon nowadays.'

'But surely wizardry is all about magic,' Slaton protested.

'How little you know,' the other replied sadly. 'Wizardry is about not letting magic get in the way of profit – or anything else the Cartel wants. Why do you think that the so-called wizards you see are such pathetic creatures? What threat could they possibly pose? The Cartel have managed to turn a once decent system into something corrupt and ineffectual. And they've done it quite deliberately.'

Several of the others were gathering round now, and Keredin went on before Slaton had a chance to absorb these new ideas.

'But to cut a long and tedious story short, my final, unforgivable sin was to admit to love.'

'What?'

'Surely you're aware that wizards are meant to be celibate?' Keredin asked, grinning.

Slaton nodded, feeling embarrassed as he recalled the tasteless jokes that surrounded this aspect of wizardry.

'Intimate contact with women drains a wizard's power, you see,' Keredin announced, affecting a pompous tone. 'Such hypocrisy! Perhaps it was like that once; maybe the old magic *needed* purity or self-denial, but by the time I was apprenticed, it was just a joke. There were *houses*. The best of them were very discreet, and the girls were quite something too – and well paid. There was only one rule. No attachments were to be formed, no contact in the real world outside. That's where I erred.' He paused, remembering. 'We ran away together. It was the worst thing I could have done.' His eyes were haunted now.

'And the girl?' Slaton asked reluctantly, sensing tragedy.

'She was killed by the ruffians they sent to bring her back. Even my powers couldn't save her.' There was obviously bitterness in the memory still. 'After that, I was informed that I could no longer call myself a wizard. I didn't care. Magic didn't seem so attractive any more.' He paused again, and Slaton tried in vain to think of something to say. That he should try to heal that long-ago pain suddenly seemed very important, but he knew the task to be beyond him.

'And anyway,' Keredin went on, 'they couldn't take away the knowledge I already had.'

His meticulous preparations for the fire now complete, he pointed both forefingers at the pile of wood and muttered a few words. With a sudden roar, flames burst from the kindling and spread quickly to the rest of the wood. Slaton jumped violently, but Lisle seemed quite unconcerned. The boy merely smiled and stretched his hands out, palms first, to warm them.

'That's a useful trick,' Slaton said, once he had recovered from the shock.

'*Tricks* are about my limit,' the ex-wizard replied. 'Which is a dreadful shame when so much more is possible.'

This time, his cynical tone had been replaced by genuine regret.

Most of the group were now gathered near the fire, their tasks complete. The horses had been tended, wood gathered, and water bottles refilled. Their bedding had been unpacked and the best sites chosen. Now it was time for food. Langel and Ross brought the supplies to the fireside.

'Slim rations tonight, lads,' Langel announced. His words were greeted with an assortment of groans.

'Where's Hawk?' he asked, looking round.

'He went hunting,' Bair replied.

'In this light? He won't be able to hit a barn door in this,' Langel said scornfully.

'If he's hungry enough,' the veteran responded, 'that man'll hit anything, even in pitch dark.'

'Quite right,' came a voice from the gloom. 'Just because you're half-blind from studying your eternal lists, Langel.' The speaker moved closer, invisible in his dark clothes until he reached the firelight. Then a slim, sharp-featured man was revealed, a bow slung over his shoulder. He tossed two game-birds down, each neatly skewered by an arrow.

'Small barns they have round here,' he remarked.

The sight of fresh meat put heart into the others. Although it wasn't much between many, their talk grew livelier nonetheless. Ross was soon regaling them with a series of absurd jokes – at which he laughed louder than anyone. Hawk, meanwhile, lay down and appeared to go to sleep.

'Amazing,' Slaton said quietly to Keredin, indicating the birds. 'It really *was* dark.'

'Aye. Hawk is a man of many talents – and just as many mysteries,' the former wizard replied dramatically. 'Apart from his apparent ability to see with cat's eyes, no one knows his real name, and he keeps his past veiled in secrecy.'

'Unlike yours, wizard!' Hawk commented, his eyes still shut. 'No doubt you've already been boring the new lads with your life history.'

There was no animosity in either's tone, but Slaton had no wish to return to Keredin's sad tale, and was keen to know more of his new comrades.

'Why Hawk?' he asked.

'It suits me,' the prone figure answered simply. 'Is a name any the worse for being self-styled?'

Unexpectedly, Lisle chose this moment to speak for the first time that evening.

'Worse for being self-styled?' he repeated, mimicking the hunter's lazy drawl.

Hawk sat up and stared, his face angry.

'You have a problem with that, boy?' he demanded.

'No. Let me explain . . .' Slaton began quickly.

'Boy?' Hawk repeated loudly, not shifting his gaze. Lisle still watched the fire, his eyes unfocused.

'Shut it, Hawk!' Brostek ordered.

The cat's eyes shifted first to Brostek, then to Varo.

'What's he here for anyway?' Hawk challenged. At his words, the entire group fell silent.

In the haste of their departure from the Rim, Varo had had no chance to explain his decision about the newcomers. Now he had no choice. He knew that none of his men would dispute his authority, but he wanted to convince them of Lisle's worth – something about which he himself was not wholly certain. Choosing his words carefully, he began a succinct explanation of the boy's talents, with emphasis on his premonitions. Brostek and Slaton added their comments when appropriate, but when they had finished, many of the men still looked puzzled.

'He didn't see the boar coming, did he,' Ryker chuckled. 'He was shaking like a leaf.'

'The least said about *that* incident the better,' Brostek said firmly, and Ryker subsided, carefully fingering the ear that had taken Varo's blow.

'If I'm *right*,' Varo said, ignoring the interruption, 'Lisle may be able to help us get to raids before they happen.'

Although several sceptical glances were exchanged, there was no outright dissent. Slaton began to realize that this group was indeed dedicated to their self-appointed task – and intensely loyal to Varo. Anyone who could weld such disparate characters together had a formidable unit at his command.

'You say the last eclipse was two days ago?' Bair said thoughtfully. 'I didn't see it.'

'How could you?' Ross exclaimed. 'You never go outside! But it happened.' Others nodded in agreement. 'It was nothing much to speak of,' the twin went on. 'The sun went slightly dim around noon, but only for a few moments.'

There was a chorus of agreement from most of the group. 'Seemed more than that to me,' Slaton put in. 'And we were only ten leagues to the west.'

'Me too,' Ryker added. 'Quite spectacular, in fact.'

'So the eclipse appeared stronger the further north or east you were from the crater,' Keredin surmised. 'What does that mean?'

No one could provide an answer.

'And yet there was no sign of it from *inside* the crater,' Brostek added.

'We need a witness who was to the west or south,' Ross suggested. 'That would tell us . . .'

'What?' Hawk asked, grinning maliciously.

'Who cares?' Langel put in. 'We don't *have* a witness. And dinner's ready.'

As they ate, several people watched Lisle's messy progress with his portion. There was little conversation for a time, but when the meal was over, talk turned to their immediate plans.

'So where are we headed?' Ross asked.

'Avranche,' Varo replied, naming a remote mountain village. 'It's just a hunch, but we've not been there for months – and neither have they.' He had no need to specify who *they* were.

Ross nodded. 'If nothing's happening there,' he said eagerly, 'we can cut over Drymist Pass to Grassmeer.'

Unnoticed, Lisle stiffened abruptly at the mention of the second name. Ross continued.

'Then we can head for Penberry. There are plenty of vantage points along the way, so we'd cover a huge area. Why don't we . . .' He stopped abruptly. 'Why's he shivering?'

Lisle was trembling, even though the night was

mild and he sat close to the fire.

'Are you all right?' Slaton asked, as puzzled as the others. 'What *is* it?'

Lisle did not respond; his eyes flickered as though he was seeing another world – or the contours of a dream.

'Get a blanket,' Bair said.

Lisle screamed, his eyes rolling up.

'Water! Quick!' Bair ordered, as Slaton gently lowered his cousin to the ground.

After a little while, Lisle grew quiet, appearing to take comfort from the blanket draped over him. He sipped some water, and soon seemed to have recovered entirely. His head wobbled like a baby's when he sat up again, and his eyes were vague, but he was no longer in distress. More puzzled and uncertain looks were directed his way.

'We'll reach Duncery tomorrow morning,' Varo stated, deliberately distracting the group's attention. 'Maybe they'll have news for us there. We'll decide on our route then.'

Duncery was one of the places where messages were sometimes left by their look-out network. Many uplanders regarded Varo and his men as heroes, and collected any information which might be of use to them – indications of unusual movements in the mountains, which passes were blocked by snow, the unexplained disappearances of animals, and so on – passing the reports by word of mouth with people travelling from village to village. Although the news was often vague, and frequently too late to be of much use, it was still welcome.

Varo's decision signalled preparations for sleep.

'What about a lullaby from our musician?' Hawk suggested slyly. All eyes went to Lisle, but he did not react.

'Will you play for us, Lisle?' Brostek asked gently.

'Play for us, Lisle?' the boy echoed, nodding.

Slaton fetched the lute from their pack, and handed it to his cousin.

'The Witchwood,' he said.

Lisle grinned, his face suddenly animated, and gently ran a finger over the strings. After minutely adjusting the tuning of two of them, he began to play.

Within moments, the drab, firelit glade had been transformed into an enchanted realm. Liquid music poured forth, its droplets seeming to catch the flicker of the flames, turning them into rainbow-hued creatures of myth: dragonflies danced with iridescent fire-drakes, kingfishers flew with tree-sprites, and the forest itself drew close to watch and to listen. Every man there saw a different confusion of images, but each was held spellbound.

As the last note died away and commonplace night returned to claim their camp, the collective sense of awe was palpable. While Varo's decision to include Lisle in their party had not been challenged openly, there had been some resentment. The recent explanation had done a little to remove such feelings, but Lisle's music had swept them all aside.

Keredin was the first to recover.

'Gods!' he breathed. 'I haven't heard anything like that since . . .' He snapped his fingers suddenly, and mumbled a few strange syllables. Sparks and flame shot up into the air from the centre of the fire, making all except Lisle retreat hurriedly or shade their eyes. The boy just smiled, and played a lightning-fast, delicate sequence of notes which *shaped* the newborn flame. The image lasted only an instant, but was unmistakable.

Magara's spectral face smiled back at each of them.

CHAPTER TEN

'Where does Langel get the money for all your supplies?' Slaton asked. Because he wanted to prove his own worth to the group, he had volunteered to join Bair on guard duty. Now that all was quiet, he took the opportunity of learning more of their way of life.

'You mean we don't exactly look like your idea of well-heeled merchants?' the old soldier asked, grinning.

'Not really,' Slaton admitted.

'We manage,' Bair went on. 'Some of the villages we've helped are generous, within their means. And when we've been too late to save a place, we've taken anything of value that was left. The dead don't resent that!' His face was serious now, and Slaton could see the awful memories reflected in his eyes. Then he shrugged. 'And we manage as best we can. Langel can make a little go a long way. Some of us work in what free time we have – and some of us are not above stretching our resources in . . . less obvious ways.'

'Such as *borrowing* from those who can afford it?' Slaton guessed.

'That's one way of putting it.'

'I was trying to be tactful.'

'You were,' Bair replied, grinning once more. 'But Kerwin, for one, wouldn't mind in the least being called a thief.'

'Which one is he?' Slaton asked, trying to match the name to a face.

Bair pointed into the gloom.

'Over there. The blond one whose eyes are never still. Don't let him get too close to your pockets if there's anything you value in them!' He laughed quietly when he

97

saw his companion's startled expression, and added, 'Don't worry. Varo has cured him of his worst excesses, but sometimes he just can't help *acquiring* things – never from us, though. And we don't investigate too closely. He puts his stealth and quickness to other uses with us, and his talents have helped us many times.'

Their conversation was interrupted by a movement within the camp as a figure rose from his bed and trod carefully towards them. Slaton recognized Brostek, and knew immediately why he could not sleep. The sight of Magara's face in the flames had disturbed them all – even those who did not know her by sight. After the initial excitement had died down, Varo had forced them all to get some rest. His quiet insistence had calmed most of the men, but his partner had obviously been badly affected by the incident.

'Couldn't sleep,' Brostek muttered unnecessarily as he joined Bair and Slaton. Magara's flame-image still haunted his eyes.

'Company is always welcome on a night watch,' Bair replied stolidly.

A few moments passed in silence.

'I didn't dream it, did I?' Brostek blurted out. 'You saw her too?'

Slaton nodded.

'A pretty lass,' Bair commented. 'Wonder how *she* felt about it?'

The other two stared at him. They had both been so preoccupied with their own reactions to Magara's spectral appearance that neither had considered the possibility of any effect on *her*.

'You don't think . . .' Slaton began. 'Surely . . .' He gave up, knowing that his query could not be answered.

'Keredin can't or won't explain what happened,' Brostek complained. 'He won't even tell me who did it, him or Lisle. Look at him – snoring happily away!'

'And Lisle's not likely to be much help,' Bair remarked. Slaton winced at the soldier's matter-of-fact

98

tone, and was aware that Brostek eyed him hopefully.

'Don't look at me,' he said. 'I've no idea. Lisle's never done anything like that before. It shook me up too.'

Brostek nodded, disappointed.

'There's more to Keredin than meets the eye,' Bair reminded him. 'You should know that. He'll talk when he's ready. Go back to sleep now.'

Brostek hesitated, apparently on the point of speaking again, then accepted his comrade's advice. He turned away and walked carefully back through the prone figures to his own blanket. He lay down, but sleep still would not come. There were too many questions echoing inside his brain. How had Magara's face been conjured up? And why? It seemed pointless, almost cruel – and cruelty was a trait not associated with Keredin – nor, as far as he could judge, with Lisle. And who *had* done it? Lisle had only met Magara the night before, but Brostek knew that Keredin had *never* seen her. And the likeness had been exact. So it must have been Lisle. But according to Slaton, the boy had never done anything like this before. Besides, when he had played for them earlier, different visions had been conjured up for each man – and yet they had *all* seen Magara's face. It made no sense.

Brostek almost got up again then, wanting to shake the truth out of Keredin. But he restrained himself; as Bair had said, the ex-wizard would talk when he was ready. Instead, Brostek's thoughts returned to the subject of the mirage.

I love her, he told himself, thinking the words that he had never spoken aloud. *Yes, but am I* in *love with her?* His mind refused to answer his own question. *Is there a difference?* The distinction had never seemed important before. *Does she know? What does she feel for me?* Their friendship was unquestioned, but could it – should it – ever be more than that?

If it weren't for our work . . .

Brostek left this thought unfinished, deliberately

turning his mind to other things. His glance fell on Varo's peacefully slumbering form. Brostek knew his partner better than any man alive, yet he had been unable to fathom his reaction to the vision. Outwardly as unmoved as ever, Varo's internal turmoil had been betrayed by his hasty and determined insistence on sleep, giving the men little chance to speculate. *He loves her as much as I do*, Brostek realized suddenly. *I wonder if he even knows.*

Then his thoughts turned to Slaton, Magara's childhood friend. He seemed honest enough, but perhaps he knew more than he was telling. Brostek wondered what had happened during the night the two had spent together, and felt his own face grow hot as he realized that he was jealous.

Don't be so stupid!

Feeling rather ridiculous, he finally fell asleep. His last waking thought echoed Bair's words.

I wonder how she *felt about it.*

*   *   *

The next morning, Slaton rose, bleary-eyed from two late nights, to find his horse already tended and saddled. He roused Lisle and set off in a tired daze. Only later did Slaton notice that Keredin was riding alongside again. The former wizard proved just as forthcoming on the subject of Magara's image as Brostek had predicted, so Slaton abandoned that topic. He wondered belatedly about the care of his mount.

'You've Jed to thank for that,' Keredin told him. 'Him and his kin.' He nodded to a group of four large men who were riding together behind the leaders.

Slaton remembered the men working as a team at the camp, their gentle touch with the animals contrasting with their obvious strength. He named them, dredging his memory. *That's Jed and his brother Lorimer. The two behind are their cousins, Chase and Neal.* The quartet had spoken little in Slaton's hearing, seemingly content with their background role among so many more noticeable characters.

'Theirs was one of the first farms to be raided by the Knifemen,' Keredin volunteered.

'How did they escape?' Slaton asked.

'They were working in a far-flung meadow, and got home too late. By then, everyone else was dead or had disappeared. They tried to trail the attackers but never even caught sight of them. After that they wandered, but could never settle to the employ of any big land-owner, so they returned to the uplands and lived as hunters and scavengers. That's when we came across them.'

'They look like handy men to have on your side in a fight,' Slaton said.

'They are,' Keredin confirmed. 'And they've also got a personal score to settle. Joining up with Varo and Brostek has given their lives a purpose.'

'We're all here because of those two,' Slaton said thoughtfully.

'Even you?'

'Even us,' he agreed. 'Though what help we're going to be . . .' Slaton shrugged.

'Varo wouldn't have asked you along if he hadn't got some sort of plan for you.'

'Is he always that calculating?'

'You've seen him. What do you think?' There was a hint of challenge in Keredin's words. 'Something died inside him when his family and home were destroyed. The only person he feels anything for is Brostek – and you have to look hard to see even that. But there's a very strong bond between them. Someone described them as "brothers in blood".'

The track they were following left the forest then, emerging on to open heathland. A third rider drew alongside.

'What nonsense is the wizard filling your head with?' the newcomer asked. He grinned, showing a remarkably fine set of white teeth in an amiable, broad face. Mischief sparkled in his wide-spaced blue eyes.

'Ignore him, Slaton,' Keredin advised before the other could answer for himself. 'Vilman is the exception that proves the rule. I don't know *why* he travels with us. Certainly not out of dedication to our cause or to our leaders . . . and he wouldn't recognize *real* nonsense if it came up and bit him.'

The young man's grin widened.

'Wizards always talk too much,' he remarked. 'My taste is for action – and where better to find it than with this happy band?'

'This happy band?' Lisle repeated unexpectedly.

Vilman laughed.

'Must be like living with your own personal echo,' he observed drily, then grew serious. 'Think he'll be able to handle the fighting?'

'It won't come to that,' Keredin put in quickly.

'Lisle is *my* responsibility,' Slaton replied firmly. 'We want no special treatment. We'll fight if needs be, as best we can.'

Vilman nodded, then his mercurial smile reappeared.

'Perhaps he should play something for the Knifemen,' he suggested. 'Charm them into submission. Can you play the Dance of Death, Lisle?'

At first there was no response. Then Lisle emitted a high-pitched squeal and a cackle of insane laughter. Several men turned to look, surprised by the unnatural sound. Vilman just chuckled, apparently satisfied, and spurred his horse on to join the riders ahead.

Slaton twisted around in the saddle, a worried expression on his face, but Lisle was already calm again.

'Are you all right?'

The boy smiled and nodded in his own, awkward fashion, his strange eyes giving no hint of what was going on inside his head.

*   *   *

The party reached the large village of Duncery late that morning. The halt was welcome, as Varo had set a good pace, but the respite proved to be short-lived when they learned that news had been received about unusual omens at Avranche. A wolf-pack that had been sniffing around for days, much to the villagers' disquiet, had suddenly disappeared. Game had become very scarce in the region, odd lights had been seen in the forest above, and the mountain eagles had been unusually active. All of this served to confirm Varo's hunch about the area, even though no definite sightings of the Knifemen or their troops had been made.

In spite of Langel's grumbling, the group were on their way again within an hour of their arrival, heading ever upwards. The mountains grew closer as they rode with a renewed sense of urgency.

Two days later, shortly before noon, Varo and his men arrived at Avranche. Slaton had become increasingly anxious about Lisle as they approached. The boy had seemed fretful, and on several occasions had tried to tell Slaton something, gesturing towards Varo. However, no sense could be made of his garbled words and there seemed to be no reason for his unease. Avranche appeared peaceful, its people going about their daily business – although the group's arrival disrupted that. The village elders came to talk to Varo and Brostek, confirming the reports of recent strange events, but insisting that everything had now returned to normal.

The tension within the group drained away, leaving frustration and disappointment in its place. And, in Slaton's case, relief. But before any decision could be made about what they should do next, Lisle, who was still mounted, set up an unearthly keening. His voice rose and fell in an ear-splitting wail that was shocking in contrast to his usual musical grace. The boy was instantly the focus of all attention; the villagers were frightened, and many covered their ears with their hands. Some even made the furtive hand-signs against madness and evil. Then Lisle pointed waveringly with an outstretched arm, and all eyes went to the vale above the village. Drymist Pass was living up to its name; a dull grey fog had filled the upper end of the valley and was rolling down towards them.

Brostek and Varo glanced at each other.

'That's not mist. It's smoke!' Varo exclaimed.

'Grassmeer!' Ross shouted, his eyes wide.

'Let's go!' Brostek yelled as he leapt into the saddle. The urgency in his voice was unmistakable.

They had a fight on their hands after all – providing they could get there in time.

CHAPTER ELEVEN

Afterwards, Slaton would remember very little of that hectic ride to Grassmeer. At first, he had held back, knowing that both Lisle and his own inexperience made them a liability, but his horse was soon infected with the general fever and flew along as fast as any. Behind him, Lisle was singing, a wordless wail that spoke of dread and anger but also of a terrible eagerness. Slaton wondered fleetingly if this was his cousin's battle cry.

Ahead, some of the men shouted, urging more speed from their mounts or encouraging others, but most were silent and intent, their thoughts lost in the roar of the wind and the thunder of hooves. The acrid tang of smoke stung their nostrils, but Lisle's song never faltered. Then, before Slaton realized what was happening, they crashed in upon Grassmeer – and his view of the world shattered into a hundred fragments, each one a scene of confusion, horror or desperation.

Half the houses in Grassmeer were ablaze. The choking air was full of screams and curses as people ran wildly in all directions.

A woman stumbled from a burning hut, her skirts aflame. Behind her staggered a small boy, his face covered by his arms. The child was immediately seized by a soldier wearing a dirty green headband, which bore the insignia of a capital M crossed by a horizontal line. The child's mother turned, screaming, forgetting her own peril, but another soldier thrust at her with a sword and she fell, clutching her stomach. The boy was carried off, but Varo caught up with the abductor, and the steel edge of his sword sliced deeply into the raider's neck. The man slumped to the ground in a splatter of red.

The boy landed heavily and lay still, cowering.

More green-banded soldiers were herding unarmed villagers – most of them elderly or very young – either towards the mountains or to the wooden hall that was the village's main building. As it became clear that they were being opposed, many raiders cut down some of their defenceless prey before joining the battle in earnest.

Other villagers, both men and women, were still resisting, and renewed their efforts now as they saw fresh hope. However, the raiders outnumbered them and were better armed: staves and hoes were no match for swords and iron spears. At the same time, the invaders changed tactics. Before the intrusion of Varo and his men they had been trying to capture as many people as possible; now they just went for the kill. For a few moments the carnage was terrible, but then the new-comers stopped the slaughter. The momentum of their charge scattered them widely, but they used their mounts to advantage, riding some of the enemy down and using their own greater height to full effect. Even so, it was clear that, sword for sword, they could not match the raiders' numbers.

The first onslaught, with its element of surprise, brought a good deal of success. Many green-banded raiders went down as Varo and Brostek cut a swathe through the middle of their number, seemingly careless of their own lives amid the clashing blades. Shadow, running beside them, added to the terror they inspired. Ross and Rogan also worked together, their mounts circling in unison, twin swords cutting like a double scythe.

The senior members of the party also formed a team: Langel, Bair and Keredin fought side by side – though less closely than the brothers – guarding each others' backs and warning of unseen perils. Others were less organized; Jed and his kin had become separated during the wild ride and now each fought alone. Too far away to help, Slaton saw two of the farmers dragged from their horses while their companions struggled to their aid. Vilman too was in the thick of things but Hawk did not enter the fray directly. Instead he hovered on the fringes, shooting arrows from the saddle. Each deadly shaft found an enemy target.

Kerwin and Ryker were nowhere to be seen. Then Slaton realized that both had dismounted, and caught an occasional glimpse as they moved within the chaos, striking, retreating, and striking again – as fast and as deadly as venomous snakes. Ryker's small dark face seemed lit with a rapturous fire, and his eyes shone with an unholy joy.

Then Slaton had no time to watch his colleagues' progress; he and Lisle were in peril themselves. Two enemy soldiers bore down on them, brandishing spears. Slaton cursed his own stupidity and made to draw his sword but before he could do so, Lisle screamed. The searing, high-pitched note was of such cutting clarity that their horse reared and the raiders stopped in alarm. That hesitation was all that Brostek and Vilman needed to fall upon them, and both soldiers died instantly.

'Keep out of this!' Brostek gasped, then wheeled his mount away again, with Shadow at his side.

'Having fun?' Vilman asked, his eyebrows raised, before he too returned to the fight.

A blue-robed figure emerged from the hall, standing still and calm amid the tumult. Cold eyes surveyed the scene, shifting from one horseman to the next. A slight smile played on the watcher's lips, as though he approved of what he saw. His implacable gaze rested longer on some than on others. Keredin and Brostek received special scrutiny, as did Varo, before his attention settled upon Slaton and Lisle. Slaton had quietened his horse and held his sword protectively, but now he felt naked and defenceless. He could see the malice of that stare and was certain that Lisle felt it too. The boy trembled and fell silent in the face of what was surely one of the Knifemen of Bari.

Varo had now noticed the impassive observer, and his steely expression grew even more determined. He urged his horse towards his adversary but was blocked by a wall of desperate men. He set about them but was forced back, and turned to look for help.

'Hawk!' he yelled, fighting to be heard above the roar of the flames and the clamour of steel. 'Hawk!' Varo pointed urgently at the impassive enemy.

Hawk heard. Quickly he nocked an arrow, aimed and let fly, and the bolt sped unerringly towards its target. The robed figure did not move, did not even flinch, as the arrow smashed squarely into his chest. The shaft went straight through him and embedded itself, quivering, in the wood behind. The Knifeman was completely unharmed.

His cold smile intensified. He turned his back on his attackers in a gesture of utter contempt, and pointed with both forefingers at the door post. A sudden blaze of blue light blinded everyone, and a horrible crackle rent the air. When they were gone, so was the Knifeman. He had vanished completely.

If Varo felt any rage or frustration, it did not show on his face. He crashed towards the wooden structure, casting enemy soldiers aside like dry leaves. With their leader's disappearance, many of the raiders gave up and ran, easy prey for their enemies. Others fought on, but their fighting skills were now half-hearted. Many died, adding their sorry remains to the existing litter of corpses.

Varo reached the hall, dismounted and went inside. As expected, there was no sign of the Knifeman, but lying within were several bloodless bodies. His face still expressionless, Varo strode outside again. On the wood, the familiar brand glowed blue; beneath it, one symbol was repeated.

*   *   *

By evening, some sort of order had been restored, but
Grassmeer would never be the same again. Although the
arrival of Varo and his group had saved the village from
total devastation, every family had suffered losses and
many of those left alive were injured. Everyone with any
healing skills – Keredin, Bair and some of the local
women – had been fully occupied that afternoon. Even
those who were not physically hurt were distraught and
suffering from shock; the raiders had spared no one,
however young or old, man or woman. The saddest sight
of all was that of tiny bodies being gently placed on the
communal pyre.

Varo's men had also suffered. Lorimer and Neal were
dead, their hacked corpses almost unrecognizable. Jed,
Chase, Langel and Vilman were wounded, but would
recover, and almost all the others had minor cuts and
bruises. Even though their casualties were minimal compared to the thirty or more raiders who had been killed,
they all felt a deadening sense of loss and grief. This was
made worse by the mystifying escape of the Knifeman
and by the knowledge that if they had arrived just a little
earlier, so many of the villagers might have been saved.
As usual, none of the raiders had been captured alive,
and so there was no hope of learning any more.

'Well, we're getting closer,' Langel commented.
'We've never seen one of the seven face to face before.'

'Didn't seem to worry him too much, did it?' Vilman
remarked.

They had all seen the gloating smile with which the
angular-faced man had regarded their efforts.

'I'll swear my arrow hit him square,' Hawk muttered,
shaking his head in disbelief.

'It did,' Keredin stated flatly.

'Then how . . . ?'

'The man – if he *is* a man – has powers,' the ex-wizard
replied, scowling.

109

'Sorcery,' Brostek said.

'It has always been possible to use magic for evil as well as good,' Keredin agreed. 'I, of all people, should know that. I can't even look at that . . .' He waved a hand at the blue brand on the hall which was glowing in the failing light of dusk, '. . . without wanting to vomit.'

'I'll cut it out,' Brostek decided.

He strode to the hut, sword in hand. As he hacked at the wood, splinters flew in all directions until nothing remained of the hated sign. Satisfied, Brostek returned to his colleagues, who were sitting some way apart from the villagers, respectfully leaving them to their mourning.

Bair finished checking Jed's bandages and turned to Slaton.

'Is the boy all right now?'

Lisle had been silently shivering ever since the Knifeman had looked at him. He was calmer now, but it had proved impossible to coax a reaction from him.

'A little better, I think,' Slaton answered. 'I . . . I'm sorry we got in the way. We'll do better next time.'

'You'd have been in trouble if he hadn't screamed,' Vilman remarked with a sly smile.

'Leave it, Vilman,' Brostek ordered. 'We all learn by our mistakes.'

'Will Lisle play for Lorimer and Neal?' Jed asked suddenly. They were his first words for a long time.

'I don't know,' Slaton replied.

'Get the lute,' Keredin said firmly.

Ross jumped up eagerly, fetched the instrument and laid it before Lisle, who looked at it uncomprehendingly.

'Will you play, Lisle?' Jed repeated. 'For my brother and cousin?'

'Lisle?' Slaton prompted when his cousin did not react.

Then the boy picked up the lute with trembling hands and settled it in his lap. He seemed certain of the world once more. He tested the tuning, then looked questioningly at his guardian.

'"Into the Night",' Slaton suggested.

As Lisle began to play a stately, elegaic tune filled with an eerie sadness, the listeners were all moved by the music and found themselves glancing at the still burning pyre. The cousins' bodies lay side by side, next to the villagers they had not been able to save. The song had no need of words to tell of their journey into the unknown, or of the grief of those left behind. While he played, Lisle's face seemed lit from within – not by joy, but by a strange, almost unearthly rapture. Long before he finished, many of the remaining villagers had gathered round to hear and they, like Jed and Chase, were crying openly as the last notes faded away.

'Thank you,' Jed said eventually in a broken voice.

As the villagers slipped silently away into the darkness, Keredin spoke quietly.

'Your music eases many pains, Lisle. I just wish it could take *that* away.'

He pointed to the doorway of the hall. There, on the newly bare wood that Brostek's sword had exposed, the blue brand glowed once more. Its malevolent brilliance mocked them all.

CHAPTER TWELVE

Varo and his group stayed in Grassmeer for another two days, partly for the sake of their own wounded and partly to help the surviving villagers. By the end of that time, the evil sign had faded to a few tiny blue sparks.

No decision had been made about what they should do next. Even Varo seemed unsure, which was unsettling for the others. His incisive leadership usually gave them all a sense of security, but he appeared now to be waiting for outside guidance. Brostek knew that his friend was hoping that Lisle's peculiar talents might come to their aid, but the young musician was even more uncommunicative than usual. If Lisle had any ideas about their next destination, he was clearly unwilling or unable to tell anyone about it. Indeed, the only times he seemed to come alive were each evening, when he played his lute for the benefit of his new companions and the villagers. Then, for a while, both he and his wondering audience were transported by the boy's unique wizardry.

There had been some discussion about pursuing those few raiders who had escaped. Ryker and Hawk, together with a few of the villagers, had chased and killed some as they fled, exacting a last, bitter revenge, but there seemed little point in a time-consuming hunt for a handful of the enemy when any that were caught either fought to the death or died without any apparent cause. But, for once, the argument had not ended there.

'If I thought we'd catch up with the Knifeman again,' Brostek admitted, 'I'd be all for it. But he obviously does not travel by conventional means.'

'That's putting it mildly,' Ross commented. 'Blink and

you'd miss him. Wherever he went, he moved as fast as a scolding tongue. Almost like—'

'And we know that they don't return to the same area for some time,' Brostek went on, interrupting his loquacious colleague. 'So the few that survived should pose no immediate threat.'

'But they *do* travel by conventional means,' Bair commented. 'On foot.'

'Yes.'

'So we could track them if we wanted to?'

'Yes,' Varo put in. 'But they always scatter after a defeat. You know that. So we'd have to split up, and we need to keep together.'

'Agreed,' Bair went on. 'But maybe just *once* it would be worth tracking one of them. Not to capture him, but just to see where he goes.' He paused while the others considered this idea. 'We know that they never attack the same area for at least a few months, so where do they get their instructions about where to go next?'

'They must go to some meeting place,' Ryker answered.

'Exactly! And perhaps the Knifemen are there!' Bair concluded triumphantly.

There was a short silence. Glances were exchanged, and then the objections started.

'Such a place would surely be guarded,' Hawk began. 'We'd be walking into a trap.'

'It might be all the way over into Bari,' Ross added. 'We could be stuck in the mountains for months.'

'Anyway, it may not be that easy to follow them,' Varo said. 'A man on foot can travel routes no horses can climb.'

'And it'd be hard for us to remain undetected,' Brostek put in.

'But surely it's worth a try!' Vilman exclaimed. 'We're not exactly making much progress like this, are we?'

'The ones that ran,' Langel asked. 'Which way were they headed?'

'North-east,' Ryker answered promptly. 'Not many of them got far,' he added in a satisfied tone.

'To the high passes,' Langel confirmed, making his point. 'And we're not equipped for an expedition into that wilderness. It would be madness, even if we were all fit.'

'Not this time,' Varo told Bair, closing the subject. 'But we'll bear it in mind for the future.'

*   *   *

On their third day in Grassmeer, Ross and Rogan were commissioned to make the short journey to and from Avranche to replenish their supplies. Langel often used the twins for such tasks when he did not go himself; the combination of Ross's quick wits and voluble tongue and Rogan's stony, disconcerting presence made them an excellent bargaining team. On this occasion they would have plenty to bargain with, because although Lorimer's horse had perished with her master, Neal's was unscathed and would fetch a good price. Langel dispatched his helpers with a list of goods he wanted in return. However, when the brothers returned to Grassmeer, they brought with them more than supplies.

News had arrived in Avranche of unrest and several strange incidents in another village three day's travel to the south. The account had an ominously familiar ring to it, and Varo decided there and then to head in that direction at first light. He glanced at Lisle as he told the others of his decision, but the boy did not react.

As soon as they set off, however, Slaton noticed that Lisle was becoming fretful again, and seemed to worsen with each passing hour. Brostek and Varo reacted grimly to this news and pushed the pace, fearing that they would once again arrive too late.

On their second day south, as midday approached, Lisle became markedly worse. He slumped down behind Slaton, burying his head in his arms and his guardian's jerkin and whispering unintelligibly. No amount of prompting could relieve or explain his terror. All they could do was press on. It was perfect travelling weather; the sun was bright but the upland air was cool. There was nothing obvious to justify Lisle's fear.

Until midday.

It was then, at the time when the sun should have been at its zenith, that the chill in the air became greater. Lisle emerged from his hiding place and pointed upwards. Shading their eyes, the others looked, stricken with horror. As they watched, the sun went out.

No one could tell whether the darkness came from one side or the other, or whether the entire burning circle dimmed all at once, but each man felt a measure of panic as the glare turned to orange, then blood red and then to black. A false night came to Levindre.

The eclipse lasted a while, and in that time, the cold and fear made even the hardiest men shiver. Lisle screamed, adding to the terror.

'So soon?' Varo breathed. They had never known two attacks so close before.

'Is it *really* happening again?' Brostek wondered aloud.

They had only to look at the agonized expression on Lisle's face to know the answer.

PART THREE

SHADOW-MAZE

CHAPTER THIRTEEN

Magara turned from waving goodbye to the travellers on the cliff top and walked slowly back to her home. Once there, she felt distracted and restless, so busied herself with mundane tasks. She tidied away the visitors' beds, washed plates and bowls and swept the floor, singing quietly to herself all the while. Finally, however, she was forced to admit that she was feeling miserable and uneasy, and the thoughts that she had been trying to avoid all afternoon made their presence felt.

As she had done on many previous occasions, Magara found comfort in the silent and unquestioning companionship of Talisman. The heron was standing quite still, apparently asleep, at the end of the walkway. He opened one eye as Magara came outside, and ruffled under one wing with his long beak as she sat down next to him.

'I wish I had wings like you.'

Talisman turned to regard her solemnly.

'All right,' she admitted. 'I wish I had wings *sometimes*. Hands do come in useful. But there's so much I could do if I could fly.'

The heron turned his head away again and appeared to stare out over the lake, but Magara knew he was still listening.

'For a start, I could fly over Nevern,' she went on. 'Perhaps I'd find Celia that way.' She shivered, though the day was still warm. 'Gods, I don't like the sound of that place.' She doubted whether she would have had the courage to try and enter the hidden valley as Slaton had done, but his story had intrigued as well as frightened her. 'Why did Celia go there in the first place?' she asked aloud. 'She must have been desperate, poor woman, but what good could such a place do her – even if she succeeded in getting inside?'

Talisman did not answer.

'Perhaps she thought the old magic might help Lisle,' she continued. 'Or at least explain why he was so afraid of the eclipses.' She paused for a moment. 'And that's another thing,' she exclaimed. 'These eclipses aren't right. There shouldn't be that many. It doesn't make any sense. And why haven't we seen them here?'

Talisman ruffled his feathers as if shrugging in response.

'I don't know either,' Magara admitted quietly.

The oddly matched pair sat in silence for a little while. Magara wriggled her bare toes in the water of the lake and her companion watched carefully, making sure that the small white objects were not fish. Eventually, her feet grew cold, and she drew up her legs and wrapped her arms round her knees.

'It's bad enough . . .' she began, then paused. 'But then Slaton – of all people – turns up and reminds me of ho— of Arenguard. And then he goes off again, just like that!' she added indignantly. 'Men!'

Magara glanced at Talisman to see whether he had taken offence, but the heron was still calmly gazing out over the lake.

'Don't you have a family?' she asked. 'Aren't you ever lonely? Or feel the need of . . . of . . . a lady heron?'

Magara had never seen another heron within the crater, but Talisman showed no signs of wanting to leave. *Perhaps you're better off this way*, she thought, suddenly envying the bird's self-containment. Slaton's brief visit had reawoken long-buried memories, and Lisle's enigmatic presence had added a further disturbing note. Magara found herself beginning to resent their disruption of her usually placid life, and quickly scolded herself for being so ridiculous.

'There's quite enough *real* evil in the world,' she told herself aloud, thinking of the Knifemen, 'without you

120

getting all worked up about trivial nonsense.'

Talisman clacked his beak twice as if in agreement, then moved to the edge of the walkway and launched himself out over the water. Magara watched him fly away, the strong, slow wingbeats lifting him ever higher. She felt an unreasonable sadness at this latest abandonment.

'I hadn't finished,' she complained, then smiled to herself, hoping that none of her neighbours had heard her absurd, one-sided conversation. *They'll think I'm going mad*, she decided, as she stood up to go inside. *If they don't already!*

But the restless unease remained within her, so she changed her mind and strode purposefully down the walkway.

Iro's hut was one of the few buildings in Trevine to be set on solid ground. Even more unusually, its floor was solid stone, painstakingly constructed and levelled from the larger slabs on the scree slope. The reason for this was obvious enough when the alchemist was seen at work. Fire and all sorts of peculiar and dangerous chemicals were Iro's stock in trade, and the spillages from his various experiments had scarred and pitted the floor. Anything less resilient than stone would have been destroyed long since.

No one knew exactly how old Iro was, but Magara sometimes felt that he was genuinely ancient. His face was pale and wrinkled, and his thinning hair had turned white some years before, the result, some said, of a chemical reaction that had been far more violent than expected. Yet his hands were those of a much younger man and his blue eyes were clear and permanently inquisitive. The rest of his body was always enshrouded in a long, many-pocketed robe which Iro insisted on calling his working coat. At one time this garment may have been white, but its underlying hue was now grey, with an impressive array of many coloured stains – or, as Iro would have it, decorations.

Magara had never quite grasped exactly what it was that the alchemist did, or how he had persuaded the council to let him stay. He always replied, when asked, that he was following in the line of many venerated forebears in the age-old quest to turn base metals into gold. Whether this was true or not, it most certainly was not the whole truth, and Magara knew that several of Iro's 'accidental' inventions were in use within the crater. He had become something of an institution in Trevine, having lived there longer than most people could remember, and no one ever questioned his right to remain.

The door of the hut was open when Magara arrived, but it was dark within. She was about to call out softly when the alchemist's voice sounded from inside.

'Stay where you are!' he ordered sharply.

Magara froze. Within, a small flame flared briefly, then there was a sudden crackle, and a shower of silver and gold sparks brightened the gloom. At first it whirled round in a circle, like a fiery dog chasing its own tail, but then it careered around the interior of the hut, apparently out of control. There was the sound of rapid movement inside the hut, and Iro emerged, scuttling along on all fours, while the sparks continued to fly.

Magara stepped aside, fascinated but a little afraid, but Iro ignored her. He turned back to watch his creation burn itself out.

'Fascinating,' he murmured. 'Perhaps with a little more fixing . . .'

The last sparks fizzled out and silence returned. Smoke drifted lazily out of the doorway.

'What were you trying to do?' Magara asked quietly. 'Make gold out of lead?'

Iro looked startled at the sound of her voice, as if he had forgotten that he had a visitor, but then smiled when he realized who it was.

'No,' he replied. 'Just slightly less lead than I had to start with.'

'Very useful,' she said, grinning herself now. 'Your face is covered in soot.'

Iro produced a dirty rag from one of his pockets and rubbed his cheeks, spreading the grime more evenly.

'Better?' he asked hopefully.

'Much.'

'To what do I owe this pleasure?' he asked, accepting her hand and being pulled to his feet.

'I need to talk,' Magara answered seriously.

'Rather more your line of work than mine, I'd have said,' the alchemist commented thoughtfully. 'But I suppose I can listen as well as most. Come on in.'

He turned into the doorway, paused, then thought better of it.

'Perhaps we'll sit outside for a bit,' he suggested. 'Would you like something to drink?'

'No. Thank you.'

'Don't trust my distilling expertise, eh? Probably wise.'

'Well, you *do* produce some strange brews in there,' Magara commented.

'Sometimes,' Iro admitted, nodding. 'What did you want to talk about?'

'Have you ever heard of a place called Nevern?'

'Oh, yes,' the alchemist said. 'One of the most famous of the magical places. That's what most people call them of course. The Linking Lords used to call them nodes.'

'Nodes?'

'Places where several lines of magic – or power – meet,' Iro went on. 'Lines that criss-cross the whole country, or so the wizards would have you believe. Where several of them intersect is called a node. They're supposed to be places where magic is commonplace, where you can make anything happen if you only know how.'

'They're part of the Linking?' she asked. 'And so all the magical places are joined to one another?'

'Yes. The wizards usually appoint themselves guardians

123

of the nodes. Not that they could guard much more than their own beer money nowadays,' Iro remarked contemptuously.

'Are they dangerous then, these nodes?'

'So the wizards said. The Link has potential for evil as well as good, of course,' the alchemist replied. 'Normal folk like us would soon be corrupted,' he added sarcastically. 'Why do you want to know about Nevern?'

'Because it's not there any more,' Magara replied. She repeated Slaton's story about Celia and the fog, hoping that Iro would be able to provide an answer. He listened, obviously intrigued, but was unable to help.

'The history of wizardry is full of messes like this,' he concluded. 'I'm afraid I've no idea what it means.'

'But it's not good, is it?' Magara persisted.

Iro shrugged.

'What do *you* think?' he said.

'That's not fair!' she exclaimed. 'You're not supposed to use my own techniques on me.'

'It seems to work when you use it.' Iro grinned at her indignation, then relented. 'All right,' he admitted. 'It doesn't sound healthy to me. But what are *we* supposed to do about it?'

'Something horrible is happening,' Magara said, serious again now. 'Not just there, but everywhere. It's worrying me.'

The unease had built within her until she could no longer escape it. She had always known that there was evil in the world, but all of a sudden it seemed that it was encroaching upon *her* world. And yet there was nothing specific that she could point to as the cause. It was a combination of things that had led to her fear.

'Talk,' Iro commanded, watching her closely. 'That's what you came for.'

So Magara told him about Lisle and the eclipses – and the questions connected with both – and of her worries about the Knifemen's border raids. Iro listened attentively, even though he had heard some of it before, but

Magara knew that he could not see why she was connecting all these things together.

'Life is full of mysteries and wonders,' he concluded, 'but all this doesn't really amount to much, does it?'

Magara knew that he was wrong, but felt incapable of explaining why.

'Are you sure there isn't another reason for your being upset?' the alchemist added.

'What?'

'How about the fact that Varo and Brostek have gone?' he asked simply.

For a few moments, she did not understand, then blushed at her own slowness.

'You think I'm moping!' she accused him, smiling ruefully.

'The human race has known such things,' Iro replied. 'Those two are obviously important to you.'

'How can you tell?' she asked, half-mocking.

'From what you don't say about them.'

'Oh.'

They sat in silence for a while.

'Well?' he prompted.

'I'm confused,' she admitted.

'They *are* a strange pair.'

That's certainly true! Magara thought. *Could that be the* real *reason for me feeling so odd and unsettled?*

'I've learnt to be at ease with Varo,' she began, 'but I don't understand him. He's so *cold*.'

'Very handsome, though.'

She nodded, not meeting Iro's gaze.

'And Brostek?'

'*He* never takes anything seriously, and that's almost as bad. I . . . I like him very much, but—'

'But?'

'He's fun to be with . . . and I think he likes me . . .'

'But you see him just as a friend?' Iro suggested.

'Something like that.'

'And you miss them both.'

125

'Yes, I do. They're both obsessed – and with good reason, I suppose – but I wish they'd stayed longer. Now that they've gone, my life suddenly seems empty and pointless.'

'That, young lady, is the most arrant nonsense,' Iro said firmly. 'They've chosen their lives. You have your own.'

'Such as it is,' Magara said mournfully.

'Listen,' the alchemist went on, a touch of exasperation in his voice now. 'I'm no expert, but even *I* can see that you have talents in abundance. And I'm not the only one to tell you this, so you can't dismiss it as the ramblings of an old lunatic!' His vehemence shocked Magara, and she watched with wide eyes as he continued in full flow. 'You're a healer and a teacher, and people *pay* you to tell stories. If that isn't enough to give someone a full and worthwhile life, then I don't know what is! You're bright and attractive—'

'In that order,' Magara interrupted, laughing. 'My sisters were the beautiful ones. I was the *intelligent* daughter that nobody noticed.'

'Piffle,' the alchemist explained. 'If I were a few decades younger . . .' He smiled, then grew stern once more. 'Look, Magara, you always seem to get to the heart of things when other people come to you for help and advice. Why not apply some of that to yourself?'

'It's not that easy.'

'Whoever said that it had to be easy?' he challenged. 'Stop wasting my time with your self-pity, and go and do something useful.' His harsh words were offset by the sparkle of amusement in his eyes, and Magara did not take offence.

'Such as?' she asked.

'Your head's full of all those old legends and myths at the moment,' Iro responded. 'Why not consult your books and see if they can tell you anything about Nevern?'

'They can't,' Magara replied. 'I'd have remembered.'

'Are you sure?' he persisted. 'Books don't always call things by their real name.'

She considered this, then thought of something else.

'Why don't the old tales tell us about the way the magical places are all joined up?' she said, half to herself.

'Perhaps because most of them were written by wizards,' Iro suggested. He watched as Magara considered this, and congratulated himself on prising her out of her self-absorption.

'Maybe . . .' she whispered, and got to her feet. 'Thanks, Iro.'

And with that she left. The alchemist watched her retreating form fondly, then disappeared into his hut and lit a lamp. He had reading of his own to do.

* * *

It was growing dark when Magara returned to her home. She went straight to the trunk containing her precious store of books and rummaged around, looking for a particular volume. Having found it, she stretched and yawned expansively. Although it was still early, she was tired, having slept little the night before, so she decided to take her reading to bed.

As she climbed in, she felt something hard by her pillow, and pulled it out. It was a small slice of the rust-coloured rock from the crater wall. Small sections of the red outer layer had been chipped away, exposing the black stone beneath. The message read:

Thinking of you, little one. B.

That's typical of Brostek, she thought, a sudden lump in her throat. *Nothing serious lasts for long.*

Magara knew, as all the people of the crater knew, that such messages would soon fade, as the black turned back to red and the letters became invisible again.

She propped the stone on her bedside table and lay down, a curious mixture of happiness and sadness welling within her. The book was forgotten. Laughter and a few tears passed before she finally fell asleep.

* * *

That night, Magara dreamt that she was in a woodland glade. A group of men were staring at her, their eyes wide in amazement. She recognized them as Varo and Brostek and their band, as well as Slaton and Lisle, who was playing his lute. They were all bathed in a strange, flickering light that seemed to emanate from her.

Tonight, the stars will shine from my eyes, she thought, and the dream faded to darkness.

CHAPTER FOURTEEN

Magara did not usually remember her dreams, but she woke late the next morning with the image of the woodland scene still vivid in her mind. It seemed almost real to her, as though it had actually happened. She was still trying to work out what it might mean when the house rocked gently, always the sign of a visitor's arrival. Footsteps sounded closer as Magara glanced at the now fading stone message and wondered, without much hope, whether her friends might have changed their minds and returned.

She was already out of bed and had donned a robe when the expected knock came at her door. Hewitt stood outside, his face haggard, and his hair and clothes even more unkempt than usual.

'I need your help,' he said in a hoarse whisper.

'Come in,' she replied, willing to try and help him, in spite of her still sleepy head. 'You look exhausted. When did you last sleep?'

'Three days ago,' Hewitt muttered as he entered.

'Then you need your bed more than anything,' she told him.

'No. I need to talk.'

I know the feeling, Magara thought as she waved him into a chair. 'So talk.'

'I . . . haven't been able to sleep or eat or play,' he began, 'since . . . since . . .'

'Lisle,' she completed for him. Hewitt nodded dumbly, then sighed. 'However,' Magara went on, 'you *do* seem to have managed to keep on drinking.'

The musician grinned sheepishly. 'I seem to have retained that ability,' he admitted. Then his face became

129

drawn once more, his eyes haunted. 'He played that song better than I could ever hope to, and he'd only heard it once! You were there. You know I'm right.'

'You are.'

'Then what's the point?' he wailed. 'All my life, I've only ever been good at one thing. And then Lisle came along – it's as if the gods were mocking my ridiculous efforts.'

'I'm sure they have better things to do,' Magara said gently.

'But don't you see!' Hewitt exclaimed. 'I *know* what music can be like now, what incredible peaks it can scale. And I know I can't reach them.' There was real anguish in his voice. 'And to have it shown to me by . . . by a . . .'

'By a dribbling idiot?' she prompted.

'No!' he cried, red-faced. 'I would never . . . I don't have the words,' he concluded miserably. 'But Lisle isn't like you or me.'

'Surely that's the point,' Magara said quietly. 'He's very special, perhaps even unique, and he's certainly been cursed in many ways. But maybe the gods made up for that by giving him that one incredible talent.'

'I would give *anything* to play like that,' Hewitt said fervently.

'Would you be like him?' she asked.

The young man stared at her as if her words made no sense, then slowly shook his head. Magara explained Slaton's theories about the workings of Lisle's mind as best she could, while Hewitt listened, growing calmer as she spoke.

'So you see,' Magara concluded, 'Lisle is a true genius in some narrow ways, but in others he'll always be a small child. And just because someone else can play better than you, does that make your music bad?'

'But I was always the best,' he whispered.

'Which is more important, to be the best, or music itself?' she asked, and went on without waiting for an

130

answer. 'You're a wonderful musician, Hewitt. You've given pleasure to hundreds of people, myself included. I've seen you when the rapture takes you, when you're lost in the sound. Do you really think all that is worthless – just because someone plays better than you?'

'I suppose not,' he answered eventually, 'but—'

'But nothing. You've put effort and skill and love into your music, and you mustn't let that go to waste.'

'It'll never be the same, though,' he said in a small voice.

'None of us ever stays the same,' Magara told him gently. 'That's what being alive means.'

Hewitt looked at her as if he did not believe this, then he nodded and whispered, 'Tell me what to do.'

He's like a lost little boy, Magara thought sadly. Aloud she said, 'Go and sleep. And when you wake up, eat. Then tomorrow, when you feel up to it, go to Newberry and ask to play. Get him to pay you in food in advance. That way, you'll *have* to do it.' She grinned. 'All right?'

'I'll try,' he said weakly.

'Good. I'll come and hear you,' she promised. 'When I hear you play your new song again, then I'll know you're all right.'

'Never,' Hewitt stated. 'It's his song now. I couldn't—'

'We'll see,' Magara interrupted. 'Now get going before you fall asleep in my chair.'

As she ushered him outside, Hewitt blinked rapidly, surprised that there was daylight outside.

'It's hot,' he commented and, with that profound observation, staggered off down the walkway, clinging on to the handrail. Magara watched until he was out of sight, then realized that it must be nearly noon and she wasn't dressed yet, and it *was* hot. The sky was a cloudless blue and the small breeze that ruffled the surface of the lake seemed only to accentuate the day's heat.

Acting on impulse, Magara threw off her robe, leaving only her thin underclothes. She looked around, hoping that no one would witness the exposure of what she considered to be her bulging and overweight flesh, and then slipped quickly into the water. She gasped at the initial shock of the cold, but forced herself to swim energetically and soon grew accustomed to it. Before long, she was floating on her back, with her eyes closed, more relaxed than she had been for days – though she still held her stomach in, just in case anyone was watching from the shore.

A shadow fell upon her for a moment, and she was instantly alert, filled with a sudden dread that it might be an eclipse. But when she opened her eyes, she was almost blinded by the sun. After some ungainly splashing, she looked round and saw that it had been Talisman, who had glided past on his silent way to her home.

There were several boats out on the lake, most of them in the areas between the central deeps and the more shallow waters of the periphery. One of them was quite close, so Magara swam towards it. She soon recognized two of the divers, Cole and Pera, and kept her distance, not wanting to disrupt their work. As she watched, a third diver, Rayne, surfaced beside the boat and apparently began to issue instructions. Magara could not hear what was being said, but nevertheless waited eagerly to see what would happen next. Then Pera spotted her and called out in greeting.

'Magara! Come and join us. We might have something interesting here.'

For a moment, Magara was too surprised to respond – the divers did not usually invite company while they were working – but then she realized that the rare chance to see them at work close to was too good to miss, and she accepted eagerly. Feeling rather self-conscious about her swimming stroke, which suddenly seemed very laboured, she approached the boat and was pulled aboard by the two inside. Once there, she could not help but compare her scantily clad curves with Pera's lithe shape, but the divers did not notice her awkwardness.

'You're interested in old stuff, aren't you?' Cole asked her. 'History and all that?'

'Yes. Why?'

'Because there's something down here,' Rayne said from the water. 'And we'd like you to take a look at it.'

'Of course,' Magara responded. 'Bring it up.'

'We can't,' Pera said. 'You'll have to go down to it.'

'Don't be silly!' she exclaimed. 'It's *far* too deep for me here.'

'We'll help you,' Cole explained. 'You can see it from about twenty paces down.'

'Only twenty paces?'

'The bed's much deeper, of course,' Cole went on, matter-of-fact. 'But the light's good today.'

'Of course,' Magara muttered.

'It's amazing no one's found it before,' Rayne added. 'It must have been unearthed by Craig's excavations last hand.'

'There've been some odd currents since then,' Pera agreed, nodding. 'Perhaps the silt has been washed away from it.'

'What *is* it?' Magara asked.

'We don't know,' Cole replied. 'That's why we want you to go down.'

'But you must have *some* idea,' she insisted.

'It's rock,' Rayne said, relenting. 'And not like most of the stuff round here.'

'And?' Magara prompted, knowing there was more to it than that.

'It's been worked,' Pera said. 'There are definite groove marks in places – as if it had once been part of a building.'

The men nodded their agreement.

'And in one place there's some sort of symbol carved into the surface,' Cole added.

'It's too symmetrical to be natural,' Rayne agreed.

'Lettering?' Magara suggested, intrigued now.

'Don't think so,' Cole said. 'Come and see.'

'But—'

'We'll make it easy for you,' Pera said in a business-like tone. 'Watch me. Follow the way I breathe.'

As Magara did as she was told, Rayne gave her further instructions.

'Hold on to our belts,' he explained. 'One hand on each. And don't kick on the way down. Your air will last longer that way. Pera will go down first and point out what you're looking for. The globe will last for a little while, so make the most of the extra light.'

'And coming back up?' Magara asked in between long breaths.

The divers laughed.

'You can manage that on your own,' Rayne reassured her. 'Just head for the sun.'

'And don't breathe in until you've reached the air,' Cole added.

'Thanks a lot.'

A few moments later, Magara was back in the water, flanked by the two men – who had each taken rocks from the bottom of the boat and attached them to their belts with thongs.

'Ready?'

'As ready as I'll ever be.' Magara felt light-headed with apprehension.

'One more deep breath,' Pera instructed. 'See you down there.' So saying, she dived from the boat and disappeared. Then the two men dived, taking Magara with them, and water rushed past her as she trailed between their powerful bodies. Sunlight dimmed and the cold intensified. She could not believe how fast they were sinking, yet Pera was far below them, the glow from her enclosed oil-wick globe like a magical beacon within the deeps.

Blood thundered in Magara's ears and she remembered to release a little air. Silvery bubbles disappeared upwards, and she felt the pressure begin to build. *No further*, she pleaded silently.

Then Cole was pointing urgently, and she peered into the gloom, trying to see what Pera was outlining below. At first nothing made sense, but then she saw the straight edges and angles, the grey rock jutting from the duller greys that surrounded it. And then she saw the symbol she had been told to look for. Pera held the globe close to it, her fingers outlining the grooves – but an instant later, the light failed. Magara's lungs were screaming for release; she had seen enough.

Cole and Rayne released the rocks from their belts and turned towards the surface. Magara clung on for a few strokes, but then her own instincts took over and she struck out on her own.

She emerged into the longed-for air, gasping desperately, to find all three divers around her, ready to help if need be. They were all grinning.

'Easy, eh?' Rayne remarked.

'No trouble at all,' Cole added.

Magara had no breath with which to argue, so contented herself with punching at them feebly.

'Back in the boat,' Pera decreed.

Once they were all aboard, and Magara had recovered the use of her tongue and limbs, they discussed their find.

'Did you see it?'

'Yes.'

'And?'

'I'm sorry,' she said through chattering teeth, 'but the sign means nothing to me.'

The divers' disappointment was plain on their faces.

'Are you sure you saw it properly?' Cole asked.

'Four circles, each touching two others, in a sort of square shape,' Magara replied.

'We thought it might be a secret symbol of some kind,' Rayne said.

'Well, if it *is*, its secret's still safe,' she commented. 'I've never seen it before.'

'Not even in any of your books?'

Magara shook her head.

'Isn't it enough of a mystery for *anything* like that to be down there?' They nodded their agreement. 'Either it's unimaginably ancient, or someone's playing a very elaborate practical joke.'

'It's no joke,' Pera replied with certainty. 'No one could have done that much rock-cutting without us all knowing.'

'And the stone is far too heavy for someone to have brought to Trevine and put down there,' Rayne added.

'Then the mystery must remain unsolved,' Magara concluded. 'The history of this place only goes back a few centuries. Perhaps that stone belongs to a much earlier age. I'll check what I can, though,' she promised, seeing their dejection.

'Perhaps if we could uncover more of it,' Cole suggested, 'we might find more signs.'

'I'd like to hear about anything you *do* find,' Magara said, then added quickly, 'but don't expect me to dive again. I'm not built for it.' She patted her stomach, smiling.

'Don't complain,' Pera said. 'That provides you with buoyancy and protection from the cold!'

'At least you can see what's there, unlike some people, who pretend not to.'

'You look fine,' Rayne reassured her.

'I saw something else down there,' she said, changing the subject. 'Something near the other end of the rock. It glittered.'

'Oh, that,' Cole said dismissively. 'It's a shatterstone. Worthless.'

'But it was beautiful.'

'Down there, yes,' Rayne agreed. 'But if we brought it into the air, after a few days all you'd have would be a pile of sand. It needs the weight of water on top of it.'

'When they were first found,' Pera explained, 'people tried to preserve them, but it's hopeless. And anyway, the jewellers can't shape them. Cut one crystal and they all shatter. We don't bother about them.'

Magara was fascinated.

'Would you get it for me anyway?' she asked hopefully.

The divers glanced at each other, and Cole shrugged.

'Why not?' he said and dived into the water with scarcely a splash.

A few moments later he resurfaced, and held out his prize. Magara took the fist-size shatterstone gingerly, but it felt solid enough. The sunlight sparkled in the many irregular crystals, and miniature rainbows hovered in the air.

'It's lovely!' she gasped.

'Keep it in water,' Pera told her. 'It'll last a bit longer that way.'

The divers rowed Magara back to the walkway, and she went inside to change and to put the shatterstone in a bowl of water. Then, feeling strangely tired and still a little chilled, she took a rug out on to the boards and lay in the sun, thinking about the events of the day. She believed that Hewitt would soon recover his healthy self-respect – which had previously bordered on arrogance – but the mystery of the carved stone in the lake was something she could not even begin to solve.

CHAPTER FIFTEEN

Magara was still sitting outside when the sun disappeared below the western cliff-tops. She watched the shadow creep closer and closer along the walkway, then forced herself to move. She went inside and checked up on the shatterstone; it was still intact, but seemed less beautiful without the sunlight to spark its fire. She wondered briefly if Iro could help her find a way to preserve it – perhaps he had already tried? – but then she remembered the alchemist's advice and went in search of her book.

To save lamp oil, Magara went outside again to read. Although sunset came early to Trevine, there would be light enough for some time yet. Skimming the pages was difficult, because she kept recognizing well-loved passages and wanting to re-read them, but Magara stuck to her task and looked for references to Nevern, eclipses and – just in case – the symbol on the structure in the lake. She could find none of these, and was just about to fetch another volume and start again, when her eye was caught by a short paragraph she did not remember ever having read before. It was headed 'Shadow-Maze' – and that in itself was intriguing enough for Magara to want to read on.

The passage told, in somewhat archaic language, of a test once set by the Linking Lords in order to determine the rights and wrongs of an unspecified case. They had magically cloaked a lonely tower in a grey, enveloping cloud, and within this cloud, or shadow-maze, they set various tasks which could only be accomplished by the true and pure of heart. All unworthy contestants would wander within the shadow-maze, hopelessly lost, eventually emerging no nearer to their goal and none the wiser.

However, the competitor with right on his side would win through to the tower, at which time the cloud would disappear and the judgement be made.

I wonder if there's a tower in the valley at Nevern, Magara thought. The obvious similarity between Slaton's experience and that of an unsuccessful suitor in the shadow-maze had not escaped her. Nor did the fact that the comparison implied, unhappily, that Slaton had not had right on his side.

The description was frustrating, and gave very few details of the tests within the maze, which meant that Magara's imagination took over. She soon found a story taking form in her head, and recalled that Hewitt would not be playing at Newberry's that night. She wondered if the inn-keeper would employ her instead. Her day-to-day needs were few, but her recent guests – especially Brostek – had depleted her stocks, and a free meal and a few coins would be appreciated. More than that, the tale had taken on a life of its own; when that happened, Magara had little choice but to try and find an audience.

*   *   *

'The last test but one almost proved to be Morten's downfall. He was weary now, and the sight of the ogre standing menacingly in his path made his heart sink. The monster was standing guard in the middle of a narrow bridge that spanned a crevasse so deep that the bottom could not be seen. The chasm was wide, and the bridge was the only way across.

'"What do you require so that I may cross?" Morten cried.

'"Gold!" the ogre replied, its small eyes narrow with greed.

'Morten knew that the sun was setting behind him. If darkness fell before he reached the tower, then his chance would be gone for ever. And he had no gold.

'However: "I have gold," he promised. "Wait here."

'"What else would I be doing?" the ogre remarked contemptuously.

'Morten turned back, and ran to fetch the sack of straw he had left behind with his horse. The cloud swirled around him as he retreated, as though it rejoiced in his defeat. Between him and the tower, the shadow-maze closed in.

'He quickly arranged a hard-packed layer of straw on the top of the sack, and turned back towards the bridge. When the ogre was in sight, Morten began to stagger, as though the weight of the sack was almost too much for him. When he was still a score of paces away, he lowered the sack to the ground, groaning with the effort. Then he straightened up and addressed the monster once more.

'"Here is my gold. It is yours if you will let me pass. But first I must wash if I am to see my love."

'Morten had artfully laid the top of the sack open just a little, and the rays of the setting sun glinted on the golden straw. The fiend's eyes narrowed still further as Morten strode to a pool of water a little to one side. He began to wash, splashing his face and arms, but kept a careful eye on the ogre as it squinted suspiciously at the false gold.

'At last, as Morten had hoped, the creature's avarice grew too much for it; it lumbered towards the sack, intent on claiming its toll. Morten waited as long as he dared, then sprinted to the bridge and dashed on to it, almost losing his balance. Terrified of those hidden depths, he desperately found his footing.

'The monstrous creature roared with fury, aware that it had been duped, but its shambling gait was too slow for it to catch its fleeing prey. Consumed with rage, the ogre hurled a boulder at the bridge – but it flew harmlessly past and crashed into the ravine below. And Morten was across!'

Magara's enraptured audience breathed a collective sigh of relief. The storyteller waited for a few moments before continuing.

'As soon as Morten reached the far side, the crevasse, the bridge and the ogre all disappeared in an instant, the monster's final scream of fury echoing in the emptiness.'

Again Magara paused, letting the listeners savour the prospect of the final test. In her invented story, it had been devised by an arrogant landowner, who had arranged for the shadow-maze to choose between suitors for his only daughter. He had employed corrupt wizards, whom Magara had deliberately made figures of fun, to ensure that the tasks were biased towards men of power and, more especially, of wealth. However, unknown to her father, the girl – who was now locked away in a lonely tower – had befriended one of the wizards. This mage still had a streak of decency in him, and he had agreed to secretly ensure that at least some of the assignments were true tests of love and worth.

Much to the landowner's chagrin, all the preferred suitors had so far failed, either through stupidity, greed or over-confidence, and he was finally forced to allow his daughter's true love to brave the shadow-maze. And Morten, through his courage, ingenuity and a generosity of spirit conspicuously lacking in his predecessors, had succeeded – so far. But he was now to face the greatest test.

'Morten was near her now. He sensed his love, but could not see her. Ahead of him, the shadow-maze was a dense fog, unrelenting, dark as an eclipse . . .'

For the first time, Magara's tale faltered. She had meant to say dark as night, but the words had formed themselves. She recovered her poise quickly enough and went on.

'Behind him, the way out was clear. In front, he was blind in the face of unknown terrors. For all he knew, there could be huge drops ahead of him, unseen monsters, snares of all kinds. To go on was to abandon himself to trust, to prove that his love, his goal, was worth any risk.

'The sun was almost half gone now, and still he

hesitated. He had only moments to decide. For the first time, fear touched him with its clammy hand – but then he caught the faintest waft of her familiar scent, and that was all the encouragement he needed. Morten strode on fearlessly into the darkness. And found himself in silence, weightless and alone.'

The people in Newberry's tavern were hushed and breathless, sharing with Magara the perils of her hero.

'How far he walked or how long it took, Morten would never know, but he emerged at last from the cloud just as the eclipse ended – and there before him was the tower, bathed in the last of the day's sunlight. Looking back, he saw that he had walked across a causeway. Had his course not been true, he would have been dashed on to the rocks below, where the restless sea swirled and foamed.

'Eager now, his heart full, he unlocked the door to the tower with the key won from the dragon, and ran up the winding staircase. And there, in the topmost room, from whence you could see both land and ocean, Morten and Julitta fell into each other's arms, reunited for all time.'

Newberry led the applause as Magara's tale came to an end and she took her bows, smiling at the appreciative cheers. A hat was being passed round and there was a healthy chink of coins. Amid the congratulations were several cries for more, but Magara fended off the requests with a hidden but growing impatience. She could hardly wait to escape.

She had just remembered that she *had* seen an eclipse while living in the crater. But it had not been in the sky.

CHAPTER SIXTEEN

Magara hurried home, a mixture of foreboding and excitement in her heart. Lighting a lamp, she went straight to the makeshift chest where she kept her old clothes. Rummaging almost to the bottom, she found what she was looking for, and dragged it out. It had been a long time since she had last looked at the tapestry, and it had been hidden away well wrapped, not only to protect the delicate needlework, but also out of frustration. As well as her recognized talents, Magara had tried her hand since coming to Trevine at other, more practical crafts, among them tapestry. But she had never been able to produce anything remotely as good as the one she had brought from home.

Home? It had been a long time since Magara had thought of Arenguard as such, and she paused, considering the memories awoken by Slaton's unexpected visit. Until a few days ago, life had seemed so simple. Now everything was uncertain.

Carefully unwrapping the tapestry, she laid it out on the floor. Then she brought the lamp closer, and stared intently at the bottom left section. Yes, there it was! Always before, she had thought that the sun was partly obscured by the lowering cloud. She was sure now that it was an eclipse; once she knew what she was looking for, the bright halo effect was unmistakable.

The tapestry had fascinated Magara since her childhood, and now she found her interest rekindled. It had been designed and executed with exquisite attention to detail; each leaf and petal, each animal and bird, every drop of water and flash of light was alive in a way that no mere reproduction could achieve. The seamstress of long ago had been a master of her craft, but had also possessed the eye of an artist. No one knew exactly how old the tapestry was. It had apparently been in Magara's family for many generations and, as her prized possession, had been one of the very few non-essentials that she had permitted herself to bring from Arenguard.

The tapestry was rectangular, taller than it was wide, and divided into four equal rectangles, each of which was a self-contained portrait of a country scene. At the central point of the tapestry was a small circle of flowers. There were patterns within each quarter and within the overall design which made it clear that the views depicted were closely linked, but none of these patterns was entirely consistent. There were unexplained oddities, hidden incongruities, and the eclipse was linked to one of these strange quirks. Although the sun – whether obscured by eclipse or by cloud – was in the sky, reflected in the still waters of the lake below was the shimmering image of the moon. As if to emphasize the unusual point, a lone grey wolf was shown next to the lake, its muzzle raised in a howl that Magara could almost hear.

So what does that tell me? she mused, thinking of Shadow, and wondering whether Brostek's wolf ever howled at the moon – or at an eclipse. *Not much!*

However, this scene was in the bottom left quadrant, which Magara thought of as the last of the four, and so she returned to the beginning, to see if the whole tapestry might have more meaning now that she had seen the eclipse.

Her starting point was always the upper left-hand quarter, for two simple reasons. Firstly, the four sections clearly related to the four seasons, and the first of these was spring. Plants were budding, trees were in blossom, and the weather was a deliberate mixture of sunshine and rain, indicating the changeable nature of the most mercurial of the seasons. The colourful arch of a rainbow completed the scene. But there were peculiarities that could be seen if the viewer chose to look closely enough. Hidden among the spring flowers were dandelions in seed, their feathery messengers ready to fly away – rather earlier than was usual. And a patch of grass was shown to be strewn with fallen leaves.

Nevertheless, the overwhelming majority of the evidence showed that the top left quadrant was indeed spring and, next to it, in the top right section, was summer. Here, the sun shone in a clear blue sky, a profusion of flowers were in full bloom, and the foliage was dense and green. The whole impression was one of heat and fullness, compared to the energy and promise of spring. And yet, among the extravagant colours of marigolds, lupins and roses, the shy petals of snowdrops could be seen quite clearly in the foreground.

Continuing the sequence, autumn was in the lower right-hand portion. The trees here were a mass of mellow reds and golds. Fallen leaves lay glistening in the diffuse orange light of a misty sunset. Fruit and berries decorated most branches and bushes, but a weeping willow was caught in a time of its own, covered with the pollen-laden catkins of early spring.

The cycle was completed by winter, the eclipse shown peering through a gap in the cold grey mass of cloud that swept across the pale sky like a great wave. Snow lay on the ground, and the gathering storm promised more to come. Most of the trees were bare; only a group of pine trees were still green. The howling wolf added the final touch to a chilling scene. And yet, in the centre of this desolation, almost unnoticed amid the snow, a white rose bush flourished impossibly in full bloom.

The second sequence, which was contained within the four seasonal pictures, showed the progress through life of a woman. In spring, she was shown as a young child, running through the garden with her arms flung wide in excitement, her dark hair flowing freely. In summer, she was a young woman, demure now and pretty, still filled with the joy of youth as she stooped to smell the flowers.

In the third quadrant, she was a full-grown woman, truly beautiful, with an air of quiet calm about her. She stood erect, looking up at a long-necked swan flying overhead. And finally, in the winter of her life, she was an old woman, her hair silver, calm in repose as she sat within her garden, working on a tapestry. Magara had no doubt that this last figure was a self-portrait of the seamstress, and that the others were memories of the woman's earlier life. What had prompted her to devote such time and effort to this meticulously executed yet vibrant work? And why the obvious anomalies within the conventional pattern? Magara had often tried to find an answer to these questions, yet she was no nearer a solution now than when she had first set eyes on the tapestry. Perhaps there were clues that she had missed.

She had also noticed other sequences, concerned with the position of the sun and the perspective of each of the sections. These two things were linked, but neither pattern was straightforward. Each of the four pictures showed a different aspect and lie of the land – which meant that either they depicted different places or, as Magara believed, they were four views in different directions from the same spot. The occasional correspondence at the borders between quadrants seemed to support this view.

For instance, a small stream swirled and tumbled from left to right in spring, disappeared at the border but re-emerged a thumb-span away in summer. A copse of fir trees in the background seemed to spread over the line between autumn and winter. However, more convincing evidence was available elsewhere. In summer, the sun was just above the horizon, the clear gold light suggesting sunrise – which meant that the seamstress and the viewer were looking east. Similarly, in autumn, the sun was again low in the sky, but this time the colouring clearly suggested sunset – which supposed that this prospect faced west. This was confirmed by a V-shaped formation of geese, flying high in the sky from right to left – or south – which was indeed what migrating birds would be doing at that time of year.

That left north and south for the other two sections, but this time the sun's position was of no help. In spring, the sun was high and would have looked much the same from any direction. In winter the eclipsed light was also high, but the issue was further complicated by the reflection of the moon. Nevertheless, Magara had decided that spring showed the northern aspect because there, in tiny detail in one corner of the sky, another group of geese was flying away from the viewer – and in spring they would logically be travelling north.

That meant that, if taken in the order that had been established by the seasons, these two sequences were lop-sided. Midday, sunrise, sunset, midday again – or night, if the reflected moon was more relevant. Whichever way she looked at it, the progression was not obvious, nor was the outlook of the four views. North, east, west, south. Surely it would have been more consistent to have travelled round the points of the compass in one direction; north, east, south, west. Although Magara could not make sense of either pattern, there were so many other points of interest and small delights in the pictures that she was prepared to forgive the ancient seamstress any number of idiosyncracies. Which was fortunate, because there were many more to be found.

Apart from the plants which blossomed in defiance of the natural order of the seasons, several other items were not quite as innocent as they seemed. Among the woodland bluebells of spring, a number of rabbits hopped along, seemingly quite unafraid of the bushy-tailed fox in their midst. The fox in his turn appeared perfectly content in this unlikely company. Dominating the middle ground of summer was a ruined building of honey-coloured stone. Empty windows and archways were covered with ivy, and broken statuary was scattered as though it had been deliberately smashed. In what had obviously once been a courtyard was an ornamental pool, a golden fish caught in mid-leap above the lily-covered surface. Above the pool was a stone fountain, still functioning in spite of the obvious dilapidation of the building. Further back, a kingfisher shimmered in flight.

In autumn, the low-flying swan was travelling in the opposite direction to the geese, but that did not seem too significant. Magara was not even sure whether swans migrated, but had always felt it a pity that the elegant white creature was alone, knowing as she did that swans paired for life. Grazing on the grass near the woman's feet were several colourful ducks, which did seem odd, as this was the only quarter in which no surface water could be seen. But strangest of all was a squirrel, hanging upside down from the huge red apple he was eating. Sooner or later he would eat away the very thing he was clinging to so precariously, and fall. Magara had certainly never seen any squirrel behave in such a perverse way.

But perhaps the most chilling incongruity of all was the sight of a grey stone tomb in the centre of spring, and it was to this that Magara found herself drawn after she had studied the eclipse. That such a stark reminder of mortality should be included in a work of art that otherwise brimmed with life was surprising enough, but surely it would have been more appropriate within the sombre tones of winter. Or perhaps that would have been a little too relevant for the artist in her old age – and so she had shown the little girl dancing next to the grave, blissfully unaware of her eventual fate.

An extra mystery was provided by the inscription just visible upon the sculptured face of the tomb. In tiny lettering it read:

NEVER
THE PLACE

Never
  the time

148

In the past, this strange epitaph had seemed to Magara like a despairing cry, as though the person buried there had not been able to complete their appointed tasks in life. She had mentally added exclamation marks to the second and fourth lines, emphasizing the frustration implied by the words – and somehow making them more defiant at the same time.

On this occasion, however, she was suddenly struck by the peculiar layout of the letters, and by the fact that only the first letter of the second couplet was a capital. Perhaps, like so much else in the picture, this message was not quite what it seemed. Perhaps it was a clue to a puzzle she could not even begin to fathom? Mentally taking the N from the third line, she repositioned it in the now obvious place:

NEVERN
THE PLACE

   ever
   the time

Could it really be that her remote ancestress had recorded the magical place called Nevern? Was it really a coincidence that Slaton had brought her news of that fabled place at this time? Was the ancient seamstress still there in some way – *ever the time* – and did the tapestry have some connection with Celia's disappearance? And could it be that all this was somehow linked to the mysterious eclipses?

Could it really be?

The night was half over when Magara forced herself to put aside her endless speculation and surrender to sleep. Her last waking thought was unnerving; if she was ever going to find any answers to her questions, she would have to go to Nevern herself.

CHAPTER SEVENTEEN

In the cool early morning light, Magara's thoughts of the night before seemed far-fetched and fanciful. She lay in bed, feeling quite wretched from lack of sleep, and thought it over again. There was no real reason for her to make the journey to Nevern, even if she could find the place, yet the feeling persisted that she should at least make the attempt.

But what would that achieve? she asked herself. *Even if I got in . . .* She remembered that Celia had apparently been able to enter the hidden valley, but there was no telling what had happened to her since. *Perhaps I could help her.* Casting herself in the role of heroic rescuer seemed quite ludicrous to Magara, and she smiled at the idea. *And there's nothing I can do, either there or anywhere else, that will stop the eclipses from happening! So what's the point?*

The only point, she soon decided, was that she might possibly clear up one or two of the mysteries that had suddenly been thrust into her life. Was that enough reason to set out on such an absurd expedition?

And how am I supposed to get there? Magara owned no horse, her old mare having been sold years earlier, had no money to speak of, and few possessions worth selling. Even her house was not her own, being on loan from the town of Trevine itself.

Eventually, Magara got out of bed and dressed, then forced herself to have some breakfast before going to visit Iro again. She took the tapestry with her, carefully rolled in its protective cover. The alchemist's hut was dark as usual, and there was no answer when she called his name. Magara was on the point of giving up when she heard a faint rustling inside. She called out again, rather more loudly. There were more shuffling sounds, a loud yawn and a fit of coughing as Iro woke up. It transpired that he too had been up for much of the night, working on his experiments. Her apologies for disturbing his rest were brushed aside. Iro was curious to hear what she had discovered.

'Did you find anything about Nevern?' he asked gruffly.

'Not in the books,' she replied, then went on to describe first the passage about the shadow-maze, and then the tapestry and its apparent link with Nevern.

The two of them spent a long time kneeling in the doorway, poring over the unfurled picture and remarking upon its various peculiarities. The alchemist disappointed Magara – he agreed with all her observations but was unable to add any further insights.

'Fascinating!' Iro concluded, straightening up then stretching painfully. 'It's almost enough to make an old man want to travel again.' He glanced curiously at Magara.

'Do you think I should go there?' she asked.

'What do *you* think?' he replied, smiling.

'Don't do that again!' she retorted, laughing. 'Give me a proper answer.'

'Even if this *is* Nevern,' the alchemist began, 'and we're by no means certain of that – then it's not like *this* . . .' and he pointed at the tapestry, '. . . any more. We know that from Slaton's tale. Going there could be dangerous.'

The same thing had occurred to Magara, but she wanted to hear Iro's reasons.

'Why dangerous?'

'You, of all people, must have heard the legend about the place that was too dangerous even for wizards,' he answered. 'It's one of the most famous myths in the history of magic.'

'Of course,' she responded impatiently. 'In the version I read, the place is called the Vortex, and anyone who

151

was a strong enough wizard to gain admittance would be given enough power to enable him to rule the world. But that story has nothing to do with this. You can't *seriously* believe that Nevern and the Vortex are one and the same!'

'No, obviously not,' he said calmly. 'But if magic is that dangerous in the Vortex – *wherever* that might be – why should we assume that it will always be safe at the other magical sites? Any sound philosophy takes as its basis the fact that every action, or power, or thing, has an opposite of equal potential. If magic can be used for good, as history and the old tales would have us believe, then it can also be used for *bad*. Honourable people don't have a monopoly on ingenuity, you know. Perhaps someone got into Nevern for the wrong reasons and, either deliberately or by default, they have corrupted the place.'

Magara glanced at the tapestry again.

'Destroying something like this,' she said quietly, 'would be real evil.'

'It's all speculation, of course,' Iro pointed out in a lighter tone.

'Anyway, the Vortex is only a myth,' Magara added. 'It can't really exist – can it?'

'You know better than I do that all legends are based on *something*,' the alchemist replied.

'Yes, but that bit about ruling the world can only be superstition,' she argued. 'Legends are always being embellished! I've done enough of it myself to know that's true.'

'A fair point,' Iro conceded, although he did not sound wholly convinced.

'Do you know where Nevern is?' Magara asked abruptly.

'About six or seven day's ride north of here, I believe,' he answered, watching her closely.

Magara thought for a few moments, then asked, 'Are there any other magical places nearer to the crater?'

'The closest that I know of is Whistling Hill.'

'I've heard of that,' she said, frowning.

'I'm not surprised,' Iro commented. 'It's only a few leagues from your old home. To get there from here, you'd practically have to go through Arenguard.'

'I remember it now!' Magara exclaimed. 'It had the reputation of being the coldest spot in the area. Lots of gloomy old stones. I never wanted to go there. But then no one had ever told me about it being magical,' she ended resentfully.

'I've never been there myself,' Iro said, 'so I can't comment on its temperature, but I do know that there's a stone circle on top of the hill, supposedly older than the first settlements in Levindre. So of course no one knows who built it. Legend has it that the stones are the children of a god who disobeyed their father; he turned them into rock as punishment – so that they would have plenty of time to contemplate their wickedness.'

'Even my parents weren't *that* bad,' Magara said, grinning.

'Well, I suppose there's always a chance that Father will turn up again and change them back,' Iro added.

'That I would like to see!'

'Legend also has it,' Iro went on, 'that there are secrets in the whistling of the wind on the hill – if you have the skill to hear them. Hence the name.'

'If it's to the north of here, then it would be on the way to Nevern, wouldn't it?' Magara asked thoughtfully.

'More or less.'

Iro waited in silence, watching his companion. She was deep in thought again.

'How do you know all this?' she asked eventually.

The alchemist smiled. 'The same way *you* get to know things,' he replied. 'By being inquisitive. I've been around long enough to take an interest in many things.'

Magara resisted the temptation to ask how old he actually was, knowing that he would not give a true answer.

'Now my active pursuits have shrunk to trying to get

153

this wretched fire-wheel to work properly,' Iro went on. 'It's already taken far too long.'

'Why the rush?' she asked.

The alchemist had evidently known before Magara that her mind was made up.

'Because I want it ready for your farewell celebration,' he told her.

* * *

Magara went to Newberry's tavern that evening, surmising correctly that at least one member of Trevine's ruling council would be there. Rothar, one of the senior divers, was having a drink with a few friends. When Magara asked if she could have a word with him, she was invited to join their party, and accepted, although she would have preferred to talk to him privately.

'What can I do for you?' The councillor's voice was deep and resonant.

'If I wanted to leave Trevine temporarily,' Magara began, 'would the council allow me to return?'

'Of course,' he replied. 'We do not change our minds that easily, and besides, you are a valued member of our community.' There were nods of agreement around the table, but Magara did not notice.

'Would you keep my house for me?' she asked.

'How long do you plan to be away?'

'Three, four hands maybe. No more than a month, I'm sure.'

'Then I don't think there will be a problem,' he reassured her. 'May I ask why you are going?'

'A friend of mine . . . is in trouble,' Magara said awkwardly. 'I'd like to help her if I can.'

'I'll pry no further,' Rothar said kindly. 'Do not worry about your welcome here, Magara.'

'Thank you.'

'Are you staying for the music?' he enquired, nodding towards the stage.

Magara was delighted to see that Hewitt was among the musicians, and she stayed to hear them play, moving to a smaller table and ordering a little wine. She had not intended eating there, meaning to save her coins, but Newberry gave her a free meal 'for getting Hewitt back to work'. She returned home that night tired but determined, her spirits lifted by her friend's generosity.

*　　*　　*

Magara rose early the next morning, thinking of all that she must do to set her affairs in order before she left. Her biggest problem was transport – her resources would not stretch to her buying or even hiring a horse for such a journey, and paying her way on carriages and carts would be expensive, laborious and time-consuming. She ran through the list of friends who might be persuaded to help her obtain a mount; she would have to work out how to repay any such loan later.

She was about to leave and begin her search when footsteps sounded on the walkway outside. She opened the door before her visitor had a chance to knock and found herself looking into Hewitt's slightly startled face.

'Hello. You played well last night,' she said, hoping that he was no longer plagued with self-doubt.

'Not bad,' he answered, some of his old cockiness showing in his smile. 'I hear you're leaving.'

'News travels fast,' she said, taken aback.

'You shouldn't be so surprised,' he told her. 'Musicians are the worst gossips.'

Magara smiled, glad to see him cheerful again.

'I'd like to go with you,' Hewitt said then.

For a moment Magara was too surprised to respond. 'Why?' she asked eventually.

'It's time for me to move on,' he replied seriously. 'And you . . . you understand me.'

Less than you think, she thought, not sure of his real motives.

'Don't you even want to know where I'm going?' she asked.

'It's all the same to me. Look, don't worry. I won't be a problem. As soon as you've had enough of me, tell me to get lost and I'll go. I'd just like some company at first, that's all.' There was a note of pleading in his voice.

The thought of having company on her travels appealed to Magara but, in spite of the young man's claim to the contrary, she did not know him very well.

'Come in. Sit down,' she ordered. Hewitt obeyed meekly. 'I'm sorry to be so blunt,' she said firmly, 'but you haven't got any silly notion about being in love with me, have you?' She had had problems of this sort before with people she had helped. The infatuation never lasted long, but could be powerful at first – and a great nuisance.

'No, no! It's nothing like that!' he exclaimed. 'I wouldn't try anything. Truthfully.'

Magara did not know whether she was relieved or sorry at this patent honesty.

'I need to leave Trevine,' he went on. 'But I've been here so long . . .'

'The outside world frightens you?'

He nodded.

'I know just how you feel.' Hewitt looked up at her in surprise, but Magara went on quickly. 'How soon could you be ready to travel?'

'I'm ready now,' he replied, then amended his response by adding, 'As soon as I pick up my viol. How are you travelling?'

'That's a problem at the moment,' she told him. 'I need to find someone who'll lend me a horse – or the money to hire one.'

'I can help there,' he said eagerly, adding in the face of her obvious scepticism, 'My brother lives on the Rim now. He's a merchant – he'll have horses to spare.'

On Hewitt's tongue, the word 'merchant' sounded like a curse.

'You sound as though you don't approve?' she prompted.

'I don't. All he cares about is money.'

'But you think he'll help us?'

'Yes.' The musician grinned. 'He has a soft spot for me – I *am* family, after all.'

'That would be wonderful,' Magara said. 'Thank you. We'll leave first thing tomorrow.' *I hope Newberry forgives me!*

'Right. See you later then.' Hewitt got up and walked to the doorway, hesitated, then turned back. 'By the way, where *are* we going?'

CHAPTER EIGHTEEN

With the problem of finding a mount unexpectedly solved, Magara then had time on her hands. She spent the morning going through her belongings, deciding what to take with her. Wanting to travel with as little as possible, she settled upon a small amount of travel-clothes – plus, of course, the tapestry. This decision was helped by the thought of having Hewitt with her. There was always the chance of a good musician finding work in exchange for bed and board along the way, thus reducing the need to carry their own equipment and provisions. In fact, the more she thought about it, the more Magara liked the idea of his company. What was it Slaton had said of himself as a landowner's son? 'Very good at getting people to work for me.' *Perhaps I haven't lost the knack either.*

Just before noon, as she was thinking over what she should do next, Magara began to feel rather odd. At first she thought it was just tiredness and the heat, but she was soon feeling stranger still, and sat down, thinking she might be going to faint. And then her discomfort became almost tangible. Although she remained conscious of the fact that she was still in her own familiar room, there were other visions before her eyes, other sounds in her ears.

It began with an unearthly wail and a sudden premonition of fear. Then she felt the wind rushing by her face. The acrid smell of smoke was in her nostrils, and she heard a dreadful keening, a sound that went on and on. After that, flames, panic, people everywhere. Blood and terror. The cries of women and children. Soldiers in green headbands. Horrible scenes that she could not shut out.

Keep out of this! A voice she knew.

Having fun? A stranger.

The images of battle fell away, and a deeper fear crept over her. A blue-robed figure shimmered in her lakeside room, outlined in a shifting halo of livid green. The man was looking around at unseen objects, his eyes moving with calm deliberation. His gaze settled on Magara, and he smiled horribly. The malice in his stare made her tremble. Then there was a bright blue flash – and he vanished. The vision passed, but though Magara knew she was safe in her own home, she was left feeling weak and shaky. *Lisle, why are you showing me this?* She knew somehow that she had witnessed Varo, Brostek and their men in battle through the boy's eyes. But the how and the why of it were beyond her. The paralysing fear had gone now, but she felt jittery for some time. If Lisle had indeed faced that terrible blue-robed figure in reality, then he must surely be feeling even worse – and that thought did nothing to allay her fears for the other travellers.

Hewitt returned during the early part of the evening to tell her that he had organized the mounts with his brother, and they arranged to meet again at first light. Magara hid her unease from him, and he went to complete his farewells. Some time later, she heard a tune running through her mind, one that she did not recognize. The music was graceful and elegaic and filled with an eerie, peaceful sadness; it eased her troubled thoughts and stilled her trembling.

She prepared a last meal, then walked outside to see if Talisman was there. The heron was nowhere to be seen, but the starlit lake reminded her of the shatterstone and she went back inside to look at it. Even in the dull lamplight, it was immediately obvious that something was wrong. Unknown to her, the bowl in which she had placed the glistening crystalline structure had been cracked, and the water had slowly drained away. As the divers had told her it would, the shatterstone had disintegrated completely, leaving what looked like a dull pile of sand.

Feeling rather disgruntled, Magara was about to throw the debris away when she noticed something shiny buried in the grit. She pulled it out and wiped it clean, hardly able to believe her eyes. Here, impossibly, were four delicate circles of a silver-coloured metal, each joined to two of the others in a sort of square. It was a perfect miniature representation of the symbol on the slab of rock in the lake. And it had been embedded inside the shatterstone! *So I was right to think it was important*, Magara congratulated herself. It seemed to her that she had been given a beautiful gift by the crater, a lucky charm to take with her on her journey. She felt that she had obviously been meant to find it, and was unreasonably happy that she had done so.

Each of the four 'rings' was the same size, and far too small to fit on even her little finger, so Magara found a thin leather lace and threaded it through one of the circles, then tied it round her neck like a pendant.

Magara slept well that night, ready to face whatever adventures might follow, and for a few hours at least, blissfully unconcerned about the mysteries that continued to surround her.

*　　*　　*

Magara and Hewitt left as planned, at first light the next morning, rising up into the sunlight on the Rim while Trevine remained in the shadow of the far cliffs. To Magara's secret delight, Talisman circled lazily overhead as they made their ascent, bidding her farewell before swooping back down to the lake. Both travellers found it strange to look down on the town from the Rim, and it was hard for them to turn and walk away.

Hewitt proved as good as his word about the horses, though his brother grumbled and fussed, and they were soon on their way north. Magara's plan was simple. They

would head for Arenguard at first, although she had no
intention of actually visiting her old home. From there,
finding Whistling Hill – a place which now intrigued her
greatly – would be easy enough, and thereafter, she
hoped that Iro's brief instructions and the help of local
people would be enough to get them to Nevern. She
refused to even think about what would happen then.

When she told Hewitt of her intentions, he asked her
why they were not going to stop at Arenguard.

'I've borrowed some money from my brother,' he
added, 'but it's not much, and free lodgings are always
welcome when you're on the road.'

'It's a long story,' Magara said wearily.

'We have plenty of time,' he prompted.

So Magara told him of her estrangement from her
family, and of her reluctance to go back unannounced –
especially as she would have to leave again at once on
her strange errand.

'Mind you,' she finished, 'I'd be glad of a few hours in
the library there. You wouldn't believe how many old
books they've got.'

'Why don't you, then?'

'I've just explained that!'

'Then go in disguise,' he suggested promptly. 'Does
your father ever employ musicians?'

'Yes. He likes them, but—'

'Then you can be my assistant,' Hewitt decided,
looking at her speculatively. 'With a beard and the
appropriate clothes, we could make it so that no one
would recognize you. I can play, while you pay a visit to
the library.'

'It'll never work!' Magara told him, laughing at the
very idea. But she was tempted – and Hewitt knew it.

*   *   *

When they mounted the crest which first brought
Arenguard into sight, Magara wanted instinctively to

161

turn away. For a while, the thought of Hewitt's plan had seemed plausible, even fun – and the thought of the library was powerful bait – but now, with the reality only an hour or two away, the whole thing seemed utter madness. While spending the previous night at a tavern, they had completed her disguise, much to the bewilderment of the landlord the next morning. Magara was now dressed in Hewitt's spare clothes, which fitted surprisingly well, but which were even more ragged than the musician's normal attire. Her hair was tied back with a dirty rag and her eyebrows had been darkened and thickened with boot wax. Her face was already much darker than when she had left Arenguard, and it was now covered with an uneven, stubbly beard made of horsehair and stuck on in matted strips with paste. Although it was a different colour from her own hair, Hewitt had pronounced himself satisfied with his creation. Magara felt both uncomfortable and wholly ridiculous, expecting everyone they met to see through the illusion immediately. However, no one had paid her much attention, and for a time she began to feel better. But now, as they neared her old home, she felt distinctly uneasy.

'I'm not sure I can go through with this,' she said.

'You've got no choice,' Hewitt replied cheerfully. '*I'm* going, and I've got your clothes.'

He was wearing one of Magara's shirts, which was more respectable than his own; it combined with his freshly washed, long hair to give him an unconventional but artistic appearance. The rest of Magara's clothes were now hidden at the bottom of Hewitt's saddle-bag.

'Why waste this opportunity?' he went on, clearly relishing the adventure. 'But you'll have to speak in a much lower voice, or pretend to be dumb.'

'I can't imagine why I ever thought I liked you,' she remarked.

'You mean apart from my charm, talent and extraordinary good looks?' he responded, grinning.

You are fully recovered! Magara thought. Aloud she said, 'Don't make me laugh. I can't even smile in this lot without the risk of it all falling off.'

'Don't worry,' he said. 'The only problem you'll have is getting it off afterwards. I take a pride in my handiwork, you know. You may have to stay like that for a while!'

'*Now* you tell me.'

The conversation had done a little to temporarily assuage Magara's feelings of anxiety and guilt, but as they drew even closer, the doubts flooded back and her stomach knotted at the prospect of her deception.

And so it was that, in the late afternoon of another warm and sultry day, Magara returned to her childhood home. A thousand memories assailed her, a mixture of pain and pleasure, sadness and joy. Here were the fields where she had played and learned to ride, the gardens where she had been so careful not to tread on the baby plants, the beehives where she had spent so many happy hours with her grandfather. And closer still she could pick out the individual buildings that made up the sprawling place that was Arenguard: the stables, where she had first seen new life come into the world, watching wide-eyed as a foal took its first shaky steps; the granary and the mill, powered by the great water-wheel with its pond where she had swum each summer; the mass of out-buildings and smaller houses that clustered round the centre; and, of course, the great, two-storey house, with all its extra annexes and wings added by each new generation.

She longed suddenly to see if her room was still as she had left it, to visit the kitchens and her old nursery, to talk to all her old friends, to her family – especially her sisters, whose children must be growing up now. And her parents . . .

'Come on, Gorman. Let's see if they can use our services here,' Hewitt said loudly.

Magara responded belatedly to the name they had

163

agreed on for her, coming out of her reverie and back to the present with a bump. Hewitt had spoken for the benefit of some men who were working in the gardens. As they passed by, she steeled herself to play her role, feeling quite sure that the first person who saw her close to would recognize Arenguard's errant daughter and have her thrown out as unwanted and unpardonably discourteous. Even arriving as her own self would surely not have been as bad as this!

At the entrance to the main courtyard, they were hailed by a burly man whom Magara did not recognize.

'You have business here?'

'Might your master have use for fine music tonight?' Hewitt answered. 'We ask only lodgings and a meal for myself and my servant here.'

The man looked them up and down.

'Wait in the yard,' he decided eventually, and walked away.

They rode in, acutely aware of the regard of several curious onlookers. Magara was hot and perspiring. Her face itched intolerably, and she hoped fervently that her beard would not begin to peel away. The man returned and beckoned to Hewitt. The musician followed him, carrying his viol, while Magara dismounted, trying to be masculine in her movements, and waited with the horses. After a short while, Hewitt returned.

'Put the horses in the stables, Gorman,' he commanded. 'I'll meet you in the kitchens when you've finished tending to them.' He smiled and winked at her.

As Magara led their mounts away, she reflected that Hewitt seemed to be enjoying his new role rather too much.

CHAPTER NINETEEN

Magara trudged towards the kitchens, grateful that dusk had made the day a realm of lamplight and shadows. She had been shown to the stables and told where the horses' food and water were kept – even though she already knew that well enough – and had then been taken to the bunk room which she and Hewitt would share. She was relieved to find that they had been given a private bedchamber; if they had been put in one of the main dormitories, escaping to the library would prove even harder.

Throughout these exchanges, she had answered all queries with inarticulate grunts, and once their gear had been stowed away, the stable boy had seemed glad to point her towards the kitchens and leave the company of the surly stranger.

Inside, the kitchens were much as Magara remembered; steamy, hot, and full of rich smells, ringing with the clash of pans and voices raised against the clatter. Hewitt was already eating, chatting away to the cooks. Magara recognized several of them, and her heart skipped a beat. This was her first real test.

'There you are, Gorman,' Hewitt exclaimed. 'Come and eat. Vale here has provided us with a feast!' He smiled at one of the maids, evidently already under his spell. Magara joined him and sat down wordlessly, her eyes lowered.

'Gorman's a man of few words,' Hewitt explained, 'but I'd be lost without him.'

No one paid Magara much attention, but she was still nervous, expecting to be discovered at any moment. However, the kitchen staff were far more intent on going

165

about their work or talking to the vastly more interesting musician, and did not give his morose servant a second glance. She began to eat, realizing that she was hungry, but found it hard to swallow.

'We've picked a good time, Gorman,' the irrepressible Hewitt went on. 'The master here, Danyel—' Magara flinched at the sound of her father's name, '—has an important guest. What's his name, Vale?'

'Bullen,' the girl answered importantly. 'He's very high up in the Cartel.'

'Some audience, eh, Gorman?'

Magara grunted, wishing he would leave her out of the conversation.

Hewitt grinned. 'It'll obviously take more than that to impress you!' he said jovially. Vale and several others laughed with him.

Magara was feeling increasingly uncomfortable, but knew that Hewitt would keep on until she said something.

'Food's good,' she muttered, in as gruff a voice as she could manage. ''s what matters.'

'Spoken like a true traveller!' Hewitt exclaimed, amid more laughter. 'It *is* good – I'll have some more if I may.' Vale hurried to oblige. 'I play better on a full stomach,' he told her, smiling sweetly.

*　　*　　*

An hour later, Magara lay on her bed, wondering when she should make her move. Hewitt had gone to play, and she had left the kitchens when he did, not wanting to be drawn into conversation. The cooks had paid no attention to her exit, and her confidence in the disguise had risen slightly. Bullen's visit was helpful. It meant that the evening meal would be a lengthy affair, involving most of her father's staff, thus giving her a better chance of reaching the library undetected. She knew that the dinner was well under way now, and as it was already dark outside, there was no real reason for her to delay any longer. The route to the library was clear in her mind. Her first objective would be to gain access to Stead's index; without that, she would have no hope of finding what she wanted in the short time available to her. The old librarian had once been a great friend, appreciating the young girl's love of books, and had shown her the secrets of the great drawers of cards – references to all the volumes in the library, and his life's work. *I hope he still keeps the key in the same place!* she thought, steeling herself to move. *If I'm ever going to go . . .*

She left the servants' quarters, and crossed the courtyard. It was as deserted as she had hoped, and she slipped easily into the alleys that surrounded the main house. Although she was passed by two men, they ignored her, and she was otherwise unnoticed. When she finally arrived at the West Wing, her heart was beating fast with mingled fear and relief. The side door was open, and she slid inside. No lamps burned in the hallway so she stood quite still for a few moments, allowing her eyes to adjust to the faint light that filtered through the windows. Calmer now, she crept along the empty corridor that led to the library.

At last she reached the door she wanted. No light could be seen through the cracks around it. *Please let it not be locked!* she prayed, and turned the handle carefully. With a loud, heart-stopping click, the door opened and she tiptoed inside, closing the door gently. Faint rays fell from a distant skylight, casting a silver glimmer over the library's outer room.

A lamp stood to one side as Magara had expected – old habits die hard – together with chemical tapers to light it. *No going back now*, she thought as the wick flared into life and a yellow glow filled the room.

The cabinets were locked, and Magara glanced up at the small shelf above the door to the main library. As a child, this shelf had always been way out of her reach, and even now she needed a stool to reach it. She climbed

167

up, feeling along the shelf with her outstretched fingers. At last they closed upon the cold metal, and she breathed a huge sigh of relief.

The cabinets and their contents were arranged alphabetically, and Magara went at once to the third one, which began with the letter N. She had three things she wanted to look up; Nevern, eclipses, and the symbol of the four circles. She could not think how to find the last of these, so began with the magical valley. The relevant card was soon found, covered with tiny letters and numbers that referred to the location of the appropriate books in the main room. *So many!* Magara thought helplessly. *How can I hope to read them all? And why don't I remember them from before?* She pocketed the card, then unlocked the first cabinet and began to rifle through the next set of cards.

Echoes, Eclecticism, Eclegme, Ecology . . . *Nothing* about eclipses?

She went through them again, sure that she must have missed the entry. Still nothing. And it would not be like Stead to have misfiled anything. She was just about to widen her search, just in case, when someone spoke, making her jump violently.

'Keep very still. I am armed.' The voice behind her was calm but terribly stern. 'I trust you have a good reason for being here, young man.'

Magara could not speak, could not even think clearly. She stood stock still, trapped in a nightmare, her heart racing.

'Turn around very slowly,' the man ordered, 'and keep your hands where I can see them.'

She did as she was told, dreading the next few moments. She had recognized the voice now.

Stead's eyes narrowed at the sight of the intruder's face. 'Who are you?' he demanded.

For a brief moment, Magara considered trying to keep up the pretence, but she knew it to be hopeless, and gave in to the inevitable.

'Stead, it's me,' she said, in her natural voice. 'Magara.'

The librarian's face registered shock and disbelief, and in the ensuing silence, the war between the evidence of his eyes and his ears was clear in his changing expressions. The long, thin blade in his hand wavered.

'This is stuck on,' she added desperately, touching her face. 'It really *is* me. I still need a stool to get your key down from the shelf.'

Stead glanced at the stool, then the shelf, then back at the intruder. He was obviously still bemused.

'Magara?' he whispered eventually.

'Yes.'

'What . . . ?' Stead began, then was silent again, quite unable to formulate a sensible question.

'I'm sorry,' she said quietly, taking a tentative step towards him. 'I hated to do this behind your back, but—'

'Your family—' he blurted out.

'They mustn't know,' she said quickly. 'Please, Stead. It's very important.'

'But . . .' He was still struggling to come to terms with the situation.

'Shut the door,' Magara suggested gently. 'I'll do my best to explain.'

The librarian turned slowly, closed the door and locked it. Under his practised hand it made no sound. When he turned back he had regained some of his composure, and although his first words were harsh, his actions had already given Magara the hope that he would not betray her.

'What's all this about?' he demanded resolutely. 'Why that ridiculous disguise? You should be ashamed of yourself. In your own home!'

'It's not my home any more,' she said softly.

'It grieves me to hear you say that,' he replied with a first touch of anger. 'Some of the things you've done have been hard to forgive, but you're still a part of this family. This—' He waved his sword at her, indicating her outlandish appearance. 'Kindly explain. And give me one good reason why I should not take you straight to your father.'

'Won't he be too busy with Bullen?' Magara asked without thinking, regretting the words the moment they were out.

'Don't be impertinent, young lady!' Stead half shouted, his face darkening. His bluster was tacit acknowledgement that there was an element of truth in her words, but Magara was quick to try to repair the damage.

'I'm sorry. Let me explain.'

'I'm listening,' he said expectantly, placing his sword on a table.

As concisely as she could, Magara told him about Celia, Nevern and Lisle, and then about Varo and Brostek and their work, the tapestry – which Stead remembered – her mission, and finally the reasons for her disguise. Throughout it all, the old man listened patiently and never interrupted, his face giving nothing away. When she finished, Stead was silent for so long that Magara wondered what he expected of her, and cast around in her memory for anything that she might have missed.

'So you came here,' he said at last, 'to get information about Nevern?'

Magara's hopes leapt. He had accepted her explanation.

'Yes,' she answered eagerly. 'There was nothing in the few books I have. But there's plenty here.' Shamefaced, she pulled the index card from her pocket.

Stead merely nodded, his face serious.

'True enough,' he confirmed. 'Though whether any of it will help your friend is another matter. What else do you need?'

'I need information about eclipses.'

The librarian nodded again, as if he had been expecting this.

'So you're worried about them too?'

'Who else is?' she asked.

'The Cartel,' he replied, surprising her. 'This library is one of the reasons for Bullen's visit. He had the same idea as you, obviously.'

'They're actually taking the eclipses seriously?' Magara could hardly believe her ears.

'They're affecting livestock,' Stead answered. 'Milk yields are down and there have been too many still-births.'

That explains it! she thought cynically.

'Add all that to the wagging of superstitious tongues,' Stead went on, 'and you have a recipe for unrest. The Cartel doesn't appreciate that, and they've been talking about doing something about it for a few hands now. They've got nowhere, of course.'

'Is that why the card is missing?' she asked.

It was Stead's turn to produce a slip from his pocket.

'What have you found out?' Magara wanted to know.

'Nothing. All we have is astronomical detail,' he answered. 'A few facts, based on observation of the skies and the calendar. All we know for certain is that there are far too many of the wretched things. The moon can't be causing them *all*.'

'Then what is?'

'No one knows.'

'What do the wizards think?' she asked, clutching at straws.

'Pah! You know perfectly well that wizards rarely think at all,' he replied. 'They've tried various spells and invocations, so I'm told, but with no success. If this is magic, then it's way beyond them.' His voice was thick with contempt.

Magara could not hide her disappointment as another avenue proved to be a dead end.

'It frightens me,' she admitted quietly. Her sense of foreboding was greater now.

'You're not alone in that,' Stead told her. 'But I don't see what can be done about it.'

'Do you think it might all be connected?' she asked hopefully, longing for some pattern to emerge. 'The eclipses, Nevern, the Knifemen?'

'I don't see how,' the old man said. 'Your tapestry is the only link, and that's tenuous at best. As for the Knifemen, I wouldn't put much store by the tales of mountain folk.'

'But I *know* these people!' she objected indignantly. 'They're not lying.'

Stead shrugged dismissively.

'I still don't see a connection,' he stated.

Lisle, Magara thought. *He's the connection, but how can I explain that?* She felt utterly dejected.

'It's hopeless,' she said miserably. 'I don't even know what I'm trying to do – or why.'

'You're trying to help a friend,' Stead replied. 'Which seems like a good enough reason to me.'

The thought of Celia trapped in that grey valley restored some of Magara's resolve. Here at least was something tangible for her to work on.

'Will you help me then?' she asked hopefully.

'If I can,' he answered. 'I don't approve of your methods, mind you. Sneaking about in this disgraceful way – but you've reasons enough in your own mind at least, I can see that.'

'I'll come back here – properly – one day,' she promised gratefully.

'Be sure that you do.'

'You can even tell my parents about all this if you like, after I've gone,' she went on. 'Though I'd rather you didn't.'

'I don't think they'd take too kindly to my part in your "visit",' he replied, smiling for the first time. 'Best to say nothing.'

'Thank you.'

'May the gods forgive me. Your father probably wouldn't,' he remarked. 'Come on, we've got a lot to do. I assume you'll want to leave first thing in the morning?'

Magara nodded, and Stead picked up the lamp. They went into the main library, a massive hall with countless rows of shelves.

'Why aren't you at the dinner?' Magara asked.

'They've got some young dorkin, smug as you like, screeching away on a viol. I couldn't stand it. Can't think what anyone sees in that racket.'

Magara stored the description away for later use, and was still smiling when Stead ushered her to a table.

'I'll fetch, you read,' he instructed, taking the index card from her. 'It'll be quicker that way.'

*   *   *

Several hours later, irregular piles of books formed battlements on the table around Magara. Her eyes were sore, and there was a dense fog inside her head. Stead was still scurrying back and forth, his speed belying his age, replacing earlier choices on the shelves and finding yet more. Of all the multitude of references, most were only passing mentions of Nevern, from which they learnt little. A few were more expansive, but even these became repetitive after a time. After half a night's work, all the two researchers had really ascertained was that the tapestry almost certainly did depict Nevern. The mage-garden was frequently referred to as a place where all seasons could be found at once, where time passed in a strange, unpredictable fashion, where roses could bloom in the snow and fruit ripen in spring. There were also some pieces about the Guardians of Nevern, wizards or people appointed by them, who cared for the place and chronicled its ever-changing state and the mysteries therein. Magara was convinced that the woman who had created her tapestry must have been one of the Guardians, using her skills to form a lasting portrait of that strange place. She longed to find some mention of the seamstress, to learn her name, but could find nothing that specific.

After the history came the legends, and there were many of those. Most concentrated on the healing powers of Nevern, or on its supposed gift of eternal life to those who either dwelt within its borders or ate of its fruit. Yet more spoke of its extraordinary beauty, which could entrance even the most dour of men. Others were more elaborate, seemingly far-fetched, while some were clearly pure fantasy, but two struck chords with Magara. The first was the oft-repeated statement that only the innocent or pure of heart could find their way to the centre of the garden – an echo of the shadow-maze again. The second was the widely held belief that the world would be safe from evil 'as long as the sun shines on Nevern'. If the garden was indeed under a permanent cloud now – its own unique eclipse – then that boded ill for everyone. This idea, whether myth or not, did little to allay Magara's growing fear.

Midnight had long since passed, and the deepest part of the night held all in its cold, dark spell. The rest of Arenguard had long been abed.

'That's all, I think,' Stead groaned, laying one last tome before her. 'Find anything new?'

Magara had kept him apprised of her findings as she went along.

'No, just more repetition,' she replied, disappointed.

'No sudden blazing revelations then?'

'No.'

'That's usually the way,' he remarked stoically. 'You should get some sleep now.' He sat down heavily.

'You too.'

Stead nodded.

'Thank you,' Magara said with feeling. 'At least this has made me even more determined to go there.'

'Be careful, Magara,' he said, the anxiety showing in his tired eyes. 'I feel responsible—'

'I'll be careful,' she promised.

'To bed then.'

'One last thing,' she said quickly, fishing out the

silvery pendant from beneath her shirt. 'Does this mean anything to you?'

Stead peered at it closely.

'Pretty,' he commented wearily.

'The shape,' she persisted, 'does it *mean* anything to you?'

'Hmmm, yes. Now you come to mention it. Some wizards have used it – it's their symbol for light, I believe.'

'Light?'

'Yes. But that's all I know,' he said. 'Where did you find it? In the belly of a fish?'

'Something like that.'

They both stood up, then embraced awkwardly.

'I won't kiss you,' Magara said, fingering her beard, and they smiled at each other.

*　　*　　*

All about her was still and quiet, and the journey back to her own chamber was uneventful. But when she reached the servants' quarters, she could see that a lamp still burned within her room. She could hear two voices; whispers, sighs, the sounds of movement.

Vale obviously took even more of a fancy to Hewitt than I'd thought!

Quietly, too tired to feel any rancour, Magara retreated. Going wearily down to the stables, she found an empty stall next to their own horses and fell into an exhausted sleep in the hay.

CHAPTER TWENTY

Magara was awoken early the next morning by the usual bustle of the stables. She was cramped and chilled, and was glad when two of the lads suggested that she go with them and take breakfast in the kitchens. The warmth and food were welcome, although she reinforced her reputation for surliness by hardly speaking a word. Hewitt came in later, all smiles and good humour. Much to Magara's disgust – she was now anxious to leave – he ate a hearty breakfast before collecting their belongings and loading the horses.

'How did you get on?' he asked, once they were on their way.

'Not very well.'

'But we're still going to Nevern?'

'Yes.'

Magara did not feel like elaborating, but her answer seemed to satisfy Hewitt's curiosity.

'That Bullen's an arrogant swine,' he remarked happily. 'He talked all through my playing! Still, he's not short of money. Threw this at me.' He held up a large silver coin. 'Had a pet wizard with him, too.'

Magara did not respond, finding his cheerful demeanour repulsive.

'Are you all right?' he asked.

'I've been up most of the night,' she retorted, 'and what little sleep I *did* get was on straw. The pitiful amount I learnt from the library has only made things worse. I feel dreadful about leaving Arenguard like this – and I need to get *this* off!' she added, tugging at her beard. 'Apart from that, I'm fine!'

'Sorry I spoke,' he muttered.

They rode on in silence for a while.

'I'm sorry I snapped at you,' Magara apologized eventually. 'It's not your fault that I have a lot on my mind. Let's find some water. There should be a stream up ahead.'

She had remembered correctly, and they led their horses into a thicket of trees, which was divided by the brook. Magara spent some time washing off her beard and peeling away thin layers of paste. It was a painful process and left her face feeling very sore – which did nothing to improve her temper – but it was an immense relief to be herself again. Then she changed back into her own clothes, with Hewitt decorously turning his back.

'You obviously weren't so gallant last night,' she teased him. 'What if I'd walked in on the two of you?'

'We wouldn't have minded.'

'You exhibitionist!' she accused. 'I'd have got *no* sleep with all the noise you were making!'

'I'm sorry you had to sleep in the stables,' he said, sounding contrite.

'It was comfortable enough,' Magara told him, completing her transformation. 'Let's get on.'

They rode slowly northwards.

'Was it worth it?' Hewitt asked, some time later. 'Going home, I mean.' He sounded genuinely concerned.

Magara thought for a while before replying.

'On balance, yes,' she said eventually. 'It confirmed several things for me, even if I didn't learn anything new. But I won't ever do things that way again. It felt very wrong.'

'It all comes,' he remarked, grinning, 'from choosing irresponsible travelling companions.'

'Especially a smug young dorkin like you,' she agreed.

'A what?'

Magara took great pleasure in explaining.

'Some people have no taste,' was his only comment.

*　　*　　*

They ate their midday meal in the open air, enjoying the food Hewitt had brought with him from Arenguard.

'I can't imagine who provided us with this feast,' Magara said innocently.

'Even dorkins have their uses,' he countered.

*　　*　　*

Dusk saw them arrive at a lonely farmhouse. The haggard wife was only too pleased to provide them with a simple meal and space in an attic room in exchange for a few coins; being a smallholder was no easy life under the Cartel. The shared mattress presented no problems. The travellers were both too exhausted to think of anything but sleep, and in any case, as Hewitt had already pointed out, he did not think of Magara 'in that way'.

They rose early the next morning, and rode on with renewed vigour, knowing that they were near Whistling Hill.

The knoll first came into view about an hour before noon, and even from a distance, the hill had a forbidding aspect. Most of the open land in this part of the country was green and the farmland lush and fertile, but Whistling Hill was barren, almost grey. As they got closer, they could see that the grass was dry and patchy on the upper slopes; even the bracken and heather seemed lifeless.

'There's not much magic *here*,' Hewitt commented as they began to climb.

Magara was inclined to agree, but stubbornness drove her on. The horses plodded slowly towards the top. Although the way was not steep, the climb seemed endless, and a restless breeze made the air feel very cool, in spite of the clear sky overhead.

At last, just as the sun was directly overhead, they

came in sight of the stones – which looked no more magical than their surroundings. But there was mystery here. The stones stood in a ragged circle, some twenty paces across, sentinels that guarded nothing. Within the circle there was only thin, dry grass. Each stone was irregular, worked only by wind and rain, yet each had obviously been placed deliberately and with some precision, part buried in the brown earth.

Magara dismounted and led her horse to the edge of the circle, wondering why anyone would expend such effort in building an apparently pointless monument. She reached out and pressed her palm against the nearest monolith, which stood almost as tall as she did. She half expected some reaction – a tingle, icy cold or heat – but it was just rock, cool and covered in lichen.

Magara stepped within the circle, thinking dejectedly that coming to the hill had probably been a complete waste of time, when the air around her seemed to waver and grow dark. Both horses whinnied nervously, and the chill of the place deepened.

The eclipse came suddenly, but was not complete. Within moments, the sun was reduced to a dark red, lopsided halo that made the stones glow eerily. At the same time, terror filled Magara, and though she remained still, she felt the rush of wind in her face, heard the thunder of hooves. *I don't want to see this, Lisle*, she pleaded silently, but was given no choice.

Another blue-robed figure appeared before her, outlined this time in shimmering crimson. As he stared at her, Magara quailed, but this time the Knifeman's gaze was neither calm nor arrogant. There was a trace of fear in his cold eyes and his body, far from being relaxed, was locked in an unnatural, rigid position. There was a scream and a blur of movement. The man staggered, clutching his shoulder. *Sing, Lisle, sing!* cried an unknown voice. A blinding blue flash. The crackle of fire and the stench of death. Rage like a midwinter storm. A fountain of blood, soaking everything, everything . . .

Red fell to black.

* * *

When Magara came to, she was lying near the centre of the circle. Her head throbbed painfully and her whole body ached. Hewitt was kneeling beside her, offering her water from a flask. Above them, the sun shone serenely in a clear blue sky.

'Drink,' he told her.

'What happened?' she croaked, then sipped.

'The eclipse began just as you went into the circle,' he answered, smiling and obviously glad to see her awake. 'You started shaking and making a *very* strange noise. Then you walked over here and collapsed. My horse nearly threw me and it took me a while to control him, but I got to you as soon as I could.'

'Did you *see* anything?' she asked.

'Like what?' he replied, looking puzzled.

'A man in a blue robe.'

'No.' He was frowning now. 'Did you hit your head when you fell?'

'You saw nothing?' she persisted.

'Only you and the stones in the red light,' he answered, shivering. 'The wind made them wail too – it made my skin crawl. I don't mind telling you, I don't like this place!'

'Me neither,' she said with feeling. *What had happened?* She shuddered at the recollection of all that blood.

'What did *you* see?' Hewitt asked cautiously.

She gave him a brief description of her vision, and then reluctantly explained where she believed it came from. The young musician obviously found her words hard to take in, but recognized her sincerity.

'Let's get you out of here,' he said. 'Can you walk?'

He helped Magara to her feet, then took her arm, and as he guided her out of the circle, Magara felt her spirits lift.

'Do you want to get down off the hill?' Hewitt asked.

'No. I'm all right now,' she reassured him. 'But I'd like to rest for a while.' She was weary now, and was touched by his concern. They reached the horses and sat down.

'No feast today, I'm afraid,' he announced, rummaging in his pack. 'Bread, cheese, water – that's it.' He passed over her portion, and regarded her seriously. 'Are you still sure you want to go to Nevern?'

'Yes.' She began to eat, taking comfort from the plain fare.

'*This* magical place didn't do you much good,' he pointed out. 'Who's to say Nevern won't be worse?'

'Nobody.'

'Then why risk it?'

'I have to.'

Hewitt shrugged, accepting her decision.

'How long will it take us to get there?' he asked.

'Two days or so.' Magara's research in the library had given her a better idea of Nevern's location, but they still did not know the precise route.

They ate in companionable silence for a while, each lost in their own thoughts. Then Hewitt suddenly began to search in Magara's bag.

'I've got an idea,' he exclaimed, pulling the tapestry out and unfurling it carefully. Magara had shown it to him soon after leaving Trevine, and the artist in him had been fascinated by its beauty and originality. 'If you're right about this,' he went on, 'and we approach Nevern from the south, then the view beyond it will be this one.' He pointed to spring. 'That's the one you reckon faces north, isn't it? The skyline is beyond the garden, so it should be visible as we approach. We can look out for it. See the shape here . . .'

Then Hewitt realized that Magara was not paying him any attention. She was looking at another section altogether.

'It's changed!' she blurted out. 'Look!'

At the centre of autumn's setting sun was a small but

definite black dot. The sight made Magara feel quite sick.

'What do you mean?'

'That black dot,' she answered, pointing. 'It wasn't there before. It's the beginning of another eclipse!'

'Oh, come on,' he objected. 'It can't have changed all by itself.'

'It has!' she insisted shrilly. 'I swear. One sun's already been eclipsed, and now there's another one.' She was poring over the tapestry, trying to see if there had been any other changes. She knew she was right about the black dot, but was relieved to see that the other two suns remained unmarked.

'This is ridiculous!' Hewitt exclaimed. 'It's been in your bag the whole time.'

'There!' Magara pointed, her heart sinking even further. 'Remember the white roses in winter? The ones out of season?'

'Yes.'

'Look at them now.'

Hewitt did so – and was rendered speechless by what he saw. Two of the blooms, which had previously been perfect, were now wilting, their petals discoloured, nearly dead.

'Gods!' he whispered eventually. 'That's horrible.'

But Magara had already noticed something else. At the centre of the tapestry, where the four quarters met, was the small pattern of flowers. But now a sort of border had appeared around them, so that they were separated from the pictures in four symmetric curves. Breathlessly, Magara reached into her shirt and pulled her pendant over her head. She laid the silvery metal on the tapestry. The outer shape matched the stitched outline exactly.

'That border wasn't there before,' she told him.

Hewitt was no longer inclined to argue. Indeed, he could not think of anything to say. Magara slipped the pendant back on, feeling shaken and unnerved. This last development had somehow made the dangers in the world suddenly much more *personal*.

'Well, that answers one question at least,' Hewitt said eventually.

'What's that?'

'Magic is *definitely* still alive,' he answered.

'But something is horribly wrong,' Magara added, nodding.

'And if we're going to Nevern,' Hewitt concluded bleakly, 'we'd better get there sooner rather than later.'

They sat for a little while longer, looking for more changes in the tapestry, but it was only when they had given up and were about to be on their way, that Hewitt spotted the last difference.

'Doesn't a rainbow have seven bands?' he asked uncertainly.

Magara looked quickly at spring, and saw that the uppermost arch had disappeared.

'The red's gone!' she confirmed.

Neither of them had any idea what that might mean.

* * *

That night, Magara dreamt of a world lit by a blue sun, but that too meant little, and she forgot about it as their journey continued.

CHAPTER TWENTY-ONE

In the end, it took them almost three days to reach Nevern. They studied the tapestry at each stop along the way, but could see no further changes.

'Do you think the eclipse caused them?' Hewitt asked, 'or was it because we were at Whispering Hill?'

'Perhaps it was both those things,' Magara replied. 'I don't know – your guess is as good as mine.'

As they rode, they asked frequently for directions. Most of the people along the way were surprised that anyone should want to go to Nevern, and regarded the travellers with some curiosity; others professed no knowledge of the place, while the instructions from the locals who were more forthcoming were at best contradictory. Eventually, however, Magara and Hewitt made their way to the valley.

'Does that skyline look familiar?' Hewitt asked excitedly.

Magara nodded, hope – and dread – welling within her.

'It's a good job you had me to find the way for you,' he remarked.

'I don't know *what* I would have done without you,' she replied, trying not to smile.

'Oh, you'd have got here – eventually,' he acknowledged carelessly, 'but you wouldn't have had half as much fun doing it.'

'Or half as much trouble!' she retorted.

'Such gratitude!' he complained, pretending to be offended.

When they finally saw the valley, viewed from the surrounding hills, their mood changed completely. It was as though a gigantic soup bowl had been filled with a pale grey gruel. Even in the strong afternoon sunlight, the place looked cold and still, with none of the beauty of natural, early morning mist.

'How long has it been like this?' Hewitt asked quietly.

'I don't know,' Magara said, trying to remember what Slaton had told her. 'Several hands at least. Maybe even months.'

'I wouldn't want to spend an *hour* in that lot,' he responded, 'let alone a month.'

Magara was beginning to feel the same way, but knew that she had to try. She owed it to Celia, to Lisle and Slaton, and most of all to herself. The two travellers rode on in silence, feeling the atmosphere around them grow oppressive. *No wonder people prefer to ignore this place*, Magara thought gloomily. As they drew closer, they saw that the surface of the fog undulated slowly, like the coils of a giant snake or the swell on a calm sea. It appeared unaffected by wind, and the grey edges remained well-defined and constant.

The horses began to grow fretful, so Magara and Hewitt dismounted, tethering their mounts before going on on foot. It was deadly quiet. There was no birdsong here, and even the sound of the breeze was muted. A few paces from the edge of the fog, they came to a halt and stared.

'Are you really going in there?' Hewitt whispered.

'If I can. Yes.' Magara spoke firmly, refusing to be intimidated by the gloomy silence.

'Then I'm coming in with you,' he said.

'No. Someone has to stay here to look after the horses, and I may need help when I get back out again.'

'You may need help in *there*!' he exclaimed, still not willing to let her go on alone.

'I appreciate the offer,' she said gently, but with great determination. 'But this is *my* task.'

'Spurn me then,' he told her dramatically. 'I shall pine away here until you return.' He gave her a forced smile, but real hurt showed in his eyes.

'Play for me,' she suggested. 'Even if I can't see through the fog, I'll be able to hear you and keep my bearings. Something tells me I'll be glad of a friendly sound once I'm in that lot!'

Hewitt stared at her intently for a moment, then stepped forward and gave her a brief, fierce, brotherly hug. Just as suddenly, he turned away and strode over to the horses, leaving her unable to respond. He unstrapped the viol, then took something from her saddlebag.

'Do you want this?' he called, holding up the tapestry.

'No!' she shouted back. 'You keep it. It'll be no use to me in there.'

Hewitt stowed the roll away again, and returned to her side.

'Now?' he asked.

'Now.' Magara knew that any delay would mean risking the loss of her nerve.

'Good luck,' he said, settling the instrument under his chin.

'I'll see you soon,' she promised, smiling as brightly as she could, then turned towards Nevern.

Hewitt began to play – a lyrical, jaunty tune, quite out of keeping with their situation – and Magara walked through the edge of the mist. Tendrils of grey swirled around her boots; soon she could not even see her own feet. She went on slowly, feeling her way carefully across the unseen ground. The fog crept up to her waist, then covered her arms and chest.

Into the shadow-maze, she thought apprehensively.

Magara took a deep breath and stepped forward. She did not look back.

*   *   *

Hewitt watched Magara's every step, feeling a mixture of terror and sadness as she was slowly enveloped – but kept the music determinedly light. It was a hard task for a musician whose playing was normally shaped by his moods. Soon, only her head remained visible, a golden flower floating on a sea of grey. Then she stepped forward suddenly, and was gone.

At the same instant, the sunlight faltered, and Hewitt looked up in panic, momentarily blinding himself. *No!* he implored silently. *Not now!* He looked back at the spot where Magara had disappeared – but there was no sign of her. *Not now, Magara!* The eclipse grew darker, casting a pall over the uncanny scene. At its height, Hewitt thought the corona was tinged with blue, but he put this down to his overwrought imagination. Then the eclipse was over and the sun reappeared – but the darkness did not leave Hewitt's heart. There was still no sign of Magara.

He played on, but was acting on instinct alone now, his fingers moving of their own accord.

*   *   *

From the moment her head was submerged, Magara was utterly blind. It was not the blackness of true dark that filled her eyes, but a pale, opaque miasma. So sudden was the change that she staggered, instinctively thrusting her hands out in front of her. She could not even see her own arms. Steadying herself slowly, and fighting against the almost irresistible urge to turn round and make her way back to Hewitt, Magara deliberately brought one hand close to her face. Her palm touched the end of her nose – and still she could not see it. She was filled with panic, and again had to stop herself from going back. Then she forced herself to listen to Hewitt's music, to concentrate on that and that alone. It was fainter now, but behind her still. She heard him falter for a moment, play on, and was thankful.

She breathed deeply, overcoming an irrational fear that the mist would poison her lungs, and tried to calm herself. A damp chill began to envelop her, and she felt droplets form on the bare skin of her face and hands. It no longer seemed possible that, somewhere, the sun still shone.

She steeled herself for another step forward, and moved cautiously, her arms outstretched in front of her. For a moment the music grew quieter, then sounded again – but from her left this time – though she was certain that she had not turned. Magara listened for a moment, wondering if the place was in fact turning about her, then decided to trust her own sense of direction. She took another step forward. The music was louder again now – and directly in front of her! *No, that's impossible!* she thought angrily. On impulse, she squatted down, deliberately immersing herself deeper in the maze, and tried to cut out all thoughts of the outside world. *Here you play by Nevern's rules.*

The music vanished, and Magara was enveloped in utter silence. Putting out her hands, she felt the ground beside her, touching grass and the stem of a small flower. *Slaton said it was bare rock.* She broke the stem and lifted it to her nose, inhaling the sharp, slippery tang of sap. *Something still grows here.* Magara tried to smell the flower itself, then sneezed as her nose was tickled by feathery fronds. *Dandelion seeds.* That seemed right for the time of year in the real world, but in the tapestry they had been depicted in spring. *Is that where I am? In spring?* The idea gave her heart. The tapestry had led her to this place. Could it guide her to its centre?

The sudden, sing-song voice of a young girl startled Magara, and her heart raced. The invisible presence drew nearer, accompanied by the sound of skipping footsteps. *It's her! The child in spring.* The words of the girl's repetitive refrain were audible now.

> 'Nature needs no reasons,
> For following the seasons.
> Seed, leaf, flower, fruit,
> Twig, branch, bower, root.'

Magara turned as the little girl went past, longing to see her and to share in her innocent joy. She instinctively tried to follow her unseen companion and took a few hesitant paces, her arms outstretched, but the voice had faded now. *Slow down!* Magara pleaded silently, unable to use her own voice. But to no avail.

Then her hands encountered cold, hard stone, and she stopped suddenly. Its surface was smooth and flat. *The tomb.* Magara shuddered as she ran her fingers along the ridges of the lid, then down to the inscription on the side. She traced out the letters of the well-remembered epitaph.

NEVERN
THE PLACE

    ever
    the time

Follow the seasons, she thought. *So if this is spring, I need to get to summer. And if I'm by the tomb, then I'm in the centre of the quadrant. So which way should I go?*

Over to her left, a fox barked unexpectedly. In the tapestry, the animal had been among the bluebells under the trees, near the left-hand edge of the picture. *So presumably*, Magara reasoned, *I should go in the opposite direction to get to summer.* She turned to her right, and set off carefully. She soon heard the bubbling of a small stream, and felt her boot splash into shallow water. *That's right*, she remembered hopefully. The stream ran from left to right in the tapestry, and reappeared later in summer. She bent down, and checked the direction of the water's flow with her fingers. Then she followed its course, treading cautiously on the wet stones.

After some time, Magara was beginning to wonder whether her reasoning had been mistaken. But then the air grew warmer, and was suddenly filled with the rich scents of summer. Bees buzzed industriously, and birds sang. *If I follow the stream*, Magara decided, *I should reach the ruined building.* But to her dismay the brook vanished; she could not hear it in any direction.

A sudden plop sounded ahead and to the right. Magara realized that this must be the fish flopping back into the pond, and headed towards the source of the noise. She heard the sound of water dripping from the stone fountain and hurried on, anxious to complete the next stage of her journey.

Then she stumbled, tripping over a heavy piece of broken statuary, grazing a knee and both her hands. The fall frightened her badly. Everything had seemed to be going so well, but it was brought home to her again now that she had cast herself adrift in an unknown void – with attendant unknown dangers. Nevern was reminding her not to take anything for granted.

She got to her feet carefully. *Now where?* She dared not think of anything other than how to solve the puzzle. To think of the alternative would be to invite madness.

A sigh of pleasure sounded to her right, and she immediately knew what it was. Magara dearly wished to see the young woman as she stooped to smell the fragrant blooms. She headed towards the source of the noise, knowing that the woman appeared in the foreground of the picture, and would thus lead her to autumn. At one point, Magara even felt the air stir, heard the swish of a full skirt as it passed close by. It was the oddest of sensations, and she shrank back, as if from a ghost. *Does she know I'm here?* she wondered. *Am I a ghost to her?* Magara's pace faltered. *Concentrate!* she ordered herself fiercely. *Keep going!*

A plant crunched under her boot and she knelt to find out what it was, feeling guilty about the unavoidable destruction. The flower was damaged beyond recognition, but beside it, her fumbling hands found several familiar, slim tubular shapes. *Snowdrops*, she thought triumphantly. *The ones that are out of season. I'm nearly there.*

She stood up and went on, then stumbled again and fell. Landing heavily, she was instantly afraid, and near to tears. Then she realized that she had fallen on soft, wet leaves. The air was noticeably cooler now, and damp. *Autumn*, she decided, much relieved, and picked herself up, wiping her stinging hands on her clothes. *Now, how do I find winter?* She remembered that there was a thicket of fir trees straddling both pictures, but she could not smell them. Listening hard, she could hear the faint quacking of ducks, but could not recall where they had appeared in the tapestry. Desperately trying to remember anything else that might be relevant proved hopeless, and she nearly gave way to panic again. She wondered briefly whether she was doomed to wander blindly for ever. *Get a grip on yourself!* she commanded. *Think! What else is in autumn?* She ran through the items in her head: the out-of-season catkins, the squirrel on the apple – neither seemed of any use. The woman here was stationary, gazing up at the swan. *The swan!* In the tapestry, the white bird flew from left to right, towards winter. As if on cue, slow, heavy wingbeats sounded overhead. Magara looked up automatically, but of course saw nothing. She heard the swan approach, pass over and then fly away. She turned to follow the bird's direction. A few moments later, she bumped into a tree, banging her head painfully. She felt better when she knelt to investigate the springy ground underfoot, and found it to be covered with pine needles. Their scent was obvious now. She edged onward, feeling her way between the trees.

Then Magara was suddenly gripped by a real chill; snow crunched underfoot and a wolf howled nearby, making her jump. She was still blind. *I've reached winter. So where is the centre of the shadow-maze?* The wolf howled again, and Magara's skin prickled with fear. Surely the phantom beast could not harm her . . .

Then she remembered the lake, and was suddenly too frightened to move. To fall into that icy water could prove disastrous, even fatal. *What should I do now?* As she despaired, wondering what to do next, the cloying scent of decay reached her nostrils, and her hands sought out and found the dying roses. She pricked an already sore finger on a thorn and sucked it, her lips trembling. *Where now? What more do you want?* she asked desperately.

Hopelessly seeking anything familiar, her hand slipped inside her collar and pulled out the shatterstone pendant. She clasped the metal rings tightly.

For the first time, there was a faint variation within the grey, a silvery glimmer that beckoned her on. Almost hysterical with relief, she stumbled towards the light. The glow brightened, took shape. And she stepped through the shadow-wall . . .

. . . into a beautiful, sunlit garden. Looking around in utter amazement, Magara saw plants and trees that were flourishing, birds and animals that added colour, movement and song to the scene. The fog had completely disappeared.

Magara almost wept with sheer joy. She had done it! She had proved worthy of the test. She could see again – and her voice had come back.

'Celia!' she called, half expecting the woman to appear immediately. 'Celia!'

A voice behind her said, 'Ah, good, you're here at last. I've been expecting you.'

Startled, Magara spun round, then froze in horrified disbelief. The blue-robed man was smiling, but his violet eyes were colder than ice.

PART FOUR

THE DANCE
OF DEATH

CHAPTER TWENTY-TWO

None of them had ever experienced so complete a blotting out of the sun before. The only light came from a thin red corona – all else was darkness. Each of the riders looked up into the sky while Lisle continued to scream and Slaton tried in vain to calm him. The boy's violet eyes were open wide as he stared fixedly at a copse of trees about a hundred paces ahead of them. His cousin tried to see what was so obviously terrifying his young charge, and glimpsed an eerie red glow amongst the shadows. The incarnadine light pulsed dully under the trees, just to the side of the track.

'Look!' Slaton yelled, pointing. 'Over there!'

A single glance was all that Varo and Brostek needed, and they spurred their horses on, charging recklessly in the midnight gloom. The rest of the group followed. When the leaders were as close to the light as the trail would allow, they brought their mounts skidding to a halt. Varo dismounted, drawing his sword in the same movement, and launched himself into the thicket. Brostek was close upon his heels. The others followed, but were already some paces behind. Slaton and Lisle remained in the saddle, Lisle trembling violently.

No more than twenty paces from the track, the trees stood around a small circular glade. At its centre was a man, standing in an awkward, rigid pose, his blue robes, bare head and outstretched hands outlined in a shimmer of crimson – a spectral echo of the sun's unnatural halo. Around his neck was a pendant in the shape of a capital M, elongated vertically and underlined. It was one of the symbols the men had grown to loathe. The Knifeman was shouting angrily, and his face twitched violently.

Unlike the calm contempt which had marked the gaze of his colleague in Grassmeer, these eyes held fear as well as malice.

When he saw the approaching swordsmen, he roared with rage, filling the air with vile threats and the promise of unimaginable horrors. All but Varo faltered at the cry, and even he only managed a few steps more, just reaching the edge of the clearing. There, his limbs became as heavy as lead, and his whole body was suffused with a terrible weariness. His strength deserted him; he could not move. His companions suffered the same fate – all were held motionless, cursing and struggling but to no avail. As he waited for release, Varo's face remained impassive, cold hatred burning in his eyes.

The Knifeman's gaze swept the others in the band, settling on someone to the rear. His fear intensified and more dreadful syllables filled the air as he appeared to struggle with the invisible bonds that held him captive. And still he stared at the back of the group, gimlet eyes boring through the darkness.

Lisle screamed, but the noise he made was unlike any human sound. It was a long, pure, drawn-out note, composed solely of pain. It was the music of madness. As the noise cut through the murk, each man felt a moment's respite in the restraining force, and one of them at least had time to act. An arrow flew from Hawk's bow, a red blur in the false night. In spite of his last-moment attempts to ward it off, the bolt caught the Knifeman in the shoulder. And this time it slammed into real flesh. Their blue-robed enemy staggered, clutching at the wound, but he still yelled angrily, trying to keep his hold over his attackers – though it was evident that the effort to do so was becoming more of a struggle.

From the gloom, Keredin's voice was raised in an agonized, half-strangled shout.

'Sing, Lisle. Sing!'

The boy instantly set up an unearthly keening, his

voice rising and falling like a siren of death. All those who heard him shuddered, but the effect on the Knifeman was remarkable. The last threads of his control fell away and he screamed incoherently, ravening eyes seeking out his nearest foe. He raised his good arm dramatically, pointing straight at Varo. The men were suddenly released from their paralysis, and were about to react when they found that another had reacted even faster.

Shadow leapt from the undergrowth and sprang at the Knifeman like an avenging fury. Her savage jaws closed on the sorcerer's neck as blue fire erupted from his fingertips. Unbalanced by the unexpected attack, the thunderbolt flew wide of its mark. Pine needles crackled and blazed, and a man cried out in mortal agony.

The Knifeman spun round, flinging the wolf from him – though the ugly tears in his neck were already bleeding profusely – and prepared to attack a second time. But he was too late. Free now, Varo whirled round like an acrobat; his blade sliced round like a midwinter scythe of doom, slashing into his enemy's neck. The blow was so violent, yet so precise, that the Knifeman's head was completely severed and sent spinning into the air. His body remained standing for a few moments, as though it were not sure what it should do next. Its red corona vanished as it collapsed to the ground. The head landed with a dull thump an instant later.

And the sun shone again, illuminating a scene of pure horror. As blood fountained from the terrible wound, sheeting out in all directions, Varo was drenched within moments. Soon the entire glade was glistening red, yet the deluge did not stop. The onlookers retreated in revulsion as the impossible geyser continued to spew forth. It was as though the earth itself were bleeding. By the time the repulsive bloodfall abated, so much blood had been spilled that it seemed like the massacre of a hundred men; the stench of it filled the onlookers' nostrils. Only the sorcerer's still-staring eyes were not coated in red – and the dead man's glare of accusation added a final macabre touch to the scene.

The tree that had been set ablaze by the sorcerous fire was charred and smoking now, but the fire had been quenched. Kerwin, who had caught the blast meant for Varo, was dead, his once restless eyes reduced to pools of dark ash and his body burnt almost beyond recognition. As they began to recover from the shock, the others dragged his remains away from the vile clearing. No words were exchanged as his friends prepared to bury him on the far side of the track.

Varo was left alone, staring at the glade. Although his face betrayed no emotion, he seemed unable to move, and was eventually pulled away by Brostek. Silently, the two men went in search of water to rid themselves of the all-engulfing red. Some time later, with the worst of the stains removed, they joined the others by the trail. Slaton and Lisle were out of the saddle now. Lisle had stopped singing at the moment of the Knifeman's execution, keeling over in a dead faint. Slaton had stopped him from falling, and someone had helped them both to the ground. When the boy had come to, his eyes had been helpless and afraid, but he was calm now. He even smiled.

'He recovers quickly,' Vilman remarked admiringly.

'His memory doesn't work like ours,' Slaton told him. 'To him, *that* may never have happened.' He waved a hand towards the glade.

'A useful trick,' Bair said.

'How did you know to get him to sing?' Varo asked Keredin.

'I've seen that sort of holding spell before,' the ex-wizard explained. 'But only the most powerful of my former colleagues could manage it, and then only on one person at a time.' Such talk of wizardry would normally have been greeted with sarcasm and outright derision, but everyone there had felt the force of the sorcerer's power. 'The theory is that each human mind is part of the Link,' Keredin went on, 'the network of the world. If you have the strength to alter the Link itself, pervert it to your own ends, then you can act on another person's mind and so control his body.'

'But Lisle?' Varo prompted as the others considered the ex-wizard's words.

'Evidently, something in Lisle's mind – or perhaps something missing from it – makes it impossible for him to be controlled as we were. Or perhaps controlling him would just take too much power,' Keredin replied thoughtfully. 'In any case, Lisle was obviously the one who most frightened the Knifeman, and we all felt the release when the boy screamed that first time. I just took advantage of that.'

'Good thinking,' Ross put in.

'And you moved pretty fast, Hawk,' Ryker commented. 'That was a good shot.'

'No,' the archer replied earnestly. 'A good shot would have taken him in the heart, head or neck. And Kerwin would still be alive,' he added bitterly.

'We don't *know* that,' Brostek said firmly. 'We don't understand magic like that.'

'Kerwin was just unlucky,' Keredin explained. 'The blast that killed him was a desperate last resort to random power.'

'But why was the Knifeman stuck here in the flesh?' Varo asked, still hungry for understanding. 'Why was *he* vulnerable when the man at Grassmeer wasn't?'

'I wish I knew,' Keredin answered.

'Could it be because of the eclipse?' Ross said eagerly. 'There was a red ring around the sun, and he was surrounded by a sort of red aura.'

'There must be a connection,' Brostek agreed, 'but why should that make him vulnerable?'

'Who cares?' Vilman exclaimed suddenly. 'Aren't we all being just a bit defeatist about this? The point is, we *got* one of them! We should be rejoicing!'

199

'We still have six to go,' Varo told him evenly. 'When they're all dead, *then* we'll rejoice.'

'Well, it's still better than anything we've managed before,' Vilman responded sullenly.

'If they all come to such a sticky end,' Ryker said, his eyes agleam, 'we'll have quite a show before we've finished. Did you see his head?' With one hand he mimicked the spinning arc of the sorcerer's skull.

Varo abruptly turned and walked away. After a moment's hesitation, Brostek followed, leaving the others to continue their discussion. He found Varo at the edge of the fateful glade, staring in disbelief. The corpse of the Knifeman was now a blackened, rotting husk, hardly recognizable as human. But the shock of that ugly putrefaction was nothing beside the fact that every drop of blood had vanished. Everything that had been coated and dripping red a mere hour earlier was now unstained, as though nothing had happened.

*   *   *

That night, Keredin felt himself being shaken awake by hands that were gentle but urgent on his shoulder. He felt a tingle of unease as he saw the glow in Lisle's strange eyes.

'What do you want?' he whispered.

Lisle's head nodded awkwardly, and he pulled insistently at the ex-wizard's arm. Keredin got up, wrapped a blanket around himself, and followed the beckoning Lisle to the slow-burning campfire. Bair and Langel, who were on watch, noticed the movement and came to join them.

'What's up?' Bair asked curiously.

'I don't know,' Keredin replied. 'Lisle woke me up. He wants something.'

The young musician pointed waveringly at the glowing embers of the fire, then flapped his arms upward, making whooshing noises with his tongue. It was a grotesque performance, but its meaning was clear.

'You want flames?' Keredin asked.

'Play,' Lisle said, nodding urgently. 'Play.'

'Wake Varo and Brostek,' Bair whispered. 'Quick!' Langel hurried to obey.

Lisle picked up his lute and settled himself, sitting cross-legged and waiting patiently, his eyes fixed on the smouldering remains of the fire. Varo, Brostek and Slaton, who had also been roused, soon gathered round, asking quietly what was going on.

'I don't know,' Keredin told them. 'Lisle wants some flames.' He had no need to remind them of the last time this had happened. 'It's obviously important to him.'

'Go ahead,' Varo said softly, no trace of sleep left in his voice or his eyes.

Keredin performed what he called his 'party piece', and orange flames burst from the embers. As they cast their flickering shadows far and wide, Lisle played a lightning fast sequence of notes, without tune or rhythm, but with a beauty and power all of its own. To the onlookers' astonishment, the flames responded, first slowing down and then becoming fixed and still, as though frozen in time. But Lisle continued playing, fast and then slow, sometimes mellow, sometimes discordant; his music seemed to mould the captive flame. A ball of fire formed in mid-air, darkened, then turned blue.

'An eclipse!' Langel breathed.

Below the blue sun another picture formed, overlaying the fire. As Lisle's music went on, the onlookers saw a miniature green hill, a tall grey tower on its summit. The top of the tower was in ruins, though the rest of the structure appeared sound enough. It was the haunt of rooks, tiny black specks that wheeled about the turret. The image was so real that the watchers each felt as though they could have reached out and touched it. Then, suddenly, it was gone. The normal red glow of the embers returned and silence claimed the night once more.

'Play,' Lisle said, in a satisfied tone. 'Play.' He looked at Keredin, Varo and Brostek in turn, as if expecting a response.

'You want us to go to this place?' Varo asked.

Lisle nodded, his expression alternating between pleasure and fear.

'Is that where the next eclipse will be?' Brostek ventured.

Lisle just looked at him, wide-eyed.

'Did anyone recognize that place?' Varo demanded, looking round.

'It looked like the tower above Jordanstone,' Bair replied, 'but when we were there last it was whole. *That* place was half ruined.'

'I remember it now,' Varo said. 'Anybody got any other ideas?'

'Could be Aberr,' Langel suggested.

'No, the tower there looks pretty similar, but it's surrounded by other buildings,' Bair pointed out. 'Jordanstone is the only place I can think of where the tower is out on its own like that. I'll get my map. Perhaps Lisle will recognize something.'

They showed the map to Lisle, hoping for some sort of confirmation, but either he did not see the place he wanted or the concept of a map meant nothing to him. After a few moments he ignored the chart completely, and kept pointing to the fire, growing somewhat distressed. Bair gave up.

'What do we do, then?' Brostek asked.

'We go to Jordanstone,' Varo replied firmly. 'As fast as we can.'

CHAPTER TWENTY-THREE

Jordanstone was to the south-west, no more than twenty leagues away as the crow flies. It was much further on horseback, however, because the route crossed two jagged ridges that ran down from the high mountains and in that terrain, many detours were necessary. Lacking any proper tracks, speed was difficult at the best of times. The men travelled as quickly as they could, but as darkness fell two days later, they had still not reached their destination. Brostek gave vent to his frustration, knowing that the tower was probably only a short distance away, but Varo remained calm, and ordered the men to make camp. He knew that trying to travel through that boulder-strewn landscape in the hours of darkness would be to invite disaster.

Throughout the night, the lookouts reported seeing strange lights, flares and flashes, coming from the direction of Jordanstone. Although this increased the group's anxiety to get there as soon as they could, they were helpless until dawn. And as luck would have it, sunrise the next day was later than normal as – for the first time in several hands – dark clouds rolled down from the mountains and the sun was hidden behind banks of grey. Thunder growled overhead as the rain came, warm torrents that lashed down in the wanton fury of a summer storm. The ground underfoot was made even more treacherous, and the last league of their journey seemed to take an age.

As they neared the hill at last, it became clear that further caution was necessary. A large number of men could be seen on the slope below the tower, so, leaving their horses with the others, and keeping to the shelter of woodland, Varo, Brostek, Bair and Hawk crept forward to get a better look. The rain had stopped now, but the air was still moist, and the muddy ground glittered in the new-born sunlight.

'The village is on the far side of the hill?' Varo asked, and Bair nodded.

'Yes,' the veteran replied. 'They may not even have seen them yet.'

'They *must* be aware of that lot!' Brostek exclaimed. 'There's too many of them to miss! And what about all those lights in the night?'

'Can you see headbands?' Bair wanted to know.

'Yes. Blue,' Hawk confirmed. Although his was the sharpest eyesight in the group, Varo and Brostek had both seen enough to agree with him.

'But no blue robes,' Varo said.

'What are they doing?' Bair asked, squinting into the distance.

'Nothing much,' Hawk replied. 'There doesn't seem to be much organization up there.'

'Then we have work to do before that happens,' Varo said. 'Let's get going.'

'There's a lot of them,' the old soldier said warily. 'More than we've ever seen before. Must be fifty or more.'

'And there's only twelve of us,' Brostek added. 'Thirteen if you count Slaton.'

'Fourteen,' Varo corrected him. 'In this fight, Lisle may be the best soldier we have. Remember his song?'

'The Dance of Death,' Hawk quoted grimly.

They made their way back to the others, and Varo began to issue instructions. Ross and Rogan were detailed to ride in a wide arc to warn the villagers – if they were not already aware of their peril. The rest of the group would also circle round to the other side of the hill, and try to gain the advantage of the high ground before beginning any attack.

'Is the tower intact or broken?' Slaton asked as they set off.

'The top's in ruins,' Hawk replied. 'Lisle got that right. Looks as though a lot has happened here since our last visit.'

They rode on slowly, using what cover they could – partly for their own protection and partly to allow the twins enough time to reach the village. The riders all glanced frequently towards the enemy when the terrain allowed, but the blue-banded raiders gave no sign of spotting the horsemen.

'They haven't even got any sentries posted!' Langel noticed incredulously.

'Easy pickings then,' Ryker commented.

'No real sport in that,' Vilman added with disgust.

'Don't be so sure,' Bair reprimanded them sharply. 'That sort of thinking can get you killed.'

They managed to get all the way round to the far side, in sight of the village – which appeared very quiet, without any reaction from the enemy – and were thus able to begin their climb out of sight of the raiders' camp. But before they reached the top, Ross and his twin rejoined them.

'Well?' Varo prompted.

'There's no one there,' Ross answered.

'No one at all?' Brostek glanced down at the village.

'Are we too late?' Varo asked.

'I don't think so,' Ross said. 'There were no signs of any fighting, and none of the houses is damaged or burnt. But we found this.' He handed Varo a ragged piece of parchment on which a message had been scrawled.

'"Master Wizard. It's in the tower. Save us."' Varo read.

'It was nailed to a post in the main street,' Ross added. 'Couldn't miss it.'

'What's in the tower?' Brostek asked as they all looked towards the lonely building.

'I don't know,' Ross answered, 'but it's my guess the villagers all simply ran away from it.'

'And is it – whatever *it* is – still in the tower?' Varo wanted to know.

'It looks deserted now,' Brostek replied. 'I'll go and take a look. You two come with me,' he added to the twins, then turned to Varo. 'Tell Hawk to cover us.'

'Can you get in without being seen?' Varo asked, indicating the troops on the far side of the hill.

'I think so. We'll go carefully.'

He and the twins set off on foot, while Varo went back to report to the others. The group watched their friends' progress nervously, ready to go quickly to their aid should it prove necessary.

Brostek reached the door of the tower in a crouching run, using the dark, silent building itself to screen himself from the army below. Ross and Rogan were close behind, their swords already drawn. Nothing stirred within, but the stout wooden door hung askew on its hinges. Beyond it lay total darkness.

'On my count,' Brostek whispered. He held up three fingers, then two, then one. As the last finger closed into his fist, the twins reacted in unison as always, flinging back the door and springing to guard either side of it, their backs against the inside wall. Brostek went in low at the centre, his blade at the ready, and quickly scanned the gloomy chamber. It was empty.

The only sound was the constant drip of water, coming from above. A stone staircase led to the next level, and Brostek led the way cautiously, peering up through the bannisters. What he saw made his blood run cold, but it was obvious that the room's occupant presented no threat. The man was seated in a chair as though merely resting, but his face was frozen in abject terror, his eyes almost popping from their sockets, his hands clamped tightly over the armrests. Whatever had caused his death, it had clearly been neither easy nor painless. The twins pressed up behind Brostek, staring as they entered the room.

'Go on up,' he told them. 'I don't think there's anyone else here, but check it all. I want to take a closer look at him.'

The brothers obeyed, and Brostek was left alone with the macabre corpse. Except for the multi-coloured cape often affected by wizards, the man wore ordinary travelling clothes. There was no sign of physical injury anywhere. Whatever – or whoever – had killed him, had used more subtle means. *Master Wizard. It's in the tower*, Brostek thought. *But you weren't even able to save yourself*. He caught sight of a chain around the corpse's neck and pulled it out. It held a pendant, in the shape of four touching circles. It proved impossible to slip the chain over the dead man's head so, with a silent apology, Brostek broke it and pocketed the necklet. Ross and Rogan returned.

'It's empty,' Ross said. 'The top part's wrecked – looks like there's been a fire. And the rain's got through on to everything.' The brothers both cast worried glances at the dead body.

'Could you see anything of that lot below?' Brostek asked.

'Of course,' Ross answered, brightening a little. 'They're still in their camp, such as it is. They seem to be wandering about aimlessly, but they're staying within a certain area. There are no fires, no tents.'

'No noise,' Rogan added tersely.

'That's right,' Ross went on. 'There's no conversation, no orders, nothing. It's weird. And they obviously haven't a clue that we're here.'

'Good,' Brostek responded. 'Let's get back.'

They left the tower quickly, glad to get into the open air. Joining the others, Brostek made his report.

'If there *was* a Knifeman here,' he concluded, 'then he's gone now.' Rogan nodded in confirmation. Brostek took the pendant from his pocket. 'The dead man was wearing this. Does it mean anything to you, Keredin?'

The ex-wizard reached out, then withdrew his hand suddenly.

'What's the matter?' Varo asked sharply.

'I don't want to touch it,' Keredin replied. 'It might release powers I can't control.'

'Explain,' his leader demanded.

'That symbol stands for light,' Keredin went on. 'But it was also the sign used by an ancient group of wizards who were convinced that they had to be ever-vigilant against an evil darkness. They believed it could destroy the world. The wizards of light were supposed to be very powerful, but I thought they'd died out centuries ago.'

'Perhaps not,' Brostek said quietly, looking at the pendant with renewed interest.

'But if the dead man *is* one of them,' Keredin went on shakily, 'then either they're no longer powerful, or *it* is more terrible than we can imagine.'

'The Knifemen are pretty terrible,' Langel pointed out.

'Well, whatever *it* is, Knifeman or not,' Varo said, 'it's gone now. And we have work to do. Let's clean up that maggot hill.'

There were general murmurs of agreement and they mounted up. Slaton and Lisle were told not to go any further than the crest.

'If Lisle feels like singing, then that's fine by me,' Brostek commented. 'But we want you both to stay out of harm's way.'

Slaton knew better than to object, and kept to the rear as the group walked their horses towards the hilltop. At that point, further stealth was meaningless, and all but Slaton spurred their mounts into a furious charge down the grass-covered slope.

The enemy did not react immediately. There seemed to be no one in any position of authority, and though each man registered alarm, there was no attempt to organize a concerted defence. Varo accounted for five soldiers before they had had a chance to seize their weapons, and his fellow riders exacted a fearful toll in that first rush. Then Slaton, watching from above, found it difficult to follow what was happening. Varo and his men seemed to move through a swirling mass of soldiers, each wearing a blue headband marked with a symbol that looked like a T set above and touching an O. Some tried to escape, but Hawk's arrows accounted for most of them. A few managed to reach the shelter of nearby trees, but the vast majority stood and fought, as if they had no other choice. Although their numbers were greater, the individual soldiers were no match for their mounted assailants, veterans now of many such encounters.

Varo was a white whirlwind of death, his expression one of icy calm as he scythed his way through the enemy ranks. Brostek and Shadow made a formidable pair, man and beast working as a team to disconcert and then destroy their foes. As usual, the twins fought together in a ferocious assault, in which each knew the other's moves even before they were made. Keredin, Bair and Langel also made an effective unit, but Ryker and Vilman chose to pursue their individual, murderous courses. Jed and Chase fought together, but without their former comrades, they seemed ill at ease, and even got in each other's way at times. Before the battle was over, Jed had taken a spear thrust in the back and had fallen from sight, and Chase had suffered many wounds.

Lisle watched the fighting silently, apparently quite calm. Slaton sensed that the end was near now. The last resistance had broken, and the few remaining soldiers were either cut down, joining the litter of bodies on the field, or had fled – to be hounded mercilessly by Hawk and the ever-eager Ryker. Then Slaton's attention was drawn elsewhere as a sudden flare of blue light erupted from within the upper levels of the tower. Lisle screamed, and Slaton yelled at Varo and Brostek, trying at the same time to control his frightened horse.

A cry of rage came from the tower, and another flare burst forth, lower down this time. All the riders who could do so now abandoned the battle, leaving the last

209

of the stragglers to flee, and made their way up to the tower.

Another flash, this time accompanied by a deafening thunderclap, roared out from the base of the tower. The remains of the door flew out on a wall of blue flame, and Slaton's mount reared, almost unseating his riders. Moments later, as Slaton controlled the terrified creature with difficulty, a Knifeman strode out into the open, his blue robes flying in the wind. Slaton could have sworn that no one had entered the tower during the battle, and it had certainly been empty earlier – but that mattered little now. The sorcerer looked round, stared at Slaton and Lisle, then glanced down at the horsemen labouring up the slope.

'Sing, Lisle,' Slaton hissed, but his cousin did not react.

The Knifeman laughed, seemingly unconcerned by the loss of his men, and stood with his hands on his hips, watching his would-be attackers with contempt. Hawk's arrow flew – as true as ever – but the sorcerer did not even blink when it passed right through his skull. Instead, he waved his hands and blue fire leapt up, spitting and crackling in a circle about him. The riders' charge faltered and died as their mounts shied away from the blaze.

Lisle chose that moment to begin his song. It was a sweet, haunting melody without words, and seemed oddly familiar to some of his companions. The Knifeman gazed at the boy, fascinated but obviously unperturbed.

'Very pretty,' he acknowledged patronizingly, then his eyes narrowed and his voice grew harsh. 'Especially from such an empty head.' He listened for a few more moments, while all around him waited breathlessly, then commanded, 'Enough!' He waved a nonchalant hand again, and Lisle fell silent. And the world about them changed . . .

The afternoon sun, which until now had been clear and strong in the rain-washed air, darkened a little. The

Knifeman looked up, and worry flickered in his eyes for an instant. Brostek felt his pocket grow hot, and pulled out the broken chain. He held both ends so that the pendant would not fall, and was astounded to see that the silvery metal was glowing with a fierce white light – clearly far too hot to touch.

'No!' the Knifeman roared, still staring up at the sky. 'It's too soon. You gave me your word!' He snarled with rage, uttering the most appalling oaths.

The sun turned blue.

Then darkness fell, leaving a blue halo in the sky, mimicked by the fiery outline of the now-transfixed sorcerer. The only real light was shed by the metal symbol held by Brostek.

'Now!' Keredin cried. 'This is our chance!'

The riders all started forward in the half-light. Fear filled the Knifeman's face now, replacing the earlier anger. He muttered darkly, and blue balls of flame grew in each of his palms, then flew towards the riders. The first shot was aimed at Brostek, but an answering flare of white came from the pendant and diverted the flame, sending it spinning up into the sky.

Lisle was singing again now – the same, ghostly tune – and this prompted the second thunderbolt to be directed at him. His horse reared and the flame caught Slaton instead, flinging both him and Lisle to the ground. Then it turned and sped towards the other riders, who scattered in panic. Rogan was caught and thrown down before the fire lost its power.

By then, Brostek and Varo had mastered their horses and were charging at their enemy. He stared at them venomously but had no chance to launch the growing fireballs in his palms. Two swords flashed down and the paralysed sorcerer fell to the ground. As the sun reappeared, his two attackers quickly retreated, expecting the worst, then wheeled back to watch the results of their work.

The Knifeman's gaping wounds did indeed pour forth

untold quantities of blood, but this time it flowed straight *upwards*, into the air, where it vanished without trace.

The onlookers watched, horrified but mesmerized, until the cries of distress from their comrades drew them away.

CHAPTER TWENTY-FOUR

It was a sombre group that took advantage of Jordanstone's empty homes that night. Although they had succeeded in routing the ill-prepared enemy force, and had killed a second hated Knifeman, they had also suffered heavy casualties of their own. Jed had still been alive when they found him, but had died before they had been able to move him from the bloodstained field. Chase was so badly wounded and had lost so much blood that Keredin – who was himself unscathed – did not expect him to survive the night.

Rogan too was barely alive. His clothes and hair had been singed by the sorcerous fire, and the skin of his face burnt pink, but these injuries were not enough to explain his state. The quieter of the twins was deeply unconscious, his body cold and limp. His breathing was the barest whisper, his pulse was weak and slow, and nothing anyone could do provoked the slightest reaction. Ross, who had suffered only minor cuts and bruises, was struck dumb by his brother's plight, and remained constantly by his side.

If anything, Slaton was in an even worse state. He too was in a coma that could not be explained by the light burns on his face and left arm – and he had also bruised himself very badly when he had fallen from his horse. Slaton showed no sign of regaining consciousness; the blue fire evidently did more than just burn.

Miraculously, Lisle had remained physically unharmed, but he seemed to be in a world of his own. The boy stared into space, seeing nothing and reacting to nothing. The only way to move him was actually to manhandle his unresisting form, and they had had to carry him down from the hill. Now he lay on a bed next to his cousin, gazing at the ceiling and shivering spasmodically. Every so often, his lips would work feverishly and a strangled whisper would emerge – but no one could understand what he said.

Brostek's left hand was badly burnt, damaged by the white light that had flared from the pendant, but he was otherwise unharmed. Bair had a deep gash running the length of his right forearm, and his sword hand was swathed in bandages, effectively useless. The others had been luckier, escaping with only small injuries at most, all easily patched up.

With Bair partially incapacitated, it was Keredin's responsibility to tend to the wounded. They had all been gathered into the largest house in Jordanstone, with Varo and Ross willing helpers. The other four men had been left to find their own accommodations. The ex-wizard was kept busy until dusk, but then there was little more that could be done. After tending to their obvious physical injuries, he knew that he had no idea how to treat Slaton, Rogan and Lisle. All that their friends could do was wait and hope.

'I'm going up to the tower,' Keredin announced wearily. 'I want to take a look at that wizard.'

'I'll come with you,' Varo said, picking up a lamp.

The two men went out, waving to Hawk and Vilman, who were on watch at either end of the village street, and began to climb the hill. Near the tower, they stopped to look at the Knifeman's corpse. It was blackened now, decomposing horribly – which was no more than they had expected.

'We must burn that,' Keredin stated. 'Or it could infect the village.'

'I'll see to it,' Varo replied.

They went on to the tower. The empty doorway led into a room in which all the stone had been blackened and everything else reduced to ash. Treading carefully, they climbed the stairs to find that the upper chamber had also been burnt beyond recognition. The wizard's chair was merely a remnant of charred wood, on which a dark skeleton still sat. A few black shreds of flesh clung to the bones.

'We won't learn much from *that*,' Keredin remarked.

'Why would the Knifeman have done this?' Varo wanted to know. 'What would be the point?'

'Too much power for his own good?' the former wizard wondered aloud. 'Or perhaps he just didn't like this place.'

They went up to the higher levels, but found nothing of note.

'How do you think he got in here?' Varo asked. 'I'm certain Slaton would have warned us if he'd come in during the battle, and the tower was empty before that. There's nowhere he could have hidden.'

'I have a theory about that,' Keredin said thoughtfully. 'But the pieces don't all fit together yet.'

'Tell me what you know.'

'I don't *know* anything. I'm just guessing.'

'Whatever.' Varo managed to show no sign of impatience.

'I'll tell you as we go,' Keredin said. 'We need to get some wood.'

They went down the stairs and retraced their steps to the village.

'I believe that what we normally see as the Knifemen are simulcrums, or wraiths,' the ex-wizard began. 'A sort of mirror-image, if you like. While the real sorcerer is somewhere else entirely.'

'In Bari?'

'That's as good a guess as any.'

'Which means that they are invulnerable here,' Varo concluded.

'Yes,' Keredin replied, 'except that during an eclipse they actually become *real*.'

'We've proved that twice now,' Varo said, nodding.

'Somehow,' his companion went on, 'while an eclipse

215

is taking place, either both "halves" become real, or the genuine man transfers to his double.'

'I hope it's the latter,' Varo said seriously. 'I'd hate to think we'd only killed half of those two.'

'I don't think they'd have been so obviously frightened if that was the case,' Keredin responded.

'If it's so dangerous for them,' Varo said, 'then why do they appear during the eclipses at all?'

'The two we've just met didn't seem to have much choice. They certainly didn't seem too happy about it.'

'You mean they may have been trapped?'

'Possibly.'

'But who would want to trap them?'

'I don't know.' Keredin paused as another thought occurred to him. 'On the other hand,' he said, 'perhaps they *need* the eclipses.'

'What for?'

'*That* is the all-important question.'

'But the eclipses are tied in with the attacks on the villages,' Varo said.

'So it would seem,' Keredin replied. 'Perhaps they're some sort of preparation for whatever vile rituals the Knifemen perform.'

'The draining of blood,' Varo said coldly. 'Those two certainly had enough inside them.'

'But not any more,' Keredin commented wryly.

'Where did it go, do you think?'

'I can't even begin to *guess* the answer to that.'

They had reached the village now, and went in search of a wood store. Collecting two armfuls, they set off back up the slope.

'Then there's the different colours,' Varo prompted. 'The light of the eclipse and the light round the Knifemen correspond – and so do the soldiers' head-bands.'

'I think the eclipses must be specific to each man,' Keredin replied slowly. 'The last two were the darkest and most complete we've ever seen. Correct?'

'Yes. Easily.'

'And each time we've been very close to the sorcerer.'

'So the eclipses are somehow centred on them?' Varo concluded.

'It seems logical,' the ex-wizard answered. 'Perhaps they gain power from the false darkness.'

'Power from an absence?' Varo found the notion hard to swallow.

'It doesn't make any sense, does it,' Keredin said. 'There's always the possibility that making themselves real allows them to accept the power of the blood.'

They were back near the tower now.

'And the wizard in there?' Varo asked.

'The pendant. Light again,' Keredin said thoughtfully. 'There must be a connection somewhere.'

'Perhaps the darkness those early wizards feared is actually coming,' Varo suggested.

'A permanent eclipse,' the other whispered, shuddering at the thought.

When they reached the Knifeman's shrivelled body, they piled wood all round it, holding their breath to avoid the stench, then stood back. Keredin brought the fire to life, but was startled to see an answering flicker from one of the tower windows. As the pyre began to burn fiercely, the two men went to investigate – and found that the last remains of the wizard were also burning.

*   *   *

Later that evening, as the macabre pyre burnt low on the hill, and after Varo had told the others of their discussion, Keredin tended to his patients once more. He found, as expected, that there was little he could do for them, so he joined the others as they gathered to eat. During the desultory conversation that followed the meal, the former wizard sat apart, working with his knife on a flat piece of wood.

217

'What are you doing?' Brostek asked eventually, peering over his shoulder.

'Trying to see some sort of pattern in this,' Keredin replied.

Carved on the wood were the seven symbols of the Knifemen, laid out in a row.

Even without the hated blue glow, Brostek felt a quiver of revulsion at the sight.

'And can you?' he asked quietly, as Varo joined him, his face a mask of stone when he caught sight of the carvings.

'Not at the moment,' Keredin replied. 'There's something familiar about them, but . . .' He shrugged. 'Anyway, we know that these two are dead.' He pointed to the two symbols on the left of the row. 'And that their colours were red and blue respectively. The next was the one we saw at Grassmeer.'

'Green,' Brostek added.

'But we don't know anything at all about the other four,' Keredin went on. 'Any ideas?'

'That's the one I want,' Varo said, pointing to the symbol at the other end. He had no need to explain why. Everyone in the group knew that it belonged to the Knifeman who had been responsible for the destruction of Varo and Brostek's own village.

'They were enclosed in a large circle on the brand,' Brostek said, trying not to think about his partner's words. 'Could that mean anything?'

'I can't see what,' Keredin replied. 'There are so many different shapes here; circles, triangles, letters, even the heart shape. But I can't tie them all together.'

The others had been listening to the exchange, and now Hawk spoke up.

218

'Surely the point is not to *solve* puzzles like that,' he said. 'What we need is to anticipate where and when the next eclipse will occur. So that we can catch the rest of them and put a stop to this once and for all.'

'That's what we *all* want,' Varo answered.

'Well, now's our chance,' Langel put in. 'It's all been happening so fast recently. We've got to take advantage of that.'

'But we need Lisle,' Brostek countered. 'He's the only reason we got the two we did.'

'I can't do a thing for him,' Keredin said, as several men glanced his way. 'There's nothing to treat. My guess is that he'll have to heal himself.'

They all looked over at the prostrate boy – who chose that moment to move his lips, mumbling unintelligibly. Keredin hurried to his side.

'Is he trying to tell us something?' Varo asked hopefully.

Keredin shrugged. 'I couldn't make out what he said. We'll take it in turns to sit by him. Maybe we'll hear something then.'

'Aren't we all forgetting something?' Bair asked. 'I'm not going to be of much use for a while.' He held up his bandaged arm. 'Chase is in a pretty bad way, and these three can't even move, let alone fight. How do you expect to be a match for any of the Knifemen, even if you *do* catch them?'

'We have to try,' Varo said, after a moment's silence. 'You can all stay here until you heal. The villagers may be back soon. When Lisle recovers you can get a message to us.'

'*If* Lisle recovers,' Bair said pointedly.

'He has to,' Varo said as though there was no doubt of this. 'In the meantime, we'll do the best we can with the men we've got. Just like before.'

Lisle spoke then, louder than before, his tone suffused with anguish and fear.

'Maga.'

'What is it, Lisle?' Keredin asked gently, as the others gathered round.

'Magra.'

'Magara?' Brostek suggested.

'Magaaara,' Lisle wailed, elongating the second syllable. 'Magaaara!'

The onlookers glanced at each other as he lapsed into silence again. Brostek knelt beside the bed and whispered urgently in the boy's ear.

'What about her? Is she in danger?'

There was no response. Lisle's eyes were completely blank.

'Perhaps *she* can heal them,' Hawk suggested. 'From what you tell me, she has a way with people's minds – and if you ask me that's what needs healing here.'

'But we can't all troop off to Trevine now,' Vilman protested. 'It's too far from the action.'

'Without Lisle, we won't *find* the action,' Langel pointed out.

'But what use will he be like that?' Bair said. 'Let me take them back to Trevine. Maybe Magara *can* help them, and then we'll rejoin you. The crater can't be more than two or three days' west of here. It's got to be worth a try.'

Varo had been about to protest, but then he saw the logic of the old soldier's words.

'You'll need help,' he stated.

'Ross and I will be able to manage between us,' Bair answered. 'Eh, lad?'

For once, Ross said nothing. He was obviously torn between wanting to continue the fight, and the desire to stay with his brother and do what he could to help him recover.

'Isn't this a bit hasty?' Vilman asked. 'For all we know, they might all be absolutely fine again in a few days' time.'

'In which case, we'll turn round and catch you up,' Bair replied promptly, 'and we'll have lost almost nothing. What do *you* say, Keredin?'

The ex-wizard hesitated before speaking.

'I don't know,' he said eventually. 'I've never seen anything like this. They could recover in the next hour, or they might be stuck like that for months. There's no way of telling.'

'Then taking them to Magara must be worth a try,' Varo decided. 'Ross?'

'I'll go,' the twin answered softly.

'What about Chase?' Langel asked. 'He's going to be difficult to move, and we can't leave him here on his own.'

'One of us must stay here with him until the villagers get back,' Varo decided.

'That only leaves six of us,' Hawk said ruefully. 'Not much of a force.'

'It can't be helped,' was Varo's uncompromising response.

In the event, this problem was solved – to no one's satisfaction – when, despite Keredin's efforts, Chase died during the night. The following morning, he and his cousin were laid on another pyre outside the village, and the others bid them a last farewell. Then they helped secure Rogan, Slaton and Lisle to their respective mounts, and the two groups went their separate ways.

CHAPTER TWENTY-FIVE

Hewitt had played until his fingers knotted with cramp. Then he sang, not caring about the words, while he worked his hands back to life. Then he played once more, a stream of liquid sound flowing out over the cold grey sea. Hours passed. Night fell, and he could see nothing except the distant stars that illuminated his lonely vigil. All through the hours of darkness, he played. He no longer knew where he was, or why he was playing – he only knew that he must. When his fingers rebelled again, he sang until he was hoarse.

Dawn came and with it, silence. Sleep claimed the musician, unwilling but helpless. He lay curled in a ball beside the garden that was no more.

Hewitt awoke near noon, and was immediately swept by a wave of despair. A rapid survey of the area confirmed that Magara had not returned. He tried not to think about what might be happening to her, and for want of something better to do, picked up his dew-stained viol, cleaned it carefully and retuned the strings. He thought of playing again, but knew that it would be useless. She would never be able to hear him now. And his hands cramped at the mere thought.

He went to the horses, speaking to them softly, and led them to a nearby stream to drink. He washed and drank himself before tethering them again by fresh grass.

'Looks as though we could be here for a while,' he told them. 'Better get organized.'

Making full use of what little equipment he had, Hewitt built a rough shelter, glad that the season was warm, then took stock of his provisions and ate a frugal meal.

Now what?

He investigated the area around him, and found a few berries and a pear tree whose fruit were too hard to eat. That would not be enough to survive on, and Hewitt was no huntsman. He did not even know how to make a fire. Racking his memory, he recalled that the nearest village was about a league away, and that they had passed a farmhouse after that, maybe half a league nearer. He counted his money. Thanks to Bullen's careless generosity, he reckoned he had enough to buy food for several days if he was careful – and if he could find someone willing to sell to him without having to travel too far from Nevern. But that decision could wait until later; he had no intention of leaving yet.

He returned frequently to the spot from where he had watched Magara disappear, looking out over the unchanging, rolling fog while he wondered miserably whether the latest eclipse had affected her as badly as the previous one. The timing of it – coincidence or not – still worried him.

As darkness fell, he ate sparingly again and then prepared to sleep, taking a blanket and extra clothes from his saddle-bag. As he did so, he noticed the tapestry, and cursed himself for not having checked to see whether there had been any further changes. It was too dark to pick out the details now, and he promised himself that he would look at it in the morning. He slept fitfully, unaccustomed to the open air and to the nocturnal noises of the countryside, and was grateful when dawn came, and then the sunrise.

He attended to the horses' needs first, stretching and warming his own stiff limbs, then took out the tapestry. It was obvious as soon as he unfurled it that further changes *had* taken place. His heart sank when he saw that the black dot in the centre of the autumn sunset had grown larger, and now obliterated three-quarters of the orange globe. An unnatural darkness was falling over that quadrant.

The next thing he noticed was that another colour had

223

vanished from the rainbow; blue this time, from the middle of the pattern. Hewitt wondered briefly about yesterday's eclipse and the flash of blue he had thought he'd seen in its halo, and wondered whether there was any connection between the two. The rainbow looked very odd now, split as it was into two sections, with the sky peering through the gap.

Only later did he notice the other three changes – all of which seemed to be for the worse. Two white roses had been wilting in winter; now the entire bush was dead, a sad dark mess on the snowy ground. The lone wolf had been joined by others, the animals' predatory air even more fearful in a pack. And lastly, the apple which the squirrel hung from now showed patches of dark brown rot.

Whatever is happening, Hewitt thought, *it's not good.* He looked out over the strange mist. *Magara, where are you?*

Suddenly, he conceived the notion that he must go in and look for her. An internal argument ensued; fear battled against loyalty, reason against need. In the end, the power of friendship won, so he went to the edge of the fog and stepped timidly into the shallows. Nothing happened. And so, terrified but determined, Hewitt waded in.

Many long moments passed before he could find the nerve to take the final plunge and enter that grey mass fully. When at last he did so, the instant blindness appalled him, but he forced himself to go on, in spite of the utter dread in his heart – only to find himself emerging again a few paces from where he had started. Two more attempts produced the same mystifying result, and Hewitt gave up, feeling an unsettling mixture of frustration and relief.

He sat down to wait. There was nothing else he could do.

*   *   *

'You've brought the tapestry with you, I trust?'

'No.' Magara could see no point in lying.

'A pity. Still, there isn't a wizard left with the skill or courage to use it, so there's no real harm done.'

Magara's mind was still reeling from the way her triumph had so swiftly turned to disaster. How could her hard-won success have led to such horror – and in the midst of such beauty?

As she faced the man in blue robes, her eyes were drawn to the pendant around his neck. It was shaped like a triangle pointing at the ground, and the sight of it filled her with nameless dread. All about him was the faintest shimmer of colour, the delicate violet reminding her of Lisle's eyes.

'Of course, it means that you'll have to work even harder,' the man continued. 'Start from the very beginning, in fact.'

'Who *are* you? What are you doing here?' Magara blurted out.

'I am here because I love things of beauty,' he replied, looking amused.

'But you're a Knifeman of Bari!' she exclaimed. Beauty was incompatible with the horror of the man who stood before her.

'I have heard that we are sometimes called by that name,' he answered. '"Knifeman" is apt, in a way. But "Bari"? Hardly.'

'Where are you from then?' The very foundations of her world were crumbling.

'Here.'

'From Nevern?' she asked, astonished.

The sorcerer laughed, as though she had made a joke.

'Actually,' he replied, 'when I still lived in the world of men, I lived in your own country – in the great and powerful state of Levindre,' he added sarcastically. 'Such a wonderful land, eh? I'm surprised that you, of all people, could stomach it.'

225

'Why me "of all people"?' she asked, even more bemused.

'So you deny it even to yourself,' he mocked her, smiling unkindly. 'How weak the bonds of heritage have grown. No wonder you all capitulated so easily.'

'What are you talking about?' Magara was thoroughly bewildered now, but in the back of her mind was the thought that if she could just keep him talking, there was a chance that she might be able to attack him – or even to escape. But she had no weapon.

'I saw the way things were going before any of the others,' the Knifeman said, launching into a diatribe. 'The Cartel running everything, money ruling all, wizards reduced to begging and scraping for favour. The old ways forgotten, the nodes neglected, the Lords a laughing stock. No respect!' He was angry now, shouting. 'You can't deny it,' he accused, turning on her. 'It's all around you.'

Magara was stunned. She had heard similar arguments advanced by others, but they made no sense coming from the lips of this man. And what was it leading to? She listened, hoping desperately for a way out of this terror.

'I knew a different way was possible,' the sorcerer ranted on, waving his arms as though making an impassioned speech to an appreciative crowd. 'And I was right! They said it couldn't be done, but I proved them wrong. And look at them now!' He laughed scornfully. 'Of course, once I had set foot on the pathway, it was to my advantage that wizardry had become enfeebled. I even helped it on its way a little – and took great pleasure in doing so!'

He's mad. Quite mad, Magara realized, but held her tongue. The longer he raved on, the longer she had to plan. If she could only reach those trees over there . . .

'The Vortex was the key, of course,' the Knifeman continued, catching her attention once more. 'Ah, I see you recognize the name. Yes! The Vortex – a remote, dangerous place of fabled magic, too perilous even for wizards. Hidden from the world and holding forbidden marvels. I found it! I made it mine!' he gloated, his eyes shining with insane fervour.

'Where is the Vortex?' Magara asked weakly, dreading his answer.

The blue-robed man smiled knowingly.

'You're in it,' he said.

'But this is Nevern,' she protested.

'And everywhere else,' he replied.

'The Vortex couldn't be this lovely,' she claimed. The scene was too natural, too peaceful and warm. Such beauty could not possibly be the seat of ultimate power.

'Would you prefer that it looked otherwise?' he enquired.

Without waiting for an answer, he snapped his fingers, and the idyllic scene was replaced in that instant by an endless plain that stretched away for ever, flat and featureless, shiny as steel beneath an iron sun.

His fingers snapped again, and the two of them stood on a narrow ridge of shingle, waves of foaming sea crashing into either side. The noise filled Magara's ears, and a salt wind whipped her hair.

Snap again, and mist-enshrouded mountain peaks reared majestically all around them. A bitterly cold wind rose from the frozen lake before her, whipping the snow from the branches of the pine trees that clung to the lower slopes of the valley.

Once more his fingers snapped – and they were back where they had started.

Magara felt dizzy, sick and helpless. Her legs were on the point of collapse. *Am I going mad?*

'Stop it!' she pleaded, bringing her hands up to cover her eyes.

'There's no pleasing some people,' he remarked, laughing. 'Would you like to sit down?'

Magara felt something nudge the back of her knees and she staggered backwards, finding herself sitting in a chair that had come from nowhere. She wanted to scream, but her lungs were having enough trouble just breathing. *Get me out of this!* Her silent prayer went unanswered. All thoughts of escape, of resistance, had gone. The taste of defeat was bitter.

'Once inside the Vortex, it was all simple enough,' the sorcerer continued, apparently enjoying his lecture to an audience of one. 'Progress was inevitable – and extremely hard work at times. That's why I allowed the others in. But *I* was the first! My plans were laid from the very beginning – and they're starting to realize that now.' He sniggered, his tone like that of a triumphant child. 'Of course, there was resistance from those so-called wizards of light.' He spat out the words with absolute contempt. 'But they were no match for me. Too little, far too late. Pitiful really, when you realize what wizardry had finally come to. And the last of them came to *such* a tragic end, only yesterday.' He sighed theatrically.

Magara was no longer really listening. She slumped in her seat, only wanting the nightmare to end.

'Pay attention!' the blue-robed man snapped in schoolmasterly tones. 'I'm just coming to the part that concerns you.'

Magara's own body betrayed her. Without volition, she sat up, raised her head and opened her eyes to gaze, unblinking, at the Knifeman. *He could just as easily stop my heart from beating*, she thought hopelessly.

'That's better. Now, where was I?' He paused, and having no choice, Magara considered his physical appearance for the first time. She had assumed, from what he had been saying, that he was old, but his face was youthful, soft-skinned and unlined. The boyish features were topped by wavy brown hair. *But that's just on the surface. He can change whole worlds – so why not his own appearance?*

'My plans worked to perfection,' he went on. 'And I made no mistakes! Reaching ever outward. Connecting, converting. All the nodes, all the lines. It was beautiful.

And it's almost finished now. Just a few loose ends to tie up, and one last fly in the ointment.' He paused again, then bent down towards Magara, bringing his face close to hers. The madness in his young eyes was horrible to see, but she could not look away.

'Of all the magical places,' he hissed, 'Nevern alone refused to submit, despite all my efforts. It took me an age to find out why.' He stood up again, and his voice returned to its good-natured manner. 'Very clever. Of course, it presented no *real* threat. It was simple enough to cut it off from the world so that no one could use it against me.'

The shadow-maze.

'The tapestry was a brilliant idea,' the sorcerer conceded. 'And created all those centuries ago! No one these days has that kind of creativity or skill. Yes, ingenious, as I said, but you are my answer.'

'Me?' Magara croaked.

'Of course. You are the last in a direct line of descent – of the youngest children – from the Guardians,' he told her. 'Even the choice of succession was clever. So many false lines. It took *years* to find you, but in the end I knew you'd come to me. And your sense of timing is immaculate. I need you to unmake the protection of the tapestry – and to help with one other small matter. Those are your tasks. Come, it's time to begin.'

'What makes you think I'll help you?' Magara asked, using her last speck of defiance.

'When you see what I am about to show you,' he replied, crooking a finger so that she found herself rising unwillingly to her feet, 'you will be overjoyed at the prospect of doing everything you can to help me.'

He smiled and turned to lead the way.

CHAPTER TWENTY-SIX

The transformation happened more slowly this time, and was even worse than before. As they walked, the perfect scenery about them faded away, and in its place was the ring of mountains that Magara had seen before. Although they were wrapped in clouds, the actual peaks were clear, rising above the layers of mist and glittering in the sunlight. The enclosed valley was vast and cold, but not entirely barren. There were thousands of pine trees on the lower slopes, and hardy upland grass showed through the snow in the central areas. Marking the lowest point of the valley was a line of three lakes, and it was towards the nearest of these that the Knifeman headed. The lake was frozen, its surface dusted with a fine layer of snow.

Magara shivered as the chill wind caught her, and the sorcerer responded with an impatient gesture. A thick woollen cape appeared around her shoulders and she wrapped herself in it, no longer caring how such things could happen.

Her captor led her on to the ice and she followed cautiously, sliding a little as she tested its strength.

'It's quite safe,' he assured her. 'It's completely frozen.'

Some twenty paces from the edge – still some distance from the middle of the lake – he stopped and turned to face her.

'Don't you feel it?' he asked, breathing deeply as though he relished the bracing mountain air. He seemed to have grown in stature; even the violet shimmer around him shone brighter.

'Feel what?' Magara asked dejectedly. 'Why have you brought me here?'

'Scrape away a little snow,' he suggested.

Reluctantly, she knelt and did so, then recoiled in horror. There, a handspan below the surface, distorted by the all-encompassing ice but more than clear enough, was the face of a man. His mouth was open as if in a scream; his eyes stared upward, open wide.

Magara shut her eyes, feeling sick, but instead of retreating into darkness, the image of the man remained. Impossibly, her vision expanded, and she saw not one, but hundreds of bodies embedded in the frozen lake – row upon row of people entombed in ice. She was standing on top of a bizarre and hideous graveyard.

'What kind of ghoul are you?' she asked in a wretched whisper.

'Your misapprehension is quite understandable,' he replied cheerfully. 'But they are not dead.'

Magara opened her eyes and stared in horror at the man beneath her feet.

'Now that you've seen them,' the sorcerer went on, 'would you like to hear them too?'

And Magara's head was filled with a dreadful cacophony of wailing, a multitude of voices, each one heartrending in its terrible pain and lonely madness.

Help me.

Cold, so cold.

Will it never end?

I can't move. Why can't I move?

Where is the sun?

So cold.

Help me, please.

Shrieking, crying, groaning. The wordless sounds of nightmare and agony.

'Stop it, stop it!' Magara screamed, covering her ears and trying to hide from the horror, fearing that she would go mad.

The noise stopped abruptly, but she knew that even though she could no longer hear it, it continued still. She was overwhelmed with pity for the prisoners of the lake,

231

and hatred for their cruel captor. Straightening up slowly, she faced the Knifeman. He smiled nastily.

'You can set them free,' he told her. 'Or you can join them. The choice is yours.'

'How?' she whispered, though she already knew the answer.

'If you do as I ask,' he replied, 'I will no longer need them, and they will be released. If not . . .'

Magara shivered, chilled to the bone in spite of her warm covering.

'Of course, only the strong and healthy were able to complete their journey here,' he continued, his pride in his vicious scheme obvious.

Part of Magara's brain registered the hidden import of his words. *This is real. The Vortex really* is *in the mountains. How can I be here?*

'It was always much easier to take the power from them where we found them,' the Knifeman went on. 'The children, the old and the weak would never have made it this far.'

Magara thought of the horrible tales that Varo and Brostek had told her of the raided villages: of the bloodless cadavers of both young and old, and of the disappearance of all the able-bodied men and women. *Now I know where they are*, she thought miserably.

'I made some of the early trips myself,' the sorcerer told her, 'but dividing my power like that was wasteful. I have left it to others for a while now. It is much the better way, and means that I can ensure that the transfers of power to the Vortex are done properly. Captured light is a potentially dangerous medium, after all. I wouldn't want any of my "colleagues" to get ideas above their station.'

Captured light? Magara wondered. *He must mean the eclipses.*

'However,' he resumed, 'the effort of bringing these good people to the Vortex was certainly worthwhile.

232

Because once they are here, they provide many advantages. Blood, mind energy, the complete linkage – all welded together in one force. It's so much more powerful a source.'

You're not only mad, Magara thought, *you're irredeemably evil. But you obviously weren't always like this. What turned you into such a monster?*

'The far lake has also been filled,' the sorcerer said, pointing into the distance. 'But I still have room for more!'

The central lake, the largest of the three, was calm and still, but its waters were not frozen.

'Of course that won't be necessary, *if* you obey me.' He spat the words into her face, his eyes holes of depthless malice, and waited for her response. However, Magara remained silent; with another of his disconcerting changes of mood, the Knifeman returned to a more conversational tone.

'We kept some of the men for escort duties. The more suggestible minds were, of course, the easiest to use, and we made sure that none of them ever returned to the areas of their former homes. Having such a force with us was never *really* necessary, but it helped disguise our true purpose. And the tales that were spread about those visits! You would have appreciated them!'

Why are you telling me all this? Magara wondered. So many things were clear to her now, but she realized hopelessly that she could do nothing about it.

'What do you want me to do?' she asked quietly, knowing that she did not have the strength or the courage to condemn herself to an icy, living death.

'Use your talent,' he replied promptly. 'I want you to tell a story. Write a book, in fact. That should appeal to you.'

'What story?'

'I'll show you,' he said dismissively. 'Let's just say that it'll be your equivalent of the tapestry.'

Magara did not believe herself capable of creating

anything of such power. *There's no magic in me.* Her doubts must have shown in her face, because the Knifeman hastened to reassure her.

'Don't underestimate yourself, my dear. Your talent is real. Rewriting a little bit of history shouldn't present any problems for you. After all, you've done it before!'

But that was just a game, she protested silently. *For entertainment.*

'Of course, if you're still undecided,' the Knifeman added slyly, 'I should point out that the fate of your friends also depends on your abilities.'

'What do you mean?'

'Varo and Brostek?' he prompted, eyebrows raised. 'Such barbaric names – but it has been amusing to watch their antics.'

Magara had begun to feel almost numbed with misery, but this latest blow hurt more than she had thought possible. *Them too?* she despaired.

'Ironically, they've actually made themselves very useful recently,' the sorcerer continued, as though he were talking about kitchen utensils. 'My colleagues have been becoming increasingly difficult. While a little ambition is good, too much can be a dangerous thing. And so it has proved – for them. They are expendable now, and so I have allowed your friends some measure of success.' He laughed at her shocked expression.

All this time and effort, Magara thought, *only to be duped by this fiend!* Her heart ached for them.

'Luck even provided them with a guide recently,' the Knifeman explained, 'but he is useless to them now. Such an *unfortunate* accident.'

A guide? Does he mean Lisle?

'I will show you how to take his place,' he went on. 'You will help your friends to satiate their own pathetic desires and aid me in the process. Your alternative is to leave them to their own devices. And if any of my colleagues find them – and they will – I can assure you

234

that your two young men will die very horribly indeed. And to no purpose.'

Magara had a fleeting vision of Varo and Brostek facing the hideous power of one of the sorcerer's 'colleagues' and her whole being cried out against it. She realized that the two men meant more to her than she had ever imagined. Did she *really* love that ill-matched pair, each in his own way? She knew she would do anything rather than have them suffer any more.

A yearning stronger than anything she had ever known held her in its grip, and she longed with all her heart for the simple world of just a few days ago. Longed to tell them how she felt, before it was too late. Longed to be with them again.

Brostek, where are you? It was always him she talked to, but always Varo's face that she saw.

'Well?' her blue-robed tormentor demanded. 'What's your answer?'

'Show me what you want me to do.' Magara felt the humiliation of defeat engulf her.

The Knifeman smiled.

And in that instant, Magara was alone in a garden, the garden of her tapestry. Nevern was indescribably beautiful; everywhere she turned there were new vistas of joy, tranquillity, and the ever-changing cycles of life. She recognized the views from the four points of the compass; the trees and plants, the animals and birds, all were familiar to her. For a moment, she experienced a brief flash of happiness, a moment to wonder whether she had awoken now, the terrible nightmare behind her. But then the changes began.

Flowers shrivelled and died before her eyes, plants collapsed into rotting piles of pulp, fruit fell to stinking decay. Lightning rent the trees, leaving blackened, lifeless husks. Grass shrivelled to dust. Birds fell from the sky, their blighted carcasses soon no more than ragged piles of broken bones and feathers. Animals fled, or turned on each other, teeth and claws stained red.

Streams that had once seemed like liquid crystal now turned to oily filth, scum clogging their banks. Fish suffocated, their bloated corpses floating on the surface of rancid pools.

In all this, there was no sign of the woman from the tapestry, but the tomb was different now. The stone vault was tiny, obviously housing the bones of a very young child. The inscription on the side read simply HALANA.

She never lived beyond spring. She never completed her work.

As the sun died behind a total eclipse, and eternal night fell, all light, all warmth vanished. Nevern became a place of icy cold and darkness. Wolves prowled until even they shunned its isolation.

There had always been a garden here. But now it had died. All life had gone. Only utter desolation remained.

As the end came, Magara found herself back on the frozen lake. She was crying helplessly, doubled up with pain, but she knew that every terrible detail of Nevern's decline was firmly imprinted on her memory.

'Good,' the Knifeman commented, regarding her distraught face with approval. 'A true artist always feels his work.'

'I . . . I can't . . . write that!' Magara breathed, half choking.

'You can, my dear,' he replied confidently. 'You have no choice.'

Magara slowly brought her sobbing under control. When she thought of the alternatives, she truly believed that she had no choice.

'What happens . . . if I do?' she said weakly.

'With Nevern finally under my control,' he answered promptly, 'I can concentrate all power, all magic, in the Vortex. The Link will be mine – and mine alone! I will be all powerful.'

'Aren't you that already?' she pleaded, looking into

his shining eyes. *Isn't this enough?*

'Here, yes,' he replied smugly. 'But the rest of the world is waiting for me. Have *you* never wished to be a god?'

Without waiting for an answer, the sorcerer changed the scene again, and Magara found herself seated at a table in a library. Before her were pens, ink and an unopened book. There was no title on its cover or spine. Looking round, she saw that she was alone, then realized with a jolt that the room was familiar. It was an exact replica of the library at Arenguard.

The disembodied voice of her captor sounded in her ears.

'It seemed appropriate. You may begin.'

Magara tried to stand, thinking that maybe, just maybe she really *was* at Arenguard, and if she could just get to another part of the house . . .

But her legs would not move and she gave in to her despair. Falling forward on to the table, she buried her face in her arms and wept. Eventually, after what seemed like hours, she sat up, wiped the tears from her swollen eyes, and opened the book at the first page. She was faced with a blank sheet.

Magara took up a pen, dipped it in the inkwell, and began to write.

CHAPTER TWENTY-SEVEN

When they bade farewell to their injured companions and left the deserted village of Jordanstone, Varo and Brostek had no idea where they should go – but felt they must go somewhere; to remain idle was inconceivable. When no inspiration came to them, they headed eastward, ready to go north, towards the highest, distant mountains. There were plains which straddled the ridges on the upper levels, making them easier to cross.

They had even thought of splitting into two or three smaller groups, reckoning that it only needed one man to kill one of the Knifemen if he was attacked during an eclipse. However, this idea was discarded on the basis that their enemies might have the banded soldiers with them. Against such numbers, even their seven swords would hardly be enough.

Enquiries were made at each tiny hamlet and homestead along the way, but they learnt nothing of significance. They decided to camp that night in the open; there was no sign of rain and the weather remained warm enough, while they were still at a relatively low altitude, for them not to need tents. But the next day would take them into the sparsely populated high uplands where the nights were cold, and this prospect did nothing to help the general air of frustration. Their route was without definite purpose, and they all knew it. Their recent successes, even though won at considerable cost, had made them impatient for more. The enforced removal of Lisle – the most obvious source of their success – made things worse, and so all the group, with the possible exception of Varo, were feeling irritable and argumentative. The seven represented a volatile mix at the best of times, but now the mixture was explosive. Several petty disputes erupted as the camp was set, with Vilman and Ryker, perhaps the most unpredictable of them all, at one time shouting and even threatening each other. Varo's single-mindedness and present preoccupation meant that he had no time for such trivialities, and so it was left to Brostek to calm things down. Although he was not in the best of moods himself – his burnt hand still hurt, and had made riding difficult – he was acutely aware of his responsibilities. Trying to lighten the atmosphere with his usual banter brought only a partial, and temporary, success, and he wished that Ross and Bair were there to help him.

The evening meal was quiet and tense. Varo and Keredin were continuing their discussion of the ex-wizard's theories, but reached no new conclusions.

'Looks as though these Knifemen have succeeded in creating the real magic that you're always going on about, eh, wizard?' Vilman said pointedly.

'Yes,' Keredin replied. 'In a way, I envy them.'

They all looked at him in disbelief.

'*What*?' Hawk exploded. 'Envy that scum?'

'Not their methods,' Keredin hastened to explain. 'But the result. Being able to project wraith images over vast distances. Darkening the sun itself. Those are marvels that wizardry could have been capable of, if it hadn't become too lazy, too corrupt.'

'Are you saying the Knifemen aren't corrupt?' Vilman asked.

'No. It's perfectly obvious that they're *totally* corrupt. But if magic can be used by them for evil, then there must be the reverse side – its potential use for good. They found the way. We lost it. *That's* what I envy them.'

Varo, his face white, stood up and moved away from Keredin. Turning back, he said, 'Anyone who envies such filth has no place with us. Take your horse and go.' His voice remained calm, his expression set.

239

'No! You don't understand,' Keredin exclaimed, shocked by his leader's response.

'Go! I never want to see you again,' Varo said. Although his words were delivered in a cold, flat tone, his whole frame was locked in anger, the tension in his muscles betraying the tension within. 'If you stay here, I will kill you.'

At this, Brostek leapt to his feet, knowing that he must act quickly, and placed himself between the two men. The others watched, stunned and silent.

'I only meant—' Keredin began, pleading.

'Be quiet!' Brostek ordered harshly, and turned to face his partner. 'You have no right to speak to Keredin that way,' he stated fervently.

Varo opened his mouth to speak, his gaze set hard, but Brostek gave him no chance to speak.

'He's been with us for *years* now,' he went on. 'And his loyalty has never been questioned. Without him, we could not have achieved all we have. Without him, we'd be blind to what we face. What did *we* know of magic?

'His envy is based upon a dream. Will you condemn a man for that? His life has been spent regretting that he could not make magic all it could be, all it should be. He would no more use the Knifemen's methods to achieve his dream than *you* would! To suggest otherwise is utterly ludicrous. You'd know that yourself, if you'd just think about it.' Brostek's fury burned in his eyes. He had never before had reason to confront Varo in this manner. And never before had a disagreement between them been aired so publicly. Brostek was shaking, inwardly afraid, but sure of his own position. 'Keredin's been through thick and thin with us,' he concluded. 'Risked his life for us. Is this how you reward him?'

Varo stood quite still, but for once the signs of the war that raged within him were plain for everyone to see. The group waited in a tense and fearful silence. At last, he simply turned and walked away. He offered no words, and his expression never changed. As he disappeared into the gloom, the six men breathed once more.

'What should I do?' Keredin asked.

'You stay,' Brostek replied firmly. 'He'll soon see he was wrong.'

'Are you sure?' the ex-wizard said, not able to hide his nervousness. 'I'd be no match for his sword.'

'He'd have to match mine too,' Brostek told him determinedly.

'Ouch! Some minds round here obviously need a touch of Magara's help,' Vilman said, as lightly as he was able.

'Leave her out of it!' Brostek snapped, then regretted his hasty words and waved a hand at Vilman, shaking his head sorrowfully. The adventurer shrugged, accepting the mute apology. No one was willing to restart the conversation. They tried to settle, but it was impossible. After an hour had passed and there was still no sign of Varo, Brostek took a deep breath and went to see if he could find his friend.

Varo was only a short distance away, sitting with his back against a tree trunk, staring at the ground between his boots. He did not move when Brostek came close.

'Are you all right?'

Varo did not stir, did not make a sound. It was as if Brostek wasn't there.

Deal with it any way you can, Brostek thought. Aloud, he said, 'Come back when you're ready. I'll be on watch.' There was no reaction. He had expected none.

Brostek returned to the camp, reassured Keredin, and ignored the obvious curiosity of the others. He told them to go to sleep, and for once was glad that no one had any further comments to make.

Varo returned several hours later. Brostek, tired himself now, looked up and smiled in relief.

'I'll take over the watch,' Varo said evenly.

'No,' his partner replied. 'You need to sleep. It's Keredin's turn.' He doubted whether the former wizard would be getting much sleep tonight anyway.

241

Varo nodded meekly, and went to his own bed. Brostek watched his friend go, knowing that there would be no apology, no admission that he had been wrong, but he was also certain that Varo – by whatever internal means – had come to terms with what had happened. It would not trouble them again.

*   *   *

The next day began uneventfully, with everyone treating the others very carefully. By noon they were on much higher ground, and the snow-bound mountains were visible to east and north. The group had now reached the point when they had to choose between several different directions; north towards the highest peaks, further east on the approaches that eventually led to Bari, or south, though they knew of no raids that had taken place in that region.

'Any ideas, Keredin?' Varo asked, his voice betraying no sign of the previous night's events.

'None,' the ex-wizard replied. He had been quiet and watchful all morning, still not quite sure of his position.

'Anyone else?' Varo called over his shoulder.

'Anywhere with a good tavern!' Vilman answered.

'Up here?' Brostek exclaimed, laughing with the others.

'There's always Skiviemoor,' Langel suggested. 'They might have seen something there.'

Skiviemoor was a remote hamlet, further to the east, which had once been a staging post on the long, arduous journey across the mountains. It was little more than a ghost town now, though a few hardy souls still clung on.

'The Halfway House is *not* a good tavern,' Vilman protested, his understatement provoking more laughter. The dilapidated inn was not even truly named, sited as it was only a fraction of the way over the mountain pass.

'But at least it'd be a roof over our heads,' Hawk pointed out.

'Providing it didn't blow off last winter!' Vilman said.

'Or collapse under the weight of snow,' Langel added.

'We might get some information there, if nothing else,' Varo decided. 'Let's go.'

Two hours later, they were beginning to think they had made a serious mistake. Thunder clouds were massing again ahead of them. The riders watched the approaching storm closely, paying no attention to the sun at their backs until a sudden darkness made Brostek turn around.

'Look!' he yelled, pointing.

His companions swung round. The eclipse came suddenly, but was uneven, far from complete, with a strange green streak in the halo. Several of the riders swore, knowing they were leagues away from the green Knifeman, and filled with frustration at being unable to attack him while he was vulnerable.

'Can you tell where it's centred?' Varo asked.

No one could, and they all knew that even if they had been able to pinpoint its focus, that would be no sure indicator of where the next one might be. Their frustration increased. Lacking anything better to do, they went on to Skiviemoor.

*　　*　　*

That night, Brostek lay on his straw pallet, knowing that sleep would be a long time coming. The landlord of the Halfway House had been flabbergasted by the arrival of so many guests, and had been hard-pressed to provide them with a simple meal. As Hawk pointed out, however, it was at least a roof over their heads. The night was cool and the rain still threatened, so they were glad of the shelter.

I'd be more comfortable in the open, Brostek thought, shifting restlessly and trying not to think about any creatures there might be in his mattress.

When he finally did get to sleep, it was to fall into an unusually vivid dream. As he floated in endless darkness, a voice said, 'Tonight, the stars will shine from our eyes.' *That's me!* he thought. *But I didn't say anything.* Then he felt something warm near him, and the shape of the dead wizard's pendant, four touching circles, appeared. 'Like mine.' Then the voice said, 'Thinking of you.' *Little one*, Brostek completed, recognizing Magara, and smiling in his sleep.

Another picture appeared in his mind. This time it was a cliff face, grey rock streaked with horizontal bands of red, with caves at its base. A vivid orange ball burned in one of the cave mouths, like a miniature sun. He felt drawn towards it, swooping down from the void – but never reached it. At the last instant it felt wrong, and he recoiled. The four circles were there again, and there was another flash of warmth. Another picture. A village, with a hill beyond. The figure of a horse, cut crudely from the turf, exposing the chalky soil below.

The dream vanished abruptly as he woke up. Varo was shaking his shoulders, speaking urgently.

'I've seen where the next eclipse will be,' Varo said, his face as animated as it could ever be. 'There was an orange sun, in a cave at the bottom of a cliff.'

Brostek did not know what to say.

*   *   *

They were all up before dawn. The astonishment that Varo and Brostek felt at sharing the same dream had turned rapidly to excitement as they both realized that this was the sign they had been hoping for. In their eagerness, neither considered where the dream might have come from.

The grey and red cliffs were quickly identified as Salem's Divide, some two or three days' ride to the north. Consulting Bair's maps produced a route through a high pass which was almost a direct line there, and which was agreed upon by all – until Brostek remembered the white horse.

'No,' he said, surprising the others. 'We must go via Marestone, here.' He pointed to the village on the map.

'But that will take us all the way round the Wistman Range,' Langel objected. 'That's another day's riding.'

'It was in the dream,' Brostek insisted. 'The white horse cut in the chalk.' He looked to Varo for confirmation, but only received a slight shake of the head. 'We must go that way,' he persisted. 'I'm sure of it.'

'Positive?' Varo asked.

'Yes. And in any case, it'll be an easier trail after Marestone. We can make up time then. And there are villages along that way, so we'll have more chance of picking up some news.'

'Marestone it is, then,' Varo said, ending the discussion.

*   *   *

The visit to Marestone, which they reached a day and a half later, proved very eventful. The village elders knew of the group from previous journeys, and rushed out as soon as they arrived to tell them the astonishing news that one of the dreaded Knifemen had simply walked into Grassmeer two days ago – during the eclipse that they had witnessed on the way to Skiviemoor. He had apparently been moving oddly, as though his limbs had not been under his own control. The surviving villagers, recognizing the hateful murderer of their kin, and finding him helpless, had promptly slaughtered him in a frenzied blood-bath of revenge.

'It's almost as if the Knifemen wanted to die,' Keredin commented.

'Or someone is forcing them to,' Brostek said thoughtfully.

Then the elders presented them with another piece of

news, almost equally amazing. A party of six men from Bari – of all places – was currently staying in Marestone, resting after the exhausting mountain crossing, before heading further west.

'They say they're going to try and get help from the Cartel,' the senior elder informed them.

'They'll be lucky,' Hawk said caustically.

'Seems no harm in 'em, though,' the old man continued. 'Peaceable as you like.'

'Let me see them,' Varo said.

The Barians were still asleep, although there was less than an hour until noon, but their leader, a man called Lynton, was soon roused. He was obviously nervous as he faced Varo and his men.

'I know what you think,' he began before anyone else could speak. 'The Knifemen come from Bari. Yes, I thought so,' he said, on seeing their expressions. 'Well, it's not true! We've been attacked as well.'

The travellers exchanged glances.

'How do we know that you're telling the truth?' Varo asked.

'I've come here unarmed,' Lynton responded. 'Would I do that if I was part of a conspiracy? We need help. The raids are becoming more frequent, and most of my people think the attacks are from Levindre. And now there's the eclipses. We're afraid, and we don't have your country's resources. I took a chance on coming here. If the Knifemen truly *aren't* from Levindre, then your Cartel and its wizards are our last hope.' The evident sincerity in his voice was convincing.

'Our wizards are not what they used to be,' Keredin said, aware of the irony of his words.

'That is bad news,' Lynton replied, downcast. 'Ours too have fallen. The last mage of any power has gone into the high mountains. It was his advice that we contact the wizards in Levindre. He gave me this as a sign of those whom I was to seek out.' The Barian took a small box from his pocket, opened it and showed the contents

246

to his audience. A slim, silver ornament, in the shape of four circles, lay within.

Wordlessly, Brostek drew the pendant from his pocket and placed it beside the other. The two were identical.

'Then at least I am among friends,' Lynton said with relief.

'You are,' Varo confirmed. 'What else did your wizard tell you?'

'He said that the best hope for us all lay in a great, red-walled crater and the lake within it,' Lynton replied. 'Do you know of such a place?'

*   *   *

'Somehow I know it's helping them,' Brostek insisted.

'Killing the Knifemen is helping them?' Hawk asked incredulously.

'Perhaps the death of one makes the others stronger,' Keredin suggested.

'There's no evidence for that,' Vilman responded. 'After we killed the first two, a set of villagers with picks and scythes killed the third. *He* hadn't got any stronger!'

'But what happened when all the blood disappeared?' Brostek wanted to know. 'All that power must have gone *somewhere*.'

'You go to Trevine with the Barians if you want to,' Hawk said stubbornly. 'I'm going to Salem's Divide. If he *is* there, then all it will take is one arrow. You follow your dreams. I'll do the killing.'

'I'm going with Hawk,' Ryker told the others.

The argument had already raged far into the afternoon. Since meeting Lynton, Brostek had become convinced that something was horribly wrong with their plans. Now he was arguing, with Keredin's backing, that they should head straight for Trevine. Hawk, Vilman and Ryker were arguing with equal vehemence that they should not. Langel was undecided, and Varo, for once, took no part in the debate. He was obviously torn. The

247

dream, as Brostek had explained, had felt wrong somehow – in retrospect Varo recognized that too – but to turn away from the Knifemen now was to deny the whole point of his adult life.

'I don't want us to split up,' Brostek pleaded. 'We'll need your help.'

'Then come to Salem's Divide,' Ryker answered. 'Then we'll go on to the crater – and with one less Knifeman to deal with.'

'No. They're being forced to die. There's something behind it. And *that's* the real enemy.' Brostek despaired of convincing his colleagues, but his own conviction grew stronger by the moment.

'Rubbish,' Hawk retorted. 'If something is forcing them, then it's doing *us* a favour.'

'My enemy's enemy is my friend,' Vilman said.

'You're wrong. I know it,' Brostek said despondently.

'You don't think you're getting a bit carried away by the silver pendants and the advice of wizards, do you?' Ryker enquired sarcastically.

'Perhaps they're better weapons than your swords,' Keredin responded.

'I know which I'd rather trust,' Hawk said.

A few moments passed in silence.

'Then we split up?' Hawk asked eventually.

'Yes,' Brostek said heavily.

They all looked at Varo.

'I go to Salem's Divide,' their leader said.

Brostek was horrified. The seeds of division had been sown only recently – how had they come to fruition so soon?

'So be it,' he said, still unable to believe that the bond between them, forged over years of trust, was now to be severed. *Brothers in blood.*

They left the inn in numb silence and went into the yard, joining the Barians who were preparing to leave. And then the unthinkable happened. Horses whinnied nervously and men gasped as the sun disappeared, leaving a vivid orange glow around the dark circle in the sky.

'Too late!' Hawk said in disgust.

'We'd have been there if we'd taken the direct route,' Vilman moaned.

Varo spoke then. It was impossible to tell from his voice what he thought of this latest development.

'The decision is made for us,' he said. 'We go to Trevine. Together.'

No one argued with him, but each man knew that it would take more than a few words to heal the rifts within the group. Brostek rode in silence, hating what had happened, unable to take any pleasure in getting his own way by default. He began to question his own motives. Magara had been part of the fateful dream, and he wondered if somehow his thoughts had been influenced by that. After all, if he returned to Trevine, he would see her again.

*　　*　　*

As the thirteen travellers left Marestone, Bair, Ross and their party of invalids reached the crater's edge at last. The journey had been long and hard, and the condition of those attacked by the Knifeman's fire had not improved. Bair made arrangements for them to stay in Melton, while Ross made the journey down into the crater. He returned with the devastating news that Magara had left Trevine over two hands ago, and no one knew when she was expected back.

CHAPTER TWENTY-EIGHT

After his abortive attempt to follow Magara into Nevern, Hewitt became restless, irked by the waiting. But he would have chosen anything other than the distraction that shook him from his enforced idleness. The eclipse came some two hours after midday, taking him by surprise, but he reacted quickly this time, and looked to see if it was stained by a specific colour. The green taint was unmistakable, and as soon as the eclipse was over, Hewitt hurried to look at the tapestry.

The green band of the rainbow had disappeared, as expected, although this was the only change in spring. Elsewhere, the variations were more marked. *It's happening so fast!* he thought, staring in dismay at the garden's accelerating decline. The setting sun of autumn was now fully eclipsed, leaving only a slim, shimmering corona; worse still was a tiny black dot at the heart of the summer sunrise. Several pine trees in both autumn and winter were now little more than lifeless black stumps, looking as though they had been split and scorched by lightning. The large apple had fallen, splitting open on the ground in a revolting, oozing pile. The squirrel was nowhere to be seen. The swan was now diving from the sky, its beak open and eyes red, as though it were attacking the woman – who was now cowering, arms raised to protect her head, all her earlier serenity vanished. The ducks at her feet were flapping their wings, obviously startled. Overall, autumn now seemed much darker, cold and bleak, and the sense of decay was far more pronounced than was natural for that season. Winter already appeared very inhospitable, and although the small back dot was the only thing affecting summer so far, Hewitt knew that it too would soon be doomed. He dreaded what would happen with the next eclipse, imagining that the real Nevern, beneath the mist, must be similarly afflicted – and knowing that he could not help Magara.

*　　*　　*

The next day, Hewitt decided to risk leaving the immediate area, believing that riding around the perimeter of Nevern was the next logical step. Leaving Magara's horse and their possessions behind seemed safe enough; he had seen no sign of anyone for nearly three days now, and theft seemed unlikely.

He wrote a note for Magara, just in case she emerged while he was away, and pinned it to his makeshift shelter, then set off, keeping the mist on his right-hand side. Watching the shifting grey surface proved a futile exercise, as it appeared just the same from any direction. Even the land around it was the same quiet mixture of empty heathland as the area where he had camped. And the small thickets and copses were devoid of any animal life. It was obviously not only mankind that shunned Nevern.

It took Hewitt about an hour to reach the far side of the fog, and he estimated that the circle of the bowl-shaped valley was over a quarter of a league wide. Continuing his circuit, he was almost halfway back when he spotted a strange construction at the base of a lone oak tree. Sticks, twigs and leaves stuck out at all angles; it looked just like a giant, messy rook's nest. This was the first thing Hewitt had seen that suggested that he might not be alone in the entire area, so he decided to investigate.

While still a few paces away, Hewitt was startled to see a head suddenly emerge from one end of the heap, regard him with birdlike intensity, then disappear again. Hewitt dismounted and approached cautiously.

'Hello?'

There was a rustle of movement. A woman came out, crawling on all fours, and sat down cross-legged on the dry earth. She was painfully thin, and dressed in dusty rags. Her face was gaunt and her lips were stained with berry juice; the blue eyes beneath her unkempt, matted hair were bright as she stared at him.

'I can't tell you the secret,' she stated firmly.

'What secret?'

'*The* secret.'

Hewitt was taken aback by this strange greeting. 'Do you live here?' he asked.

'Yes.'

'How long have you been here?'

'Forever.'

'Has the fog always been here?'

'What fog?' the woman asked, frowning.

'That,' he replied, pointing.

'That's not fog!' Her tone implied that he was being utterly ridiculous.

'What is it, then?'

'It's a *secret.*'

'Oh.' Hewitt was beginning to think that the odd hermit was even more eccentric than she at first appeared. 'Have you been in there?'

'Oh yes! Many times.' There was a touch of pride in her voice.

'How do you get in?' he asked, trying not to sound too eager. *Or is that a secret too?* he wondered silently.

'You wait for the lights,' the woman answered, as though Hewitt should have known this obvious fact.

'What lights?'

'The riding lights.'

'I don't understand,' Hewitt said, thinking that the old woman was as cracked as a summer mud-flat.

'The lights come out and you ride them,' she explained patiently, talking to Hewitt as though he were a small child. 'They take you inside. But they won't take *you.*'

'Why not?'

'You have to be special,' she replied knowingly.

'What's it like inside?' he asked, trying a different approach.

'Cobwebs.'

Her one-word answer was an uncannily apt way of describing Hewitt's own experience within the clinging grey nightmare. Then another thought occurred to him.

'What's your name?'

The woman seemed surprised by his question, then thought for a while, trying to remember the answer.

'Celia,' she said eventually.

Hewitt cursed himself for not having realized the truth at once. Although this woman did not immediately match Magara's description of Celia, that was hardly surprising if she had been living like this for any length of time. The irony of his discovery hit him with the force of an avalanche. Unless he was very much mistaken, Celia had never succeeded in penetrating Nevern's defences, and that, combined with her earlier troubles, had driven her insane. Magara was risking everything – and for no reason! He glared at the fog, hating its very existence.

'I can make it all go away if you like,' Celia told him brightly.

'How?'

She turned to face the mist, then shut her eyes tight, and giggled.

Hewitt was now convinced that this woman was utterly mad. In spite of his own worries, he felt desperately sorry for her, and tried to persuade her to come back to his camp. But she would not budge. Even her son's name provoked no more than an uncaring shrug. She explained over and over again that she had to wait for the lights, and eventually he gave up. If Celia had survived this long in the wild, then a few more days would surely not harm her. Besides, Hewitt could see no way of helping her, and he dared not leave the camp for too long in case Magara returned.

* * *

The following day saw the last of his food, so he amended his note to Magara and set off. It took him some time to locate the nearest farmhouse, and when he did, the farmer and his wife regarded Hewitt and his money with deep suspicion. They had nothing to spare, so the musician was forced to go on to the village.

He returned, impoverished but fully laden, in the early afternoon. He took some food to Celia, but she was nowhere to be seen so he left it by her 'nest' and went back to his camp. The tapestry had accompanied him on all his travels – he knew Magara would never forgive him if anything should happen to it – but it had not altered in any way for two days now. While he was unpacking his provisions, however, he felt a strange foreboding, and looked up. The eclipse happened abruptly, and the orange colour of its halo was obvious. *Waiting for the lights*, he remembered, wondering.

As soon as the eclipse was over, Hewitt studied the tapestry again, but the orange curve of the rainbow was still intact, and he began to question his previous assumptions. Nothing else had changed either – but that was only a small comfort.

CHAPTER TWENTY-NINE

Time had ceased to have any meaning for Magara. Locked in the phantom library, there was no night or day, no sunrise or sunset. There were no eclipses. She was unable to move from the table most of the time. Even her food and drink were brought to her, by an unsmiling man who remained silent no matter how she tried to prompt him, and who was the only other living creature she saw – apart from the Knifeman on his periodic visits. Whenever necessary, she was allowed the use of her legs so that she could go to the adjoining rooms – which did not exist at Arenguard – to wash and attend to her other needs. Other than that, she had no freedom at all. She even slept in her chair, waking cramped and uncomfortable, The Book in front of her the whole time.

Although desperately reluctant, Magara was transcribing the vision of the decayed garden shown to her by the sorcerer. She spent as much time as possible describing the wonders of the undefiled Nevern, but her captor soon grew impatient. So, fearfully, she began to paint pictures of destruction with her words. Lightning crashed, trees and flowers died, fruit rotted and fell. The process sickened her, but as the Knifeman kept reminding her, to disobey him would be to risk far greater perils.

On one occasion, however, he visited her for another reason altogether. Waking from her dream-laden sleep, she muttered, 'I can't write now. Exhausted.'

'I have a different task for you tonight,' he replied.

Magara waited, mute with apprehension.

'You are to issue certain directions to those friends of

yours,' he explained. 'I would have made you do it earlier, but one of my colleagues has been very careless of late. His death was almost too easy.'

'How do I send these directions?' she asked miserably.

'Use the Link,' he replied. 'Don't forget where you are. All lines go through the Vortex, and they are all available to you.'

'Why don't you do it yourself?'

'I could,' he said carelessly, 'but it would be so much better *this* way, don't you think? You will be able to find them easily, and they know you. They trust you.'

'How do I know it won't be leading them into a trap?'

'You don't.' His smile made Magara shudder.

'What must I tell them?' she asked, resigned for now.

'Show them this picture.' He touched a finger to her forehead, and in her mind's eye she saw grey cliffs, streaked with red, with caves at their base. An orange fireball burned in one of the cave mouths.

'They should be grateful for the advice,' the sorcerer remarked. 'If they hurry, they will find another of my erstwhile colleagues. And he will be quite helpless.' He sounded almost exultant.

If they kill another Knifeman, then they will make this one even stronger, Magara realized. *But what can I do?* Aloud she said, 'All right. How do I use the Link?'

'Shall I draw you a picture?' he said mockingly. At a snap of his fingers, the library vanished, and Magara found herself floating in endless darkness. Then the darkness revealed patterns; endless lines of light, faint at first then growing stronger; an infinite web that crossed and recrossed; intersecting, dividing, coalescing, neverending. 'Behold the Link,' the sorcerer announced in the darkness. He sounded amused.

Magara felt dwarfed by its vastness, helpless in the face of its complexity, yet knew this was the stuff of reality. Here was the true life of all her world; everything was contained here, everything past or still to come.

Control the Link, she knew, and you would truly be a god.

She was filled with conflicting emotions. *Surely I could use this to defeat him!* But the dangers of such power were painfully obvious. *Look what it's done to him. Use it, and I become like him.* Ambition, fear and greed all lashed at her, but overriding all these was an overwhelming surge of compassion. The Link was sick, perhaps even dying – with all that that implied for her world. Magara wanted to help however she could, to heal it, restore the faltering balance, but she knew such a task was beyond her. She was shaken rudely from this dream by her tormentor's voice, his words echoing her thoughts eerily.

'Do not think to abuse my gift. The Link does not allow the uninitiated to plunder its secrets at will. If you overreach yourself, there would be a heavy price to pay. And I shall be watching.'

'What must I do?' Magara asked, her voice sounding tiny, lost in the void.

'Think of your friends, think of something unique to them,' he instructed her. 'The Link will find them for you. Then show them the picture I gave you.'

Varo? Brostek? she tried tentatively.

Lines shifted and swirled, patterns formed and reformed. *Something unique to them,* she thought, feeling slightly dizzy. There were so many possibilities, and so many pitfalls. Magara merely watched for a time, contemplating. She reviewed memories, and found Brostek's phrase running through her head. She sent it spinning out into the Link.

Tonight, the stars will shine from our eyes.

'That's me!' someone said. 'But I didn't say anything.'

Magara recognized Brostek's voice, saw a glimpse of his sleeping face, and smiled. Varo too was nearby. Then something between them caught her attention. Warmth drew her to the four touching circles. *Like mine,* she thought, then shied away, frightened of letting the Knifeman see it.

257

'Complete the contact,' he ordered irritably.

Thinking of you, Magara sent, and heard Brostek respond.

'Little one.'

They were both aware of her now, so she sent the cliff scene, felt them accept it – and knew an instant's revulsion at what she was doing, knowing that it was wrong. But then she was overcome by another source of warmth, another shape like the pendant. Her vision closed in upon it, and she saw a remote village, the shape of a horse carved into the chalk hill beyond. She knew all three locations; her friends, the cliffs, the village – but then they all vanished and she was back in the library, disorientated.

The violet shimmer around the sorcerer was flickering wildly as he glared at her, suspicion in his cold eyes.

'What were you doing?' he demanded. 'At the end?'

'You . . . you said they needed to hurry,' she replied. 'Their most direct route to the cliffs was snowed in, so I told them to go a different way.' She waited, not knowing whether he would accept her hurriedly improvised account. His face was unreadable.

'Congratulations,' he said at last. 'It seems you have a talent for such work. I may use it again.' He spoke pleasantly, but she heard the threat implicit in his words. 'Let me see the pendant,' he went on unexpectedly.

'W-what pendant?' she stammered, not able to hide her dismay.

'Come now.' He held out his hand. 'Do not try my patience.'

Reluctantly, Magara pulled out the pendant and passed it over. The Knifeman inspected it, smiling, but she noticed that he was careful to touch only the lace, not the metal itself. After a few moments, he tossed it back to her.

'If such trinkets help you,' he commented derisively. 'Sleep now if you must, then get on with your writing.'

After he had gone, Magara was left wondering

whether the four circles were of any significance. Her captor's condescending tone had been convincing, and surely, if she could use it against him, he would not have returned it to her. And yet . . .

*　　*　　*

Time passed – but the only way Magara could prove this to herself was by the slow progress of The Book. Hating every word, she made excuses to delay her work. She changed passages time and again, repeated herself, and pretended to forget certain details. And she made the curious discovery that the Knifeman became annoyed by this, yet did nothing about her malingering. She wondered why he did not force her to hurry. She slept as much as she could, and did as little fresh work as possible, but knew that she was only delaying the inevitable.

While she played for time, her thoughts often strayed to Varo and Brostek, and she wondered what they had made of the vision they had been sent. She hoped her true feelings had come across, and that the two men would go to the chalk-horse village. There, if any-where, they might find help. *Gods, I wish I was with them now!* She imagined Varo's perfect features, felt his strong arms enfold her and lift her effortlessly from the ground. She heard Brostek laughing and joking, telling her not to be so silly. What would he tell her to do now, she wondered. *Stop daydreaming and try to think of a way out of this!* she answered herself. *But how?*

Much later, the idea dawned on her that she might be able to use the Link on her own. It was a terrifying prospect, but if what her gaoler said was true, then the possibilities were endless – should she succeed. The more she thought of it, the more she believed she *must* try. And the more terrifying the prospect became. *It seems you have a talent for such work.* But Magara did not know where to start. *Shall I draw you a picture?* How could she draw her own picture?

All lines go through the Vortex, and they are all available to you.

For a moment, Magara sat perfectly still, her heart racing. The words had been familiar, but the voice had not been that of the sorcerer.

Who are you? she pleaded. *Talk to me.* She was suddenly aware of the immensity all around her, real though unseen. The Link had come to *her*.

An image formed in her mind; a woman, instantly recognized as the one from the tapestry. *Halana.* She was somehow the little girl, the grown woman and the old seamstress all at the same time, but Magara chose to see – or perhaps Halana chose to appear as – the young woman, strikingly beautiful, her long black hair flowing about her shoulders.

You are treading on dangerous ground, Magara. In your world, this is known as the realm of the dead. Her tone was faintly hostile.

Help me, Magara pleaded.

You must choose your own path.

But I have no choice.

There is always choice, Halana contradicted her. *Why are you betraying your talents in this way? You are a healer, but this . . .* she indicated The Book, *. . . this is sickness, perhaps even death. In the past, your stories touched many hearts, and your insight has helped many troubled minds. With this you deny both.*

But if I don't . . . Magara cried, hurt beyond measure by the accusations, *. . . those poor people in the lakes will never be released – and I will join them.*

And if you do, Halana countered, *we will* all *join them. The price of your success will be not only the destruction of Nevern, but the death or enslavement of everyone in our world. If he gains total control of the Link, there will be darkness everywhere except the Vortex – and for ever.*

No!

You know in your heart I am right, Halana went on relentlessly, ignoring the desperate denial. *Be yourself, Magara. He needs your help. Deny him, for all our sakes.*

The contact ended then, as it had begun, without Magara knowing how it had happened. She put down her pen and stared at the writing on the page before her. In her words she saw cowardice and guilt, and she shivered, feeling the ice harden around her.

CHAPTER THIRTY

Bair and Ross stabled their horses and wondered what they should do, now that their main reason for coming to the crater had gone. As they returned to the dormitory where Rogan, Lisle and Slaton lay, they speculated on the chances of there being another healer in Trevine, someone who could help their stricken friends.

'There are many talented people down there,' Bair stated.

'We'll make enquiries,' Ross agreed. He was greatly distressed by his brother's malady, but was determined not to give up hope.

When they arrived at their room, they found no change in the patients' condition. Moments later, they were distracted by a visitor – one of the wallmen who had just taken Ross in and out of the crater.

'The council has invited you all to stay in Trevine,' he told them. 'Will you come?'

'Gladly,' Bair replied, gratefully accepting this unexpected offer.

'Then I'll make the arrangements,' the wallman replied, looking at the three still figures. 'Wait here.'

'I wonder what prompted that?' Ross said as the man left.

'I don't know. But I'm glad of it, all the same,' Bair responded.

The wallman returned later with several of his colleagues. They placed the three casualties on to solid stretchers, strapping them in carefully, then carried them to the rim. Bair and Ross followed, full of admiration for the wallmen's calm efficiency.

By the time they reached Home Platform it was dusk,

but there was nonetheless quite a reception committee waiting to greet them. Among them was a tall, heavily muscled man with an unmistakable air of authority. He stepped forward once Bair and Ross were free of the rope cage.

'The council welcomes you,' he said. 'I am Rothar.'

Bair introduced himself and Ross, then the three wounded men.

'Lisle and Slaton we know,' Rothar replied. 'They are good friends of Magara, and remarkable in their own right.'

'We others can make no such claims,' Bair responded. 'We are merely friends of Magara . . .' Even that was stretching a point. '. . . and had hoped that she would be able to heal our companions.'

'Magara's friends are welcome here,' the councillor said. 'She is a valued member of our community. As you know, she is not here at the moment – Iro can tell you more about that.' He indicated a white-haired man in a grey smock who stood nearby. 'But first, let us install you in Magara's home. It seems fitting.' Rothar led the way. 'We have others with healing skills here in Trevine,' he told them. 'Perhaps they will be able to help your comrades.'

It was not until later that evening that Iro finally got the chance to speak to Bair and Ross. They were all settled now in the lake-borne dwelling, and had already received several visitors. No one had yet been able to determine what ailed their friends, or to suggest any treatment, but some of them had promised to do what research they could, and return the next day.

The alchemist told the two men of Magara's decision to leave and the circumstances leading to that. He also related all he knew about her destination.

'Unless she and Hewitt were unaccountably delayed,' he concluded, 'they should have reached Nevern several days ago. But I have no way of telling when she'll be back, other than to say that she had planned to be away no longer than a month.'

The two travellers did not know quite what to make of all this, but they were in agreement about one thing; Brostek and Varo should know about it as soon as possible.

'I'll leave first thing in the morning,' Ross said. 'Look after them for me.' He glanced at his brother.

'Of course,' Bair replied, appreciating the younger man's ready acceptance of the task. 'Go to Duncery first, then leave word at the other usual message points. That way we'll either get word to them or get news of them before too long.' Turning to Iro, he added, 'Thank you for your help.'

'It's the least I could do,' the alchemist replied. 'I know something of your work. And I want Magara back safely just as much as you do.'

*   *   *

Ross had already been gone a full day – a day in which the condition of the three invalids had not changed, in spite of all the efforts of the citizens of Trevine – when Lisle stirred. Exhausted by travel and the care of his charges, Bair slept on.

'Magaaara,' Lisle breathed, a gentle smile lighting up his face.

He sat up slowly, looked around, then got quietly out of bed and cautiously picked up his lute before tiptoeing across to the open door. So light were his normally clumsy footsteps that the house did not rock at all. It was almost as if the boy too were floating.

Reaching the walkway outside, he stared intently at the lake. Its surface was mirror smooth, showing perfect reflections of the gradually lightening sky, the dark rock of the crater's rim, and the other dwellings of Trevine. But Lisle was looking deep into the water, his eyes moving constantly.

A boat was moored to the side of the walkway a short distance away and, after a little while, Lisle, moving with

264

a stealth that belied his normal ungainliness, climbed into it. He gazed solemnly at the knot securing the bow rope for a long time, then gave it several exploratory tugs. The knot held fast. Then Lisle began to sing under his breath; his fingers danced to the tune, deftly untying the knot and setting the boat free.

Few people were up yet, and those who were gave the lake no more than a cursory glance; the long-held tradition was that no one disturbed its tranquillity on the 'mirror-days', those times when not even the wind ruffled the water's immaculate surface. So no one saw Lisle slowly and laboriously propel the small craft into the deeps, using one oar as a paddle. He was still singing softly; the gentle ripples of the boat's wake spread over the otherwise motionless water.

When he was fifty paces or so out, Lisle stopped, apparently satisfied, and laid down the oar. Picking up his lute, he sat quite still and gazed out over the water. The ripples that had marked his progress still distorted the mirror lake, and he watched them carefully before beginning to play. A quiet, soothing melody sprang up, like a lullaby for the wind. The ripples seemed to react, gradually becoming still as the music flowed gently over the whole surface. At last it was all perfectly smooth again, and Lisle's boat was matched by its mirror image in the water. Silence returned as the boy laid down his instrument, then stood up and jumped deliberately into the mirror.

He vanished instantly, ineffectual arms and legs flailing as he sank from sight. Soon only a few silver bubbles, wriggling their way to the surface, marked his passage. Then they too were gone, and absolute stillness returned to the crater.

*   *   *

When the empty boat was spotted soon afterwards, it was the cause of great consternation. No one could imagine who had defied tradition; nor could anyone work out what they were doing now. The divers were certain that it was not one of them, but no one else was capable of staying underwater for so long. The boat's owner swore that it had been moored properly.

It was only when Bair was roused by the commotion and realized that Lisle had gone, that the truth was suspected. Even then, the divers hesitated to break with custom in order to launch a rescue, but Bair was adamant. Then a small breeze blew up, so that the lake's surface was already ruffled, and the boats went out immediately. The discovery of Lisle's abandoned lute confirmed their worst fears. Divers went down, scouring the area where the boy had vanished, but they found nothing. If indeed he had drowned, then his body must have sunk to the deepest, most inaccessible part of the lake, and it might therefore be some time before it was recovered – if it ever was.

Speculation as to why Lisle had done it proved useless. There seemed no rhyme or reason to his actions. Everyone mourned the loss of such a unique person.

Bair returned to his two other charges, who remained comatose, grieving for Lisle and feeling the guilt of his own incompetence as a guardian. He had known the musician for only a few days, but, like all his companions, had formed a tremendous regard for the young boy. The only bright note in all this was the fact that Lisle had apparently recovered consciousness without outside help – and that augured well for Rogan and Slaton. But even this thought brought sorrow. When – if – Slaton awoke, he would have to be told of Lisle's loss.

*   *   *

Magaaaara.

Lisle knew that she was somewhere near, and wanted to find her. Although he could not have put his feelings into words, he knew that the music that was his life sounded sweeter when he was close to her. He did not think of her as being in the lake, indeed he did not really know what a lake *was*, but he heard her song, and it came from that direction. And so he followed.

He was not frightened as the water rushed past him; the consequences of his fall into the deep were unknown to him. The silvery bubbles fascinated him, but it hurt to breathe in, so he stopped. Instead he watched and listened, still hearing her song – which seemed to grow louder – over the rushing in his ears.

Down, down. Darker and darker. And cold. Pains in his chest, ears, face. Blackness. Down, down . . .

Magaaara.

Then, without any change of direction, he was going upwards. It was brighter now. The pains hurt more, and he was still cold, but the blackness had gone. Up, up.

Lisle's head broke the surface, streaming icy water as he spluttered and gasped in the cold air, waving his arms and legs to keep himself from sinking again. The pain receded, but the bitter cold remained.

Lisle looked around, not at all surprised to see that the lake was now surrounded by a vast ring of snow-covered mountains. He knew she was here. But although her song was louder now, he still could not see her.

Magaaara.

The lake he was in was flanked by two others, but they were frozen and their songs were ugly. They hurt Lisle's ears, so he shut them out and looked further afield. A brooding, grey-stone castle stood at one end of the valley, and it was from there that Magara's song was coming. Lisle had begun to splash his way towards the bank when the song stopped abruptly.

No, Lisle! Get away. Bad *here.*

Stopped in his tracks by her voice, Lisle did not struggle. He let himself sink back into the icy water, the pain of her rejection stilling the song in his own heart.

Down, down, he fell, into darkness.

CHAPTER THIRTY-ONE

Ross arrived in Duncery in the late morning, a little over a day after leaving Trevine. He was both astonished and delighted to see the men he sought riding towards the centre of the village from the opposite direction. Varo and Brostek were at the head of a surprisingly large group, and Ross wondered who the strangers were. In the exchange of news that followed, he found out about the envoys from Bari and much more; he also became aware of the tensions among his colleagues. The last two days had not fully resolved all their differences. His own news was greeted with mixed reactions.

'So Lisle *was* saying that Magara was in danger,' Brostek said. 'Not that he needed her.'

'You can't be sure of that,' Hawk pointed out.

'If she's in trouble, then how did she get that message to you in the dream?' Ryker wanted to know.

Varo cut in before Brostek had a chance to respond.

'How do you know all this?' he asked Ross.

'An odd fellow called Iro told us,' the twin replied. 'Magara talked to him about it before she left.'

'Tell us everything,' his leader instructed.

Ross began by repeating Iro's explanation of nodes as best he could, adding that Nevern was one of these. Then he told them of the mysteriously named shadow-maze which Magara believed was enveloping the magical place. This matched Slaton's earlier description, which Varo and Brostek remembered only too well. Then Ross described the tapestry, told them of Magara's intention to travel via Whistling Hill, near Arenguard, and that she was accompanied by a musician named Hewitt.

268

'Magara believed it's all connected somehow,' Ross concluded. 'Nevern, the eclipses, and the Knifemen.'

'Well, we know she's right about the last two,' Brostek said.

'But how does Nevern fit in?' Hawk asked sceptically. 'Sounds to me as if she's gone on a wild goose chase.'

'I don't think so,' Keredin responded.

'Why?' Varo asked quickly.

'If Magara's right, and the tapestry *does* depict Nevern,' the former wizard replied, 'then I'd wager it's an image-key.'

'A what?' Brostek asked.

'An image-key – it's something which protects a node from change,' Keredin explained. 'It can take many forms, but basically it's a representation of the true form of the place. If anything threatens to harm it, then the image-key automatically restores it to its rightful state. If you like, it's the memory from which the node itself can be recreated. If I'm right, then the tapestry must be *very* old, because the secrets of magic that strong were lost centuries ago. And to defeat an image-key would take a power just as strong.'

'But someone has, with this shadow-maze?' Varo prompted.

'Not necessarily,' Keredin answered. 'I think someone is trying to make it invisible, to hide it away so it can no longer be effective.'

'Who would want to destroy it anyway?' Ryker asked. 'And why?'

'The Knifemen have proved to be sorcerers of considerable strength,' the ex-wizard replied. 'Perhaps Nevern is somehow opposing them.'

'How can a garden oppose *anything*?' Vilman wanted to know. 'It just doesn't make sense.'

'And if there are a lot of these magical nodes,' Ryker added, 'why pick on Nevern?'

'It's obvious by now that we are fighting a magical as

well as a human battle,' Varo said. 'Wizardry has its own rules, and I'll be the first to admit we don't understand them.'

'Can't argue with that!' Vilman conceded, shrugging.

'The tapestry showed an eclipse,' Langel pointed out. 'Perhaps that's the connection.'

This argument sounded thin, even to Keredin, but he was thinking further ahead.

'If I'm right,' he said, 'then the tapestry might also act as a guide to get into Nevern and defeat the shadow-maze.'

'And if Magara succeeded in getting in?' Brostek asked.

'Your guess is as good as mine,' was the reply.

Varo and Brostek exchanged glances. This time they were in complete agreement.

'We have to go to Nevern,' Brostek stated.

'Wait a moment,' Hawk objected. 'Two days ago you wanted to go to Trevine. Now, when we're only a day's ride away, you want to head off somewhere else?'

'Brostek and I will go to Nevern,' Varo confirmed calmly. 'The rest of you must choose your own paths. The envoys from Bari want to go to the crater. Will you escort them?'

'Magara is our friend,' Brostek added. 'We must help her.'

'I never thought I'd see you step aside from the fight because of a woman,' Vilman said, half sour, half mocking.

Brostek was on his feet in an instant, his eyes blazing. They had never seen him so angry.

'We are stepping aside from nothing!' he exclaimed, his voice cold with controlled fury. 'You are a *fool* to think that!'

Vilman remained silent, taken aback by Brostek's ferocity, but the accusation did not leave his steely blue eyes. Brostek sat down slowly.

'If Magara's not in Trevine, and Lisle's condition

hasn't changed,' Langel said, 'then what's the point of going there?'

'Lisle may recover, or there might be others there who can help him,' Varo replied. 'And the Barians want to go there. They believe it's important.'

'I can't see either Trevine or Nevern helping us much,' Hawk commented, 'when the Knifemen are in the mountains.'

'So will we be,' Brostek vowed, 'as soon as we've dealt with this.'

'Do we have time to wait?' Langel asked. 'They may not stay in the mountains for ever. The eclipses are awfully close together now. I think this is leading up to something, and it's going to happen soon.'

'Leading up to what?' Hawk asked pointedly.

'The eclipses *help* us,' Ryker added. 'That's when the Knifemen are vulnerable.'

'But what if *I'm* right?' Brostek put in. 'What if killing the Knifemen isn't the whole answer? If killing some really does make the others stronger? The power of the last one doesn't bear thinking about.'

'That's only a theory,' Hawk said. 'You've no evidence for it, only your feelings. Personally, I'd much prefer one Knifeman to five.'

'Well, I'm going back to Trevine,' Ross put in. He hated listening to the disagreements among his friends, and wanted it to end, wanted decisions to be made. 'Rogan's there,' he added.

'I'll come with you,' Langel said wearily. 'Now that we're so close.'

Ryker, Hawk and Vilman exchanged glances, and the archer answered for all three.

'All right. Trevine it is.'

'I'm going to Nevern,' Keredin decided. 'I'd like to see it for myself.'

So the group split up once more; as he rode away, Brostek wondered ruefully whether this time the separation was final.

In the afternoon of the following day, the remnants of the group came in sight of the crater. The Barians looked down in awe.

'This is the place!' Lynton exclaimed. 'Exactly as it was described to us.'

'Well, if the answer to all our problems is here,' Hawk told him, 'I for one don't know where to look.'

Ross went to see the wallmen at Rimgap One, and returned with the news that they were all invited down.

'Them too?' Langel asked, indicating the Barians.

'Of course. They'll do anything for me here,' Ross answered, grinning. 'Must be my persuasive manner.'

'They probably just wanted to shut you up,' Vilman remarked.

The Barian's amazement increased as they made the heart-stopping journey down into the crater. News of their arrival had obviously preceded them; several councillors were waiting to greet them, and the foreigners were invited to discuss their purpose with the council. Iro was there too, and it was he who led the five others to Magara's house and their reunion with Bair. When they walked in, Lisle was sitting in the middle of the floor. He was wrapped in a blanket and shawl, but his arms were free, and he was quietly playing a melancholy tune on his lute.

'He's better!' Ross exclaimed, and looked hopefully at Rogan.

'There's no change in the other two, I'm afraid,' Bair told him, 'but Lisle has recovered. And that's not the half of it.'

After he had been brought up to date with all their news – including the orange eclipse which neither Ross nor Bair recalled seeing – Bair told them of Lisle's disappearance and apparent drowning the day before.

'But then, when we'd given up all hope,' he went on, 'he pops up in the middle of the lake and the divers fish him out. He's been chilled to the bone ever since, but otherwise he's back to normal – or at least what passes for normal with Lisle.'

'But where *was* he?' Langel asked.

'No one knows,' Bair replied. 'The divers are completely baffled. They swear he couldn't have been in the lake all that time. He'd have drowned.'

'It's impossible,' Ryker said, shaking his head. 'I'll wager he can't even swim.'

'Has he said anything?' Hawk asked hopefully.

'Only one phrase, over and over again, as if he was talking to himself,' Bair answered. 'It seems to make him sad, but no matter how we've tried to coax him, he won't say anything else. He says, "No Lisle. Get away. Bad here."'

As if on cue, Lisle stopped playing and spoke.

'No, Lisle! Get away. *Bad* here.'

They were the same words, but the intonation was different this time. And Iro recognized it immediately.

'That sounded just like Magara!' he said.

CHAPTER THIRTY-TWO

The three days that followed the orange eclipse were uneventful for Hewitt. He contented himself with small tasks, aimed at making his living conditions more comfortable, and whiled away long periods practising on his viol. He wondered how much longer he was going to have to wait.

He visited Celia's hovel several times, but she was rarely there. The food he had left her was untouched, and when they did meet, she made it very clear that his help was not wanted. Although he tried to persuade her to join him at his camp, she refused – to his secret relief; the hermit unnerved Hewitt far more than his continued solitude. There were a few times when he thought he detected movement in the undergrowth near his tent when he was making music, but he resisted the temptation to call out or investigate.

He checked up on the tapestry periodically. The eclipses had progressed no further, and the black dot in the summer sunrise remained unchanged. The rainbow – or what was left of it – was also no different, but the musician thought he could see other odd, seemingly insignificant, details which altered from day to day. However, they were so small that he could never be sure they were not just figments of his imagination.

* * * *

While Hewitt waited patiently for her return, Magara's resolve slowly hardened. Halana's message had terrified her, and she believed every word of it implicitly. The real evil of the man she dared oppose had been brought home to her, and she realized at last that there was no hope for her. If she completed The Book, the sorcerer's victory would be complete, and that would mean the doom of all the world. It was unthinkable. But if she did not . . .

Although she could not bear to think of the horrors that he could impose upon her, she had always known in her heart that what she was doing was wrong. Halana had merely confirmed that fact. Magara's own fate now seemed inconsequential, and in a way that made it easier for her to face.

Her only hope lay in delay, and in the wildest of speculation. She knew from Halana's hints and from her own observations that the Knifeman could not simply force her to write what he wanted. *Be yourself, Magara. He* needs *your help.* He needed her 'willing' cooperation – presumably because the magic to counteract the effect of the tapestry would not otherwise be effective. *Deny him, for all our sakes.* That meant that her captor could only go so far in his threats to her. Anything which left her incapacitated would deny him the chance of reaching his ultimate goal. Theoretically, therefore, she could put back the completion of The Book almost indefinitely.

However, she must make some show of progress in order to mollify him. She did not want to test his fragile patience too closely in case he decided to try to do without her, and entomb her in the lake before she had a chance to put her ideas into practice. Magara was determined never to finish her task, hoping that she would find the courage to go screaming into the ice rather than capitulate to him. In the meantime, she knew that even the slimmest of chances was worth pursuing.

The first of these stemmed from a remark the sorcerer had made just after she had come face to face with him for the first time. It had been about the tapestry. *Still, there isn't a wizard left with the skill or courage to use it, so there's no real harm done.* The implication of his words had not sunk in at the time; now, desperate as she was, Magara began to wonder if perhaps the Knifeman was right.

Even if a wizard could get into Nevern, what could he achieve? Her enemy obviously feared such a possibility, so perhaps the mage-garden – while it remained un-conquered – possessed its own magic, powerful enough to oppose the sorcerer's domination of the Link. What was it he had said? *It was simple enough to cut it off from the world so that no one could use it against me.*

But did such a wizard exist? They were all held in such low esteem now, and wizardry as a whole was regarded in Levindre as something of a joke, so it seemed unlikely. Yet Magara had managed to enter Nevern – and she was no wizard – so how much talent was actually needed? And then again, her ancestral connection with the place may have been more significant than she realized.

One thing gave her a little hope, and that was the existence of at least two more four-ring pendants, seen during her excursion into the Link. Her own had been the final key to unlocking the shadow-maze, so if others had them . . .

One was apparently with Brostek and Varo. Although this was encouraging in one way, she knew they were no more magically talented than she was. However, she had no idea who owned the one she had sensed in the chalk-horse village. Perhaps it was the wizard she sought. Perhaps the sorcerer had been mistaken when he said that the last of the wizards of light was dead. After all, the four circles represented light, and would be the obvious symbol of recognition for such a mage. And her captor had not been willing to handle her pendant directly, so it must hold some power of its own.

Magara was left with two problems. The first was how to let any would-be rescuer know that they should come to Nevern. Apart from Hewitt, only Iro and Stead had known of her destination. She wondered briefly what the musician was doing, but decided that he must have given her up by now. She did not blame him, and smiled for a moment at the memory of his quicksilver nature and unexpected generosity of spirit. *Stop reminiscing!* she ordered herself sharply.

It was unlikely that any of the three men would make contact with the people she sought, unless Varo and his group returned to Trevine. And the chances of that were slim. So she would have to try to contact them, or the unknown wizard, herself. And that meant using the Link.

The Link does not allow the uninitiated to plunder its secrets at will. There would be a heavy price to pay if you overreach yourself. Even if she could find the Link again, would she be able to use it without the sorcerer's direction? Would she overreach herself? And yet could the consequences of doing so be any worse than what she faced now? *You are treading on dangerous ground, Magara. In your world, this is the realm of the dead.* Perhaps Halana could help her again. But how was Magara to reach her? Last time, Halana had approached her; she had sensed nothing since.

She half hoped that her enemy would ask her to use the Link again for his own vile purposes. It would be too dangerous to try anything while he was acting as overseer, but she could study the process more closely, and perhaps learn how to initiate it on her own. One way or another, she was determined to try.

Her second problem was to make sure that if somebody *did* eventually come to Nevern, that they were able to get in. Having had the clues in the tapestry to follow, she hoped that Hewitt might not have left, and could therefore pass on the information. But there was no guarantee of that. However, Magara knew that the tapestry had been changing even before she had started The Book, and she was convinced that this was due in some way to the sorcerer's evil purpose, and to specific events such as the eclipses and the deaths of other Knifemen. Therefore she could not be sure that the clues she had noticed would stay the same. And so she began to devise a way of *planting* new ones.

If the purpose of The Book was to counteract the tapestry, then it seemed logical that what she wrote would affect either Nevern itself, or the tapestry – or possibly both. Thus, if she could hide indicators in her tale in a way that would not arouse her captor's suspicions but which others would recognize, then there was a chance that she might be able to guide them through the shadow-maze. The ideas were beginning to germinate in her mind, and Magara set about her task with renewed vigour.

* * *

Magaaara.

Her concentration was broken by the sudden cry, far away but still very clear in her head. She had a brief vision of silver bubbles disappearing upwards, of the world growing cold and dark. Pain. She gasped involuntarily, as though she could no longer breathe.

Magaaara.

Louder now. It was Lisle, she knew, but how could that be? After those first distressing scenes of battle that he had shown her, there had been no contact since she had entered the shadow-maze. What had changed? The pain grew worse, but the darkness receded. Light flooded abruptly into her vision, the light of snow and sky. Sheer amazement filled her as she saw the circle of mountains, the frozen lakes, and realized that Lisle was in the Vortex.

Magaaara.

His eyes showed her the grey castle in which she was imprisoned, and she felt his relief and intent; she also knew that the Knifeman must surely be aware of the stranger's presence.

No, Lisle! Get away. Bad *here,* she pleaded silently, fearing for his life.

278

Magara sensed him slip away, his pain redoubling in sadness and hurt. Guilt assailed her, but she was glad that he had left the Vortex. She thought about the boy's astonishing appearance for a long time. How had he got there? Or had he just been an illusion? What had he been doing in the lake? The questions multiplied in her head, and nothing made any sense. If she was right, and the Vortex was located in the very highest mountains, then there was no way that Lisle could have reached them travelling by conventional means. So he must have come via a magical place – as she had done – spirited away by the Link. Could Lisle be in Nevern? And if so, where were Slaton and the others? If not, then he must have come from somewhere already controlled by her captor – an uncomfortable thought. But then again, if he could get here, perhaps others could too.

She kept expecting the sorcerer to come and question her about Lisle, and had no idea what she should say when he did; it was not until much later, however, after she had slept and started what for her was a new day, that he paid his next visit.

'Get up.' Magara felt the life come back into her legs. She obeyed, wobbling as her underused muscles protested. Her legs tingled agonizingly as she walked around the room, but she enjoyed the painful movement, relishing this temporary release from her confinement. Meanwhile, her enemy was leafing through the last few pages of her Book.

'Your progress has slowed again,' he commented. 'I'm disappointed.' There was a cold menace beneath his mild words, and he stared at her with shrewd eyes before speaking again. 'You're intelligent enough to have realized that I cannot force you to write,' he said, surprising her with his candour. 'But I can force you to *want* to write.'

Magara said nothing, dreading what was to come next.

'It's obvious that the fate of the people in the ice does not move you,' he continued. 'I had not thought you so

279

callous. Perhaps it would be different if I let you listen to them more often. Perhaps even while you sleep. How have your dreams been recently?'

Magara swallowed hard. She knew that he was capable of doing what he threatened – and that it would drive her mad.

'If you give me dreams like that, I'll be too tired to write,' she protested weakly. 'I need proper sleep. Creating this Book is exhausting – and I'm going as fast as I can.'

The words sounded desperate, even to her.

'Really?' There was a long pause as he watched her, a faint smile playing on his lips. 'Your work is truly excellent,' he said eventually. 'I can almost see it all happening. Indeed much of it already has,' he added, confirming Magara's earlier thoughts. 'But you are capable of *so* much more, I am sure. For instance, if I were to arrange for you to witness the unfortunate demise of your very dear friends, would you not rush to lessen their agony by completing your task?'

Magara saw in his words the opportunity that she had hoped for. Perhaps now she could contact Brostek and Varo. The danger to them was only too obvious, and she did not know if she could bear to see them suffer. But she knew that she would have to take the chance if it was offered. However, it was not to be.

'Or perhaps the threat should be more personal still,' the Knifeman went on. 'It occurs to me that you could write just as well with one eye as two.'

Excruciating pain lanced through Magara's skull, and she lost all vision in her left eye. Screaming, she brought her hands up to her face, expecting to find blood streaming from an empty socket – but her eye was whole, unharmed. Yet still the unbelievable pain stabbed her. Then the sorcerer made a small gesture, and Magara almost fainted with relief as the pain vanished and her sight was restored.

'I have some experience with knives,' her tormentor

added, his face blank, without his usual sardonic smile.
'Do you really want me to demonstrate?'

Magara shook her head, bathed in a cold sweat.

'Then write!' he commanded.

CHAPTER THIRTY-THREE

On the first morning after their return to the crater, Bair and the remnants of Varo's group met again at Magara's home. The four newcomers had been given lodgings elsewhere, as there was no room for them in Magara's small house.

'We should come here more often,' Vilman proclaimed as he entered. 'That meal last night was the best I've had in years. No wonder Varo and Brostek made friends in this place.'

'Our hosts seem to be breaking all the rules for us,' Hawk said. 'They're usually very strict about who they let stay down here.'

'They even let *me* in, you mean,' Ryker added, grinning.

'There've always been visitors,' Ross put in. 'But I don't know how long they'll let us stay.'

'As long as we like, according to Rothar,' Langel answered. 'And no one's going to argue with *him*!'

'I think they sometimes like to show an interest in what's happening in the world at large,' Hawk said. 'Bringing the Barians with us probably helped.'

'But this sudden interest *is* strange,' Ryker commented. 'I mean, Varo and Brostek must have been telling them about the Knifemen for years.'

'Perhaps, as this is the only place we know of that isn't affected by the eclipses, they imagine there's a more important role for them,' Bair suggested. 'At least now they want to find out what's going on.'

'They certainly spent long enough getting the facts out of us last night,' Hawk agreed. 'If it hadn't been for the food and drink at Newberry's, I'd have fallen asleep on them in the middle of it!'

'*Why* doesn't the crater get the eclipses?' Ross asked. 'Perhaps the Barians are right and this place is special.'

'So special it's the one place we're *never* going to get the chance to kill any Knifemen,' Ryker remarked caustically. 'Or anything else for that matter,' he muttered to himself.

'Well, we're here now,' Hawk said. 'So what shall we do?'

'Lisle's better. That's what we wanted, isn't it?' Ryker replied. 'Why not go back to the mountains with him?'

'What's the rush?' Vilman exclaimed. 'We have a table at Newberry's tonight!'

'This is serious, Vilman,' Langel said.

'So am I!' he responded.

'We'd have problems if we went now,' Bair pointed out soberly. 'Slaton's still unconscious, and I don't know if we could cope with Lisle on his own.'

'He seems all right here,' Ryker pointed out.

'Travelling is different, though,' the veteran replied.

'I want to stay with Rogan for a day or two,' Ross put in. 'If Lisle has recovered, then there's a chance the other two will soon.'

'I'd still be no good in a fight,' Bair added.

'And Keredin's not here either,' Langel said.

'So what?' Ryker demanded.

'Lisle needed Keredin's flames to show us where to go,' Langel explained. 'He may not be able to do anything without them.'

'We can give him flames,' Hawk said.

'It may not be that simple,' Bair stated.

'So we just sit here and do nothing?' Ryker was pacing up and down like a caged animal.

'At least we could wait until we get word from Varo,' Ross suggested.

'But we've no idea how long he's going to be!' Hawk objected. 'It could be hands! And while we're stuck here, we'll never know how many eclipses we're missing.'

'Maybe someone else will do the job for us,' Vilman said. 'We didn't kill the Knifeman at Grassmeer, after all. Of course,' he went on, 'we could all jump in the lake and disappear for a while, like Lisle did. That would save us having to decide what to do.'

'If you can't be serious, then just shut up!' Bair snapped.

'I'm going for a swim,' Vilman decided. 'It's too hot to stay in here, and the water looks good. Let me know when you've decided our next move.'

'Are there any fish in there?' Ryker asked.

'Yes, but you kill them at your peril,' the other replied. 'That's the divers' prerogative.'

'I'll just look,' Ryker promised, grinning.

The two men went out.

'Call us if it comes to a vote!' was Vilman's passing shot.

The others looked at each other.

'Gods!' Langel breathed. 'We're going to have trouble with those two if we stay here much longer.'

The sounds of splashing came from outside, and Lisle looked up at the noise.

'Maybe they have the right idea,' Hawk said. 'Enjoy this holiday while we can. I've a feeling there won't be much of a chance afterwards.'

'Then we stay here for the time being?' Bair looked round, and received nods of agreement.

'For the time being?' Lisle echoed, looking sideways at the old soldier.

Then the boy began to play. The others listened for a while, but the song was so mournful and the sun so bright outside that first Hawk, then Langel and Bair drifted away, leaving Ross to watch over the unmoving invalids.

*   *   *

However, the whole group soon gathered again, shortly after midday, when a deputation came to Magara's house. The visitors were Rothar, another diver called Rayne, Lynton, and his second-in-command, Tagila. The room was crowded when everyone was inside, and filled with an air of expectation. After asking after the health of the patients, Rother explained a little of what he had been discussing with the Barian envoys.

'Gentlemen,' the councillor began, 'from what Lynton and his team tell me, and from what I have learnt of your own recent exploits, I think the time has come for Trevine to enter the fray, so to speak. I confess that when Varo and Brostek spoke to us before of the Knifemen's raids, I could not see how such things could affect us here. I hope you will forgive my short-sightedness, for it is clear now that Levindre and Bari are both in some peril, and our community can no longer afford to stand aloof. The very fact that the unnatural eclipses do not affect us here is reason both for gratitude and anxiety. We do not know whether this marks us as a haven of safety or as a place of special danger, but either way, we must act.'

The travellers exchanged glances. They had waited a long time to hear someone in a position of authority speak like this – and even if it was only in Trevine, it was at least a start.

'But *our* resources alone will not be enough,' Rothar went on, echoing their thoughts. 'We all know that the Cartel holds the power in this country; they have the men, money, arms and all the other necessities for the large-scale operation that may be needed. I am therefore proposing that we send a joint delegation to the Cartel's annual gathering at Mathry, which will be held next hand. We can then present our various cases together. I myself intend to represent Trevine; Tagila and a lieutenant will be spokesmen for Bari. Lynton and the rest of his party will remain here, for reasons we will go into in a

285

moment. It is only right that one or more of you should accompany us. Your first-hand knowledge will be of paramount importance.' Rothar paused and held up his hands to forestall any comments, then continued. 'I know that Varo and Brostek have tried this before, but they had much less evidence then. It is time to try again. And, in the absence of your leaders, you must choose a representative.'

'Bair?' Hawk suggested immediately, and Rothar turned to the veteran.

'Your seniority and the fact that your injury makes it impossible for you to fight in the near future suggest you as the ideal candidate,' he said.

'I want nothing to do with the Cartel,' Bair stated grimly. 'And they'd not exactly welcome me in their midst.'

His colleagues were surprised. Although they had always known that the old soldier's antagonism towards the Cartel ran deep, this was surely too important to let a mere grudge hold sway.

'Don't you think—' Langel began.

'No!' Bair said with a tone of finality. There was an awkward pause.

'Anyone else?' Rothar asked eventually.

'Anyone else?' Lisle mimicked.

The Barians looked at him in surprise, not understanding, but the others did not explain.

'Langel's your best bet,' Bair said at last.

'Me? Why?'

'Because you're calm, rational, and well-organized,' the other replied promptly. 'If anyone can get something out of those bastards, you can. Besides,' he added, half-smiling and half-scowling at the others, 'this lot here are all too hot-headed or addle-brained for diplomacy.'

Ryker laughed. Hawk just grunted, and Ross looked down at his feet, grinning.

'You are right, oh wise one,' Vilman responded. 'We are still just impetuous youths.'

Rothar clearly did not know what to make of this exchange.

'Bair's right,' Hawk told Langel. 'You're the best man for the job.'

'Will you do it?' the councillor asked, much relieved.

'Doesn't look as though I've got much choice,' Langel replied.

'Good,' Rothar said, taking this for assent. 'That's settled then.'

'Why aren't you going to Mathry, Lynton?' the newly appointed emissary asked.

'We have discovered that Trevine is even more special than we had thought,' the Barian envoy began eagerly. 'There is a giant replica of the symbol our wizard gave us carved in stone under the lake.' He would have said more, but Rothar cut in.

'Rayne here was the first one to see it,' he said. 'Let him explain.'

The diver dutifully told how he and the others had spotted the worked stone beneath the water, and had cleared away some debris to find the intriguing symbol of four touching circles carved into the rock.

'We took Magara down to see,' Rayne went on, 'but she could make no more of it than we could. It must be very old. We know now that the symbol stands for light, as used once by wizards – but that's all.'

'But it confirms our belief that we've come to the right place,' Lynton added. 'That's why I will stay.'

'To do what?' Hawk asked.

'Perhaps nothing for a while. But we are obviously meant to be here.'

'Is there anything else?' Langel asked the diver.

'Magara saw a shatterstone near the rock,' Rayne told him. 'We took it up for her, but I don't see that it has any relevance.'

'Where is it?' Hawk asked.

Rothar explained that shatterstones disintegrated soon after they were taken from the lake.

'No help there, then,' Bair commented.

'So all we really know is that there's an ancient rock down there,' Vilman summed up. 'How does that help us?'

Although no one knew the answer to his question, Lynton at least was optimistic.

'I'm sure it will all be made clear soon.'

'I hope so,' Ryker commented wryly. 'Because it's as clear as mud right now.'

'Could this thing in the lake have anything to do with Lisle's disappearance?' Ross asked.

'No,' Rayne said. 'If he'd got that far down without help he would certainly have drowned. Besides, we checked over and over again. There are no air pockets he could have waited in, nothing. What he did is just not possible.'

They all glanced at the boy.

'Who knows what's possible with Lisle?' Bair said.

*   *   *

Langel spent the rest of that afternoon and the early evening in conference with Rothar and Tagila, then joined his comrades at Newberry's tavern.

'Who's taking care of Lisle and the other two?' he asked, seeing all five colleagues around the table.

'Iro and a friend of his,' Vilman replied jovially. 'So we can celebrate your departure in style. Try some of this.' He poured wine into a glass.

'Where'd you get the money for all this?' Langel asked suspiciously.

'Always the storesmaster, eh?' Hawk teased.

'Being Magara's friends stands us in good stead here,' Vilman replied. 'Brostek's obviously not the only one who's taken a shine to her.'

'Besides,' Ryker added, 'now that you are an intimate confidant of Rothar, you should know that we are guests of Trevine's council.'

'In that case, fill my glass again,' Langel said, grinning. 'This is good – and I've obviously got some catching up to do.'

'Good man!' Vilman said approvingly.

'How was Rothar?' Bair asked.

'Impressive,' Langel replied seriously. 'He may sound like a bit of a windbag, but he can certainly get things moving when he wants. An advance party is already on its way to prepare the ground at Mathry, and he's been discussing everything in fine detail with me and Tagila. If he can't get something out of the Cartel, I'll be very surprised. We're leaving tomorrow morning.'

'It seems funny to be working with the Barians, after thinking of them as the enemy for so long,' Ryker said thoughtfully.

'Life is strange,' Vilman announced, raising his glass in a toast.

*   *   *

After bidding farewell to Langel the next day, the others returned to Magara's home. Ross was despondent over Rogan's unchanging condition, and Lisle was still miserable, so the others tried to think of ways of enlivening their stay.

'Now that we know we've got to wait for Langel,' Hawk said, 'we might as well relax and enjoy ourselves.'

'I may go up to the Rim,' Ryker decided. 'Do a little hunting. This place cramps my style.'

'I'd rather we all stayed together,' Bair said. 'When the time comes, we may need to move quickly.'

'Get Rayne to show you their fish-spears,' Vilman suggested to his colleague. 'Just don't come near me when I'm swimming!'

By early afternoon the wind died away, and the day turned even hotter. The group watched curiously as the divers all brought their boats to shore.

'What are they doing?' Hawk wanted to know.

'They can sense the stillness coming,' Bair told him. 'They call them mirror-days. No one's allowed out on the lake then.'

'Why not?' Vilman asked, standing up and going to the end of the walkway.

'I don't know,' the veteran answered. 'It's a tradition here.'

'This place is *weird*,' Ryker pronounced.

Lisle came tiptoeing out of the house, his solemn face intent. The surface of the water was now completely still.

'Not a whisper,' Vilman said softly. 'Incredible. It could be—'

Nobody discovered what Vilman was about to say, because just at that moment, Lisle gave him a sudden, heavy push. Vilman toppled over the low rail, fell headlong into the water . . . and disappeared.

CHAPTER THIRTY-FOUR

Hewitt had spent two days doing little more than watch the everlasting fog.

Ten days! he realized on waking the next morning. *I've been here for ten days. Two whole hands!* It did not seem possible. The thought that Magara had been *inside* the fog for all that time made him feel ill.

He settled into his now established routine – washing, eating, then practising on his viol – but he was thinking all the time about two events the day before that had disrupted his seemingly endless vigil.

The first had happened while he was playing. He had become aware in the middle of a piece that he had been joined by a voice, singing beautifully. He played on, trying to work out where it was coming from. Eventually, Celia came out of her hiding place, smiling shyly as she accompanied him.

'You sing well,' he told her when they reached the end. He was genuinely surprised. He would not have expected such a lovely voice to spring from this frail and undernourished creature.

'You play well,' she replied wistfully. 'You remind me of someone I once knew.'

Magara had told Hewitt of Celia's story, and he knew that she was referring to Lisle's father. He had thought it a sad tale, and had wondered whether to write a song about it.

'Do you know "Rose of Evermore"?' he asked.

'Oh, yes!' she exclaimed, clapping her bony hands with almost childlike excitement. 'It was one of my favourites.'

So Hewitt played, and she sang. For a while the young

musician forgot Magara, forgot the fog, and just took pleasure in the music they were making together. Smiling at each other, they finished the song with a flourish.

'Did you sing to Lisle?' Hewitt asked after a pause for breath.

'Oh, yes. All the time,' she answered, with a sad smile. 'He's dead now.'

Hewitt did not contradict her; Celia had evidently found some sort of peace, and he would do nothing to endanger that.

'I have to go now,' she said suddenly. 'The lights are coming.' And with that, she scurried away.

'Where? When?' he called after her, but she did not respond. He took a few steps after her, then gave up, leaving the madwoman to her delusions.

The second incident, another eclipse, had been vastly more disturbing. It had not been like any that had gone before. The darkness had been far from complete, and the lopsided corona had been two-coloured – a bright, pure yellow alternating with indigo. Shafts of these colours had flashed across the darkened sky, as though a gigantic gemstone was catching the sun's rays. It was a mesmerizing sight, and Hewitt would have thought it beautiful if he had not been aware of its possible unpleasant results.

He could hardly bring himself to look at the tapestry afterwards, but knew that he must. And it was as horrible as he had feared. The minor changes of the previous days had now been swamped by a deluge of decay. Both yellow and indigo bands had gone from the rainbow, leaving only orange and violet, looking very strange in their isolation. The summer sun was now totally eclipsed, which meant that three of the four quadrants were in semi-darkness. Spring's bright sun was blighted now, with a black circle at its centre that covered perhaps one-third of its surface.

Another change was so major that it took Hewitt some

time to work out what it was. The woman had disappeared from the three eclipsed quadrants, with only the little girl in spring remaining. And she had moved. No longer skipping happily through the garden, she was now sitting beside the tomb, her small body obscuring the inscription. There was an air of loneliness about her small figure, a sense of desolation. Hewitt even fancied he saw miniature tears glistening on her cheeks.

The rest of the tapestry showed a horrible degeneration. Only a few animals or birds were still alive. The wolves prowled in winter and the fox still barked in spring, but its fangs were stained red now, and its forepaws rested on the mangled remains of a victim. The rabbits had gone, as had the geese, the kingfisher and most of the ducks. Worse still, autumn's swan was dead, its corpse an ugly heap of maggot-riddled flesh and crumbling feathers. The remaining ducks were barely alive, their eyes glazed with a hideous white film, their plumage dull and molting. Their beaks were open, as though they were gasping for air.

Nearly all the plants and trees were dead now, except for a few sickly looking buds in spring. Blackened trunks and rotting filth dominated the other three-quarters. Summer, which until now had escaped relatively unscathed, and which had once been so abundantly full of life, was now a desert of decay. Stinkhorn and other ugly fungi had sprung up from spores hidden in the decaying vegetation, feeding off death. The stream had dried to a muddy, discoloured ooze, and the fish now floated on its side in the oily pool. The fountain was choked with brown, slimy weeds, whose drips stained the stones below. In autumn, the ground was littered with fallen fruit and berries, unrecognizable now, their flesh an evil, bubbling pulp. And trees still smoked in winter, their glowing embers a reminder of the primeval force that had destroyed them.

Even spring was badly affected now, showing few signs of healthy growth, and scum marked the banks of its stream. If the tapestry really was an accurate reflection of the real mage-garden, then Nevern would soon be dead. *And what shall I do if Magara is still inside then?* Hewitt asked himself, then rolled up the cloth and hid it away. He could not bear to look at it any more.

Now another night had passed, and he knew he must check it again. Although he was filled with revulsion at the sight of the tapestry, he could not see any more changes, and thankful for that at least, he put it away again.

Taking up his viol, Hewitt began to play, all the time watching the rolling mist that was Nevern. Then he gradually became aware of another rhythm, a pounding that seemed to come from the earth itself. He looked up.

Three horsemen were heading straight towards him, their mounts' hooves thudding into the turf. Even at a distance, Hewitt recognized Varo's blond hair shining in the sun. Beside him was the less imposing shape of his partner, the grey flash which was Shadow alongside. Hewitt did not recognize the third member of the party, but the rider had a mane of black hair that streamed in the wind as they thundered towards him. There was an air of grim purpose about their approach.

CHAPTER THIRTY-FIVE

After the sorcerer's awful demonstration of power, Magara forced herself to write more, if only to appease him temporarily. She wrote some things exactly as he wished, but she also tried to introduce her own idiosyncracies, hoping against hope that someone would follow her clues as she had followed Halana's. This new section covered many pages, but she managed to keep genuine progress towards the Knifeman's goal to a minimum. However, he saw only the increased flow of words, and was apparently satisfied.

Magara wrote, slept, and wrote again. She felt awful at the end of each 'day', the natural rhythms of her body unsettled by the constant unnatural light. She had realized now that she should try to find out what her *real* surroundings were like, so when her gaoler next appeared, Magara spoke first.

'Is it day or night?'

'What does it matter?' he asked in return.

'My mind is confused,' she replied. 'I can't concentrate. I don't know when to sleep, wake or eat. I can't write properly any more living in a false world.'

'Your true surroundings would be less comfortable,' he pointed out.

'You call this comfortable?' she responded with some spirit, glancing down at her immobile legs.

'Very well.'

The library disappeared. Her chair, the table, The Book and her writing implements were now housed in a bare stone chamber with a single door. The only windows were very high up, just below the rafters, and well out of reach. Looking up, Magara could see the night sky through them, with one or two stars just visible. Oil lamps burned on stands around the walls.

'Thank you,' she said.

'You've done well,' he remarked, looking over her shoulder. 'You'll soon be finished.'

As the sorcerer left, Magara stared at the words she had just written as if seeing them for the first time. Her captor was right. She had very little time left.

*　　*　　*

Although it began as a dream, Magara was soon aware that it was also something more. When Halana turned to face her, she saw that the young girl was very pale, and there was pleading in her eyes. She spoke with the voice of a child, but there was an older wisdom in her words.

My death will mean the end, Magara. You know that.

It will never happen, she vowed.

Only a thin line now protects my existence, Halana went on. *Tread carefully, lest you step over.*

That piece of history will never *be rewritten,* Magara assured her emphatically. *Whatever he does to me.*

Well said. The girl smiled wanly. *You are of my stock. Remain true.*

Then there's still hope?

While Nevern lives, there is always hope.

But I may not be alive to see it fulfilled? Magara asked quietly.

Halana's silence spoke volumes.

Will the wizard come to Nevern?

I cannot tell you that. Halana began to cough.

I'm sorry, Magara said, knowing that she was responsible for the girl's illness. *I'm doing my best.*

We can ask no more, Halana replied as both her image and her voice began to fade.

Don't go! Magara pleaded.

I must. My own world is calling.

How do I use it? How do I get into the Link? she called, desperate now.

Ask, came the faint reply.

Halana was gone, and the Link was gone with her. Magara awoke, cursing silently. How was she supposed to ask? Once again, the Link had come to her. Once again, she had sensed its sickness, made personal this time by Halana's own illness. Magara was sickened by the thought of what she had done to the seamstress. But what choice did she have? She had to travel so far down the Knifeman's road in order to convince him that she would arrive at the end. *There is always choice.* Magara prayed for strength. *You will not cease to exist, Halana,* she promised. *I will not let you die.*

The sky was lightening in the windows above, but Magara was desperately weary, feeling as though she had had no rest at all, so she tried to go back to sleep. At this stage of The Book, any time spent not writing was time well spent.

When she woke again, sunlight was streaming into the room. Although The Book stared at her accusingly, she would not pick up the pen. Magara brooded, waiting fearfully for the sorcerer's return and his discovery of her lack of effort.

Inevitably, her thoughts turned to Varo and Brostek. She saw again Varo's dark brown eyes, beautiful but unnervingly cold, remembered shaving him, revealing the perfect, strong face beneath the white-blond hair. Then Brostek intruded, demanding her attention, and she smiled at his homely features, his laughing green eyes. Where were they now? Could she get a message to them? *Ask? Ask who? Ask what?* she wondered. Even if she *could* contact them, how could she prevent her captor discovering what she had done?

You can't worry about that! she told herself, then reconsidered. *Even if it gets Varo and Brostek killed? But if I fail, they will die anyway,* she realized. In a world

297

where the blue-robed Knifeman was a god, there would be no room for her friends.

Try then.

Magara shut her eyes, remembering what the sorcerer had said when he had ordered her to contact the travellers. *Shall I draw you a picture?* She became annoyed as she recalled his amusement, and she tried to imagine instead the vision his prompting had formed. Endless lines in the endless dark. But this time there was only her imagination at work.

It's hopeless.

Ask.

Show me a picture. Please!

The emptiness rushed in around her. The Link was there! Magara suddenly realized that it had always been there; it had just been waiting to be perceived. She was filled with elation and fear.

Varo? Brostek?

Lines moved. Patterns formed and re-formed.

Where are you?

There was no reply.

What am I doing wrong? she wondered.

She was enveloped then by a feeling of consternation, but the confusion was not her own. She wondered briefly if perhaps she had reached them, but for some reason they were unable to reply.

Can you hear me?

There was another rush of emotion then, an odd but distinct warmth, coming from two entirely different directions.

Take the wizard to Nevern! She hoped that someone would heed her words.

'We will.'

The two words swam out of eternity, and her heart leapt with sudden hope. She had not recognized the voices, and could not be sure if it was really her friends.

'The wizard is not with us.'

A different voice then, coming from another place,

but also somehow connected to the warmth. Regret was mixed with eagerness in the man's tone.

Wait! I don't understand.

Her gateway to the Link was closing.

Don't go! she pleaded, but the contact was gone.

Magara opened her eyes to find the room lit by oil lamps, the windows no longer admitting any sunlight. *How long was I in the Link?* It had seemed like only moments. Surely a whole day had not passed? Then she realized that it was an eclipse. She could not see the sun, but flashes of yellow and indigo sent the shadows spinning, as though the two colours were warring with each other. Then it was over. The sunlight returned, making her blink in the sudden brightness.

Magara's heart sank as the door opened and her captor came in. All her earlier bravado evaporated as she imagined what he would do to her. Had he discovered that she had used the Link to try and contact her friends? Had he noticed her lack of progress on The Book? But the sorcerer did not mention either. He seemed jubilant, almost dancing about the room.

'Did you see it?' he asked. 'Wasn't it beautiful?' He threw his head back and laughed when he saw Magara's mystified expression.

'I have . . . persuaded . . . two of my remaining colleagues to fight a duel in the northern wastelands,' he explained. 'Naturally enough, such evenly matched opponents have both succeeded – and both lost. They are dead now, and I have their power, their hard-won power,' he crowed. 'And I didn't have to lift a finger!'

He just wanted to boast, Magara realized. *And I'm the best audience he has.* She hoped that his mood would last, keeping his attention away from her actions. Watching his self-obsessed display, she felt relief mingled with disgust, but she kept her face neutral.

'Only one left,' the Knifeman went on. 'And he'd have been dealt with by now if your stupid friends hadn't been so lax.'

'Should I try to contact them again?' Magara asked, her heart in her mouth.

'No. I've no more time for such trivia,' he replied. 'The game is being played for higher stakes now.'

A game? Magara thought incredulously. *He calls this a game?* At least he seemed unaware of her attempts to contact Brostek and Varo. She was not sure whether to be relieved or disappointed that she would not get a second chance.

'Not long now, eh?' he concluded jovially and went out, leaving Magara shaken and appalled. His confidence was terrifying, allied as it was with such awe-inspiring power. It was almost impossible to think of opposing it. Her own efforts seemed pitiful – the feeble attempts to turn The Book to her own purpose, and now the Link. Had she really made contact with anyone? The answers she had received had been both anonymous and contradictory. *We will. The wizard is not with us.*

Her captor had clearly been distracted by the battle between the two Knifemen, but that was over now and Magara dared not try again so soon. In any case, she felt utterly drained, and disturbed by her apparent lack of success. She tried to calm herself, to think clearly, but failed miserably as her mind was suddenly subjected to yet another vision.

Magaaaara.

Lisle had returned, but this time his voice was weak and distant, and the face she saw was not the boy's. It was broad, with widely spaced blue eyes – now open wide with shock – and he was spluttering in the water of the lake. She recognized him as one of Varo and Brostek's band, one of the men she had seen staring at her in a dream.

What's going on?

Magaaaara.

She saw a flashing image of the crater, men staring into the mirror-still lake. Then it was gone, and her mind was her own again.

Am I going mad? she wondered in despair.

*   *   *

The next morning, Magara opened The Book, too exhausted and confused to do anything else. She stared at the page, realizing that she was about to begin the final chapter.

Time was running out.

CHAPTER THIRTY-SIX

'Lisle! What are you doing?' Bair yelled, as the splash echoed around the silent crater.

'What has he ever done to you?' Hawk asked, laughing.

'He needed a wash, anyway,' Ryker commented, grinning broadly. 'Come out of there, Vilman. You'll get us all into trouble.'

They waited for their companion to surface, but after a few moments the water had become almost still again, and there was no sign of him. Good humour turned to puzzlement, then anxiety.

'Where's he gone?' Ross asked, voicing everyone's concern.

The lake water was clear as the ripples of his fall spread ever wider, but Vilman was nowhere to be seen. They were all at the rail now, staring into the depths. People were looking at them from other walkways, having heard the splash.

'Magaaara!' Lisle cried suddenly.

They all turned to the boy.

'What on earth is wrong with you?' Hawk said. 'That's *Vilman* you pushed in, not Magara.'

'He's playing a trick on us,' Ryker suggested. 'He'll be hiding under the house or the walkway. I'm going to go down and see.' And he began to take off his shirt.

'What's going on here?' It was Cole, one of the divers. He was frowning angrily as he approached them. 'Breaking the mirror will bring ill luck to us all.'

'More ill for Vilman than for us,' Ryker commented drily. 'He's vanished.'

'Magaaara,' Lisle repeated, still staring into the water.

Several people glanced his way, then went on trying to peer under the walkway, their movements causing a series of small waves on the surface of the lake.

'We can't just wait here—' Bair began.

'All right. I'll go,' Cole decided. He slipped into the water, and the others watched as he swam down strongly, then circled round below the house. He was underwater for what seemed like an age, but when he resurfaced, Cole was not even short of breath.

'Nothing!' he said, as though he found it hard to believe the evidence of his own eyes. 'He *has* vanished.'

'Like Lisle,' Bair said quietly.

'This place *is* weird,' Ryker added.

'How good a swimmer is he?' Cole asked, but no one got the chance to reply. Just at that moment, no more than ten paces away, the lake erupted and Vilman surged to the surface, gulping air and spluttering, then splashed his way frantically to the walkway. Cole stared at him as if he were a ghost while the others pulled him on to the boards. They were laughing with relief now, but Vilman's face was chalk white, his eyes wide. He was cold and trembling.

'Enjoy your swim?' Ryker enquired, grinning.

'It's . . . I . . .' Vilman stammered, then coughed and spat out some water.

'Where were you hiding?' Hawk asked. 'You gave us quite a scare.'

'Not . . . hiding,' he gasped, obviously still terrified. Their smiles turned to frowns as they realized this was not an act.

'What happened?' Cole asked, joining them.

'Who pushed me in?' Vilman demanded, ignoring the question.

'Lisle. Why?' Hawk replied.

Vilman stared at the boy, something like hatred in his eyes. 'He's been there,' he said.

'Been where?' Bair asked, but Vilman paid him no attention. He staggered to his feet and advanced on Lisle, grabbing him by the collar.

'Where is it, Lisle?' Vilman demanded, shaking the boy. 'Where did you send me?'

'Leave him alone!' Ross shouted.

'Have you gone mad?' Bair exclaimed.

They separated the two, and Lisle edged away as Vilman stopped struggling, shaking his head as if to clear it. He swore softly under his breath, still shivering violently.

'Now will you tell us . . .' Bair began.

'When he pushed me in,' Vilman cut in, 'I went under here. But when I surfaced, I was somewhere else altogether.'

'What!'

'I was in a lake surrounded by snow-capped mountains,' he went on. 'There were other lakes, but they were frozen. And there was a castle at one end of the valley. It was so cold and I was so scared, I thought I was going to drown. But though I went under, I came up again in an instant. Back here!'

'Is there a history of insanity in your family?' Ryker asked, all innocence.

'It's true – I swear,' Vilman insisted. 'Why would I make up a story like that?'

'You've made up stories before,' Hawk pointed out.

'Try it for yourself then,' the other said angrily. 'See how *you* like it.'

'Cole here went down shortly after you did,' Ross told him. 'But *he* didn't go anywhere.'

'You don't have to believe me!' Vilman shouted. His trembling had worsened, and he was still deathly pale.

'*Something* obviously happened to him,' Bair said.

Cole, who had remained silent throughout the exchange, now spoke.

'I'd swear he wasn't down there when I looked.'

'No!' Vilman responded through chattering teeth. 'That's because I was freezing to death in the mountains.'

'And Lisle disappeared before,' Cole added.

'That was during a mirror-lake too!' Ross exclaimed.

The diver nodded.

'Perhaps our tradition has more sense to it than we knew,' he said.

'You're not really taking this seriously, are you?' Ryker asked in disbelief.

'I have to,' Cole answered.

'Next time *you* go in,' Vilman threatened, but Ryker only rolled his eyes at his colleague.

'Will you come and tell the council about this?' the diver asked.

'Yes.' Vilman was a bit warmer now.

'And you've no idea where this place was?' Bair asked.

'Oh, yes,' Vilman snapped. 'It was the little pond where I used to collect frog spawn when I was a boy. Must have slipped my mind,' he went on sarcastically. The old soldier was unruffled.

'But there were mountains?' Hawk persisted.

'Yes. Bigger than any I've seen before.'

'Lisle was shouting for Magara while you were gone,' Ross said. 'Any idea why?'

'None. Unless she's in the castle. Horrible looking place.'

'Could it have been Nevern?' Bair asked.

'Not unless Levindre's geography has altered drastically!'

Their discussion was interrupted by the hurried approach of Lynton and one of Trevine's councillors.

'My friends!' the Barian envoy cried. 'Events have taken a new turn. I have had a vision.'

'Oh no,' Ryker groaned. 'Not you too.'

*   *   *

That evening, when the group was gathered together again, Iro came to visit them and hear their version of all the day's events. Vilman told his story again. He was now almost fully recovered, and the terror he had felt was obviously receding. Then the alchemist was told about the Barian's 'vision'.

'Actually, he didn't *see* anything,' Hawk began.

'According to Lynton,' Bair said, 'he heard a woman's voice in his head. First she said, "Where are you?", and then, "What am I doing wrong?" Lynton wanted to reply, but didn't know how – he was rather thrown by the whole thing.'

'I can understand that,' Ryker commented.

'Then she said, "Can you hear me?",' Ross told Iro, taking up the story, 'and Lynton thought the voice seemed to be coming from that pendant of his.'

'Made from telepathic silver, obviously,' Ryker remarked facetiously.

'When he took it out,' Ross went on, ignoring the interruption, 'it was warm.'

'Most things are in this heat,' Ryker added.

'Shut up, Ryker,' Hawk snarled.

'Next she said, "Take the wizard to never",' Ross went on.

'Nevern?' Iro asked.

'We asked the same thing,' Bair replied. 'Lynton said he thought she'd said "never", but it was probably "Nevern".'

'After that it was very confused . . .' Ross said.

Ryker opened his mouth to speak, but thought better of it when he saw the look on Hawk's face. Ross continued.

'. . . but he remembers wanting to point out that he didn't have a wizard with him. Then the woman said something about not understanding, and then "Don't go!" Lynton said she sounded desperate. And that was the end of it.'

'Could it have been Magara?' Iro wondered aloud.

'There's no way of telling,' Bair responded.

'Lisle thinks she's in the mountain valley, not Nevern,' Vilman said.

'I wonder if he's right,' Iro said thoughtfully. 'There's a legend about a place high in the greatest mountains – called the Vortex. It's supposed to be the place where all the lines of the Link converge, a place of great power, great magic. Magara and I were talking about it just before she left. Perhaps she went there instead of to Nevern.'

'But *why* would she go there?' Hawk wanted to know. 'More to the point, *how* could she? If it's really in the high wastelands, then it's damn near inaccessible. She'd never have got there so soon, even if she'd been properly equipped.'

'It was just a thought,' Iro said.

'Maybe *she* found a lake to jump into too,' Ryker suggested. It was intended as a joke, but the alchemist pounced on the idea.

'That's it!' he exclaimed. 'If it really is the Vortex, then it would be connected to all the nodes, including Nevern.'

'You mean transport by magic?' Bair asked. 'Isn't that just a bit far-fetched?'

'Ask Vilman,' the alchemist replied. They sat in silence for a while, then Iro spoke again. 'Let's assume the place Vilman – and presumably Lisle – went to is the Vortex.'

'That's a big assumption,' Hawk said.

'And wouldn't that mean that Trevine is magical too?' Ross asked.

'Yes, in a way,' Iro said, warming to his theme. 'You remember telling me about that theory of Keredin's? About the Knifemen being wraiths of the real men? Well, perhaps the lake here is the mirror image of the one in the Vortex.'

'But only when it's mirror still?' Bair completed.

'Apparently,' Iro agreed. 'There must have been a reason behind the tradition.'

'Well, it should be easy enough to test!' Hawk said.

'Rather you than me!' Vilman told him.

'How did the council respond when you told them about the other lake?' Iro asked.

'They're going to get the divers to investigate that carved stone down there again,' Vilman replied, 'but they seem as mystified as we are. If not more. After all, this is their home, and being told they don't know its true nature must come as a bit of a shock.'

'Do you think they'd help us test Iro's theory?' Hawk asked. 'They're the obvious ones to do it.'

'They'd be breaking their own taboo, and they won't be happy about that,' the alchemist replied. 'But there's no harm in asking.'

'All right, so assuming we all swim down here and pop up in the Vortex,' Ryker said brightly. '*Then* what do we do? And what's all this got to do with the Knifemen? I think all that would happen is that we'd get very cold.'

Iro told them about the other legends connected with the Vortex, and the promise of ruling the world.

'If one of the Knifemen – or whoever is controlling them – is in the Vortex, then that could be the source of the eclipses. It could also be the source of the eternal darkness the wizards of light were so worried about.'

'And when I first met you, I thought you were relatively sane,' Ryker responded. 'Do you really believe all that end-of-the-world stuff?'

'No,' Iro replied, 'but then I didn't believe that there was magic in this lake either.'

'Well, if you want my opinion,' Ryker said, grinning, 'I think all it means is that Vilman is a raving lunatic who should be locked up. And Lynton's just as bad.'

'You'd better not turn your back on me next time the lake is still,' the lunatic replied, but he was smiling as he said it.

*   *   *

The following morning, the divers all left their regular work to investigate the carved stone and the areas where Lisle and Vilman had disappeared. They found nothing, but a gentle wind was constantly ruffling the lake's surface, so no one was too surprised.

Later that day, news was sent down from the Rim that some people there had observed a partial eclipse of the sun the day before, and that strange yellow and purple flashes had been seen in the sky to the north-east. Nothing had been seen from inside the crater, but for the eclipse to have been observed on the Rim meant that it was somehow stronger than those that had gone before.

And it escaped no one's attention that the highest mountain peaks lay to the north-east.

CHAPTER THIRTY-SEVEN

The three horses came to a halt, sweating and wild-eyed, and Brostek leapt from the saddle.

'Where is she?' he demanded.

'In there,' the musician replied, pointing towards the fog.

'Alone?'

'Yes. I tried—'

'How long has she been gone?' Varo interrupted.

'Ten days.'

'Gods!' Brostek exclaimed. 'Why didn't you stop her?'

'I couldn't,' Hewitt said defensively. 'She—'

'Haven't you even looked for her?' Brostek interrupted furiously.

'I *tried*,' Hewitt answered, getting rather angry himself now. 'It's impossible – you're completely blind once you're in that. I just kept going round in circles and coming out again.'

'We'll see about that,' Brostek stated aggressively, and strode towards the grey mist.

'Wait!' Keredin had been the last to dismount, and although he was a little out of breath after their wild ride, his shout still carried conviction. Brostek hesitated, then turned and looked at his companion in silent question.

'There's more to this place than a little fog,' the ex-wizard said. 'You know that. We need to think about this before going in. Magara's already been gone a long time. Another hour will surely make no difference to her, and might mean the difference between success and failure.'

'Keredin's right,' Varo added calmly. 'We don't know what we're dealing with here.'

Brostek said nothing for a while. All his instincts were urging him to attempt Magara's rescue as soon as possible, but he finally saw the sense of his friends' advice.

'All right,' he agreed eventually, and turned to Hewitt. 'Tell us what you know.'

'And start at the beginning,' Keredin added.

So Hewitt told them how he and Magara had left Trevine, what she had learnt at Arenguard, about the eclipse and her apparent link with Lisle at Whistling Hill, and finally about the tapestry and its ever-changing state.

'Does Magara have the tapestry with her?' Keredin asked.

'No. I've got it here.'

'Why didn't you say so?' Brostek demanded.

Hewitt had been reluctant to show them the remains of the picture, but went to fetch it now. When he unrolled it for them, they were horrified.

'What a dreadful place,' Brostek breathed. Keredin's expression showed his revulsion; only Varo's gaze remained impassive.

'I wish I could show you what it used to be like,' Hewitt said. 'It was so very beautiful.'

'The changes happened during the eclipses?' Keredin asked.

'It started off that way,' Hewitt replied. 'At least, I always noticed the differences soon afterwards. And it's still mostly like that, but since Magara went in there, there have been changes at other times too. Almost all the recent awful things happened yesterday, after the eclipse with the purplish-blue and yellow flashes. Did you see it? And those colours vanished from the rainbow at the same time.'

'Two more Knifemen dead?' Varo wondered. The correspondence between the times when their enemies

311

had been killed and the disappearance of the equivalent colours had been noticed by all three travellers.

'Looks like it,' Brostek confirmed.

'Only two left then,' Keredin said. 'Obviously the orange Knifeman survived when we didn't get to Salem's Divide in time.'

'What happens,' Brostek asked quietly, 'when all the colours of the rainbow have gone?'

'Darkness,' Hewitt whispered, understanding the other's anxiety only too well.

'The double eclipse happened at much the same time as we got the message from Magara, didn't it?' Varo asked Brostek.

'Message?' Hewitt demanded. 'What message?'

'It was very confused,' Varo answered. 'We both heard her voice inside our heads at the same time. She called our names, but we couldn't understand the next part. Then she asked, "Can you hear me?"'

'And I felt this grow hot,' Brostek added. He pulled the wizard's pendant out of his pocket, and held it up.

'Magara has one of those!' Hewitt exclaimed. 'She found it inside a shatterstone in the lake.'

'In Trevine?' Keredin asked incredulously.

'Yes,' the musician confirmed. 'Iro told Magara that it's an old symbol for light.'

The three travellers exchanged glances.

'So perhaps Lynton is right and the crater *is* important,' Varo said. 'But why?'

'You were telling me about Magara's message,' Hewitt prompted impatiently.

'We think she said, "Wake the wizard of Nevern",' Varo said. 'But it wasn't clear.'

'In any case,' Brostek put in, 'she referred to this place. We were on our way here anyway, but that certainly spurred us on!'

'But then her last words seemed to be advising us to wait,' Varo went on. 'She told us not to go quite distinctly. But because that contradicted what she'd said earlier, she may have been referring to something else. We just don't know what.'

'At least it means she's still alive,' Hewitt said quietly. He had begun to have serious doubts about this. 'Did you manage to answer her?'

'We tried, but we didn't know how,' Varo replied.

'We both agreed to do what she asked,' Brostek explained, 'but then we realized that we don't really know what that was. How are we supposed to wake this wizard of Nevern?'

'Well, the first thing we must do is get in there,' Keredin answered.

They all looked at the implacable grey mist.

'Do you still think this is Nevern's image-key?' Varo asked, indicating the tapestry.

'Yes. I'm sure of it now,' Keredin replied. 'What Magara read at Arenguard confirmed it, and the changes since must mirror what's happening inside. And we already know the tapestry is somehow linked to the Knifemen and the eclipses.'

'The Cartel are worried about the eclipses too,' Hewitt put in.

'Well, that makes me feel so much better,' Brostek remarked sourly. 'We can all relax now.'

'There was an eclipse just as Magara went in,' Hewitt said, remembering that fateful moment. 'The blue one.'

That image silenced them all for a few moments, but then Varo brought them back to the present.

'All right. Let's sum up what we know. The tapestry is the image-key to Nevern, and should also be the key to unlock the shadow-maze. Magara must have got in successfully. If she was just wandering and lost, like everyone else who's tried, then she'd have come out again long before now. So perhaps we can do it too.' He sounded confident, as though he truly believed that they could follow their friend into the shadow-maze.

'But once inside, we'll be working blind,' Brostek added. 'Hewitt says we won't even be able to see a hand in front of our noses.' The musician nodded in confirmation.

'And there's something else,' Varo went on. 'If we heard Magara correctly, then there's a wizard in there. Somehow we need to wake him up; perhaps he'll be able to help us against the Knifemen.' He paused. 'Anything else?'

'Do any of the old legends help you?' Hewitt wondered. 'Only the innocent and pure of heart are supposed to be able to enter Nevern. The world is safe from evil "as long as the sun shines" on the garden. And it's a place where all the seasons can exist at once.'

'How innocent are *we*?' Brostek wondered.

'If Nevern looks like that,' Keredin said, nodding at the tapestry, 'then there's not much sunlight left, is there?'

'All the seasons at once?' Varo queried.

Hewitt explained the anomalies in the original version.

'There doesn't seem to be much like that now,' Varo commented.

'The seasons are all a mess,' Brostek added.

They stared at the ugly images.

'But the tapestry is the only real help we've got,' Keredin stated. 'And we won't be able to see it once we're inside.'

'Then we'd better know it well,' Varo decided. 'Give me a little time.'

He took the tapestry and went away to study it on his own.

'Will he be able to remember it all?' Hewitt asked softly.

'Every last stitch,' Brostek replied. 'Varo's mind is like that. His memory is phenomenal.'

'We'd better sort the horses out,' Keredin said. 'Will you help us, Hewitt?'

'Are you coming in with us?' Brostek asked Keredin as they worked.

'Yes,' the former wizard said determinedly.

'Sure? This is our job, Varo's and mine.'

'I'm doing this for me,' was the reply. 'And for Mattie.'

'Your lover?' Brostek asked. Keredin had never spoken her name before.

He nodded. 'I gave up wizardry for her. This is the last chance I have to make amends. If magic is going to be used – just once – to do some real good, then I'd like to be there to see it. I know she'd want that too, in spite of what it did to us.'

'Do you ever regret trying to run away with her?' Brostek asked.

'I never regretted the attempt,' Keredin replied. 'Only that we failed. And we won't fail Magara.'

'Not if I can help it.'

'You love her, don't you,' the older man said.

'Yes,' Brostek admitted. 'Varo does too – though I sometimes wonder if he even knows it.'

Hewitt had remained silent during this exchange, feeling as though he were intruding, but now Brostek turned to him.

'The last two hands must have been lonely for you, stuck out here on your own,' he said.

'I've had some company,' the musician replied, and explained about Celia. 'She even sang with me yesterday.'

'Perhaps she will today too,' Keredin remarked.

The other two looked round, and saw Celia approaching them. She was obviously nervous, and kept her head half turned away, watching them sideways.

'Magara asked me to play for her when she went in,' Hewitt said, beckoning Celia towards them. 'We could do the same for you.'

'We'd like that,' Brostek replied.

Celia had edged closer, glancing every so often at Shadow – who returned her gaze placidly.

'The lights are coming,' she announced.

Brostek and Keredin looked at Hewitt, and he explained her odd theory, adding quietly that he thought the hermit was mad.

'Will you show us the lights?' Keredin asked gently.

Celia nodded vigorously, like an enthusiastic child, but no amount of coaxing could induce her to say any more, and they gave up the attempt.

Then Varo returned, pronouncing himself ready. The three men took the simple precaution of roping themselves together, waved farewell to Hewitt and Celia, and took one last look at each other before wading into the opaque fog. Shadow followed close on Brostek's heels. Less than an hour had passed since their arrival. Hewitt watched them go, his heart filled with a mixture of hope and foreboding.

He played for them, and Celia sang, sounding rapturously happy. The three men and the wolf disappeared; this time, there was no eclipse to mark their entry into the shadow-maze.

CHAPTER THIRTY-EIGHT

The morning seemed endless to Magara. As the time crawled, she felt the sorcerer hovering nearby, ready to pounce once she had completed her task. He visited her frequently, and she found his eagerness obscene. Magara wrote as slowly as she could, but there was only one event of note left to record – Halana's early death – and she was determined *not* to record that. And so she filled a few pages with tiny details of decay. While this would not affect anything significantly, it would hopefully satisfy all but the most intensive scrutiny by her captor.

She wished that her writing could be like that on the rock taken from Trevine's cliffs. Then it would fade away after a time, and all the evil would simply be undone. Inevitably, she thought of Brostek's message. *Thinking of you, little one.* And of all the things it didn't say. Magara knew that Brostek cared for her, but had his message meant more than that? She hoped so.

The longing to see him had grown until it was something akin to pain. Magara no longer doubted that she loved him, and the thought that she would probably never get the chance to tell him so made her want to weep. It did not matter that his looks were so far from her imagined ideal; she knew now that her feelings for him went far deeper than friendship. She was angry with herself – why had it taken such awful circumstances for her to realize that she loved him? She berated herself for not having acted when she had the chance. Her thoughts became entangled in the hopelessness of what might have been.

And Varo? Magara could not deny that she was

attracted to him physically, although she found it difficult to look into those impossibly cold brown eyes. And what he felt for her would always remain a mystery, hidden deep within that obsessive, calculating mind. She had known for some time that the unlikely pair made such a good team precisely because they *were* so different. And she also knew that she was now pinning almost all her few remaining hopes on the two men. *Where are they now?* she wondered.

They await your signal.

The girl's voice came out of nowhere, startling Magara, but bringing with it renewed optimism.

Halana? Is it you?

They have entered the shadow-maze at Nevern, the girl went on weakly. *Make your choice now.*

Then the contact was gone, and the sickness of the Link lingered in Magara's mind like a bad taste on her tongue. She wished she could have had more of Halana's counsel, but knew that she must act now. Desperate measures were needed – and quickly. Varo and Brostek were inside the shadow-maze! She had no time to wonder whether they had brought the wizard with them. *They await your signal.* Would the clues she had put in place be enough? Should she risk everything with a direct message in The Book? How else could she send the necessary signal?

Magara turned the page and discovered that she had reached the very last blank sheet. She had no alternative now but to choose the ending. Inspiration came from the memory of the story she had made up – a lifetime ago it seemed – about the test of the shadow-maze. In that, the final obstacle to success had been a trial of faith; to prove that love was worth any risk, any unknown danger. So it was for Magara now. So it would be for Varo and Brostek. If the Knifeman discovered her treachery then she was surely doomed, but the alternative was even worse. Magara would not fail through inaction. She would keep her promise to Halana!

318

She began to write, this time believing every word, willing it to be true. And hoping that somewhere there was the power to make it real.

'The darkness that had come to Nevern was pierced by a single shaft of light. It shone like a beacon, guiding the pure of heart to the garden. And the message that the light brought with it was – Have faith.

'The same message was now inscribed upon the tomb, above a device formed of four touching circles cut deep into the stone. HAVE FAITH.'

Magara got no further. The door to the chamber was flung open and her gaoler stormed in, his face distorted with rage. Violet light sparkled and flashed all around him.

'What are you doing?' he screamed.

Grabbing The Book from Magara, he quickly scanned the last page, then ripped it out in fury, crumpling the paper and flinging it into a corner of the room. As he did so, Magara felt the pendant at her throat grow warm.

'You little imbecile!' the sorcerer shouted. 'Did you think to deceive me with such puerile tricks? You deserve . . .'

Intense pain seared through every nerve of Magara's body; she could not even scream as the breath was sucked out of tortured lungs. She knew she was going to die, and would have welcomed even that oblivion rather than endure such torment a moment longer. No living creature could stand this.

Yet it was not only her body that suffered. The images forced upon her mind were in some ways even worse. Blood spewed, the cries of those frozen in the lake rose to ever more ghastly heights, and all living things decayed horribly. She saw her own face shrivel and discolour as flames engulfed her hair. Blackness beckoned . . . then withdrew.

Magara slumped forward, beaded with perspiration, crying helplessly and gasping for air. Her torturer had relented at the last moment. In fact, the Knifeman had controlled his rage, realizing perhaps that such punishment would kill her, thus ending his chance of fulfilling his dream.

'You see what lies in store if you disobey me again?' he shouted. Then he calmed down, and added in his normal icy tones, 'You will now complete your story within one hour – or it will be the worse for you. Understand?'

'I can't,' Magara croaked. 'The last page is gone.'

She paid a heavy price for her petty defiance. A band of pain, as severe as before but now tightly controlled, ran up her body. Each part of her trembled in awful anticipation, then twitched in reaction after the agony had moved on. When it reached her neck, Magara almost fainted, but her tormentor was too calculating to allow that now. Her mouth and teeth, nose and cheeks, then her eyes and ears all shrieked in anguish. She was blind for a moment; when she could see again, the ragged edge of the page had gone, and a fresh sheet was in its place.

'Be very careful what you write this time,' the sorcerer warned her. 'And give me that pendant. You can't possibly use it, but it's obviously giving you some very stupid ideas.' He held out a hand expectantly.

Magara removed the lace and, with a shaking hand, deliberately threw it at him. The Knifeman moved instinctively to catch it, then thought better of the idea and let it fall to the floor.

'If it can't harm you,' Magara whispered painfully, 'why won't you touch it?'

He stared at her coldly for a few moments, then stooped to retrieve the pendant. He enclosed the metal very deliberately in his fist, and held it up. A tiny spasm of pain crossed his face, but this was instantly controlled. His hand began to glow red, as though it had become a miniature lamp, the bones visible as shadows within the flesh. It grew so bright that Magara almost expected to see smoke and smell charred skin. In the corner of her

prison cell, the crumpled page suddenly burst into
flames, and her last hope was utterly destroyed.

The glow died away and the Knifeman opened his fist,
revealing a small, black, shapeless lump of metal which
he tossed aside contemptuously. His hand was
unmarked.

He flicked his wrist and Magara found herself forced
to pick up her pen.

'Finish it,' he commanded. 'Now!'

CHAPTER THIRTY-NINE

Shadow growled deep in her throat as her master led her into the fog, and whined as she became the first of the group to lose her vision. Brostek bent down to comfort her, ruffling the fur behind her ears; the wolf quietened, and began to follow him by scent alone. The three men waded deeper, listening all the time to Hewitt and Celia, whose music was welcome but supremely incongruous.

They were lined up side by side, with Varo in the centre, slightly ahead of the other two. He was taller than either of his companions, and so his line of sight would remain clear for a little longer. He felt them stagger as they became blind, and heard their sharply indrawn breaths. Even knowing what would happen had not prepared them for the awful sensation of isolation and claustrophobia. And then they both pulled on the rope as they veered away in opposite directions. Varo tugged sharply then held the ropes firm, halting their wayward progress.

'You're turning away!' he said, instinctively raising his voice now that the other two were invisible.

'No, I'm not,' Brostek replied, his voice sounding slightly muffled. 'I'm going straight on.'

'Me too,' Keredin said. 'I swear.'

'You were both turning,' Varo insisted. 'And in opposite directions.' He pulled at the ropes again, shortening the distance between them. 'I'll keep my head above the mist as long as I can. Stay with me.'

His companions replied with grunts of assent, and they went slowly forward. Brostek and Keredin shuffled uncertainly, one hand on the connecting rope, the other stretched out in front of them.

'Can you see anything at all?' Varo asked, coming to a temporary halt.

'Not a thing,' Brostek answered. 'It's awful.'

'I can smell something, though,' Keredin said.

'What?'

'I don't know. It's sort of sickly.'

'I can feel a breeze too,' Brostek added. 'At our backs. Very gentle but constant.'

'That's impossible,' Varo said. 'The fog's not moving at all.'

'It *is* there, though,' Keredin confirmed. 'I can feel it too.'

'I'll be under myself in the next couple of steps,' Varo told them. He was already on tiptoe, almost at full stretch. 'Can you still hear the music?'

'Yes, it's over to our right,' Brostek answered.

'No, it's to the left!' Keredin exclaimed.

'It's still behind us,' Varo said. 'We've been going straight the whole time.'

'It felt like we were turning,' his partner replied.

'Well, we weren't. Are you ready?'

'No one could ever be ready for this,' Keredin said. 'Let's just go.'

They edged forward again. Varo took a deep breath as he became totally immersed. He immediately understood the others' hesitancy. The instant unlight was desperately unnerving, but Varo would not allow himself to panic.

'Are you in?' Brostek asked.

'Yes.'

'The music sounds as though it's in front of us now,' Keredin said tentatively.

'It's still to the right for me,' Brostek responded.

'Ignore it,' Varo told them. 'The rules are different here.'

The other two thought privately that following their leader's advice was easier said than done. The music represented their last link with the outside world, and to cast it aside would take an effort of iron will; simple for Varo, not so for them. The three men and the wolf were all totally blind now, and a chill dampness began to seep into their clothes, a false dew speckling hair and skin. The wind was at their backs as they took deep breaths, and tried to still their racing hearts.

'What now?' Brostek asked.

'Hold still,' Varo ordered. 'I'm going to duck down. I want to see what we're walking on.' They did as he asked, feeling his movements through the rope. Varo's fingers encountered grass, wet but not rotted. He told the others what he had found, and added, 'If the tapestry is an accurate guide, then we must be in the bit portrayed as spring. There's still some life here.' He paused, then went on thoughtfully, 'I can't hear the music at all down here, and the smell is stronger—'

'Ssh!' Brostek hissed suddenly. 'I hear something.'

In the silence that followed, they all heard the faint sound of a girl singing. The pain and sadness in her voice were plain, but the actual words of her song could not be heard. Varo stood up, moving carefully so that he would not overbalance.

'Let's go towards her,' he said quietly. 'It must be the girl by the tomb. Together, now.'

They drifted deeper into the maze, and as Hewitt's music faded, relieving them of its confusing pull, the girl's voice grew louder. She sounded hoarse and tired. At last they could make out the words.

> 'Nature needs no reasons,
> For following the seasons.
> Seed, leaf, flower, fruit,
> Twig, branch, bower, root.'

But then her song faltered and she began to cough, a dry racking sound which was followed by a painful wheezing and sobs of misery. Shadow whined softly, as if in sympathy, and Brostek wanted to go to her, to comfort her and ease the pain.

Without the need of words, they moved forward again, arms questing ahead. Then Brostek's fingers encountered an unexpected warmth. It was only a fleeting sensation, like feeling warm breath on a cold day, and it was soon gone, but he knew that it had been her. A shiver ran through him; he felt as though he had touched a ghost. He knew that soon even that feeble warmth would be gone. The girl was dying, and when she did the garden would surely die too. Brostek wanted to call out, to tell her that they were trying to help, but he could not. A moment later his hand hit cold, smooth stone, and he called the others to a halt.

'It's the tomb.'

His colleagues drew closer, testing the outlines of the gravestone.

'There's an inscription,' Keredin said.

'What does it say?'

The ex-wizard laboriously traced out the letters.

'H.A.L.,' he reported, then paused. 'I'm not sure what the next letter is. Part of it is missing.' After another moment he added, 'There's nothing else.'

'At least we know where we are now,' Varo said.

'Oh, really?' Brostek sounded amused.

'In the tapestry, I mean,' Varo answered seriously. 'The tomb is in the centre of the spring quadrant.'

'Do you think the girl's song was trying to tell us something?' Keredin asked. 'Should we follow the seasons too? Complete the cycle like the original tapestry?'

'Sounds logical,' Brostek commented. 'So which way is summer?'

At this strange-sounding question, the ex-wizard's fragile composure began to crumble. He had tried to remain calm, wanting to use what knowledge he had to help his companions, but now the task ahead seemed impossible – even though it had been his own idea.

'I'm . . . I'm not sure I can do this,' he blurted out, suddenly sounding very afraid. 'We could be lost in here for ever.' He pulled along the rope, and clutched Varo's hand. 'Don't leave me, for pity's sake.'

Varo did not know how to cope with this outburst, and it was Brostek who reassured Keredin.

'We won't leave you,' he told him. 'We got into this together, and we'll get *out* of it together. But we must stay calm.' The others remained silent. 'All right?' Brostek prompted.

'Yes,' Keredin said shakily, sounding embarrassed.

'You said that the tapestry is the key to this place,' Brostek went on, deliberately trying to involve the ex-wizard again. 'So if we followed that, which way should we go to get to summer?'

'To the right, I suppose,' Keredin answered, 'but how can we tell which way that is? Direction means nothing in here.' He shivered as the wind switched round.

The sudden squeal of a terrified rabbit was abruptly cut off, and they automatically turned to face the direction of the sound. A fox barked triumphantly, and Shadow growled in response. In his mind's eye, Varo saw again the bloody jaws of the fox, and placed that image in his mental picture of the tapestry.

'The fox was on the opposite side from the border with summer,' he said.

'So we should move away from the sound?' Keredin suggested, sounding a little more confident now.

'But Hewitt's music led us all over the place,' Brostek pointed out.

'That came from outside,' Varo stated, as if this explained everything.

'And the girl's voice did lead us all to the tomb,' Keredin said.

They set off gingerly, and soon found their boots sinking in mud, the sickly smell intensifying with each step. Varo stooped to touch the ground, and discovered sluggishly flowing water. His fingers came away greasy and foul-smelling.

'The remains of the stream,' he said. 'So we're going the right way.'

326

A little later they seemed to step through an invisible wall. It was much warmer here, but the smell of decay was ten times worse, and they all gagged in disgust. The sweet, cloying odour of rotting spring had been revolting enough, but it was nothing compared to this all-pervading, stomach-turning stench. Their boots squelched through soft, decaying matter, releasing bubbles of rancid gas that made them choke. Shadow whined piteously; the ordeal was even worse for her.

'Stinkhorn,' Brostek gasped. 'I'd know that smell anywhere.' He remembered Magara taking him to inspect some of these nauseating fungi, which Iro had cultivated.

'This is summer then,' Varo said, sounding pleased, in spite of the horrible atmosphere.

'The death of summer,' Keredin whispered.

The wind, which had been at their backs as they walked away from the tomb, now shifted slightly again. For a moment the stink was less oppressive.

'Is the wind following us, or are we following it?' the ex-wizard asked, and wondered what had prompted this idea.

'You think the wind might be helping us? Why?' Varo asked suspiciously.

'I don't know. Perhaps Magara left a trail behind her for us to follow?'

'In the wind?' Brostek responded sceptically. 'How would she have done that?'

'At least it can't rot,' Keredin said, gasping for air.

'We'll keep a watch on it,' Varo decided, not even aware of the irony of his words. 'Quiet now, and listen.'

They all picked out the distinct sound of drips falling into still water, and a whistling, as of wind blowing through convoluted shapes. Both came from ahead and to their right, the direction the wind was now taking.

'The ruin?' Keredin suggested.

'Yes,' Varo agreed. 'Let's go towards it. We can get our bearings at least.'

The stream had vanished under the mass of rotting vegetation, but it was still treacherous underfoot. They stumbled often, each steadied by the others, and their hands and knees were soon covered in slime. Shadow too was suffering. She stayed close to her master's legs, almost making him trip on a few occasions; her sense of smell was less reliable now in the middle of such a welter of foul odours.

At one point, the rope between Varo and Brostek became entangled in something that blocked their way.

'Look out!' Varo warned.

The two men drew back as the obstruction fell to the ground, landing with a dull splash. It sank further into the mire with an obscene gurgling noise. They edged around it carefully, feeling their way and discovering that they had knocked over one of the broken statues, its stone now eroded and coated with filth. They proceeded even more cautiously after that, none of them wanting to fall or be pulled to the ground.

'Fish!' Brostek said suddenly, as Shadow growled her disapproval. 'Gods, that's vile!'

They all noticed it then, a new thread in the all-surrounding mesh of smells. The dripping was louder too.

'We're nearly there,' Varo said. 'The fish was in the pond by the fountain.'

As he spoke, Keredin's foot sank into water and he nearly fell, putting out a hand to save himself, and grasping stone covered with slippery fronds. He pulled his boot out again.

'We *are* there,' he remarked, feeling sick.

'Then if I'm right,' Varo pronounced, 'we should turn half right to go on to autumn.'

'Down the tapestry?' Brostek said.

'Yes. It's worked so far.'

At his words, the wind shifted again to blow in the direction Varo had suggested, and that settled it for them.

The first indications that they had entered autumn were a sharp drop in temperature and the sound of ducks croaking feebly, their voices more of a hiss than a quack. Next, the three men noticed a change in the type of smells that surrounded them. This was a relief at first, but the new odours soon seemed just as bad. Above all was the sweet, sickly scent of rotting fruit – much of it obviously fermenting – so that the air was heavy, and made their heads swim. But there were other smells beneath the surface that told of viler putrefaction, and they all thought immediately of the dead swan. The wind had dropped suddenly as they crossed the imaginary border, but Varo knew where to go next.

'Follow the sound of the ducks,' he instructed the others. 'That will lead us to the swan. Then we should turn right again.'

As the dismal quacking grew louder, the smell of death grew even stronger. It was overpowering now. Varo touched something with his boot, which gave gently when he pushed, and bent to investigate. Frayed feathers brushed his arm, and then his fingertips touched the squirming mass of maggots. He shook them off, feeling no sense of disgust, merely satisfaction.

'Good,' he said. 'Tread carefully.'

He turned to the right, in the direction he had chosen, but at that moment a cool breeze sprang up, this time blowing in their faces. They hesitated.

'It *can't* be the other way,' Varo said quietly.

'The wind's been right up to now,' Brostek pointed out, then sniffed as a new scent was borne to them on the breeze. 'Smells like plum brandy,' he said. Magara had often teased him about his liking for the fiery spirit.

'Should we turn around, then?' Varo asked, uncertain for the first time.

'Remember – Hewitt told us that the perspective of the tapestry changed out of sequence,' Keredin put in.

'So?'

'Going from summer to autumn it swings right round

from east to west,' the ex-wizard went on. 'Perhaps the wind changes round too. Perhaps we need it in our faces now.'

'If it *was* anything to do with Magara, then I think you're right,' Brostek said. 'She knows my weakness for plum brandy, and she'd expect me to head towards it.'

'This way then,' Varo decided.

They went on, skirting the swan's remains and edging forward, sliding their boots over the wet ground.

Winter came like an avalanche of ice, burning their lungs. They all shook with cold. Here, the stench of decay was replaced by the lifeless aridity of frozen wasteland. Wolves howled, adding to the sense of desolation. Shadow answered in kind, her hackles raised and fangs bared in the primeval cry of her race. All three men, even Brostek, whom Shadow loved, cringed at the eerie sound.

The wind was still in their faces, but that seemed a feeble reason for any confidence. They smelt the acrid tang of woodsmoke, heard the crash of lightning and the crackle of flames, but of course could see nothing of the burning trees. A few paces further on, they all stopped as realization dawned.

'We've reached the last quadrant,' Brostek said. 'Now what do we do?'

'This should be the end,' Keredin added.

'Back to spring again?' Varo suggested.

'We'll go round and round for ever like that.' Keredin's voice rose in panic.

'What have we missed?' Brostek wondered aloud. To have come so far and still be blind was a cruel fate.

But then their blindness was lifted momentarily as a shaft of light pierced the gloom. They each saw it for an instant, felt drawn to it. Involuntarily, they all stepped towards the light, then stopped, assailed by hidden terrors.

To go that way, Varo knew, meant walking over the frozen lake, and to risk falling through the ice to drown in the unseen waters below. To die in such a way had always been his personal nightmare, hidden so deep that he had never spoken of it to anyone. Keredin alone heard Mattie's voice, pleading with him not to come to her, telling him that *they* were waiting for him, and that they would kill her if he did not obey them. Such words had never actually been spoken, but in his mind, Keredin had agonized over that fateful decision time and time again. Now it seemed that he was being given the chance to rewrite his own personal history, to abandon his chance of love and save her life. Even Shadow was faced with an image of her nemesis – a wall of fire, trees burning so that there was no way through. She snarled, shying away from the hated fire.

And Brostek knew that there was a pack of ravening wolves ahead. He was suddenly a boy again, watching the ferocious creatures which would surely tear him to pieces if he came too close.

Have faith.

They all heard it, though there had been no sound. The pendant in Brostek's pocket grew hot. He took it out, and it lit the fog around him with a dull glow. No words were spoken, and none was needed. They moved towards their own terrors, accepting whatever fate had been set for them, propelled by love and prepared to risk everything for it. The beacon which swept the shadow-maze drew them closer.

Then a sudden roar of flame made them blind again, and the beacon was snuffed out. But they had reached their goal, and they stepped through together. The fog had vanished, but they were horrified by what they saw. The shadow-maze had been defeated, but Nevern was just as the tapestry had shown it; black decay and stinking death as far as they could see. They had won through the dream; their prize was to live in perpetual nightmare.

Worse still, in all that horrible wasteland, there was no sign of the sleeping wizard – or of Magara.

CHAPTER FORTY

Hewitt and Celia continued their music-making for some while after the three men had entered the fog. And in all that time, nothing changed except the angle of the sunlight falling upon the mist. Eventually, the unlikely pair rested, and some impulse made Hewitt look at the tapestry again. It had changed. The last few signs of life had been all but obliterated. The girl lay slumped on the ground beside the tomb, and the fox had vanished altogether. The ducks were dead, mere skeletons now on the barren earth; even the wolves were skulking near the edge of the material, as if they were about to leave Nevern for good. Worse still, the eclipse of the spring sun was now almost complete. Two-thirds of the circle was black, casting a long shadow over the last remnants of the forsaken garden. Hewitt closed his eyes in horror, wondering what the three friends had let themselves in for. Then, suddenly, Celia cried out.

'The lights. Look! The lights!' Her voice was triumphant, as though she had known this would happen.

Hewitt opened his eyes. The flickering on the surface of the mist was vague at first, and could only just be seen, and he thought perhaps that it was just a trick of the sunlight. However, it grew in strength and a swirling pattern of light emerged, moving distinctly within the slowly undulating grey mass. It was the first real variation Hewitt had seen in all his time there.

'What does it mean, Celia?' he asked anxiously.

The hermit did not answer him directly, but began to dance on the spot.

'I can make it go away!' she cried gleefully, closing her eyes and giggling.

Hewitt felt a spasm of anger at her capriciousness, and was about to speak again when he realized that, this time, Celia's boast was no childish joke. As he watched, the fog thinned rapidly, fading into nothing . . .

. . . and revealed the horror beneath.

Hewitt's hopes had risen for an instant, but he was appalled by the sight of Nevern's decline. Not even the tapestry's changes had prepared him for such a shock. His legs gave way beneath him and he sat down suddenly, feeling ill.

Celia opened her eyes again and stared.

'Pretty,' she said happily, and started towards the stinking black wasteland. Hewitt watched her go, saw her stoop to pick something from the ground, and knew that he did not have the stomach to follow her.

*   *   *

Magara stared at the last page of The Book. Her hour was nearly over now, and she felt like a condemned prisoner waiting for the moment of execution. For she was sure that she would die when the hour was up – and she was adamant that she would never finish her 'task', but would rather face the sorcerer's wrath.

Since his ultimatum, she had written a few more lines, and there was room for only two or three more now. She had done this in order to appease the Knifeman, should he visit her during her hour of grace, and thus try and gain a little time. But her captor had not appeared, and Magara could not help but wonder why. There could not be long to go before the moment of the deadline – and of his triumph.

A small spark of hope suggested that perhaps the other surviving Knifeman, the one whose identifying colour was orange, was attacking her gaoler; perhaps there was a slim chance that the two would annihilate each other. Or perhaps – an even more outrageously optimistic thought – the wizard she had longed for had actually reached Nevern. Magara could not allow herself to believe this; she was sure that she would have known, would have felt something, if he had arrived. And yet . . . *You will only see something if you are willing to open your eyes.* She remembered the phrase from her childhood; it had been one of her tutor's favourite sayings. And she had nothing to lose.

Show me a picture.

There was no response, and Magara realized that it could not be that easy. It was not a matter of words, but of intent. True commitment was needed to reach the Link.

She willed herself to relax, then concentrated her whole being on asking the Link to respond; she utilized every part of her mind and her spirit, knowing that anything less would fail. For a moment, nothing happened, but then she felt the vast emptiness surround her. This time it was full of fire and lightning – the Link was aflame with a conflict beyond her imagining. Cowering in her own small space, she asked to see Nevern, and was rewarded with a vision of devastation and black despair. But at its heart a single spark of light shone out, and she focused on this with frantic eagerness. Her heart leapt as she saw Varo, Brostek and Shadow – and another man, whose mane of hair sparkled with light. *The wizard!*

Suddenly, she knew what she had to do. She opened her eyes, looked at The Book and wrote her last defiant words. Then she sat back, sick with fear, but still strangely content, and watched the door fly open as her enemy came in. Magara prepared herself to die.

*   *   *

Far away from both Magara's prison cell and the site of Hewitt's vigil, a group of men stood watching the surface of a lake. None of them knew exactly what they were looking for, but they each knew when it would be seen. As soon as the surface became a mirror . . .

But the wind swirled round the crater, and small waves distorted the images of cliffs, sky and the town. Overhead, a heron circled lazily, and on one of the walkways, a young boy looked solemnly at the moving water, then went and fetched his lute.

CHAPTER FORTY-ONE

The three men looked around, aghast. This was a scene from the darkest reaches of nightmare. Even the newly restored sunlight seemed reluctant to illuminate such a landscape.

'Where is she?' Brostek asked hopelessly.

'No one could survive in this for one hand,' Varo said. 'Let alone two.'

They both seemed utterly at a loss, and so Keredin – surprising even himself – took charge.

'We'll split up,' he decided, 'and search the central area. If there's anything to tell us where Magara or the wizard are, then it'll be here.'

'There's no one here,' Brostek said despairingly.

'Failing that,' the former wizard went on, undeterred, 'look for anything, however small, that is still healthy and alive. Anything at all.'

'In *this*?' Brostek asked.

'The sun is shining on Nevern again,' Keredin responded with more cheerfulness than he actually felt. 'So there's still a chance that we can save it.'

Neither of the others looked as though they believed a word of this, but they moved to obey nonetheless. They regrouped some time later, but could report no sign either of the people they were seeking or of any healthy life.

'The only thing that's changed is the inscription on the tomb,' Varo added. 'It now says "H.A.L.A.N." – but that still doesn't make any sense. And there's no sign of the girl anywhere.'

'There must be *something* here,' Keredin persisted.

'Well, we can't find it,' Brostek replied. 'What do you want it for?'

'Look,' the ex-wizard began, hoping to force them out of their dejection. 'We made it *in* here, didn't we? I don't know what's happened to Magara any more than you do, but at least we have a chance to restore Nevern. That's *something*. And who knows? Perhaps if we do, it will help Magara, wherever she is.'

'How?' Varo wanted to know.

'Nevern was once magical,' Keredin replied. 'And I believe that it still is. The image-key still exists,' he went on, ignoring their expressions of disbelief, 'and on it the fourth eclipse was not full. If this place was completely dead, then we'd never have got in at all. Therefore it *must* be possible to restore it! That's what Magara wanted us to do.'

'She wanted the wizard to do it,' Brostek pointed out.

'Well, the wizard's not here!' Keredin snapped. 'I'm the best we've got! Don't you see? This is my chance to make up for all those wasted years, for all the hypocrisy, to prove to myself that wizardry isn't a redundant art, that it still has some meaning in the world. I might fail, but this is a chance I've *got* to take. And I need your help.'

His two companions had never seen him so animated, and the urgency in his voice finally cut through Brostek's gloom and Varo's incomprehension.

'So what are we going to do?' Varo asked.

'An image-key is the means of restoring a node,' Keredin explained. 'I know this one has been corrupted, but the original is still there somewhere. We have to find the way to release it.'

'But we haven't got the tapestry,' Brostek objected.

'Varo has. In his head.' The former wizard turned to the blond man. 'Think! Was there anything alive and unsullied left on the tapestry? Anywhere? If we can find that, then we can begin again. And if Nevern lives again, then there's hope for restoring the rest.'

'The rest of what?' Varo asked, still confused.

'The Link,' Keredin replied. 'Don't you see? If a

magical place as big, as powerful and as well-protected as this has almost been defeated by the evil we face – whether it's the Knifemen or not – then the rest must have been polluted too. Magara's experience at Whistling Hill tallies with that. I remember that place from a long time ago – it was famous as a site of peace and tranquillity, where dreams were always beautiful.'

'It's not like that now,' Brostek said, pointing out the obvious.

'Exactly,' the ex-wizard agreed. 'If we can turn back the evil here, then we may be helping more than just Nevern.' He looked again at Varo, who was silent for a while, deep in thought.

'There's nothing at all,' he said eventually. 'Even the last few plants in spring are already dying.'

'What about right at the centre, that small piece that joins all four quadrants?' Keredin asked, desperate for some small piece of hope.

'No,' Varo replied with conviction. 'There's nothing there. It's just like the soil here, quite bare.' For a few paces all around them, the soil was sterile; there was not even any dead grass.

'What about around the edges?' Keredin suggested. 'Should we look further afield?'

Varo consulted his memory again.

'No . . .' he said. 'I don't think . . . Wait!' The others held their breath. 'There might be something,' Varo went on. 'In spring, on the very edge on the left-hand side, there was a dandelion in seed. It wasn't yellow any more, so I thought it was dead. It might still be alive – and healthy.'

'Which way is spring?' Brostek asked, echoing his earlier question.

They all looked around but there was hardly any variation in the ruin of the former garden.

'Spring faced north,' Varo said eventually. 'So if we're in the centre now, then we should go north too.'

'But we entered the fog from the south, and went into

338

spring,' Brostek argued. 'So doesn't that mean we should go south? And which way *is* south, anyway?'

Their nightmare journey in the blinding fog had left them completely disorientated. They had absolutely no sense of direction now, so they searched for clues in the distance, trying to recognize the skylines or pick out landmarks beyond Nevern itself.

'This is north,' Brostek decided, pointing.

'No, I'd have said it was this way,' Keredin said, indicating a direction almost at right angles to the other.

'We'll try both,' Brostek said. 'Varo, you go another way, just in case we're *both* wrong.'

'We must hurry,' Keredin added. 'I don't think we've got much time.'

He and Brostek left, and Varo hesitated for a moment. Then he remembered something, and berated himself for not having thought of it earlier. The tomb was in spring! Knowing where the gravestone was, he set off towards it at a run, his boots sliding in the filth. As he passed it, he noticed that part of another letter had been added to the inscription. But he ran on, desperate to get to the flower.

While he was still some distance from the edge, Varo saw a figure wandering through the mire, and recognized Celia. He ran towards her. She was pacing slowly in the muck, black ooze squeezing up between her bare toes; in her hands she held the remains of a flower. As Varo drew close, she finished singing, brought the plant to her lips, and blew. Tiny pieces of fluff scattered on the breeze as the seeds flew away.

'No!' Varo yelled, startling Celia. She turned to run. 'Wait, Celia. Please!'

To his relief, she stood her ground warily and allowed him to approach. The seeds she had blown away were already lost in the vile mud.

'Can I have your flower?' he asked gently.

'But I haven't finished my song yet,' she told him, frowning.

339

'No, you mustn't,' Varo said hurriedly. 'I need it.' He had seen that only a single seed remained, precariously attached to the dandelion head. 'For the lights,' he improvised. 'They asked me to get it for them.'

Celia looked suspicious for a moment, then slowly nodded and passed him the flower. Varo took it carefully, feeling the fresh sap still wet on the broken stalk, and cradled the head gingerly in his hand.

'Thank you,' he said, then set off as fast as he dared, back towards the centre.

Celia trailed behind, unable to keep up with his long strides. She looked around, exclaiming every so often, 'Pretty! So pretty.'

When Varo returned to the patch of bare earth, there was no sign of his companions. He yelled their names into the deathly silence, and was soon rewarded by their hurried return.

'Did you get it?' Brostek asked breathlessly.

'I think so. But there's only one seed left. Celia blew the rest away.'

'Show me,' Keredin demanded. Varo carefully opened his hand, and the ex-wizard nodded his approval. 'It'll have to do,' he said.

'Did you say Celia?' Brostek asked then.

'Yes. She's wandering about in all the mess, but she seems quite happy.'

At that moment, Celia could be heard singing in the distance. All three men looked at her for a moment, then returned to their own business.

'What now?' Brostek queried.

'Now I try to remember what it's like to be a wizard,' Keredin replied with a rueful grin. 'Will you give me the pendant?'

'You didn't want to touch it before,' Brostek said, pulling it out of his pocket.

'I know, but it's a source of power, and I haven't got nearly enough, so I'll have to risk it,' Keredin explained. 'And that's the last thing I'll have to worry about. Even *attempting* this is meddling with things far beyond anything I know.' He took the offered pendant, holding it by the chain.

'What are you going to do?' Varo asked.

'I'm going to call on the old Guardians of this place,' he replied. 'All the nodes had Guardians once – one of Nevern's probably wove the tapestry.'

'But you said the tapestry was ancient,' Brostek said doubtfully.

'The Guardians are all dead, in our terms,' Keredin explained, 'but the Link preserves their spirits – or whatever – as it does all life. Here, of all places, I should be able to make contact. It would probably be a good idea if you two kept your distance. I don't know what's going to happen.'

'It could be dangerous?' Varo said.

'That's like asking if the sea is wet,' Keredin replied, laughing. 'Overreaching your limits is always dangerous. Powers this vast were never meant for the likes of me.'

'We'll stay with you,' Brostek stated simply, and Varo nodded his agreement.

Keredin began to object, then shrugged.

'Whatever happens,' he said solemnly, 'thank you for this opportunity. You two gave meaning to my life when there was none. It seems fitting that it should have led to this.'

'You've been the best and truest of friends,' Varo stated. It was as much of an apology for his earlier doubts as he could ever make.

'Good luck,' Brostek added.

Keredin flipped the pendant into his hand. The gesture was nonchalant, though his heart was pounding. At first, nothing happened, but then his fist began to shake, and at the same time, the perimeter of the patch of bare earth began to glow with an unearthly light. Shadow growled softly, her hackles rising.

'Get away, quick!' Keredin breathed.

'No! We stay,' Brostek responded.

'I can't control it!' Keredin's face was contorted, his eyes shut. Beads of sweat stood out on his forehead.

'It's the same shape as the pendant!' Varo exclaimed, looking at the outline of the patch of earth for the first time. The glow was brighter now, flickering like blue-white flame.

'Blow the seed . . . to the ground,' Keredin rasped, sounding as though he were in great pain.

Varo did as he was asked, and he and Brostek watched the seed float down and settle on the dark, lifeless earth.

'Guardians of Nevern!' the ex-wizard called hoarsely. 'If you hear me, help me. Your unworthy servant asks for your aid.'

Pinpricks of light began to shoot around Keredin, like fireflies in a miniature whirlwind. In the same instant, the barrier about the three men became an intense wall of light, shaped like the outer edge of the four-circle pattern. They heard Celia singing nearby, and Varo and Brostek turned to look. Keredin was unable to move. He was held almost rigid, trembling, and apparently under some terrible burden.

Celia walked towards the bright, translucent wall, apparently unaware of its existence. The two men yelled, and waved her away, trying to warn her. But she came on, still singing.

> 'Nature needs no reasons,
> For following the seasons.'

She stepped into the wall, which flared into life, engulfing her in white fire. But now it was the little girl from the tapestry who stood before them. Smiling, she continued the song.

> 'Seed, leaf, flower, fruit,
> Twig, branch, bower, root.'

Under the mesmerized gaze of the three men, she went to where the seed had fallen and cupped her hands over the spot. Then she looked up at Keredin. Although she did not speak, there was obviously some form of communication between them.

'Yes!' he gasped finally.

The girl stood, glanced briefly at the other two men and the wolf, then walked away. As she emerged from the other side of the wall, she was Celia again, wandering on as if nothing had happened. 'Pretty!' they heard her say.

Then their attention was drawn back to the patch of bare earth. Before their eyes, a green shoot snaked up, leaves grew and spread, and a stalk sprouted from the centre. A yellow flower blossomed, its petals brilliant in the midst of so much darkness. That soon faded, and was replaced by the familiar puffball. An invisible breeze scattered the feather-light seeds – and within moments, a multitude of green shoots were protruding from the earth.

'Very pretty,' a cold voice said sarcastically.

The men's amazement turned to dread as they looked up to see the blue-robed Knifeman standing just outside the wall of light. His outline was marked by a strong violet glow, and he wore a heavy metal pendant in the shape of an inverted triangle. Shadow growled, legs tensed ready to spring, and Varo's sword was in his hand in an instant. Brostek drew his weapon too, and began to advance. Their enemy took no notice of either of them. His violet eyes were fixed upon Keredin.

'It's a wraith,' the former wizard said in a strained voice. 'You can't harm him here.'

Varo and Brostek froze, but still watched the unmoving Knifeman.

'How observant of you,' the sorcerer remarked. Though he sounded amused, his eyes were hard and angry. 'It seems I underestimated you. I had not expected a renegade wizard to get as far as this.'

'I've only just started,' Keredin croaked, his voice thick with contempt.

'Come now,' his adversary said patronizingly. 'A few weeds within this shield! Surely you can't expect to do more?'

'Nevern *will* grow again,' Keredin whispered defiantly. 'The image-key still exists. And there's nothing you can do to stop it!'

'Even if that were true,' the Knifeman replied, 'you would have to release this screen to do it, and then you and your friends would be at my mercy.'

'We are prepared to pay that price.'

'But we are brothers, you and I!' the sorcerer cried. 'Your dreams were the same as mine.'

'No! Not for this.' Keredin's denial was emphatic. 'You have taken something which should have been great and beautiful, and distorted it into something ugly and vile. I want no part of it.'

'But I could make you a god!' the blue-robed temptor persisted. 'Show you magic as it truly should be. I can see the pain this puny effort is causing you. Can't you see that there are no limits to what we could achieve together?'

Varo and Brostek wanted to warn their friend against the sorcerer's blandishments, but knew that he must fight his own battle. They need not have worried. Keredin proved loyal.

'You're wasting your breath!' he spat. 'Nevern will live.'

'Then you will die,' the Knifeman warned.

'Gladly!' With a last, terrible effort, Keredin tossed the pendant to Brostek. 'It's up to you now,' he told him.

The sorcerer snarled with anger as the shield of light began to fade. Brostek caught the pendant and instantly felt the shock of its power run up his arm, suffusing his whole body. It had never felt like that before!

'Thank you, Magara!' Keredin cried inexplicably. He stood still, no longer shaking, his burden lifted.

A knife glinted in the sorcerer's hand. The shield was gone now. There was a sudden blur of movement and the blade flew towards Keredin, its metal flashing with

344

violet sparks. Varo dived, trying to intercept its flight with the blade of his sword. His timing was perfect but the spectral dagger passed through his weapon un-affected. Keredin made no attempt to avoid the knife, and it hit him in the chest. Spectre or not, its effect on him was all too real. As it pierced his heart, red blood staining his shirt, the pinpoints of light fled from him and streamed towards Brostek. In an instant, white flames sprang up, engulfing him and his wolf – and at the same moment, Varo disappeared. An instant later, they re-appeared, completely transformed. Brostek and Shadow were now surrounded by a glittering white corona, while Varo was invisible behind a black mantle that enveloped him completely. He was a void in space in the shape of a man, admitting and emitting no light. They all moved instinctively to attack their foe, but the sorcerer had vanished – and before they could react, they too were swept away into nothing.

Keredin fell to the ground, alone now on a bed of yellow. The agony passed from his face, and he smiled. There was movement all around him, and although his eyes were already dimming, he could still see the rebirth of the garden. It was irreversible now, he knew. The true image-key was reasserting itself.

Grass turned the earth green. Flowers and shrubs sprang up in profusion. Trees were brought back to life, their leaves, blossom and fruit all growing in abundance. Insects hurried between hoards of pollen, birds flew and sang, and fish swam in the freshly flowing streams. The animals had all returned. All the seasons were there, the endless cycles in their ever-changing beauty. Nevern bloomed again.

Keredin saw it all, and knew that his life had been leading to this moment. It was the fulfilment of his dream. In the instant before he died, he thought he saw Mattie's face – and she was smiling too. He went to her gladly.

CHAPTER FORTY-TWO

As magic awoke once more in Nevern, two men far to the south also woke from a long, unnatural sleep. Slaton and Rogan opened their eyes and sat up. They looked at each other, and then at the astonished delight on Ross's face.

'Where are we?' Rogan asked his twin.

Outside, someone was playing a sweet tune on a lute.

*   *   *

Hewitt could not believe his eyes. After the fog cleared and Celia had wandered off, nothing much had happened for a while. He stood tensely, watching, hoping for something more. For what seemed like an age, there was nothing. But then he could see flashes of light in the centre of the valley, and to his delight, he could see patches of colour growing in the midst of decay. Green was the first, but there were soon splashes of pink, yellow, red and blue, as all of nature's colours bloomed, spreading out from the middle of the garden in ever-expanding waves of life. Hewitt felt like cheering, but could only stand and watch, open-mouthed.

And then he thought of the tapestry, and unfurled it quickly. It was changing as he watched! From an oddly shaped patch of yellow in the centre, the tendrils of colour were spreading out, the tiny stitches moving and changing hue like living things. Before long, the entire tapestry had been restored to its former glory. All the time, Hewitt glanced back and forth between it and the real Nevern, unsure which was copying which.

Everything was back in its accustomed place. The

eclipses were gone, restoring sunlight to three of the quarters, and revealing the moon in the winter sky as well as its reflection in the lake below. The woman returned in all her ages, as graceful and serene as ever. Each season was revealed, complete with all their original idiosyncracies.

Only the rainbow was not restored. It was still a peculiar two-coloured archway, split by a curving line of sky.

When the tapestry finally stopped changing, Hewitt looked up and saw that the garden itself was just as perfect. But although it was more beautiful than anything he had ever seen, he knew that it was still not his to enter. The song that it awoke in his heart was one he would never be able to play, but he rejoiced in it anyway.

*   *   *

Celia walked slowly through the peaceful glades and scented spaces of Nevern, singing softly to herself. She came at last upon a man lying upon his back amid a blaze of dandelions. His chest did not move, and Celia was sure that he was dead, but there was no mark on him, and so she decided that his heart had just stopped. His face was serene.

Celia moved away, coming back a few moments later to lay a single white rose upon the man's breast.

'Pretty,' she said thoughtfully, and went on her way.

CHAPTER FORTY-THREE

Magara stared at her captor, mesmerized by his furious violet eyes, and waited to die. But he made no move towards her. After a few moments, she noticed that he wore a distracted expression, and that his usual corona of light was missing. His mind was clearly occupied elsewhere, and he gave no more than a cursory glance to what she had written.

'So you choose to delay my victory rather than earn my gratitude,' he said finally. 'So much the worse for you.'

Magara pushed the fateful volume away from her, and summoned up every scrap of bravado left in her.

'You cannot force me to complete this evil,' she said. 'My talent is for healing, not this . . . sickness.'

She had expected him to tear the page out, as he had done before, but instead he paid it no attention, as though it were a matter of complete indifference to him.

'I'll deal with you later,' he told her. 'You will have an eternity to regret your decision.' He smiled at the look of dismay on her face, then swept out of the room in a whirl of blue robes. 'In the meantime . . .' he added, snapping his fingers.

Magara's legs were jolted with pain, terrible grating waves that made them feel as if every bone were being broken over and over again. She gritted her teeth, knowing that there was no way to make such agony bearable. *An eternity.*

Magara had been prepared to die, but she knew now that she had been a fool to believe it could be that quick, that easy. Her enemy was capable of far greater cruelty. She fought desperately to distract herself, to think of something other than the racking pain. For some reason, the Knifeman had obviously abandoned The Book, and so she was expendable now; he could force her to endure anything. She had subconsciously been relying on his anger to make her end swift and final, but his last words had made it clear that this would not be the case. And for the first time, Magara realized exactly what she was facing.

She glanced again at The Book. The last line was written in bold, defiant letters – 'The wizard of light returned to Nevern.' Within her tortured brain was a tiny spark of triumph, and she clung to this feverishly. The very fact that the sorcerer had not destroyed the page must mean that her words had come true. Had she *made* them true, she wondered, or had she merely reported what she had seen? The wizard in her vision had seemed familiar, but she could not think why.

Thank you, Magara.

The words, a cry of gratitude and relief, came out of nowhere. The contact faded swiftly, but before it was gone, Magara understood. The man was Keredin, the ex-wizard who was a part of Varo and Brostek's group. She had known of his sad story, and realized now that he had been trying to relearn the art of wizardry in a desperate attempt to save the garden. Her inaccurate words had given him a strength beyond his own, thus allowing him to succeed. They had become a prophecy which was now fulfilled.

Tears ran down Magara's cheeks – half for Keredin, and half for herself. Her vision was blurred for a moment and when a movement on the desk caught her eye, she thought she must be hallucinating. She rubbed her eyes and looked again. The Book was writing itself! The bold script followed on from her last line, the black ink moving across the page like a living thing.

'Magic was born anew,' she read in wonder, 'and the garden bloomed again.'

But that was not all. As Magara watched, the earlier

words on the page began to fade, then vanished altogether. *Like writing on the cliff rocks.* Magara leafed through the previous pages. They were all blank again. Her tears flowed as the weight of guilt was lifted from her heart. History was indeed being rewritten – but not in the way the Knifeman had intended. The last obstacle to his final triumph was still in place. Nevern lived – and was growing stronger with each moment.

Filled with relief, Magara was soon reminded of her desperate situation when the pain in her legs intensified. Once more she was plunged into despair. *Let me die*, she pleaded, overwhelmed with self-pity. *Let me die. I can't stand this much longer.*

But then the veil of misery was lifted again as she sensed – somehow – that Varo and Brostek were near. Images flickered within her head, and she knew that they were in the Vortex, transported here as she had been. But there was something different about them. Brostek had become a being of white flame, and she could not see Varo properly at all, only a black form. Love and longing raged in her heart like a fire, and her darkness was illuminated by a small ray of hope. But then she remembered that the Knifeman was all-powerful in the Vortex, and the hope turned again to misery. Soon, she knew, her friends would be as helpless as she.

The chamber was silent; inside her mind, Magara was screaming.

*   *   *

As soon as Magara's captor had seen The Book, he had know what was happening. Using Halana's descendant to counteract the magic woven into the tapestry had been a risk, he knew, but one he had been prepared to take. He had never really believed that anyone would be in a position to take advantage of her foolish initiative. The attempt by the renegade wizard would have been pitiful but for Magara's aid – and the unfortunate

350

coincidence of the pendants of light. Even so, he knew he should have foreseen this possibility and been prepared to deal with it. He controlled his anger with difficulty, watching the remote scene through the eyes of his simulcrum.

The sorcerer had left Magara's cell, extracting a small measure of vengeance as he went, and recalled his mirror image. His violet corona was returned to him as he became whole again. For a few moments, he remained still, deep in thought. The rebel wizard was dead, but he had been able to transfer his power to his two companions, and the Knifeman had not expected that. And yet they would never be able to control it. Could such novices *really* believe that they could beat him?

The Knifeman swept them into his lair, knowing that he could destroy them at his leisure. But first he had a task for them to do, and the irony of what was to face them pleased him greatly.

*   *   *

Brostek and Varo had hardly had time to react to Keredin's death and their own extraordinary transformation, when the desolation that was Nevern disappeared and they found themselves, swords still drawn, beside a frozen lake high in the mountains. The Knifeman was nowhere to be seen. Taking their bearings nervously, they saw that there were two more lakes beyond the closest one, and that there was a forbidding grey castle further down the valley. Shadow howled, making the moment even more eerie.

'Where are we?' Brostek was completely unnerved. There were forces flowing within him he did not understand, and the world had obviously gone mad. 'What's happened to us?'

'I do not know. Are you all right?' Although his words implied concern, Varo's voice now had a metallic

351

vibration to it that stripped it of all humanity. It sounded as though it were being filtered through steel plates.

'I think so,' Brostek replied, staring at the black shape that was his partner. 'Are you? I can't *see* you.'

'I am fine,' Varo grated.

Brostek looked at the pendant resting on the palm of his left hand. *There's something inside me, and I don't have the first idea how to cope with it. I'm no wizard – I don't know how to deal with magic!*

'Perhaps this is where Magara came,' Varo said in calm, unnatural tones. 'If so, then the castle is the most obvious place to look for her. Shall we investigate?'

Brostek nodded, still trying to fight his panic, and they set off around the frozen lake. They had only gone a few paces, however, when a man appeared out of thin air a little way ahead of them. His blue robes marked him as a Knifeman, and an orange glow circled his body. He wore a heavy pendant round his neck, shaped like a heart sitting on a horizontal line. The expression on his face was one of bewilderment, as if he were surprised to be there; when he saw Varo and Brostek, this changed to anger and a little fear.

Varo reacted instantly and instinctively. He lunged at his enemy, sword raised.

'No!' Brostek cried. 'Wait!' But he was ignored. Varo had no time to listen to reason now. He had only one aim, and his need to kill his hated foe overcame everything else.

The Knifeman moved quickly, raising both arms and pointing at his adversary. Blue fire crackled and sped towards Varo, but although the salvo hit his black form squarely, it only slowed his progress for a few steps. The blue flames vanished, sucked into the black void that was Varo – and he came on.

The Knifeman looked first amazed, then terrified. He unleashed more thunderbolts, in increasingly haphazard fashion. Most missed their target but others caught some part of Varo as he ran on, weaving between the blasts.

But none halted his progress – or even delayed him by much.

Brostek had not moved, torn between his own uncertainty and the desire to help his friend. While he was hesitating, he heard a splash in the unfrozen lake but when he turned to look, all he could see were a few ripples spreading outwards from the centre.

'Don't kill him!' he yelled, then added desperately, 'There's no eclipse. He's not even real!'

But Varo knew better. He closed in, dodging the last feeble bursts of power and raised the sword that was now a dark void, an avenging blade of nothingness. The Knifeman stumbled and fell backwards, yelling unintelligibly. Varo's blade swept down, slicing into real flesh and bone. His enemy screamed, but only once, and in an instant the orange light disappeared. But Varo did not stop. The blue robes were soon in shreds and the Knifeman's body lay shattered – though there was not a drop of blood to be seen.

Brostek approached his friend cautiously, sickened by his berserk fury, wondering for a moment whether Varo might even turn on him.

'It's over, Varo,' he said. 'He's dead.'

The black shape paused, sword raised in mid-strike. He seemed to come slowly to his senses.

'Where's the blood?' the metallic voice asked. 'There should be blood.'

'There is none,' Brostek answered firmly. 'Leave it. He's dead.' *And the final Knifeman has all their power,* he added to himself.

Brostek looked up at the castle, shuddering at the thought of Magara being held prisoner there. But before they could go on, the frozen lake beside them exploded in a hundred places. Huge chunks of ice rolled lazily in the air, while smaller fragments flew in all directions, adding a strange whirring noise to the ear-splitting cracking of the deep ice. The two men watched, horrified, as it became clear that the source of each eruption was a man or woman rising from beneath the surface. As the frozen boulders and hail crashed down all around them, the strange troop clambered over the frosty wreckage. Their skin was blue white from the cold, and they were all clutching a weapon made from ice – long, sharp spikes, jagged clubs and icicle knives. They each wore a violet headband, and their eyes were all possessed by a burning, desperate hunger. They had been granted release from their frigid hell for one purpose only. Kill the intruders and their animal, the master had told them, and I will set you free. They needed no further encouragement. They would obey him or die in the attempt rather than return to their frozen prison.

As the first wave began to cross the shattered lake, moving inexorably towards the two stunned intruders, further crashes rent the air as those buried deeper freed themselves and crawled from the slithering pits to follow the others.

Brostek and Varo realized that the protection afforded them by their strange shields would be no defence against the physical fury of hundreds of ice-warriors. Brostek saw no choice but to stand his ground with Shadow and sell their lives as dearly as possible – but Varo moved forward, wading into the battle with a readiness that was akin to joy. In the face of those impossible odds, he became a dark whirlwind of death.

CHAPTER FORTY-FOUR

Hewitt sat with the tapestry propped on his knees, looking between it and the garden. He expected no more miracles – what he had already seen was more than enough – but he was still hoping to see Magara and the three men return. However, apart from the occasional fleeting glimpse of Celia, there was no sign of anyone.

His keen eye had observed one more change in the restored tapestry. The tomb was marked with a new inscription, the tiny letters now reading 'HAVE FAITH'; below that was the symbol of four touching circles. Now, as Hewitt watched, the orange arc of the rainbow unravelled itself and disappeared, as though it were sinking into the fabric itself. The violet band was left alone in the spring sky.

* * *

Rogan and Slaton staggered towards the doorway, desperately trying to understand Ross's flow of words as he told them what had happened since they had been struck down in Jordanstone. Looking out, they saw Lisle sitting cross-legged on the walkway, playing a gentle tune which grew quieter by the moment. The others around him were staring at the water. The lake's surface was almost still, only the tiniest of ripples marking the last breath of wind. Most of Trevine was also on the water's edge, crowding the walkways and the shoreline. Everyone waited, silent and unmoving.

'Tread lightly,' Bair told his newly recovered colleagues. 'It's almost there.' Puzzled, they stopped where they were.

Then the mirror was complete, and Lisle stopped playing.

'Now?' Cole asked.

'Yes,' Rayne told him. 'Go!'

Cole dived from the end of the walkway, entering the water with hardly a splash. Those around gasped as he disappeared from sight in a flash of reflected sunlight. Although the water was clear, no one could see him under the surface. The ripples from his dive spread in silence as all of Trevine held its breath. Long moments passed as everyone scoured the surface and peered below, shading their eyes against the glare of the late morning sun.

Then there was a great cry of relief as Cole suddenly reappeared, travelling so fast that he almost leapt from the water. He swam rapidly to the walkway, and eager hands helped him out as a hubbub of speculation grew from the more distant onlookers. Those nearer saw the answers in the diver's wide eyes and pale face.

'It was just as Vilman said,' he breathed.

'You see—' Vilman began, looking at Ryker, but Cole cut him off.

'There's more,' he said urgently. 'I was only there for a few moments, but I saw a man in blue robes with an orange glow about him, fighting *something* that was just . . . just black. And Brostek was there, with a white wolf beside him.'

'White?' Ross queried. 'But Shadow is grey.'

'No matter,' Hawk said. 'Could the other have been Varo?'

'I couldn't tell.'

'It's them, and they need our help,' Bair concluded.

'Then let's go!' Ryker said, his eyes agleam.

'We will come with you,' Lynton put in quickly. The four remaining Barians were among the spectators. 'This must be why we were sent here.'

'The divers will come too,' Cole said, glancing at Rayne and receiving a nod of agreement. 'The water is home to us, and some of you may need help.'

'Good,' Bair responded. 'We need all the help we can get.'

The word was passed along, causing consternation and uproar, but amid the seeming confusion, the citizens of Trevine performed a remarkable feat of organization. Council members took charge of individual sections of walkway, and those who were to follow Cole into the unknown were made ready. Surplus clothing was discarded, weapons secured, and divers assigned to accompany anyone who was not a strong swimmer. The starting signal was arranged.

When they finally realized what was happening, Slaton and Rogan both wanted to dive as well, but they were forbidden to do so. They were still very weak, and would have been more hindrance than help.

'Anyway, we need you to look after Lisle,' Bair pointed out.

'But what about your hand?'

'It's just a scratch,' was the impatient reply. There was no way that anyone could prevent the old soldier from taking part in this adventure.

And so the five members of Varo's group and the four Barians were joined by more than twenty divers and a number of volunteers from Trevine. They all stood perfectly still on the various walkways, waiting for the signal. Once again, Lisle played, seeming to understand what was required. His serene music swept out over the water, the gentle melody reaching all those who watched or waited. The last few ripples died away.

Rayne's arm was raised in readiness, then lowered abruptly, and the different groups all dived or jumped into the mirror lake. Before anyone could stop him, Lisle laid down his lute and jumped in after them.

CHAPTER FORTY-FIVE

Into the screaming came a voice that would not be denied.

Will you give in to him even now?

Leave me alone, Magara responded miserably. *Haven't I done enough?*

Why fight the battle so hard, Halana asked in return, *if you intend to surrender in the war?*

I can't *fight any more,* she wailed.

Your friends are persevering, Halana told her sharply. *For you, for their own lives, for all of us. Will you abandon them now?*

I can't do anything, Magara objected. *I have no power.*

Does my health mean nothing to you? Halana's voice was that of a grown woman, not a frail girl. *Nevern blooms again, Magara. Because of you! Wizards are not the only ones with talent. Why deny your own? What men call magic is available to all with the eyes to see. You have proved yourself – and you are in the Vortex.*

What can I do from here? The waves of pain from her trapped legs still washed over her.

You are a healer, Magara. Start with yourself! Why do you think he seeks to distract you with pain? He fears you. And we need *you.*

He fears me? she asked in disbelief.

If it weren't for you, Halana replied, *he would rule us all by now. He may still in time.* The Guardian paused, as though considering the effect of her words. *Don't be afraid to ask for help,* she concluded. *But ask it first from yourself.*

Halana's presence withdrew, but the contact did not end, and Magara still felt the vastness of the Link all around her. Within its limitless boundaries a battle was raging, wave upon wave of change, bordering on utter chaos. She had no idea what it all meant; no way of even putting it into words or thoughts. There was still a horrible feeling of sickness, but now there were also a few fragile strands of health. *Nevern blooms again.* The mage-garden had been their last hope – and it was fighting back. The least she could do was to resist as well. But how?

My talent is for healing. She had made that claim to her captor earlier in the day. *Then prove it!* she challenged herself.

Magara realized with a jolt that the Knifeman had been the first to acknowledge her talent, when he had chosen her to write the story that would counteract the magic of the tapestry. Wasn't that magic in itself? And Nevern's rebirth was surely healing of a sort.

You are a healer, Magara. Start with yourself!

My pain is false, she told herself. Her legs were not broken, nor were they paralysed. Which was all very well, but her brain insisted that they were. Magara had been very good at helping other people with their problems, at soothing troubled minds – but how could she argue with herself? This time she could hardly ask, 'What do *you* think?'

Magara smiled through gritted teeth – and saw a small strand shift within the Link. She was inside its infinite complex, a part of it as well as an observer. *All lines run through here.* Which were the lines the Knifeman was using to hurt her? Where were the strands that assailed her? She searched blindly, guided only by instinct. She sensed so much in the Link that was wrong, so much that was warped or unbalanced, that it seemed to take an age to find what she was looking for. But the instant she 'saw' the threads he had used in the manipulation of her limbs, she knew them to be horribly unnatural. In her mind's eye, she coloured the lines red, needing an image to make the task manageable. The strands could not be cut – the Link was eternal – but they could be changed. Her gaoler had mutated them, so she must find a way to reverse his vile handiwork, to untangle the knots of pain.

She gave the lines an experimental 'push' with her thoughts, and saw the colour change from red to orange. To her amazement the pain lessened slightly. Then she carefully uncoiled another loop and watched the orange fade to yellow. Magara went on, rewriting that part of the Link, and making it true. Once more, she felt her pain recede. Green, blue, indigo. She recognized the pattern that was her real self, and reached out for it. Violet. Of all the colours of the rainbow, this last made her falter. It was *his* colour. But she was nearly there now. Summoning up all her willpower, she completed the change – and all colour disappeared.

Magara sat, tense and still, waiting for the agony to return. But it did not, and she eventually managed to trust her own achievement and opened her eyes. Nothing had changed in the stone-walled chamber, but she saw it differently now. The Link was still there, as it was everywhere, an all-pervasive presence, like the grain within the wood of a tree.

Stand up, she ordered herself. To her astonishment, her legs obeyed. Joy matched her wonderment, but she was instantly sobered by the thought that this was only the beginning. Magara pushed her chair back suddenly, and it crashed to the floor. The sound was answered by an explosive cracking noise from far away, and she felt yet more patterns shift within the chaos of the Link. She strode determinedly towards the door.

*   *   *

Even though each of them had been prepared in theory for what was about to happen, the group that arrived from Trevine were left stunned and breathless by the manner of their entry into the Vortex. They all surfaced within a few moments of each other, after the shortest

360

but strangest journey of their lives. The less experienced swimmers were gasping for air, but everyone looked around hurriedly. The mountains stared back impassively, but on the frozen lake beside theirs, the scene was anything but calm.

There was no sign of the blue-robed man that Cole had reported seeing, but Brostek, Shadow and the black shape which they took to be Varo were now beleaguered by a large force wielding weapons of ice. As the newcomers splashed towards the shore, ice shattered deafeningly and more warriors emerged from the frozen wreckage.

There was no time to think, still less to understand what was happening, as they waded out of the water and went to their friends' aid. At first the enemy ignored them, so intent were they on their original prey, but the assault from the rear soon made its mark, forcing them to turn and fight. The attack was spearheaded by the five men from Varo's band, but Lynton and his men and the volunteers from Trevine were not far behind. And although they were vastly outnumbered, they made rapid inroads into the enemy force, giving fresh heart to Brostek and Varo.

Brostek and Shadow had defended themselves desperately – as the several bodies at their feet attested – but they had been driven back all the time, and were tiring fast. By contrast, Varo had cut a swathe through the ranks of the foe, killing without compunction and leaving a trail of blood freezing in his wake. His charge had been reckless, beyond all reason, but he stormed on. The ice-warriors soon learnt that they could not approach him – to do so was to meet instant death in the form of the whirling black sword – and they now surrounded him, feinting and dodging on the broken ice, waiting for the mistake that would surely come. Such tactics would have driven other men to uncontrolled fury, but Varo merely chose to ignore the odds against him and picked his targets carefully, making each thrust or swing count.

Each victim brought him a small measure of satisfaction – until he was faced by a snarling, wild-eyed woman. For the first time, he thought about where these people must have come from. His own mother had been one of those abducted by the Knifemen.

The moment's hesitation gave the woman the chance to lunge with her needle-sharp ice-spear. Varo fended it off, but its point tore into the flesh of his left forearm. Varo killed her with a clinical stab to the heart, and forced himself to be alert once more. But he never regained his former unthinking sense of invincibility, and the unexpected arrival of their allies was thus a welcome relief. Varo had not even considered the ultimate outcome of the fight before, but he realized now that, without their aid, he would eventually have been killed. And the odds were still against them.

As the last of the newcomers struggled from the water to join the fray, the air was once more split asunder by the sound of shattering ice. The second frozen lake, the one nearest to the castle, was exploding – and a second army emerged. At the same time, the third lake began to freeze over. In moments, the ice at the edges was a handspan thick and the very last member of the group from Trevine was almost trapped, his feet encased in ice. Lisle's awkward movements were nearly his downfall, but Ross spotted the boy and ran back to drag him free, cursing his brother for letting Lisle follow them.

With the freezing of the last lake, their escape route was cut off. There was nothing for it now but to fight to the death.

As their allies turned the fight into a full-scale battle, Varo and Brostek had a chance to look around for the first time. They both saw the blue-robed sorcerer at the top of one of the castle towers, and began to work their way through the turmoil, calling on their friends and slowly forming a cohesive unit to pit against the frenzied attacks of the enemy. As they drove their wedge ever closer to the castle, the second group of ice-warriors

362

stood in their path, but their ferocity and makeshift weapons were no match for the travellers' practised skills and the strength and dexterity of the divers with their steel blades.

Lisle was shepherded along in their midst, apparently unconcerned by the savage violence all around him, his violet eyes fixed on the castle.

'Magaaara!' he exclaimed in delight.

Varo and Brostek were among those who heard him, and they redoubled their efforts to reach the fortress – where the Knifeman was no longer to be seen. Eventually, they managed to breach the opposing force, and Brostek signalled Bair to organize a defensive wall as he and Varo ran on to the castle, Lisle limping behind them as fast as he could.

* * *

Magara opened the door, and looked out on to an ill-lit corridor. Sunlight beckoned from the far end and she walked towards it. She had no specific plan in mind, but wanted to try and make contact with Varo and Brostek. She had gone no more than a few paces when she suddenly felt as though her head would burst, and came to an abrupt halt. Although no voice spoke to her, Magara was overwhelmed with all the demands being made of her. Knowing that a true healer was in the Vortex, and having learnt of her small triumphs at Nevern and over her own imprisonment, the Link had come to her. All the magical places that had languished for so long under the sorcerer's foul influence were now appealing to her to save them too. The mere thought of such a monumental task left Magara feeling shattered and helpless. There was no hope of her being able to untangle the far-reaching web of evil. It was a task beyond any one person.

For a moment, she was tempted to take power from the Link, and use it to try and destroy her enemy, but she knew that even if she succeeded, such a battle would leave the Link permanently scarred and deformed. It would be vulnerable to the next sorcerer who sought to exploit the weaknesses she would have created. This power was never meant for any individual; it corrupted all that touched it.

The Link continued to plead, its infirmity and need tearing at her. All her instincts were to help – but where was she to begin? It was hopeless. Even if she could start the healing process now, her efforts would be far too little, too late. Her enemy's resources were infinitely greater, and as soon as he discovered her intention, he would move to prevent any real progress – and would probably kill her. And yet the healer in Magara insisted that she try.

She chose a tiny portion, and sensed how it had been distorted. The effort of putting it right proved exhausting – but, far away, a spring once known for its wonderful healing properties, but which had grown sullied and poisonous, now ran clear and bright once more. Magara's tiny success only increased the clamour in her head, and left her even more certain of eventual failure. *Can no one help me?* There were many others in the Link with healing powers, but there was none in the Vortex, none who could help her in time.

No more! she cried silently. The Link's agonized reaction to her despairing denial left her crushed and guilty. *I can't do it.*

Magara began to run, trying to escape the madness, running from the burden she could not possibly bear. She emerged into the sunlight of the courtyard, and stopped suddenly when she saw her captor standing in its centre, his back to her. Beyond him was a large archway, flanked by towers, through which she could see a battle raging in the valley. The clamour in her head died away as the sorcerer turned slowly. Momentary surprise showed on his face but this was immediately masked by an expression of cool indifference.

'Hold her,' he said. 'If she struggles, cut her throat.'

Two men wearing violet headbands emerged from the shadows beside Magara, and before she knew what was happening, her arms had been twisted cruelly behind her and a knife held to her throat, its razor edge just touching her skin. The men made no sound but held her in a grip like iron. They were the Knifeman's creatures; she would have no chance of overturning his domination of their minds.

Her captor turned away again, facing the open gateway, and waited calmly, his arms folded. The noise of fighting drew closer, and then the featureless black figure that Magara knew to be Varo ran through into the yard. She alone could see through the opaque cloak of darkness and sense the steely expression of deadly intent below.

As Varo charged at his mortal enemy, Brostek and Shadow appeared in the gateway. Varo closed in on his intended victim, his sword at the ready – and then the sorcerer raised a hand almost casually and blue fire pulsed in a blinding bolt of controlled power. The black shield seemed to absorb some of that first impact, but a second burst threw Varo backwards like a rag doll. He landed in a crumpled heap, and lay unmoving by the base of the archway.

Magara watched this contemptuous dismissal of her friend with dismay. Then her eyes were drawn to Brostek. Both he and Shadow were surrounded by a silvery white light that glinted as they moved. Beneath the light, man and wolf were blood-stained and Brostek's eyes were haunted, glancing first at Varo, then at Magara, and finally back to the Knifeman.

'I may have a place for your stupid friend later,' the blue-robed man remarked. 'At least I will turn his talents to good use. But for now it is *you* that I want.'

Magara heard these words with dread. She had yearned for so long to see her two friends, but now her love was helpless, and she could see no possible way of helping them. Brostek halted, some ten paces from his enemy. As he glanced at Magara again, she wondered if her presence was distracting him.

'You are no match for me,' the sorcerer went on. 'Why make this hard on yourself? Surrender your power now, and your end will at least be quick. It's all you can hope for now.'

Magara felt the truth of his words, but at the same time she saw what Keredin had done. He had taken the power she had granted him and added to it the latent potential of the pendant of light and the residue of his own strength. He had then divided it between Varo and Brostek, making them reverse mirror images of each other, hoping to make the negative strength of one the positive power of the other; dark opposed to light; intellect against intuition; cold violence divided from the warmth of love; detached reasoning compared to illogical passion.

Accentuating the pair's natural traits should have made each of them stronger, but something had gone very wrong. Varo's composure had been destroyed, and the alien confusion had robbed him of his protection. And without him, Brostek was incomplete, filled with knowledge but without the resolution to use it effectively. His sword hung limply at his side as he stared at his confident foe.

I wonder if he even realizes what's happened to him? Magara thought in helpless agony.

'I'm waiting.' His opponent's hesitation evidently provided the sorcerer with some amusement.

For his own part, Brostek was aware that he was now the focus of something he could not comprehend. He did not doubt that magic was involved, but Keredin's parting words hung heavy – *It's up to you now* – because he had no idea how to harness the power or how to use it; he just did not know what to do. He was certain that the Knifeman could not be killed in a conventional way – Varo's defeat had emphasized that – and knew that something more was needed. *But I am no wizard!*

Brostek also knew that whatever Keredin had done had afforded him and Varo some magical protection, but clearly that could not last for ever. He assumed that the ex-wizard had intended them to work as a team. His partner was stirring now, moving slowly on the ground, but if any of the ice-warriors reached him while he was still dazed, he would be dead in moments.

And, last but not least, seeing Magara there, a knife at her throat, had unnerved him. She had been the reason for their going to Nevern in the first place, a journey that had led them here – where it would end, one way or another.

'Must I waste my energy taking what you could give me with so much less pain?' the sorcerer asked impatiently.

He flicked his hand with an almost playful gesture, and a small blue fireball shot towards Brostek. He reacted instinctively, raising the hand that held the pendant. White light flared, and the attack veered away, fading harmlessly.

'So you *do* know I'm here,' the Knifeman commented, amused once more. 'Why won't you answer me?'

Brostek's stare became even more intense. He had fended off the blue fire almost without thinking, and at the same time he had felt a surge in the power that was inside him. He did not understand how this could be, but at least he now had a reason to play for time. The germ of an idea began to form in his mind.

'Why should I yield my power to scum like you?' he said.

'Bravo! It speaks!' The sorcerer clapped mockingly.

Magara held her breath. She too had felt the surge of awareness at the moment of attack. The Link had responded, feeding Brostek's defence. But so much of the Link was already corrupt; she was afraid that, in the end, it might hinder rather than help him. *Unless* . . . At last she saw her chance to act, and made herself ready.

'You are evil filth,' Brostek said. 'The world will be a cleaner place without you.'

'Do not presume to impose your pitiful standards upon me,' the Knifeman responded evenly. 'The Link contains everything. Your pathetic ideas about good and evil mean nothing to it, or to me. Such petty morality is worthless. The only truth is power, and the Link did not *grant* me my power. I *took* it.'

'Show me,' Brostek challenged. 'I don't think you're capable of *taking* the food from a blind man's plate.'

Why is he taunting him like this? Magara wondered fearfully. Then she was distracted for a moment by the sight of Lisle, who had just appeared in the gateway and was crouching beside Varo.

'Really?' the sorcerer said, still feigning amusement but with anger in his eyes.

'You have no real power,' Brostek went on. 'You delude yourself out of vanity.'

The Knifeman snarled and unleashed a blaze of blue fire. Magara was ready this time, and filtered the surge of power from the Link, making sure the healthy strands were the ones to feed her love. He blazed white in return, standing firm against the onslaught, but Shadow yelped and retreated, growling.

'Is that the best you can do?' Brostek asked.

Is he trying to match the Knifeman's power? Magara wondered hopelessly. *There is no chance of that!*

'You test my patience,' their enemy said.

'I test your *strength*, weakling,' Brostek responded venomously.

Another, even fiercer blast crashed into the answering white fire, which Magara again helped to augment, but this time Brostek staggered backwards. Pain suffused his face, though his eyes still flashed defiance. The white light around him flickered fitfully, obviously weakening.

Don't do this, Magara pleaded silently. *We can't compete with him.* She prepared herself, and appealed to the Link for one more, even greater effort.

'Had enough?' the sorcerer gloated.

For an instant, Brostek glanced at Magara and she thought she saw a note of sad apology in his eyes before he returned his gaze to their opponent.

'No,' he said calmly. 'You are no match for me. I'm coming to get you.' He stepped forward, lurching slightly as though he were drunk.

Although Magara knew what was coming, she could do nothing to prevent it. The onslaught was blinding, a roaring beast of feral intensity, fire without heat but terrible in its power. The sorcerer had lost patience finally, and was intent on putting an end to the one-sided duel. Magara did what she could, putting all her effort into aiding the Link's defence of her friend, but in the instant that the Knifeman launched his attack, Brostek deliberately cast off his shield. He shrugged aside the white mantle, and stood before them as a mere human being.

'Varo!' he cried. 'Now!'

'No!' Magara screamed, feeling the knife scrape on the skin of her throat. *No! No! No!*

The blue fire hit Brostek's unprotected body squarely, throwing him backwards like a dry leaf in a storm. His sword and the pendant flew away from his outstretched arms. Having nowhere else to go, the huge surge of power from the Link followed the symbol of light. A hand, gauntleted in black shadow, reached up and caught the pendant in mid-flight, the silver metal resting in the blood which covered Varo's left hand. He rose from the ground like a harbinger of doom, and recovered his blade. His black shape was now streaked with silver, and he was advancing on the thunderstruck sorcerer even before Brostek's lifeless body skidded to a halt.

Shadow growled, and Lisle sang a note so clear and piercing that it was almost visible. His strange eyes flashed, mirroring the colour of the Knifeman's corona. Varo stormed on with Shadow at his heels, both intent on destroying Brostek's murderer. But Magara knew that they would never reach him in time, that the Knifeman would flee, to escape and fight again on his own terms. In the midst of her stunned misery, she saw a darkness in the noonday sun and knew what Lisle was trying to do. She added what she could to his effort.

The eclipse came suddenly, darkening the world and leaving only a violet corona in the sky. But in the Vortex, a tunnel of impenetrable darkness reached down into the courtyard, the captured light creating a realm of nothingness. First the Knifeman was engulfed, then Varo and Shadow followed him into oblivion.

The black tunnel was quite opaque, admitting and emitting no light at all – until, in the space of a few mind-numbing moments, it changed from black to red, then orange, and on through all the colours of the rainbow to violet – and then beyond the range of human sight into invisibility. The sorcerer, Varo and Shadow had vanished completely, and at the same time, the two men holding Magara collapsed, and she was released. She knew without looking at her captors that they were dead.

The Link was still with her, but it was in utter turmoil now; she could not find the living strands of either Varo or the sorcerer, and so knew that they must be dead.

Stunned by this second loss, Magara found herself alone suddenly, hardly able to stand. She staggered to the gateway, where Lisle lay still. Her healer's sight told her that the boy was dead, and her fingers confirmed his lack of pulse. His final song had simply burst his heart. She closed his violet eyes, then went to join her love.

Magara knelt beside Brostek's crumpled figure, some-how more graceful in death than it had ever been in life. She cradled his body in her arms, and bent to kiss him gently. *Did you know?* she wondered in anguish. *Did you know how much I loved you?*

Then Magara gave in to the grief that hurt more than any of the sorcerer's torture. She held Brostek, rocking him gently, as the tears poured down her cheeks.

CHAPTER FORTY-SIX

Magara was still weeping when the others found her. They gathered around silently, unwilling to disturb her mourning, but eventually she became aware of their presence and looked up. She knew several of the faces from Trevine; others were vaguely familiar, and she took those standing nearest her to be members of Varo and Brostek's group. They all looked exhausted and solemn. Many of them had been injured, but the valley was quiet now. The battle was over.

'He's dead?' Bair asked gently.

'Yes.'

'Varo and Keredin?'

'Dead too.'

'And the Knifeman?' the veteran said.

'He was killed too,' Magara replied.

'Then they'll rest easy,' Bair stated.

'So where are their bodies?' Ross asked.

'They disappeared in the eclipse,' she explained.

Nothing more was said for a while, but eventually the needs of the living demanded attention.

'Do you know this place?' Bair asked.

'Not really.'

'We must get shelter before the cold and wet finish us off,' Bair explained. 'And we've several wounded that need help.'

For the first time, Magara noticed that their clothes and hair were damp, and that most of them were shivering. The heat of battle had worn off now, and the icy cold of the mountain air was chilling their blood.

'No,' Magara decided suddenly. 'I have a better idea. Gather everyone here by the gates.'

'What about our dead?' Bair asked. 'We need to bury them.'

'Not in this place,' she replied. 'Bring them up here.'

The old soldier nodded, not knowing exactly what she had in mind, but accepting her authority.

'What about the Knifeman's soldiers?' he asked.

'Are any of them still alive?'

'No. They're all dead – every last one. Those we hadn't accounted for just keeled over when the eclipse happened.' Bair shrugged off the eerie memory.

'They died when their master did,' Magara told him. 'Leave them here. They're at rest now – their nightmare is over.'

The veteran set about organizing all that she had asked for, which involved considerable effort for the surviving men and women. Of Bair's colleagues, only Hawk had been killed, but Ross and Vilman were both injured. Ryker alone was unscathed. Lynton had survived, but two of the other Barians were dead, and the people of Trevine had lost almost half their number, with many of the others wounded.

While the bodies were being brought to the castle and laid out near Brostek and Lisle, Magara forced herself not to dwell on the appalling sacrifice that had been made that day, but on what had been achieved. The evil reign of the sorcerer was over, and all around her in the Link she could discern signs of recovery. A dark shadow had passed from the world. Free at last, all the lines of life, all the magical places, were being restored. Without thinking, Magara used her healing sense to guide the progress, using Nevern as its key. Soon the process was self-sustaining, and her subconscious involvement no longer required. But she did not lose contact. She had one last request to make of the Link.

And before that, she had to ensure that their world would never suffer in such a way again. The Vortex must be sealed off completely, she decided, left as a dark graveyard of evil ambition. It had never been meant to be a place for men.

When all was ready, she called Bair over, and explained what she was going to do.

'Should we tell them all, or just go ahead?' she asked.

'Tell them,' the old soldier replied promptly. 'After what they've already been through, they can cope with anything.'

For the first time, Magara wondered just how they had all got there.

'We have much to talk about,' she said.

'That we do,' Bair answered. 'But right now, the important thing is warmth.' Magara nodded, and he turned to the others. 'Listen now!' he called.

She told the shivering group what to expect. Everyone accepted her words in silence – except Ryker.

'Beats walking,' he commented.

'Ready?' Magara asked, and received nods of assent.

She drew on her connection with the Link, focusing all her thoughts on her longing to be back in the real world. Mixed with this was an enormous sadness that some things could never be the same.

The darkness grew steadily, even though it was less than an hour after midday. The sky grew black, the sun a fading white disc. Then the sun was gone, and the entire valley became a void, admitting and emitting no light. The trembling men and women were blind, shivering in absolute darkness.

Suddenly, with absolutely no sensation of movement, the darkness was replaced by a scene of pure beauty. All of them, both the living and the dead, were now in Nevern.

*   *   *

The warmth of the mage-garden soon dried their clothes and brought colour back to the faces of the travellers. And the boundless positive energy that the place

373

bestowed helped immeasurably with the treatment of their injuries, so that by mid-afternoon, everyone was as comfortable as possible. It was time to turn their attention to the dead.

Those from Trevine would be cremated, as was their custom, and the Barians decided that their dead compatriots should be treated in the same way. Their bodies were carried from Nevern to the heathland outside, as no one felt it right to have a large fire in the garden. Hewitt was encountered on the first of these trips, and persuaded to enter the forbidden territory. He and Magara greeted each other like long-lost friends, and he cried with her over the loss of her friends. He felt an especial sorrow at the news of Lisle's death.

Magara and the surviving members of Varo's band had agreed between themselves that Brostek, Keredin, Hawk and Lisle should be buried in Nevern itself. Magara knew that the Guardians would approve. They chose a site near Halana's tomb, and prepared the graves.

After the four had been laid in the ground, each of the living said farewell to their former comrades in their own fashion. All the people from Trevine came to pay their respects. Lynton and his remaining companion did likewise, promising to tell of their exploits on their return to their own country, and vowing to banish the suspicion and enmity between Bari and Levindre. Hewitt paid his tribute in the only way he knew how, playing with an intensity of feeling that brought tears to the eyes of even the hardest of men. Yet he knew that his music did not do justice to Lisle's extraordinary artistry. Bair, Ross and Vilman saluted their fallen comrades in a few moments' silent contemplation, and Ryker laid a crude representation of a bow and an arrow beside Hawk; the archer's own had been left behind in the crater.

Magara came to say goodbye to all four, knowing that each had given their lives for the sake of something bigger than themselves. She knew of no better definition

374

of heroism. She had never met Hawk, but mourned his loss, feeling a kinship she could not explain. Keredin had been familiar to her only through their brief contacts within the Link, but she felt she knew him well. He especially deserved this final resting place, here in the garden that his sacrifice had given life to. Lisle would always remain an enigma and she grieved for the loss of his unique spirit, his talent and for the hurt his death would bring to Slaton. At least now the young boy would never again be subjected to ignorant ridicule, never again be put on show. His short life had not always been a happy one. It had changed the course of many others, though; its end seemed sad but fitting.

But, inevitably, it was Brostek's grave she lingered by. It seemed impossible that a man so full of life should be so empty, his body now only a shell. And it also felt wrong that neither of his lifelong companions, Varo and Shadow, were able to be buried alongside him. *Perhaps they're with him now,* she thought sadly, knowing that Brostek would be with her for ever.

Her final act was to kneel down and place the miraculously restored tapestry in Brostek's hands. Halana's work meant a lot to her, but she wanted him to have it – a demonstration that his friends were still with him. And it was right that the fateful image-key should remain in Nevern, guarding its future.

'He'll look after it better than I could,' Magara said to no one.

She leaned over and stroked his hair tenderly, and then, because her heart could stand the pain no more, she walked away and let others fill the unmarked graves.

*   *   *

That evening the group camped just outside Nevern's boundary. The funeral pyre burned all night, sparks flying up into the sky, blazing reminders of the lives that had been lost.

At first light, they all set off on the long journey south, leaving Nevern in the care of its new Guardians.

Only one person remained in the mage-garden, moving happily among the flowers and trees, accepted by the birds and animals as one of them. When she came upon the four fresh graves, she considered three of them, then smiled. Sitting down contentedly beside the fourth, Celia began to sing softly to her son.

CHAPTER FORTY-SEVEN

Magara had been back at Arenguard for four hands now, but she had only rarely had time to rest or recover. There had been so much coming and going, and she had been required to tell her story so many times that she often felt quite dazed with exhaustion. And she missed Brostek and Varo desperately.

She had been reconciled with her family, although her parents still found it difficult to accept her insistence that she would eventually return to Trevine.

Magara had even confessed to her earlier visit – although she diplomatically omitted any mention of Stead's involvement – and had been forgiven. Her sisters had been shocked and fascinated by her adventures, and she had rediscovered them as friends. She had also taken comfort from their children and her new role as an aunt. The young ones were much more impressed by the story of Magara with a beard than by silly tales of her adventures at Nevern and the Vortex – and that too was oddly reassuring. However, she firmly refused to give a repeat performance. All her family were concerned, and did their best to cheer her up, but they could not fill the empty ache inside her.

Most of the other travellers had long since departed. Indeed, the party from Trevine had been home long enough to send messages back to Arenguard. And so Magara learnt that the carved rock beneath the lake had disappeared again. Several of the divers had seen it on their way to the Vortex, and had described it as looking like the lintel of a door, but now it was nowhere to be found. That gateway to the Vortex was firmly closed once more – but the rule about not disturbing the mirror lake would be even more strictly adhered to from now on!

She had also received news of Slaton. He had tried to stop Lisle and had jumped into the lake after him. But he had evidently been too late. He had remained, floundering, in Trevine's waters, and had needed rescuing himself. After that, like the many others left behind, he had been able to do nothing but wait. When he had finally received the news of his cousin's death, he had decided to return home, and was there now, having promised to visit Magara soon. She hoped that he too would be reconciled with his family.

Bair, Ross and Vilman had also returned to Trevine, and had been reunited with Rogan and Langel. The five men stayed at the crater for some time, sharing in the grief and the glory of the crater's returning citizens. Magara had no doubts that they would find something to replace their old way of life, although from all reports, they were in no hurry to start. Before he left Arenguard, Bair had confessed to her the reasons for his hatred of the Cartel. It was a complicated and bitter story concerning an injustice over stolen cattle and the subsequent violence. To Magara's astonishment, the story dated back more than twenty years. She was able to placate Bair by assuring him that the landowner who had wronged him was now dead; her father's fulsome welcome also helped the veteran overcome a little of his prejudice.

Langel had returned from his duties as an envoy, feeling that he had been cheated out of his chance to help in the real fight. His colleagues did their best to make him feel more cheerful, and he took some comfort from the partial success of his own mission. The problems of the eclipses and the Knifemen's raids had of course been solved, but the Cartel had resolved in future to pay more attention to the more remote areas of the country. And relations with Bari were on the mend. Lynton and his fellow envoys were on their way home now, escorting representatives of Levindre.

No one knew where the final member of Varo and Brostek's old group had gone. Ryker was simply not there one morning, and even Vilman, who had always been the closest to him, had no idea where he was headed. They all assumed that Ryker was in search of other prey against which to pit his special talent. He seemed to have led a charmed life up until now, but no one expected to hear from him again.

Hewitt was the only one to stay on at Arenguard with Magara. His music enlivened many evenings, and she knew he was truly recovered from his part in recent traumatic events when he chose to perform the song that Lisle had played the night they first met. It was rapturously received, but Hewitt's smile of acceptance was sad, and there were tears in his eyes as he dedicated the music to Lisle's memory.

* * *

Magara had been glad to make her peace with Arenguard's old librarian. To her surprise, Stead managed to decipher the Knifemen's symbols. Although the meaning of these signs was shown to be essentially unimportant, his childlike enthusiasm on discovering the answer had overcome Magara's natural antipathy towards the subject.

'I put them in the order of their colours in the rainbow,' he told her. 'Like this.'

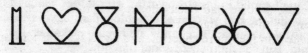

'And?' she prompted.
'Try covering up the left hand side of each in turn.'
Magara did so.
'Mirror images!' she exclaimed.
'And now think about your symbol of light,' Stead went on.

379

'Of course – it's the next in the sequence!'

'Wizardry is beyond the natural spectrum, obviously,' he commented.

'I thought you didn't believe in magic,' she teased.

'After recent events,' he replied, 'I think I'd better start.'

* * *

'There's someone to see you,' Stead told her.

Magara groaned. She had managed to escape from the seemingly endless treadmill of visitors for a few precious hours that afternoon. She had been lying on her bed, reading, but her time of peace was obviously over now.

'Who is it?'

'I don't know,' he replied. 'Your father just sent me to fetch you.'

Magara followed the librarian down to Danyel's study. He opened the door, and stood back for her to enter. Her father was standing at the far side of the room, talking earnestly with two men who had their backs to her. As she came in, one of them turned round and smiled, his brown eyes lighting up with pleasure. Magara felt an unbelievable jolt of recognition, then rising joy, as the man strode rapidly towards her, his arms spread wide in welcome. It was Varo.

Magara ran to him and was swept off her feet and whirled round in his strong arms. Her father watched in disbelief – his youngest daughter had always been sensitive about her size, and hated being picked up like a child. But she didn't care about that now.

'I thought you were dead!' she exclaimed, looking up into his handsome, bearded face.

'So did I,' he replied, grinning as he put her down.

'What happened?'

'It's a long story,' he said, 'but first there's someone I want you to meet . . .'

Magara turned to greet the other newcomer – and froze in horror. It was the Knifeman. He looked younger, somehow, and the blue robes and triangular pendant were gone, but it was the same man.

'You're dead,' she breathed.

'The man I *was* is dead,' he replied. 'I have been granted a second chance.' His voice was calm and gentle, but it still made Magara shudder.

'No!' she whispered, aghast. 'It's not possible.' She turned to Varo. 'This is madness!'

'That is no way to talk to guests, Magara,' her father remonstrated, frowning. 'Temar here is a wizard with important business with the Cartel. He goes to Mathry tomorrow.'

'Don't be afraid, little one,' Varo said. 'It's all right.'

But everything was not all right. Magara fought against the terror rising up inside her, but felt her mind go dark. Varo caught her as she fainted.

*　　*　　*

When Magara came round, she was lying on her own bed again, with Szara, one of her sisters, sitting beside her. She looked up from her sewing as Magara's eyelids fluttered.

'It's about time you woke up,' she remarked. 'Whatever came over you?'

'Where's Varo?'

'He's with Father and Temar,' Szara told her.

'Get him for me.'

'Don't you think—'

'Get him!' Magara exploded.

Szara gave her sister a long-suffering look, but left the room, returning a little while later with Varo. After one look at her sister's expression, she left them alone together.

Once again the warmth of his smile sent a jolt through

her whole body, reminding Magara just how glad she was to see him. But . . .

'Is he still here?' she asked fearfully.

'Yes,' he answered. 'But it's all right, Magara. He's not the same person.'

'How do you know?'

'Because I saw him change.'

'I don't understand,' she said helplessly.

'When the eclipse took us, I don't know where we went,' he began. 'Perhaps it was some part of the Link, perhaps somewhere *beyond* the Link. But wherever or whatever it was, it changed us both – drastically. I wanted to kill him, but I suddenly knew that there had been enough killing. If he died at my hands, then my own life would be over. I would have achieved all I'd ever wanted, all I'd ever thought about. But I couldn't do it.' He paused, remembering. 'Then I saw him as he really was, an old man grasping at power but helpless now, vile but pathetic. And he changed before my eyes. He grew younger, and I saw his history being rewritten – or rather unwritten. All the choices that had led him to the Vortex were unmade, all the evil that had built up in him was drained away. He's eighteen again now; young, untainted, and idealistic.'

There was no doubting the sincerity in Varo's voice, but Magara still found it hard to believe. Her terrors were not to be assuaged so easily.

'But how do you know he won't do it all again?' she asked.

'I saw that too!' he responded, smiling. 'This time he will make wizardry what it really *should* be. He will be the leader who will help us all find our way again, sweeping away all the bigotry and corruption. You'll see. He goes to Mathry tomorrow – and that'll shake things up, for a start!' He laughed.

'You saw the future?' she whispered.

He nodded.

'And you believe all this.' It was not a question.

382

'I have no choice. I *saw* it.'

Magara was speechless; she still could not bring herself to accept such a miracle.

'Is it really true?' she breathed eventually.

'As true as my being here,' he answered.

'And you *are* here.' She leaned forward, and they embraced. 'It is so good to see you, Varo.' But then she remembered something he had said earlier, and she sat back to look at his face. 'You said both of you changed. What happened to you?'

'I have a new name,' he answered enigmatically. 'I'm called B'varo now.'

'Why?'

'Don't you know, little one?' he asked, and suddenly his voice was more than just familiar.

Magara's eyes widened.

'Brostek?'

B'varo nodded.

'I am both Varo *and* Brostek,' he said. 'I am neither. But whatever I am, I love you.'

'What? How?' she gasped.

'I don't know,' he answered seriously. 'Perhaps both of us were incomplete as we were, and the magic just brought the two halves together—'

'Wait!' she interrupted. 'What was the last thing you said?'

'Two halves together?'

'No. Before that.'

'I love you,' B'varo said, smiling.

Can this be real? she wondered, stunned and hardly daring to hope. It was much too good to be true.

At that moment the door was pushed open tentatively, and Magara was about to curse the intruder when Shadow's muzzle appeared.

'Come in, Shadow,' B'varo commanded, and the wolf trotted in to sit happily at the bedside. 'She guided us down from the mountains,' he went on, ruffling the animal's neck. 'I'm not sure we'd have made it without her help.'

'Look at me!' Magara ordered.

Startled, B'varo did as he was told. The brown eyes in his perfect face were exactly the same as before, but there was a warmth in them now, a depth of feeling that Magara had never seen in Varo's steely gaze.

She reached out and pulled him to her. He was tentative at first, but then responded with a passion that left them both breathless. All the doubts and questions flew from Magara's mind, and she surrendered to an overwhelming happiness.

'You need a shave,' she said, the banal statement making them both smile.

'True,' he answered. 'Will you do it for me?'

'Of course.' Magara was grinning like an idiot.

'I'd better wash my face then,' he said, and promptly lay down on the floor. 'Come on, girl.'

Shadow licked eagerly at his beard as Magara laughed.

'Enough,' B'varo decided, and stood up.

Magara got up to face him, and he took her hands in his.

This is real, Magara thought, delight and sheer joy welling up within her.

'I knew . . .' she whispered. *Somewhere deep down, I knew*.

'When did you know?' he asked, in the way of all lovers.

'When I saw your face,' she answered, looking up into his eyes. 'When I saw you smile.'

'Stay with me.'

'Always.'

B'varo's grin grew even wider.

'Tonight,' he said, 'the stars will shine from our eyes.'

THE END